The Swan Garden

PARADIGM
HALL PRESS

CLOVIS, CALIFORNIA

the Swan Garden

A Novel By
Anne Biggs

THE SWAN GARDEN. Copyright © 2016 Anne Biggs

Paradigm Hall Press
An Imprint of HBE Publishing

Front cover photo copyright © 2016 Aaryn James
Back cover photo copyright © 2016 Anne Biggs
Typesetting by Dan Dunklee & Joshua Muster
Layout and cover design by Joshua Muster

CHILDREN OF LIR appears in the back, courtesy of Project Gutenberg.

All inquiries should be addressed to:
HBE Publishing
640 Clovis Ave
Clovis, CA, 93612
http://www.hbepublishing.com

Library of Congress Control Number: In Process

ISBN 978-1-943050-39-0 Trade Paperback
ISBN 978-1-943050-11-6 eBook

February 2016

HBE PUBLISHING

For every unnamed girl or woman who spent time in a mother-baby home or Magdalene Laundry against their will, you have taught me the meaning of fortitude.

THE VIOLATION

1949

ey girlie,"

A voice from behind broke the calm of the late afternoon. Before I could turn, I felt his hands on my back and the gravel dig into my cheek, as I fell to the road. His hands forcing their way under my clothing, digging at my skin. My panties tearing, as he turned me to face him.

I felt his stubble rub against my cheek, smelled the stale stench of cigarettes and alcohol. He started thrusting, forcing his way inside. His face twisting, his pointed jaw seemed to lead his motions. His yellow teeth biting his lower lip, drawing blood. He let out a groan, pushing harder, I cried out and squirmed away.

"Shut up, don't move," as he grabbed my blouse, ripping the buttons.

His eyes focused on my breasts, his calloused hands squeezing and twisting.

"You're gonna like this, girlie."

He pulled me harder, thrusting between my legs. His face contorted into spasms, eyes closed. My tears clouding his features.

His weight lifted, the air was still.

I was alone.

CASTLEPOLLARD

The Arrival

arly, on the first Saturday of June, Monsignor drove his shiny black sedan up to our gate. Before I even heard the hum of his motor, Mum came to my bedroom door, tapped lightly, and came in with a small tattered suitcase. "Here I brought this for you, to put some things in."

"Where am I going?" I pulled myself up from beneath the comforter.

"You need to get some things together. You're going away," she paused, "for a while, you know, until the baby comes." She hesitated between words, as if she forgot what she was supposed to say.

"No. You promised," I said, pushing the covers to the other side of the bed, trying not to make any noise.

"I did nothing of the sort," she said, setting the suitcase on the floor next to the bed.

"Yes, you did. You said…"

"I said, I would do what I could. Your father knows what is best, and we must abide by what he and Monsignor decide. You need to be a good girl, do what they say. You'll be home in no time, back to school and forget this ever happened."

"Forget? How could I forget? What about the baby? You do remember I'm having a baby? What's going to happen to it?"

"Alice, we can't talk about that right now. Let's just get through this."

I felt my face flush. Anger churning my stomach, moving up toward my throat, like a bit of bad chicken. How could this be happening?

"Oh, my God. I can't believe you're letting him do this."

"It's done, Alice. Get your things together. We'll wait for you downstairs. Monsignor is here and he doesn't have much time."

"Mum, please, don't do this."

She left the suitcase and walked from the room without another word, with no reassurance I'd be all right, that I'd get through this. I looked around at what had once been familiar, too stunned to believe what was happening. Believing in my heart that this time, at least, she would prevail. That she would dig deep to find the strength. My judgment failed me. I ached from the betrayal.

I didn't have much to collect. I gathered two of my favorite skirts, a cardigan, and an extra blouse from the closet, a nightgown, stockings and undergarments from the dresser drawer. I grabbed my hairbrush, and a thinly bound book of Irish legends Mum had given me one Christmas. I checked the room one last time for anything I might need, or want. Last, from a small jewelry box on top of the dresser, I pulled out a stained white string with a Sacred Heart medal attached to it. I had won it at school when I recited a poem from memory. I slipped the necklace into the pocket of my skirt.

When I came downstairs, Monsignor sat at the table drinking tea with Da. Monsignor stood to greet me, but Da walked out the front door, not bothering to look at me. I imagined he wanted me gone, so he could put this mess behind him, when asked at church, he could say, "it's been seen to."

Monsignor took my suitcase and guided me out the door. Mum stood in the doorway, waiting as always, her stoic face speaking volumes in the silence. I pulled a single white rosebud from the bush by the gate.

I took my place in the backseat. Monsignor handed me the suitcase and a sealed envelope. I brushed my hair from my face and fiddled with the door handle.

Everything would be different now. Neither Mum nor Da had said a word about how long I'd be gone, or when I'd be coming back. I turned and looked back through the tinted window, but the yard was empty. Da was nowhere to be seen. Mum stood alone in the doorway.

*   *   *

The walls of Castlepollard loomed before us, like a tower from childhood nightmares. A three-story brick building that held a history. A history even girls from Meadows Glen talked about. "Homes" where bad girls went to finish out their term. I felt the hair on my arms stand up, and I shivered at the mere thought of passing through those double doors. Four pillars guarded the entrance. The walls were a dull gray with white lace curtains hung in the windows.

A small older woman opened the car door, dressed in a faded blue smock, her hair pulled back in a loose bun.

I stepped out, clutching my suitcase and the sealed envelope as she pointed to the double doors, guiding me through the entry. As the doors closed, I heard tires spin in the gravel, Monsignor had completed his task. I had been dumped at the door.

It could have been worse, I could have been put on the bus and sent on my own. But it didn't matter how I got here, I was here, and the tightness in my stomach told me I would be here for quite a while.

"You can sit here," she said softly, more like a whisper than a direction.

"Thank you." I sat in the high back cushioned chair against the wall and waited.

She glanced over, this woman with pale sunken cheeks, and gave me a slight smile. Leaning down, she whispered, "My name is Sara."

"I'm Alice."

"We'll put your suitcase right here by the door." Sara moved it against the wall.

"What do I do now?"

"Just wait. Reverend Mother will be out in a few minutes. She'll explain everything you need to know, then I'll take you to the dormitory on the third floor. You can change and rest before supper."

I nodded.

"You'll be just fine," she said, patting my hand. "Mind your business and do everything Reverend Mother tells you."

I looked around the opulent entry, very different from the outside of the building. The tile floors glistened a polished white. A staircase, with oiled wood, led beyond what my eyes could see. A statue of the Sacred Heart stood centered on the crafted mahogany table, buffed to a bright shine.

"When do I get to go home?" I asked, looking back at Sara.

"I wouldn't be thinking about that right now. That won't be happening for a while."

Just as Sara turned to walk away, the office door opened. "You must be Alice Brennan." A tall lean woman stood in the doorway.

"Yes, ma'am."

"Well, don't dawdle, girl. I'm much too busy to wait for you to decide to stand and walk. You, wait here until we're done," she said, pointing to Sara, "then take her upstairs and get her settled in. Come on now," waving me through the door, "let's be done with this."

Framed pictures of saints hung along the walls, and a large wooden crucifix hung behind the desk.

"Stand up straight. Where are your letters?" She asked, as she walked to the desk. I handed her the envelope and waited as she reviewed the contents. From across the desk, I could smell lye soap with a scant scent of roses. Looking at her face, I found myself smiling for the first time, though she never looked up, I saw that her square face fit perfectly into her black and white habit.

"I see Monsignor's been thorough. You come from Meadows Glen."

"Yes, ma'am, that's in County Westmeath."

"That was not a question."

"I'm sorry."

"You were attacked on the way home from school."

"Yes, ma'am."

"So, your mum believed you? Never mind." She let out a snicker as she tapped a small wooden ruler against her desk. "How far along are you?" She finally looked up, instead of making eye contact, she stared at my belly.

"Three months past, maybe Ma'am."

"Your mother took you to the doctor, and he confirmed your pregnancy, but not the rape. So, how do I know that you told the truth?"

"Because, I did."

Still tapping the ruler, she sat up straight. "I'm supposed to believe someone just threw you to the ground and had his way with you?"

I didn't know how to respond. I slipped my hand into my pocket and fingered my Sacred Heart and the wilted rose. I stared up at the cross behind her desk, and prayed silently to Jesus, hoping he would get me through this. Reverend Mother stared at me in what seemed utter frustration. She got up from her desk, came around and stood in front of me, still holding the ruler in her hand.

"All right, listen carefully. Your parents signed you in, so you're here until they sign you out. You will do everything I say, and mark me, if you don't, you will be sorry. You know you've sinned and we're here to help you earn forgiveness from God." She looked at my face, took the ruler up to my chin and ran it down the front of me, until it rested on my belly.

"Reverend Mother, I didn't do anything wrong. I was never with a boy."

"Really? If you weren't with a boy, how did you get pregnant? Are you the new Virgin Mary?" I could tell she wanted to laugh out loud, but she didn't. She kept her cheeks tight, and repositioned the ruler to my chin.

"No, I'm not saying that." She leaned in so close I could feel her breath. I tried to move back, but I hit the wall.

"Let me remind you, I have control over you now, and whatever I record will impact how long you stay, where you go, and when your time is over."

"Yes, ma'am."

"We have rules around here, don't test me, girl. Never miss chapel, clean-up after yourself, and have no conversations with any of the other girls. If one of the Sisters wishes to converse with you, you stop, bow your head, do not look at them. Answer with a simple yes or no."

She moved to the door, opened it, and stood aside. I saw her hand on the knob and noticed the whiteness of her skin, and the cleanliness of her nails. I could tell she had never spent much time in a garden. Though always clean, Mum's hands were red and cracked during the cold winter months, and often filled with creases of dirt, buried deep from fall planting.

"Sara, take her to the dormitory."

She closed the door and left the two of us alone. Sara started toward the stairs and I reached for my suitcase to follow her.

"Oh, no, you have to leave that there."

"But it's mine," I said.

"No, it's theirs now. They decide whether you need any of the contents, which usually they figure you don't, and they dispose of the rest. They say everything is given to the less fortunate, but I've seen personal belongings tossed away in the garbage."

Sara took the suitcase from me, set it down, and guided me toward the stairs. She seemed even smaller than when she opened the door. Her hair thin, nails splintered, eyes vacant. Without telling me, I could only imagine she had been in this place for a long time. The smell of lye filled the stairway. Girls, all dressed the same, were cleaning the floors or polishing the rails of the stairway, barely holding their balance, .

"You have pretty hair," she said, almost like a child admiring something she wanted. Reaching out to touch my braid. "I had a braid once, longer than yours, reddish-brown, like a horse's tail," she giggled. "Did you get your name?" she asked.

"What are you talking about?" confused by her abrupt question.

"She changes your name, so no one will know you were here." Sara whispered, waiting for me to catch up.

"Did they change yours?" I asked, curious about what was to come.

"Yes, but I've been Sara for so long, it doesn't matter whether I remember or not."

"You don't remember your real name?"

"Oh no, I remember. My name was Katherine, but Da called me Katy, and Mum called me Kathy. There are some things you try to forget, but some things you never can." She turned away and continued up the stairs with her pale hands grasping the stair rail.

I didn't know this woman, but after our short walk, she seemed more than a simple-minded old woman. She had been someone's daughter, someone's mother.

"How can they take your name from you?"

"She picks a name, that no other girl has, writes it down in her book, and there you have it. Actually, they can take anything they want from you," she said, with a touch of sadness in her voice.

"It looks like they already have." Sara unlocked the door and walked toward the beds, leaving me alone in the doorway. Looking back, she pointed to a thin mattress.

"There, the one with the clothes, that one is yours. When you are finished changing, put your old ones in the wooden box by the lavatory door, then come downstairs. I have to get back to the kitchen. It's on the ground floor, the far side of the entryway, just before you reach the hallway that takes you to chapel. I'll get you some breakfast, then we'll start on supper. Do you have any questions?"

"No, I'll be fine." I didn't want her to know that I had no idea where to go.

Sara left and I looked around the cold, dark dormitory. Twelve beds in all, six on each side, between each bed stood a small night table with double drawers. The clothes reserved for me, were a blue smock, brown blouse, a pair of shoes and white socks. I picked up the smock and held it close to my nose. Though ironed and clean, it smelled sour, like old fruit. I took off my clothes and slipped into my new uniform. I took my string necklace from the pocket of my skirt and slipped it under the pillow. Afraid of someone finding it, I knew if I wore it someone would take it, and I'd never get it back.

I began to think about the days ahead. I looked around the dormitory, nothing like Reverend Mother's office with framed pictures, solid wood desk, and a window with lace curtains. The only windows here were lined high along the ceiling, the lack of light made it dark and cold. The hardwood floor polished and worn. I closed the door to the dormitory and headed downstairs. As I passed the girls still cleaning, some looked up with knowing glances. Others kept their heads bowed to their work. All were silent. Though different shapes and sizes, they all looked alike. Their faces were marked with despair, their hands red and wrinkled from the steaming water. I looked away as well, knowing that one day I would be one of them.

A Visit with God

found the chapel accidentally, going down the wrong hallway. I went inside thinking I needed a word with God about what was going on.

At home, whenever I got upset, I ran outdoors, scampered around the barn, and screamed out for anyone to hear. Then watched as my breath floated to the sky.

But I wasn't at home and there was no place to go. I pulled open the door and stepped into the silence. The small chapel felt much warmer than the dormitory, and much nicer than Reverend Mother's office. I crept up the aisle toward the altar, but stopped when I saw the glow of the votive candles flickering in the far corner. I looked around to be sure I was alone. At my church, Monsignor made everyone put a coin in the box, and then only allowed one candle to be lit. He always checked, even when the church was empty, he found a way of knowing.

With no coins, and no Monsignor watching; I lit the candle for no one else, but me. The small white candle, giving off a shimmer, filling the void. I bowed my head, made the sign of the cross, and knelt at the altar. In a barely audible voice, but loud enough for Him to hear, I prayed.

Dear God,
It's me, Alice, and you know where I am. I haven't been here
for even a day, and I'm afraid of everything. No one believes it
wasn't my fault; not Mum, not Da, even Monsignor couldn't
look me in the eye. Reverend Mother thinks everyone is a sin-

ner. She looks for the worst in people, even as she expects their best. Only Sara understands. God, I've always been a good girl. Please don't leave me here. I need You now. I have to go before someone comes looking for me. So please God, find a way to get me home.
Amen

Kneeling at the small altar, the tears came. I closed my eyes and let them spill. A volcano erupted inside me, forcing everything to spew out. I couldn't stop. Fear came from all around me; this baby that would never be mine, the rage of those who claimed to love me, and Reverend Mother. I felt every part of me tremble and shake. Like a balloon, set free to swirl until it fell, deflated. There was nothing left in me. I sensed a presence, small hands touched my shoulders, grabbing tight, as if I might slip away.

"I thought you might be here," Sara whispered. "Come on, you'll be spending enough time here. You need to get breakfast, and I need to get back to work. I have a plate ready for you." She lifted me from the altar, and led me back down the aisle. She moved quietly, then paused, turned, held onto my arm, and genuflected, an act I knew all too well. I wondered how often Sara prayed to God, and if He paid attention to her prayers.

We walked to the far end of the building. I followed Sara through the double doors of the kitchen. On a table sat a tray covered with a towel, a cup of tea setting next to it.

"Sit. You need some breakfast." Sara went to the sink and began to wash dishes, not looking over at me.

When I pulled the towel away, I found a steaming bowl of cereal and two slices of buttered potato bread. Since I had not eaten before leaving home, I was anxious to get something warm in my stomach. After a few minutes, Sara took a seat across from me warming her hands with a cup of hot tea. She watched me take spoonfuls of the oatmeal.

"Slow down. I can get you more if you're still hungry."

"I'm sorry."

"That's okay. You may as well enjoy it for now, it won't always be this way," Sara said, taking a sip of her tea.

"Reverend Mother said I'm not supposed to talk to anyone."

"Reverend Mother says a lot of things, but down here, her word doesn't mean much. She rarely comes around, and when she does, she barks orders at the door," Sara said, pointing to another set of swinging double doors. "Anything that happens inside the kitchen doesn't concern her, unless Monsignor Matthew comes for a visit, then she may consider it."

"Who is Monsignor Matthew?"

"Don't worry about him, at least not now. He comes now and again, and Reverend Mother treats him likes royalty. He usually only comes down to transfer penitents to Dublin."

"What is a penitent?"

"That would be you, me, all the other girls. It's how the Sisters refer to everyone, at least everyone not wearing a habit. "

I took a drink from the now warm tea. It was becoming clear to me how things would be. We were different, nothing would change that. We were the penitents in the blue smocks that everyone avoided, if possible.

"Where are you from?"

"I'm from Meadows Glen. My Da's a dairy farmer. I have four brothers and sisters."

"What happened? You look too young to have been in love."

"No, I didn't fall in love." I felt a blush cross my face. I couldn't tell her what happened. People I cared about thought badly of me, I didn't need a stranger to do the same.

"It's okay. I know pretty much everything about everyone. I know the ones who fell in love, the ones who lost their lovers, and the ones who never loved at all. Which are you?" I didn't look up at her, just quickly scooped up the remaining cereal, and ate the broken pieces of bread. I stopped long enough to take a sip of tea, and looked around the kitchen It was much larger than any I had ever seen. There were two doors, one leading to the hallway by the chapel and the other to the dining hall.

"All right. You don't have to tell me," Sara said, "but I imagine the worst happened to you. We won't talk about it again, but at least let me tell you how to survive in this place. You must follow the rules, the Sisters will think nothing of beating you. There's no mercy when you disobey, regardless of when your time is. Disobeying is tricky. You might not really be doing anything wrong, but if one of the Sisters thinks you are, she can become ruthless. Everything she does is to bring you forgiveness from God."

"How will I know whether I'm being disobedient?"

"Easy, you'll get pulled to the side, or tripped, or denied your meals, or the worst, sent to Reverend Mother, where she'll give you the beating of your life with a strap. The worst punishment dished out is getting your hair cut. You look pretty docile, so I imagine you'll keep your hair." She reached over and stroked the tips of my braid, then sat back.

"What do I need to be careful of?"

"Well, except for here in the kitchen, as she said, you don't talk to anyone ever. Don't let them get you angry. Don't let them catch you crying. They are good at finding your weaknesses. The crybabies have the hardest time of it. Did I tell you, no talking?"

"Yes, twice. What else?" I asked, taking the last sip of my tea.

Sara set her tea on the table and moved in as if she was about to whisper the secrets of the world. She motioned for me to lean in also. I couldn't understand why, we were alone in the room.

"Reverend Mother doesn't like things to get messy."

"What do you mean?"

"The blood. She hates to see the blood on the sheets, so if she's there, she makes the girls deliver on a porcelain commode. If Nurse Claire isn't there to stand up for you, Reverend Mother usually wins and you're stuck on the commode where your baby drops into the world."

"I don't understand." I said, more confused as she continued.

"You ever see a baby born?" Sara asked in a strained whisper.

"Yes, we had animals who delivered, but never a real baby. I always had to wait out of the room when it was Mum's time."

"Do you remember where your Mum delivered?"

"She lay on her bed, with the midwife at her side."

"Reverend Mother doesn't like messes anywhere, least of all in the infirmary. Imagine that?" Sara laughed out loud.

For the next two hours, I followed Sara everywhere. I set the plates and silverware on the long tables in the dining hall. I hauled in potatoes from the garden and peeled carrots for the stew. I carried soiled sheets from the dormitory down to the laundry room, where I dipped my hands into the steaming cauldrons where the sheets and religious garments soaked throughout the day. The hours passed quickly, as Sara filled me in on how the other girls came to this place. Later in the day as we knelt in the chapel, she gave me her rosary beads.

At supper I sat across the table as Sara began to serve the soup. The room was silent, except for hushed murmurs coming from the Sisters table.

"What is wrong with you?" One of the Sisters shouted. "This soup is cold."

"I'll get you another," Sara said, reaching for the bowl, but spilling it all over the table, and the Sister's skirt. She glared at Sara and, without a word, slapped her, causing the bowl to slip from Sara's hands crashing to the floor. Sara lost her balance from the blow, hitting the edge of the table as she went down. One of the girls ran to her, but was pushed away.

"Leave her be. She can get up on her own."

The room fell silent, everyone watched Sara. She lay still for a few moments. The Sisters went back to their supper, but a tall girl sitting at the far end of the table got up and took hold of Sara's arm, lifting her off the floor. She took a napkin from the table and placed it over Sara's eye. She led Sara back through the double doors into the kitchen.

I lined up with the other girls at the side of our beds in the dormitory for night prayers. I lay alone that first night covered by one blanket. I missed my sister and Mum's homemade comforter that kept us warm when cold winter storms blanketed the countryside. I reached under the pillow, clutching my Sacred Heart. I blessed myself and prayed He would help me find my way. Then I thought about Sara lying alone somewhere in the kitchen on her cot, and the secrets she knew about the Sisters, the building, and every girl who lived here. She knew them all, but we could do nothing for her. Like the stories in my legend book, she held the key, but these were no legends I had learned at Mum's knee. These were no fairy tales, where happy endings abound. I could see no happily ever after ever coming from these stories. I slipped the medal back under the pillow and stared up at the prison-like windows. I had survived my first day, but I had no idea what tomorrow would hold.

I closed my eyes and tried to replace the visions of the laundry room, with memories of Meadows Glen. If I could get back to the broken fence with white peeling paint and run the twig across the boards, I'd be okay. I'd help Mrs. Murphy with her foal. I'd go out to the meadow with Connor, pick up steaming chunks of peat, but I knew in time, home would only be a faint memory. My memories would be replaced with Sara darting about the kitchen, the girls dipped to their elbows in lye soap, or the Sisters issuing orders and making demands.

Each morning, after restless nights, I would find myself more tired than before. The months passed and I learned well from the frail, damaged Sara. I listened closely, rarely saying much.

I never remembered restful sleep, instead, tossing from side to side, awake, then asleep, then awake again, like blinking lights from a broken street corner lamp. I turned every way possible to get free from my prison.

One evening halfway through a warm August and still months from delivery, I went to the lavatory to wash cool water over my face, then went back to bed, slipping quietly under the thin gray blanket. I turned my head to the side and closed my eyes, forcing myself to stay still and fall asleep.

Mum had finished cleaning the kitchen, wiping down the table, putting the last of the plates away, that I had dried, but couldn't reach the shelf of the cupboard.

Da had fallen asleep with the paper crumpled in his lap like burned kindling, his cigarette smoldering in the overflowing ashtray. Mum motioned for me to fetch it, and dump it into the hearth. After doing what she asked, I watched her open the small drawer on the far corner of the counter and pulled out one of Da's already rolled cigarettes. She grabbed a matchbook and slipped out the front door, leaving it slightly ajar. I slipped out the door and saw the glow of the light between her fingers. "Go on in, girl," she said, inhaling and looking away. It had been a long time since I had seen Mum so relaxed, a soft smile and a glistening dew came from her eyes.

"What are you doing out here?" I asked, taking a seat on the bench.

"I needed some fresh air."

"But it's freezing."

"For you perhaps." She moved her arm around my waist and

pulled me close. "Is that better?" I immediately felt the warmth of her body next to mine. We sat in silence for a few minutes; neither of us said anything, just stared up into the night sky.

"Well, since you won't go in, I best tell you something, if you think you can keep a secret."

Mum was not one to keep secrets, nor to tell them. She didn't believe in secrets. Unless asked, you kept your mouth shut. She thought if it wasn't worth telling everyone, it wasn't worth telling anyone. Mum never got along well with the neighbors when they came together over tea to chat about the residents. I leaned in close and could feel her sweet tobacco breath on me.

"I'm five months past. Come late spring, I'll be delivering a baby."

I was ten and couldn't decide how I felt about another baby. There were already four of us sharing the table. If it was a girl, I'd have to share even more of our room, since having Maggie, she took up more space than I appreciated. She was just four. Mum must have seen the strain in my eyes, as if I was trying to see every star up close from the sky. Suddenly, before I realized, both her arms tightened around me.

"You'll always be my first."

"No, Connor was your first."

"But you were my first girl. All the babies in the world can't take that away." I felt myself melt like snow, there in the moonlight, wrapped in her arms.

"Your first girl. You'll will always hold that place in your heart, no matter how many come after."

I shivered under the thin blanket, far from the bench by the front door, far from Mum's hug that night. Inside I felt a flutter, wide-awake I rested my hand on my belly and tried to imagine if this were to be my first girl, and if so, would I ever forget her?

*   *   *

I rushed, as fast as my lopsided body could carry me, down to the kitchen to find Sara. The contractions had started. She looked up from the steaming pot of potatoes while two penitents ran around like clowns, preparing for Monsignor Matthew's visit.

"I think it's time. The pains are closer," I said. I leaned against the wall, and cupped my belly. I could feel the baby trying to push its way out. Before the next contraction, I shuffled to the bench by the table and laid my head down. In a few minutes, the pains diminished.

Sara stopped stirring and knelt, placing her hands around my belly. Her fingers moved in a circular motion, then she stopped.

"It's not your time yet." Sara said, getting off her knees. "Nurse Claire won't be back until this afternoon, and unless you want Reverend Mother waiting for you, you'd better find a way to distract yourself from the pain." I began to cry not for any particular reason, but for every reason I could think of.

"Stay here, but keep out of everyone's way. Here, take this bowl and break the beans apart. If Reverend Mother comes down, I'll tell her I needed extra help." Sara still wore a yellow rim around the edge of her eye from her most recent encounter with Reverend Mother. As I filled the bowl with broken pods, I couldn't help but fear that someday I'd replace Sara. This was my future.

"Monsignor Matthew will serve Sunday Mass. Just be glad she's so preoccupied, or you'd find yourself on the commode in the infirmary when your time comes."

Working in the kitchen with Sara distracted me from my pains, but in a short time they returned, sharp and jabbing. I cried out.

"Hush, girl. Can't let anyone hear you. How much time between each contraction?"

"I don't know, ten minutes, maybe less, but they're lasting longer."

"You're close girl, but we still have time."

The Dining Room

ara, is everything ready?" Reverend Mother asked, standing in the doorway surveying the kitchen.

"Yes. The tables are set and the food is ready to go out."

"Did the partitions come down?"

"The girls removed them earlier."

"Put the platters on the tables and have the girls line up. After everyone's in place, Monsignor Matthew and I will come in. Be quick about it."

Wiping the sweat from her forehead, Sara turned from the door. "At least tonight, we'll eat like kings."

"What do you mean?" I asked.

"With Monsignor Matthew here, we'll eat the same as the Sisters. Reverend Mother makes sure he sees us eating well. Go on, line up with the others."

Standing in our places, Reverend Mother came in with Monsignor Matthew. They stood side-by-side, hands almost touching. After blessing the food, he made the sign of the cross and held the chair for Reverend Mother. Nodding, she gave permission for the penitents to sit. The silent room began to fill with light chatter and the sounds of eating.

Generous slabs of beef, fat chunks of potatoes, gravy, and fresh squash made their way around the tables. Rich butter to spread across thick slices of bread. Sara caught my eye, giving me a wink.

Reverend Mother and Monsignor Matthew put down their forks. Standing, they started the procession to the chapel. Without a word, our dinner ended.

*   *   *

Walking in a single line, I kept my eyes focused on the steps of the girl in front of me. I lost sight of Sara when I slid into the back row of the chapel. I gripped my hands around the bottom of the pew to hold myself up, taking a deep breath. After everyone took their seats in the chapel, Reverend Mother stood in front, beaming with pride. Monsignor Matthew stood next to her staring at his congregation of sinners. He looked regal in his black woolen robe, and purple sash with a long gold cross hanging from his waist.

My pains intensified, so I leaned forward to control them, trying to push them back from where they came.

"Come on." Out of nowhere, Sara slid into the pew and took my arm. "I'll guide you out."

"Is Nurse here yet?"

"I just talked to her, and told her you were ready. She's preparing everything for you, but you must be quiet. I'm going to slip you out of here."

"I can't move. It's falling. Oh my God what do I do?"

"We'll start the blessing now, if everyone will stand." Monsignor Matthew said, stepping up to the altar. Reverend Mother sat straight behind the penitents and clapped her orders. We rose in unison.

As I stole out of the pew and stood in the center of the aisle, I felt a splash of water between my legs, spilling down onto the shiny glossed tile. I froze. Terrified. I looked over at Sara. With Monsignor Matthew offering absolution of our sins, I stood in shame as I waited for my sin to be born.

"God have mercy on these poor penitents." Monsignor Matthew continued. Reverend Mother patrolled the center aisle and stopped abruptly when she caught sight of me.

She lunged at me as Monsignor Matthew continued his sermon. "As Jesus blessed the wine and visited the lepers, I am here to bless you." His voice trailed off as he turned back toward the altar and his congregation of penitents.

I stood, stained with water dripping from my frock and streaming down my legs. Monsignor Matthew noticed me. "Do something with that girl," he growled to Reverend Mother. He straightened his crucifix, and returned to the altar without looking back.

I locked eyes with Reverend Mother whose cheeks flushed crimson. "God will punish you for this," she whispered. "You will pay for what you have done to me." Turning away, "get her out of here," she hissed at Sara.

THE BIRTH

ara guided me to the farthest end of the hall. Nurse Claire looked up as we entered the infirmary. "She's ready," was all Sara said.

"Bring her here," Claire said pointing to the last bed, "the further from the door, the safer she'll be."

"Where's Reverend Mother?" I asked, trying to stay calm. "Don't let her near me."

"I'll watch for her, Alice. Claire, you have to get her settled before Reverend Mother gets here."

"Where is she?"

"She's still with Monsignor Matthew, but I think she'll be here soon."

"Then watch from the door, let me know when you see her. I need to get Alice ready. It won't be long now. We need to get you out of these clothes."

Nurse helped me pull the jumper over my head, stripped me of everything else, dropping the clothes at the foot of the bed. She slipped a gown over my shoulders, and laid me down, covering me with a thin sheet and a dingy gray blanket.

"Sara, bring me some towels and a basin of water. Now, Alice, it could go quick or slow. We won't know until it happens. If you need to scream, do. It will help." Nurse doused a towel, it felt cool on my forehead.

Sara went back to the door standing guard. I felt safe and warm, no longer under the scrutiny of Reverend Mother. I looked up at the wooden cross hanging on the wall, larger than the one in Reverend Mother's office. I closed my eyes, and in a few moments I was back in Meadows Glen.

> *I looked out the kitchen window and saw Mum puttering about in the garden. Her red hair, brassy in the early-morning sun. She bent down digging at something with the trowel. I froze, not believing my eyes as she began tugging at something buried there. As she pulled my jumper from its hiding place, she turned to look at the window.*
>
> *Mum came in from the garden.*
>
> *"Sit down, Alice."*
>
> *"I was just going out. I finished in the kitchen, and…"*
>
> *"You're not going anywhere." She dropped the muddied garments on the hearth. "Explain this."*
>
> *Staring at the filthy clothes, I stammered. "They're mine. I buried them."*
>
> *"That doesn't make any sense. Why would you bury perfectly, good clothes?"*
>
> *"They're soiled."*
>
> *"Wash them."*
>
> *"I tried, they won't come clean. I can't wash the stain away."*
>
> *"Girl, you're not making any sense."*
>
> *"There was blood all over them. He attacked me on the way home from school."*
>
> *"Who attacked you?"*
>
> *"I don't know, he…"*
>
> *"What did he do? He didn't. Oh, Alice, why didn't you tell me?"*
>
> *"I was afraid, afraid you'd tell Da."*

"Alice. Wake up, girl. I need to examine you and see if it is time."

"I'm sorry Mum, it wasn't my fault."

"Alice, I'm not your Mum."

Instead of looking into Mum's eyes, it was Nurse Claire's soft green eyes that looked back at me. "I need you to slide all the way down, so your bum is at the edge of the bed. Pull your legs up as close as you can to your chest."

"Will it hurt?"

"No more than it has been hurting since you came in." She adjusted the sheet and I could feel her hand lightly rubbing my belly. "Not here yet, won't be long though."

I smelled a faint scent of rosewater.

"Where is she? Get out of my way." Reverend Mother screamed.

"Reverend Mother, you have to leave," Nurse Claire said, stepping between us. "Everything is fine here. She's about to deliver."

"Put her on the commode. She doesn't need a bed."

"I will do nothing of the kind."   The old woman reached across to yank me from the bed. Claire grabbed her wrist.

"That's enough," Nurse Claire yelled. "She's in full labor, and will remain in bed until it's over. Now, do I need to ask you again?" Nurse Claire stood firm, glaring at Reverend Mother.

"This is not over," she said with narrowed eyes, turned and stomped out the door.

"Thank you for not putting me on the commode," I said.

"No one should use a commode as a delivery table," she said, her voice muffled from under the blanket.

"You ready now, dear?" Nurse Claire asked.

"Should I be?"

"Yes, it's time, you are about to crown. I can see the head. I'm going to have you start pushing in just a minute."

"What?"

"It means your baby's coming out."

She spread my legs apart again.

His hard hands pulled my legs apart, the gravel dug into my back. He straddled me. Fumbled and tore whatever he couldn't undo. His weight and the stench of alcohol suffocated me.

The pains, like daggers, stabbed deep between my thighs. I pinched the sheets together, closed my eyes, and pressed down. It went black.

Pounding on his shoulders, I couldn't stop the ramming of his hips against me. It burned like fire. I should have tried harder. His smell folded into my skin.

The pain hung over me, and as quickly as the memory came, it disappeared. When I opened my eyes only the whiteness of the infirmary and Nurse Claire were keeping me safe.

"OK. Start now. Push. This baby is coming." I pushed, and pushed again. I listened for Nurse Claire's directions, pushing and stopping at each command, seemingly going on for hours. Tears ran down my cheeks while I muffled my screams. Something blocked the way. I felt the tearing as I pushed harder.

Nurse leaned over me, pushing down on my abdomen, but nothing happened. Sara continued wiping my face, kneeling next to me. I closed my eyes, lulled by the tenderness of her voice. I was brought back to reality with her tugging and pulling between my legs. Something was wrong I could feel it. The pains were different. Sara stroked my cheek, rounding her fingers down my chin. I reached for her hand. It should have been Mum, offering her caress.

*   *   *

"Alice," a cool hand touched my forehead.

"What happened?"

"She's here," Sara whispered in my ear.

I barely heard what Sara tried to tell me. I closed my eyes and found myself no longer in the white room, instead, sitting on our hearth, helping Mum fold clothes, safe and comfortable. A final burst of pain brought me back. I screamed. Sara returned the cloth to its place. Sleep came over me.

When I opened my eyes, the morning glare from the tiny ceiling windows blinded me. I closed my eyes to block the light, then slowly opened them again. The figure on the cross still stared down.

Nurse Claire came toward me. In her hands, wrapped in lightweight white blanket, the tiny bundle was wet, still bloody.

"She's a wee girl," she said, laying her on my chest. I touched the black matted hair.

"She's perfect," Sara said, smiling down at me, "Look, see her fingers and toes," she said, opening the blanket.

Holding my baby for the first time, I felt the rhythm of her heartbeat as she lay in my arms. I held her tight, knowing that Reverend Mother would place her on the cold stone front steps outside, as a sacrifice to God for my sins.

I turned on my side with the infant secure in the curve of my arm. I lifted her hand, her tiny fingers clutching mine. I fell asleep until I heard her whimper and felt a wiggle.

"What are you doing?" I cried as Nurse Claire moved her.

"It's okay. I'm going to bathe her, while you get some rest. I'll come back and clean you up."

Nurse Claire returned and lifted me from the bed, placing me in a straight-back chair, while Sara slipped the stained sheets from the mattress. Nurse Claire removed my soiled gown and cleaned me with a warm washcloth. She wiped the blood from between my legs. Slid a gown over my head and helped me back in bed.

Nurse Claire left the room, but quickly returned nestling the small white bundle in my arms. Seeing her, tears gushed down my face while the rain beat hard against the windows, echoing my tears.

The silence broke.

Out of the corner of my eye, I saw a swirl of black. "Get that baby away from her," she screamed.

Nurse Claire didn't move. Sara hid in the corner. Reverend Mother held my baby with one arm and stationed herself between the bed and the door, standing erect, and composed.

"You will never hold this baby again. I'll have her gone tomorrow before I let you touch her. You will never humiliate me again." Her lips tight and creased to one side. "I want you out of this infirmary by this afternoon."

"No." Nurse Claire spoke up, taking the baby from her arms before Reverend Mother could stop her. "Besides extensive tearing, the bleeding hasn't stopped. She'll pass out if you send her back to work now."

"I don't care what happens to her. I want her out of this infirmary."

"You can do what you like with me," Nurse Claire said moving across the room toward the bed. "She remains in this bed until the day after tomorrow. She deserves at least that."

"She deserves nothing." Reverend Mother couldn't contain her rage.

"With all due respect, if you send her back to work and she continues to bleed, I will be forced to call for the doctor and that will be much more bothersome than allowing her to rest for one more day."

A silence filled every corner of the room. "If she's not gone by noon, there'll be hell to pay... for both of you."

ᛗum's Arrival

on't worry, I'll take care of her. She'll be fine," Nurse Claire said. "Reverend Mother knows you're the only one who can feed her. She won't spend money on formula if she doesn't have to. You're safe for now."

I heard the words, but rolled away unable to reply. Milk leaked through my gown at the thought of the baby in the corner. Lost in my fears and a restless sleep, I heard footsteps coming back toward the bed. Nurse Claire stood there, holding my baby.

"You've been asleep for a long time. Here, hold your daughter, she's hungry," Nurse Claire said, smiling.

I pulled myself up, leaned against the metal headboard, and opened my gown. I took the baby from her arms, but I didn't know how to feed her. I didn't know what to do with these feelings that filled my heart. I couldn't distinguish between the pain and the love. I wasn't supposed to love this being that came from me, but I did. She had been created in a moment of rage, pulled from my body, but when I heard Reverend Mother say I could never have her. Did that trigger my heart, or was it her tiny fingers wrapped around mine? Her warm skin against mine? I touched her lips, moving her down, securing her in my arms.

"I don't know how to do this." I started to cry.

"You'll do grand," Nurse Claire said, moving her finger along the edge of my daughter's mouth, opening it slightly. "There, now put your nipple in her mouth. She'll take hold." The small face shifted about, trying to move into position. Suddenly, after a few moments I felt it. She took hold and began to suck. Slowly snuggling deep into my arm. Our first attempt only lasted a few seconds before she fell asleep, her mouth still holding tight. Nurse Claire stood over watching my every move.

"Go ahead, wake her up, she's still hungry. When she finishes on the one side, switch her to the other side doing the same thing."

I held her close, covering her with the blanket, almost hiding her, terrified Reverend Mother would return and take her from me.

"Will they let me name her?" I asked, as Nurse Claire sat on the edge of the bed watching me.

"I imagine so. Do you have any names in mind?"

"I want to call her Fionnuala, Finn for short. You know, like in the story, The Children of Lir."

"I know the story well, but don't you think it is a bit odd? Such a big name for a wee girl?" Nurse Claire asked, "due to the circumstance?"

"I know in a few days, or a week, or a month, and though gone from me, she will forever be my white swan. Is that too much to hope for?"

Nurse Claire looked down at me, and smiled. "In that case, Fionnuala would be grand."

An eerie calm filled the air. Nurse Claire went to the far corner of the room to tend to another girl, before I realized my arms were empty.

"She's gone. Where have you taken her?" I cried.

"Alice, calm down. When you fell asleep, I put her in a crib, over there," Nurse Claire said, pointing across the room.

"How long have I been I asleep?"

"A few hours. It's supper time. Are you hungry?"

"No, I'm just so, very tired."

"You need to eat. I'll have one of the girls fetch you a meal. When you are done, you need to get your rest. Reverend Mother will come back some time tomorrow. You'll need to be ready."

"When will I see my baby?"

"I'll bring her back to you when we are done. I'll even bring over the crib, so she will be next to you." Nurse Claire continued.

"I shouldn't love her so much, but I do. What's going to happen to us?" I asked. "They're going to take her from me aren't they?"

"You're allowed nine days, so I'm going to make sure you have them. I know Reverend Mother will be pushing things along. She'll be out for revenge, so once you're out of here, you need to watch out. I'll take care of things in here."

I knew Nurse Claire's intentions were admirable, but I also knew I had to do my share as well. I couldn't give anyone cause to come after me. The next morning one of the girls brought me some fresh clothes.

"You have another day to rest. You don't have to go yet."

"I can't let her be the one to find me. I'll go work for a few hours, and when she is satisfied that I'm back at work, I'll come back and rest."

I went back to the drying room hiding in the far corner, folding sheets and towels, all the while, remembering the touch of my daughter.

Nurse Claire sent messengers when I needed to feed Finn, but I was aware long before they arrived. I found my way to the infirmary as often as needed, even slipping out of the dormitory at night to sleep next to her, hold her in my arms, but our time together was running out. Reverend Mother had no intentions of allowing the nine days I'd been promised. On day seven, Sara came in the door.

"She wants you in her office . . . now."

"Why?"

"Your Mum is here; she came in on the train. I tried to listen from outside the door, but they whispered too low. I'm sorry, not much help."

"Thank you for trying."

"How's the baby?"

"She's wonderful. I've named her Fionnuala, but I call her Finn. Nurse Claire leaves the door unlocked and I sneak into the nursery and stay with her every night."

"Be careful. Reverend Mother has her ways and rarely does she fail."

"Have you seen her at all?"

"She comes to the kitchen now and again looking around, then walks out without a word. No one has seen her this mad since two penitents escaped and Monsignor Matthew blamed her."

As we came around the corner, we saw Reverend Mother standing in the doorway of her office.

"Don't say a word," Sara whispered, as she turned back the way she came.

*   *   *

Just seven days after giving birth I stood against the wall in Reverend

Mother's office, which, with a swipe of her hand dictated the way of my life. I had angered her, and defied her. I'd not be forgiven. She'd find a way to repay me for my insolence. When she closed the door, I knew exactly how she would do it.

Mum, her hair wet from the rain, clutching her pocket-book in her hands, her thin coat wrapped around her. I looked down at her Sunday shoes and her torn hose, splattered with mud from the gutters. It saddened me to see her in such disarray, looking lost and confused, nothing like the Mum I had known. I took the seat Reverend Mother directed me to, trying to get Mum's attention. With a quick jab, I realized Reverend Mother kept us as far apart as possible. I smiled again, trying to reach for her, but Reverend Mother swatted my hand away. I sat back, glared at Reverend Mother and in my mind, wondered how this had happened, how I ended up in this place.

Seeing Mum alone, told me everything I needed to know. Da refused to accompany her. I had shamed him before his community, his church and his God.

His daughter, a whore, his grandchild a bastard, and his wife informed, that neither would be allowed back. She didn't have to say a word. I knew. I knew from the moment he slapped me on the stairway, allowed me to be taken from my home that he'd never forgive me.

I saw his anger in Mum's face, never looking up, never acknowledging the daughter she allowed her husband to discard.

"Thank you for coming all this way, Mrs. Brennan. We'll work through this promptly, you can be on your way before dark."

"Thank you Reverend Mother. I am so grateful for what you've done for my daughter."

"We need to make some decisions about the baby's placement and Alice's transfer."

"Excuse me, what transfer?" I asked. Looking at Mum, I knew she had no idea what Reverend Mother meant.

"You know she's not returning to your home, don't you?"

"I'm sorry, I don't understand," Mum said. She twisted the handkerchief she pulled from her handbag.

"We feel," Reverend Mother continued, looking straight at Mum, "it would be in Alice's best interest to be sent to a convent school in Dublin, rather than return home."

"What would she do at a convent school?"

"She'd be educated," Reverend Mother said, making notes in a file with my last name in the corner. "You do realize if we allowed her to return home, that it could happen again?"

"That I'd be raped again? Are you saying I asked for this?"

"Mind yourself, girl," Reverend Mother snapped, leaning forward.

"Mrs. Brennan, a rape doesn't just happen. She must have done something. We just want to protect her from this happening again."

A hush filled the room. Mum sat with her handbag clasped in her lap. Reverend Mother wrote notes in a file I would never see. Me, I sat on the edge of the chair, with my future in the balance.

"Mum, you need to take me home," I tried to whisper to her.

"No. She needs to protect you," Reverend Mother shouted, standing up. "That's what she needs to do, and as is clear to all of us, that cannot be done in your home."

"Perhaps she's right, Alice. You did get yourself in trouble," Mum said in almost a whisper.

"How did I do that? He raped me," I said, trying to get Mum to look at me.

"Let's conclude this. We have much to consider, beginning with the baby's name. We need to file the birth certificate, and the baby needs to be baptized before she leaves." Reverend Mother laid out the prepared documents, beaming that she had offered up the ultimate compromise to such a sinner.

"I don't believe the child has been named. I didn't know we could," Mum said in earnest.

"She has. I know the name," I said.

Mum continued, as if I hadn't said a word. "I hoped whoever took the child, might name her, or you Reverend Mother might take the privilege," Mum said, fidgeting with the single thread hanging from her coat, but never turning to look at me.

Mum let go of the thread, slipped her black gloves from her hands and entwined them on her lap.

"You're not listening. I have chosen a name." I could have been talking to the walls.

"We don't name the babies," Reverend Mother replied putting notes on the paper in my folder. "Each family is responsible for that task, but Certificates must be completed before the transfer."

"Aren't you listening to me? I've named her," I said, sliding forward on the chair so they could see me. "Her name is Fionnuala."

At those words, Mum sat up. "You cannot do that. Reverend Mother, I am very sorry for my daughter's rudeness. I did not raise her to be disrespectful."

Mum turned to Reverend Mother. "Sister, I mean Reverend Mother," she paused, embarrassed with her error, "You see what I mean? I think we should give her your namesake. You've taken such excellent care of everything during this difficult time. Maybe your name would be a blessing to the poor child."

"I don't give my name to the babies."

"I don't need your name. I have chosen a name for my daughter," I said standing up so they'd look at me, "Fionnuala Claire Brennan."

"You will be calling her nothing of the sort." Reverend Mother said, this time staring straight at me.

"My name won't be on her birth certificate. In the eyes of the law, she will never be mine again, but God will know," I said.

"That is enough." Reverend Mother stood up.

"She's my daughter, even though I'll never watch her grow, I'll never celebrate birthdays. I'll have no right to her, she'll always be a part of me." I stared back at Mum, though she looked away.

"I'm giving her a name that means something to me." I said, moving toward Mum's chair.

Reverend Mother said nothing, but bowed her head. I saw it, a sly smile. She had won. She looked up, throwing me a scathing glare, but there was nothing more she could do to hurt me. She had done it all.

I stood behind Mum, with my hands on her shoulders. After a few moments, Reverend Mother pulled her papers together and focused her words on Mum alone.

"Alice, if you will take your seat, we have one last line to fill. The father? Mrs. Brennan, do you have his name?"

"No, I don't. He must have been a vagrant. Alice never identified him. Is that important?"

"Well, we just want to be sure we are thorough." Over and over, Reverend Mother attempted to extract a name from Mum, believing she hung on to an unspoken truth. Never once did she ask me. At the end of the conversation, the line remained blank. For a moment, seeing the empty line on the paper took me back.

Staring at the blank space, the sound of his voice came back to me, a voice I couldn't identify and would never hear again.

Reverend Mother completed the final documents, the name, Fionnuala Claire Brennan written on both the birth certificate and baptismal documents. She listed Alice Brennan as the mother. The line for the father remained blank. No honor to be had, but I took it as a small victory.

I watched my mother look lovingly at my captor. She must have thought that we had both been saved. I could easily have seen her looking up at the Crucifix making the sign of the cross in gratitude.

"Mrs. Brennan if you could wait here, we still have a few items to complete. I'll walk Alice back to her station, I'll have some tea brought in for you."

"That would be wonderful." Mum straightened her skirt and laid her purse on the table.

Reverend Mother got up, moved to the door, and motioned to a Sister standing outside to bring a tray of tea and cakes. Reverend Mother signaled for me to go out the door.

"You can see your daughter before you leave for the train, but for now we need to talk privately."

My mother said nothing. Together, Reverend Mother and I returned to the washroom. Arriving at the doorway, Reverend Mother grabbed my arm and pushed me agianst the door.

"I've had enough of you. One more outburst like that, and I'll see you never leave the infirmary. Do I make myself clear?" When she slapped me, her ring caught the edge of my mouth.

"Yes, Ma'am," I said, tasting the blood as it began to trickle.

She turned, leaving me at the door without another word. Now, neither child, nor woman, but after seven days, I was different in every imaginable way.

Sara came up behind me, pushing me through of the doorway. She took a cloth from her pocket, licked it and began to wipe the blood from my face.

"What's going to happen to me, Sara?" I asked, as she took hold of my hand.

"First off, your Mum will need to pay the ninety pounds, but by the looks of you, I imagine that won't be happening."

"What ninety pounds? What happens if she doesn't?"

"The ninety pounds is your keep, their pay for your room and board, and delivering the baby. If she doesn't pay, you'll be going to the Laundries, girl. They make no allowances."

"Why would I be sent there?" I asked

"To pay your debt. They're workhouses for women who get in trouble."

"Okay, but I didn't get in trouble," I said.

"Get it through your head. You had a baby, didn't you?" Sara whispered.

"Yes, but I didn't do anything wrong."

"Stop your foolishness girl. You ought to know by now. One, you've sinned, and two, if your family doesn't pay, you'll have to work off what has been provided for you. You're not going home. None of us go home," Sara said.

"Why didn't you get sent away?"

"No one came for me, and they decided they could use my cooking skills to their favor."

"No. They promised I'd go home. That is why Mum came today, to take me home."

"No, I imagine she never promised to take you home. She came to sign you over to another convent, not out. If you're signed in by a parent, they need her signature to sign you over to the Laundry convent."

"When will I go?"

"In a few days, maybe even tomorrow. Your baby is gone, or will be, so nothing's holding you here, and from what I can tell, Reverend Mother wants you gone."

I didn't want to listen to Sara, so I moved away.

"Leave me alone."

I didn't hear the door open, nor did I see the black swirl of a skirt, but I did feel myself being pulled up from the floor.

90 Pounds

didn't know how long I remained on the floor, my mind swirled with images of Reverend Mother, a vision of the Laundries, and every horror I could conjure. The room stormed around me, everything collapsing at my feet.

"She wants you back in her office," a girl I didn't recognize said. "Do you want some help?" With her coarse hands, she smoothed back my hair, and helped me to my feet. I grabbed hold of the sink to keep my balance.

It took a few moments to collect myself, but it all came back. I had no pocket for my memories, no place to put the pieces of my life for safekeeping. I knew in the next few hours everything would be taken from me. I'd be stripped to nothing. Perhaps Reverend Mother might leave me alone, move on to another victim.

All the while holding on to me, the girl with the coarse hands led me downstairs, to the conference room, where my future, and that of my child, had been laid out. She tapped on the door, and we waited together.

Sr. Beatrice, the oldest and shortest of all the Sisters, and the kindest, opened the door. I peeked past her and saw that everyone had taken their places at the table. There was Mum, Reverend Mother, and Monsignor Matthew in the far corner, with two empty chairs next to him. Reverend Mother directed me forward with a nod. Sr. Beatrice took the remaining empty seat.

"With Reverend Mother's help, all the arrangements have been completed. The baby has been baptized and everything is ready for her transfer to Dublin," Monsignor Matthew said.

"Wait. Why wasn't I there? She's my daughter," I said, standing to get someone to notice me.

"Sit down, Alice. You didn't need to be present. Monsignor Matthew took care of it," Reverend Mother said.

"The baby will be transferred tomorrow to St. Patrick's in Dublin. She'll be taken to a foster home in a few days." Monsignor Matthew continued, flipping through the papers. He looked up toward Reverend Mother with a simple nod of his head.

"I'm never going to see her again, am I?"

"You are simple, aren't you girl?" Reverend Mother said. Mum sat mute, letting Reverend Mother insult me. "The infant will be placed with a family, who can provide much more than you ever could," she continued. "The papers you sign today, will release you of all responsibilities," Monsignor Matthew said looking straight at me.

"I won't sign." I said, tightening my jaw, and folding my arms across my chest.

I looked over at Mum, but she stared straight ahead. I had no idea what happened between the two, but whatever had, Reverend Mother won.

"Yes, you will," Monsignor Matthew said, now speaking to the wall behind me, "You may never search for her, and she will never be told anything about you."

"This never happened, if you will," Reverend Mother added.

"Never happened? How could it have never happened? I had a baby. She's asleep in the nursery. Her name is Finn. You signed her birth certificate with my name on it. You can't say she never happened."

"My Lord girl, you are a moron. Did you not hear me?" Reverend Mother said, staring right into my eyes. "This child, you so wanted to call Finn, is nothing to you anymore. Is that clear?"

Mum fumbled with her pocketbook, rubbed her hand down her nyloned leg, licked her dry lips, but said nothing.

"When do I get to go home?" I asked, attempting to pull myself together.

"I have talked to Reverend Mother, and with guidance from Monsignor Matthew, I've decided, it would be best for you to go to a convent in Dublin. You'd live with other girls, get proper schooling, much better than anything offered in Meadows Glen."

"You know they're sending me to the Laundries, don't you?" I asked.

Reverend Mother reassured her, "it's a convent school in Dublin. She'll have a chance to see the city, be educated, and meet new friends. When she is older, and ready, she can come home. This will all be behind her."

"It would be like a holiday. You'll forget everything that happened. You'll start fresh with your life. How grand would that be?"

"I don't want to forget. I want to take my baby and go home. Pay her the money and let me go," I begged.

"What are you talking about? What money? It won't cost anything for you to go to convent school."

"Mum, They're not sending me off on holiday, or to any school." I was ashamed for being so rude, but I didn't know how else to do it. I was fighting as hard as I knew how, but with the looks on their faces, it was a battle I had lost long before it started.

"It's already been settled Alice. Your mother signed. The transfer is complete," Reverend Mother said, opening the folder in front of me, "now, if you will just sign here."

"I'm not signing."

"I don't really need your signature. I only need a parent's." I shoved the papers away. It was over. She had won from the start.

"Alice, you will be transferred tomorrow. It's the best for everyone. Your mother won't have to worry about your safety. We won't let anything like this ever happen again."

"Can I, at least, see Finn before I leave?" I asked.

Reverend Mother looked over at Mum, then back at me. Standing, she gathered the papers. "I don't think that would be a good idea, but I will give you a few moments with your mother."

"I have nothing to say to her. I want to see my daughter."

"You'll be respectful and say a proper good-bye, or I will see to it that you never leave any convent. Do you hear me?" Reverend Mother's face turned red. She rose from her chair, leaned into me, but caught herself.

In a few moments, Monsignor Matthew rose from his seat, took the folder and dismissed himself.

"You two stay for some privacy. Say your good-byes." Reverend Mother said, following Monsignor out the door.

After everyone left, Mum and I stared at each other. I felt betrayed by such ignorance, both hers, and mine. What would we have to say to each other?

"I wish you'd have been a foolish girl." Mum began. "It would've been easier. Love gets lost, and we're thoughtless for moments we can't ever get back." She began to weep for the first time, brushing my hair from my face, gripping my shoulders like she'd never seen me before.

"I was neither foolish nor thoughtless," I said. "My only mistake was not seeing his face."

"Don't you know girl, it doesn't matter what happened? The truth doesn't matter. They're taking you, and there's nothing I can do to keep you here, but it's for the better."

"Better? You think the Laundries would be better?"

She knew. I watched her push her damp hair away from her face, with her other hand she touched my cheek, leaned in and kissed my eyes. The moment her lips brushed mine, I couldn't stop the tears.

"You know, if I could, I'd take you home today, but I can't. We can't pay the ninety pounds." She stepped away from me.

"Mum you have to pay the money, so I can go home. I'll forget. I promise. I'll find a way to pay you back." Grasping hold of her, I was begging. I would have fallen to my knees if I thought it would have made a difference.

"Reverend Mother thinks maybe after time away, you'll forget. You'll find some redemption. She's worried about you and, to be honest, so am I. You're different since you've been here." She turned away and moved toward the door.

"Of course, I'm different. I had a baby." I couldn't believe what I was hearing. "Don't you remember what you told me, that night we sat outside, when you were pregnant? You told me how much you loved me and that you never forgot your first daughter, no matter how many other children you had. You said that, I remember."

"I never said that."

"Yes, you did. I was ten, and it was during the winter. We were sitting on the porch and you promised you'd always love me, because I was your first daughter. You said that."

"No, Alice you are mistaken. You must have dreamt it."

"No, I didn't dream it. You said it. I know you did. I remember. You said that you would always love your first. Well, that's how I feel about Finn. I love her. She is my first. I can't leave her. Why are you sending me away? Why won't you pay? Aren't I worth ninety pounds?"

"Your Da refused to give it to me. There, now you have it. I couldn't do anything even if I wanted to. It's over."

She leaned against the wall so she wouldn't fall, and I stood frozen in the reality. She started to cry, but I realized it was not for me, or my baby. If she let me come home, Da would throw her out. He would throw us all out, so she had to sacrifice me for the rest of the family.

"You're leaving me here. You knew it the day I left."

"It's done, Alice," she said, coming toward me as if she could close her eyes and I would disappear. The ground fell open beneath me. "Someday you will forgive me."

"No, I won't."

"We're doing this for you. Before you know it, you'll be better than ever. All this will be behind you."

"No, Mum. You want me to forget, but every day I'll be reminded. Just let me come home."

"Reverend Mother and Monsignor Matthew have already explained it to you."

"Yes, and you want me to believe it's the money. If it weren't for the money, I'd be coming home."

"Alice, enough. It's settled." Mum turned toward the door, but I grabbed her by the arm.

"Do you want to see her, before you go?" I asked as she slipped her tattered gloves over her stained, country hands. Her shoulders crumbled together, and her head dropped. Every bit of air came out of her, I watched her spirit collapse. She gathered it back.

"No, I don't think that would be a good idea. I am sure she's grand, but what good would it do?"

"She's my daughter. She's your granddaughter. That's what good it would do. No matter what happened, she is our blood."

"I'm sure she is."

"Just tell me you know Reverend Mother lied, and that the papers you signed are a lie." I reached for her hand.

Looking in her eyes, she stared beyond me. I realized, even if Da had the money, I'd still be going to the Laundries. She patted my cheek and walked through the doorway. I had been traded for ninety pounds.

Despite of the shame, or that they signed my name to the documents, Finn was my firstborn daughter, as I was Mum's. I'd never have traded her for ninety pounds.

*   *   *

I watched Mum go out the door and heard her talk with Reverend Mother in murmurs. I didn't' want to hear her explanations. The front door closed and I knew her ordeal was over.

Reverend Mother returned to the conference room, "We will finish this in my office." She waited as I walked out, then swept ahead, as her gown glided across the floor. She took a key from a hidden pocket, and unlocked the door.

"Sit there," pointing to a chair in the far corner. "We have a few things to finalize."

She took her seat behind the desk. Folding her hands, she smiled.

"You put on quite a show," she said.

"It was not a show. You told my mother she had a responsibility to me. Well, I have a responsibility to my daughter. I'm defending our lives because no one else will."

"You're fourteen. You know nothing about defending anything," she said, leaning back in her chair. She opened the top drawer of her desk, but I couldn't see what she took from it. With great earnest, she got up and moved around to the front of the desk. With her hands behind her back, she leaned against the edge of the polished wood and glared at me.

"With all due respect, I turned fifteen."

"Oh that's right, you did. So you are a woman now." Her eyes taunted me. "You're such a fool."

Suddenly, she swung and I found myself on the floor, with her standing over me.

"Please. I just want to go home," I said, trying to pull myself up.

"We are not done, girl," as she pushed me down with a kick. Her smile disappeared; replaced with pure contempt.

"Just let me be," I pleaded.

"Oh, I'll let you go, but I don't want you to forget what you are."

She began beating me with the belt she had wrapped around her hand. I brought my hands up to protect myself, but the belt came down repeatedly. There was no place to hide.

I could hear the snap and felt the sting as it cut through my clothes, into my skin. She lunged again and again, swinging with a crazed fury.

As quickly as it started, it was over.

Except for my whimpering, a silence took hold. Kneeling, she grabbed my hair, with a swift jerk, she began to hack at my braid. Sharp jabs stabbed deep into my scalp. She stood, holding my braid, as if a ransom had been won. She smiled as she dropped it in the wastebasket, and placing the scissors back on the desk.

"Get up," she said, barely moving her mouth.

"I can't." Even the slightest move hurt. "Why are you doing this?"

"I'm saving you from the fires of Hell. You must pay for your sins."

I looked up at the woman, standing self-righteous. She had once stood regal, holding the voice of authority. Now she was no better than the man who threw me to the ground and took everything.

"What do you want? Tell me what you want." I cried, pushing clumps of hair out of my eyes.

"I want you to confess your sin and repent," she said, still red-faced.

"What am I supposed to say?"

"Admit your sin against God. You've sinned. You're a fornicator, someone has to save your soul," she said.

"I'm not a sinner."

"God is the judge of that. You are all sinners."

A tapping on the door broke the moment. It opened without a response from Reverend Mother. "Oh my God," a voice said from the door. "What have you done?"

"God's will."

"We have to get her some help. I'll get Nurse," Sr. Beatrice said.

"No, just take her to the lavatory. Clean her up."

Sr. Beatrice took hold of my hand, helping me from the floor, blood running down my face.

"What did she do?" Looking over at my face and scalp.

"I will not tolerate being disrespected."

"She's just a girl. What could she have done?"

"I tried to help her, but she would have nothing of it. She cursed at me." Reverend Mother said, regaining her composure.

"She needs medical attention, regardless of what you think."

"I don't care what you do. Get her out of my sight." She leaned against the desk, her eyes filled with exhaustion. "Just know, Alice, you'll never see that bastard child again, or that hole you came from. You think I'm the wrath of God. You wait, girl. I'm nothing compared to what you will face."

Sr. Beatrice guided me out the door, and down the hall, leaning me up against the wall while she opened the lavatory door.

"Come on, Alice I'll clean you up."

"Why did she do that, Sr. Beatrice?" My words garbled with spittle and blood.

"I've known Reverend Mother a long time, since she was a novice. She wasn't always like this."

"What do you mean?"

"She had dreams . . . we all did. Hers would take her to Dublin. To work in a private school, be in charge of proper young ladies. But they never let her. Every opportunity seemed to slip away. She had a run-in with Bishop Donovan when he was a Monsignor here. They butted heads from day one and he vowed she would never leave Castlepollard. As the years passed, she has been filled with frustration and hatred. Filled to the brim."

"So this has happened before?"

"More times than I could ever imagine."

"Why don't they stop it?"

"No one ever told," washing the blood from my face and arms. "I always thought the true reason was jealousy."

"Jealousy?"

"All of you girls had something she could never have. Instead of being sympathetic, she has let the anger and hatred fester. Using our God as her excuse."

"She has no right to do that."

"She would disagree with you. In many ways she is just. But sometimes . . . she loses control. She is a good soul. She just can't see her own flaws. We are not to judge."

The explanation stopped and I stared at the tears that washed down the wrinkled face of her friend. I was grateful for her compassion. I pulled her close, seeing her pain. She returned the embrace.

Sara entered the lavatory. "Oh, no. What did you do?" Sara asked, looking from me to Sr. Beatrice.

"Sara, take her to the dormitory, wash her up, then put her to bed."

"Who did this?"

"Don't worry about that now. She needs to rest for a few hours. Later, take her to chapel."

Without saying a word, Sara guided me through the door. When we entered the bathroom, she gently pulled at my clothes. "I know this hurts, but I have to...Oh, Alice your back..." She moved me in to the shower stall and stood with me, the water washing over us. Sara ran the cloth gently over my body, taking great care with the welts on my back and thighs.

"Alice, I don't know how you're even standing," she said drying me with a towel. Wait here. Let me get you a gown and get you in bed." After changing her clothes, she sat on the bed stroking my hair, and smiling.

"It doesn't look so bad, besides it will grow back in no time."

"I know."

"You rest now. When you wake up, Sr. Beatrice wants you to go down to the chapel. I don't know why, I have to get to the kitchen, but I will keep a look out for you."

It was hard to keep my eyes open, once I allowed myself to relax. I slipped my hand under the pillow, grasping my Sacred Heart holding it close to my breast. I could not lose it.

When I awoke, it was dark and I could hear the girls breathing deep.

Good-bye

didn't remember sneaking out of the dormitory. I didn't remember walking down the stairs or finding my way to the chapel. I slid into the last pew, sat straight-backed, and took a deep breath, trying to prepare myself for what was to come. I looked around and captured the stillness. I found peace staring into the stained-glass windows, reflecting the candlelight.

I once loved a God, and all I learned about Him, but over the months, in His name, my beliefs had been beaten from me. He stared down at me in judgment. I wondered what He had told Reverend Mother to teach me. What did I need to learn?

"How are you feeling?" Asked Sara, brushing my shoulder, my skin tender to the touch. "I have some news."

"Did Reverend Mother fall down the stairs?"

"You're leaving this morning for Dublin, The Laundries," she said, looking almost excited. "We're going together."

"How can that be? Oh my God, it's my fault. I made this happen. I'm sorry."

"No, I asked to go. If I stay, Alice, I have nothing. A day will just come when one morning I don't wake up. At least I'll have you. We'll be together." Her smile was dumbfounding, how could someone be looking forward to the Laundries?

"But the Laundries will be worse, harder, won't they?" I asked.

"No, I think Hell is here." Sara said. "We'll get through this. We'll be together. Who knows what'll happen? Who cares?" resting my head on her shoulder.

"I need to see Finn before I go, Sara."

"I know."

*   *   *

Inside the nursery, we found the babies, Nurse Claire busy tending to the newest arrival. I skimmed through the cribs until I found Finn, asleep, curled in a tiny circle under her blanket. I pulled the Sacred Heart medal from my pocket.

For something with little or no value to me as a child, it became more precious than anything I ever owned. I needed Finn to have it. I had to believe it would keep her safe. It was all I had to give her. I lifted my daughter, just a touch and slipped the string around her neck, resting the medal against her chest.

Nurse Claire said nothing of my chopped hair, or the cuts and welts, but I saw the sorrow in her face. I imagined she had seen such damage too many times before.

"When your daughter leaves here, she'll have it," Nurse Claire said, gathering my body close and letting me collapse in her arms.

"I'll come back someday, but you must protect her, keep her away from Reverend Mother, and tell her I didn't do this. Please, tell her I didn't do this." I paused, looking down at the crib. "Tell her I love her," I said turning away.

"Wait," she said. I turned and watched her scoop Finn up from the metal crib. She placed her in the grooves of my arms. "Tell her yourself. Tell her before it's too late."

"Well, isn't this just grand?" Reverend Mother pushed Sara to the side. "Nurse, take the infant out of this room. I'll deal with you later."

Reverend Mother was no fool. She must have anticipated that I would attempt to see my daughter one last time. I stood in front of her, while still holding Finn. She swung her hand in a moment of rage.

"You will never touch me again." I screamed at her, catching her arm in midair and pushing her away.

"Stop. You need to stop now. You have beaten this girl beyond recognition. What is wrong with you?" Nurse Claire asked.

"She deserved it," Reverend Mother said, straightening her skirt and the gold cross that hung from her waist.

"No one deserves what you have done to her. Leave us. I'm in charge here. This is my infirmary." Reverend Mother glared at her.

"Have the baby ready tomorrow morning. Someone will be coming to transport it to Dublin." Turning back to me, "now see what you can do about it," she said.

I knew it would be the last time I'd hold Finn. I leaned in, and smelled the sweet skin. "I love you Finn," I said, nestling my head in her tiny chest. "I didn't do this," I whispered into her blanket. "Please don't forget me."

The three of us stood together in silence. I took a deep breath, and allowed myself a faint smile. I had given her a piece of me that she might have forever. I hugged Nurse Claire and left the infirmary for the last time. Sara and I walked arm-in-arm back down the hallway.

"I need to go into the chapel," I said letting go of Sara's arm.

"Do you want me to go with you?"

"No. I'll be okay. I just need to be alone."

"All right. I'll wait in the kitchen. Be careful."

"What can they do to me now?"

I opened the heavy door of the chapel and knelt at the altar. I made the sign of the cross and I looked up to the Sacred Heart statue before me.

It's Alice, you know that. I'll be leaving today, going somewhere in Dublin. You know that, too. I'm a bit disappointed in the way you've been looking after me. With my going and all, I'm hoping you'll do a better job watching over me in the Laundries than You did here. I'm quite a mess. Truth be said, I'm losing my faith in You.
I don't know what's going to happen, but I do know I'm going to need Your help. Keep my Finn safe. She is such a sweet thing. She doesn't know what is going on. And someday, bring us together again.
Amen

I heard the door to the chapel open. I turned and saw Monsignor

Matthew with a folder in his hand, and next to him, Reverend Mother.

"Well my dear, it looks like it's time. We must be getting along before it gets too late," Monsignor Matthew said as he walked up the aisle.

I stood and moved toward the door. Reverend Mother stood to the side as I walked past. The three of us walked down the hallway with Monsignor Matthew leading the way, Reverend Mother keeping step behind me.

"Thank you Monsignor for coming so early this morning."

"I'm delighted that a position was found so quickly," he said, bowing his head. Sara was standing in the entryway.

"If I could have just a moment with them alone? I'd like to say good-bye." Reverend Mother asked.

"Very well, I'll wait for them in the car." He opened the door, and quickly found his way out.

"I wanted a chance to say good-bye to both of you properly," she said, first going over to Sara. "You've been with us a long time. I will miss you, especially your cooking."

"Thank you, Ma'am," Sara said, bowing her head in reverence.

"You go on now. Have a safe trip and God be with you," Reverend Mother said, waiting as Sara went through the front door, then she turned back to me."

"Well, we had quite a time didn't we, girl?"

"Yes, Ma'am, we did."

"Anything you want to say to me?"

"No, Ma'am, there isn't." I knew what she expected . . . that would never happen.

Suddenly, she pulled me close as if in a hug, both of her arms coming in tight across my back. "I will see that your life is a living hell."

I pulled away and looked at her.

"Good-bye dear. If you thought I was bad, just wait," she whispered with a smile.

* * *

I watched the stout, whiskey-breathed Monsignor, shift in his seat, tucking the envelope that held our future, in the glove box. I could smell the alcohol mixed with stale, musky after-shave. He ran his fingers through his oily hair and straightened himself for the drive.

As we left Castlepollard behind, I turned to take a last look at the stonewalls. Were we leaving one prison for another?

"How are you today? Looks as if we'll be getting a bit of a storm," he said, staring back at me through the mirror.

I said nothing to his greeting. What was there to say?

"It will take more than an hour. I'll need to go slower with the traffic and the rain," he said, still peering through the mirror.

The rain came down harder as we drove. We passed St. Patrick's Cathedral, O'Connell Street, Cleary's Department Store, and St. Stephen's Green, places where I once dreamed of spending holidays.

I stared out the window at the blurred roadside, as we drove wondering what lay ahead. I turned toward Sara, slumped against the door, asleep with her hand covering her face.

We slowed going over the bridge connecting the two sides of O'Connell Street over the Liffy River. Looking out past the bridge, I watched swans gather at the edge of the river. As a little girl, Mum told us of the legends, how the wicked step-mother turned her children to swans in The Children of Lir, and how their voices were heard for hundreds of years. She told of swans being brought to the river's edge as a gift from a legendary king, and protected from all dangers. I wondered why we, sinners of God, as Reverend Mother called us, could not be as protected as those white plush birds; perhaps our beauty had not blossomed. Were we yet to be transformed?

Transfixed by the magnificence and enormity of the swans as they bathed in the morning sun. Their garden—their Swan Garden.

"You girls from this area?" he asked as he drove along.

"Are you now?" he asked again.

"No, Monsignor," I said, "From the Midlands."

"I've been to County Meath, an astonishing church, it has." I looked up in the mirror, and I caught him watching me again. Something in his eyes made me shiver. Reverend Mother once called him "our messenger from God." But what was the message?

*　　*　　*

A massive ivy covered wall appeared in front of us. The hedges along the street hid the landscape on each side, with a tall spiked wrought-iron gate between them standing open. Massive brick buildings with bars across the windows loomed against the darkened sky. We'd be bedded there, alone on a single sliver-thin mattress, until we had worked off our debt and set free. My parents had found a way to be straight in the eyes of God.

The driveway wound through the firs and manicured lawns, past gardens lush with roses. What the public saw. We rounded the final circle, and I nudged Sara.

"We're here. Have you ever seen the likes of this?" Monsignor Matthew asked, staring as if it were something magical.

No, and I imagine I never will. I'll be dying here. I wanted to say, but instead whispered an inaudible, "No."

"It's majestic, isn't it?"

"Like nothing I've ever seen." A pastoral prison where we'd never see the light of day. With all this beauty on the outside, no one would ever suspect.

Monsignor Matthew turned off the engine, retrieving the envelope, and his hat. Sara and I remained quiet, still too afraid to move. Adjusting his hat, he came around and opened the door on Sara's side, allowing us to step out.

"I'll be looking out for you, girl." He ran his fingers down my cheekbone, leaned in and kissed my forehead. "And the baby? How's the baby?" He didn't wait for an answer, but turned and left us standing in the gravel driveway. The rain continued to fall as he headed to the front door.

THE LAUNDRIES

MOTHER MICHAEL

 polished marble table stood in the center of the hallway with a painted ceramic statue of St. Patrick centered on top. Wooden beads looped around the neck and shoulders of the statue. Black serpents twined around his sandals and slithered up his robe. Terrifying at first, but at second glance, a fitting statue to greet visitors to this place with the official name of St. Patrick's Convent for the Lost Souls, but to the neighborhood, known simply as "The Laundries."

"You'll be meeting Superior Mother Michael. Besides Monsignor Matthew, she is in charge. Remember that," the penitent who had greeted us said, beckoning us to follow her.

"Is she mean?" I asked, hoping to learn what I was stepping into.

The woman looked around, turned and stopped, almost causing me to run into her. "She's no picnic, I'll tell you that," she whispered. "You get on her bad side and you'll be here for life. Oh, and the one who usually stands right next to her, Sr. Helen, watch out for her."

She rapped twice on the heavy wooden door, then opened it. In the far corner stood a tall imposing Sister, who took the folder from the penitent. Once we were inside, the penitent closed the door without a word. We heard the squeak of her shoes on the tile as she walked down the hall.

Another Sister, who I assumed must be Mother Superior, bulging from her black habit, stood behind a desk. She said nothing, just stared, motioning for us to sit down. The taller Sister next to her remained in the corner still holding on to the folder.

The Reverend Mother stood shorter than I expected. Her cheeks puffed like burnt biscuits, flooding out of the sides of her starched habit. Outside of the Laundries, she might have gone unnoticed, dull features except for the scars. Short, soft pink lines ran across her hands, like works of art. Here, they glorified her as religious royalty.

"Well, who do we have here? Are you simpletons?"

"No, ma'am."

"Who are you?"

"Alice Brennan, and Sara Hughes, Mother Michael," the imposing Sister from the corner said, moving over between us. Never looking at the woman next to her, as she placed the folder on the desk.

"Take the other one outside. I will meet with her later." Sara never raised her head as the Sister pushed her through the door.

"Can you speak, girl, or has your tongue been cut out?" She asked, looking straight at me.

"I'm trying to be respectful." I kept my head down so my features couldn't be seen.

"I am Superior Mother Michael, but you will respond to me as Mother Michael. I see that Monsignor Matthew and Reverend Mother have sent your papers. I already know about you girl, but I like to hear for myself, before bringing judgments."

She sat down in her chair behind the desk and folded her hands over the papers. She cleared her throat and looked up at me.

"Get on with it girl, I don't have all day," opening the folder in front of her.

"What should I say?" At a loss, I knew she didn't want the truth.

"Well . . . start with why you are here."

"I don't know." It came out before I had a chance to take it back.

"My, my, aren't you an odd one. I would think you would know why you were here. Would you like me to tell you?" She grinned, got up from her chair and moved around the desk.

"Your family didn't pay the ninety pounds owed to Castlepollard, so you must work it off here. It costs money for your room and board and care for the bastard child of yours."

"They told my mum I'd be going to school."

"I'm sure they did. Yes, you will get an education, I guarantee you that."

"When I've paid you back, can I go home?" I asked.

"Of course you can, you silly thing," she said, straightening her gown and adjusting the brown rosary beads attached to the gold cross that hung from her waist. "Tell me now. Who is he?"

"Who?"

"The father, girl. Who is the father?"

"I don't know."

"Whore, were you then?"

"No, Mother Michael, I didn't, to be sure. He raped me."

"You were now, were you? I've heard that tale many times before.

"How old are you, girl?"

"Just turned fifteen."

"Where's the baby?" Mother Michael flipped through the file from the Home.

"Being fostered out, ma'am."

"Well, that's a good thing."

"I'm a good girl." I said. "I didn't do anything wrong."

"Why are you here, Alice Brennan? Can you answer me that?"

"To repent. Reverend Mother told Mum I wasn't ready to go home, but I am. Home's where I need to be."

"Let me see if I have this right, you're a splendid girl, but you gave birth out of wedlock, and you aren't allowed to go home yet? Am I correct so far?"

"Yes, Mother Michael, you are."

"Sister Helen, I am shocked. We must have made a mistake. We have ourselves a good girl here. Did you know that?"

"No Mother Michael, they informed me otherwise. I can't imagine Monsignor Matthew would make such a mistake. I should have asked him to be sure." Still in the corner, she almost laughed out loud, covering her mouth instead.

"Well, Alice," Mother Michael said, "I do not believe in rape. I suppose any girl who says she's been raped, must have done something to bring it on."

"I just wanted to explain."

"That you are bold or simple? Which is it, girl?"

"I'm not simple."

"I'll decide that." Mother Michael said.

"How long do I have to stay?"

"Well, that depends on you. Hinges on how hard you work, and how well you get along with the others. But more important, how you get along with me. Let's go over the rules. Do you have any questions before I start?"

"No, Ma'am."

"Follow these simple rules. No talking, be on time at your workstation, do not miss Mass, do not leave a work area without permission, no talking to any of the other girls, and never go outside, unless directed by a Sister.

You'll start in the ironing room this afternoon, when done there, then off to the folding room until all garments are bagged and ready for transfer.

If you complete all the tasks before dinner, you'll polish the pews in the chapel. Cleanliness is next to Godliness. We keep it that way. Dinner is at 7:00. You'll be back in the chapel for Vigils at 7:30. Return to the dormitory by 8:00, lights dimmed by 8:15." The clock had been set and running.

"Alice what was your baptismal name."

"Mary, why?" I asked, knowing what was coming.

"No, can't be that. Do you have a middle name?"

"Margaret."

"No, we have a Margaret. I'll deal with this later. Oh yes, when I said no talking to any of the other girls, trust me, I meant it. You're always being watched. I will know. I do not like to be disobeyed."

She closed the folder, signaling that her business with me was concluded. Sister Helen guided me out the door, where a penitent waited to introduce me to my new home.

From a side-glance, the freckled girl might have been much older, but with her colorless, gaunt cheeks, her age seemed irrelevant. Her hair was pulled tight back away from her face, with no life in her eyes, no color identifying her heredity. At one time, she might have had rich thick flowing hair, a luscious brunette, with shades of red, that matched her splash of freckles, but the glow had long since disappeared.

"This is Veronica, she'll take you to the dormitory," Sister Helen said.

She led me down the long hallway and up a flight of stairs to the dormitory. Unlike the Home, thirty beds lined the walls like hedges, lockers stood between each bed. There were no throw rugs between the beds. Inside each grey metal locker hung six brown faded jumpers unraveled at the hems, along with two steel-grey cardigans. A pair of worn brown shoes sat on the bottom, with underwear and socks folded next to them. Two nightdresses and six blouses, had been placed on the top shelf.

Without notice, she pushed me down on one of the cots. I felt the coarseness of the mat through my dress and realized, I might have more than the Sisters to fear.

"The others will be here before too long," she said, glancing around the room.

"Long memories the Sisters have, especially Sister Helen. Stay out of her way at all costs. It does no good to fight them, no matter what your heart tells you. You'll not win against any of them."

Without taking a breath, she continued her guidance. "Don't trust anyone, not the Sisters, and never the girls, not even me. Because I'm talking with you, does not mean I'm being your friend. These girls will do anything to get into the Sisters' good graces or out of their bad ones, as the case may be. Stay away from Monsignor Matthew. Never be alone with him, no matter what."

"Why?"

"He is a sick bastard," she said nodding her head. "I'll take you around first, so you know where everything is. It's much larger than it looks from the outside. We're only allowed in certain areas. Dormitories are the farthest from everything, way up on the top floor. You've seen the offices. The chapel is across the hall. You'll spend the most time in the cafeteria and the laundry rooms, which are in the basement."

"I didn't know this place had so many different parts," I said.

She nodded. "On the other side of the complex, the orphanage, the school, and the rectory where Monsignor Matthew lives."

"An orphanage?"

"Don't even think about it," she admonished.

I could only wonder if Finn may have been brought there.

"Hey? Are you listening?" I turned back toward her, but couldn't help smiling. I now had something to distract me from the days ahead. There was a possibility, just a few buildings away, my daughter was snuggled warm in a bed.

"I know what you're thinking," she sighed. "All the other girls who lost their babies think the same thing. I'm serious. You can't ever go over there." She understood, but I didn't care.

"What?" I tried acting surprised.

"You think your baby is here, don't you? And you think you can find a way to get to her? Don't make that mistake."

"How can that be a mistake?"

"I've seen it happen before. If they find you there, you won't see the light of the next day. And your baby, if she is there, will be gone even quicker. Sr. Helen keeps close track of all the girls in her charge. Don't even try." Veronica said, tying her hair back with a rubber band.

"All right, I won't." I'd keep my options open.

"Where do I need to go?"

"She wants you to start in the sorting room."

"What's that?"

"That's where they bring all the soiled garments. We pull them out of their bags and sort them. You know, sheets, towels, vestments, all different kinds of garments. After sorting, girls come in and take everything to be soaked in vats of lye. After the soaking, they're put in tubs, and scrubbed with a brush till they're clean. Finally, everything is rinsed. If it's warm enough, it's hung outside, otherwise they're put in the drying room."

"I do this all day?"

"Yes. The only time you won't be working in one of those rooms is when you are eating, sleeping or at chapel. The days are long."

"Do you ever get to go outside?" I asked.

"Only if you are assigned hanging, or you bring in or take the bags to the delivery truck."

"How do you do this?"

"How do you do what?"

"This. All this." I motioned with my hands.

"You don't think about it. You just do it. You think of something else. Before we go downstairs, you need to go in to the bathroom wash your face, do something to your hair," she said taking a brush from her pocket.

"Do I look that bad?"

"Yes, you do." For the first time, offering a faint smile.

I went into the lavatory and watched the cold water fall into the yellow stained, cracked sink. I splashed water against my face and took a deep breath. I grabbed a towel off the top shelf, and wiped my face. I ran the damp cloth over my arms and around my neck, brushed my hair back, but since I had nothing to clip it with, the ragged pieces fell in my face.

"You almost done?" Veronica called out.

"Yes, I'll be there in a minute."

"Here," Veronica said, pulling a bobbi pin from her pocket.

"You can't work with your hair falling in your face."

"Thanks," I said, as I put in the pin.

"That looks better. Come on, let's go."

"How do you have a brush and pin with you?"

"Don't worry about it, I'm allowed," she said, turning from me.

We left the dormitory and made our way down the first set of stairs.

"I'll take you to the cafeteria first, before we go to work. It's almost supper time," Veronica said, walking next to me.

"What's that?" I asked, hearing a set of chimes.

"It's the bell calling everyone to meals." We fell into line behind the others, almost marching to our seats. Veronica pulled me into a chair next to hers. Together we picked up our forks, all at the same time, and ate until our plates were empty. We were each given a scoop of watery gravy with chunks of potatoes, and one slice of bread to lap up the gravy.

A partition divided the Sisters from the rest of us, the only sound from our side of the room was the clanking of the forks on the stoneware plates. Behind the partition, there was talking, laughing, and the clinking of the fine china.

I looked around for Sara, but couldn't find her in the dining room. "Veronica?"

"What is it?"

"Do you know anything about the old woman who came in with me? Her name's Sara."

"She's working in the kitchen."

"Do you think she's all right?"

"She should be, as long as she doesn't do anything stupid. Why would you care?"

"She's my friend."

"Don't. Friends don't mean anything here. Worry about yourself," Veronica said.

When the bell rang, the penitents walked in silence to the chapel.

"You'll come here twice a day, before breakfast and after supper. Actually, I like this place the best of all," Veronica whispered.

"Why?"

"Because we sing here."

As we took our seats Sr. Helen moved back and forth between the rows, tapping the women's shoulders with her ruler reminding them to sit up straight. I stared up at Monsignor Matthew as he began the service. He spoke straightforward of our damnation. I bowed my head, in a shame I couldn't explain. Standing over us, he looked much closer to God.

"What is it about him?" I asked Veronica, staring at him trying to figure out his secret.

"Never mind. Just stay away from him," she growled, turning toward me.

At the end of the service we were escorted back to the stairway. It was then that I sensed someone behind me. I looked up and saw Sr. Helen.

"You need to come with me," she said, herding me away from the other girls.

"Everyone who comes here gets a haircut. If you behave, you can earn your hair back," she said.

I ran my fingers through what I had left.

"Earn my hair back? What does that mean?"

"Stay out of trouble and your hair will grow back."

From the look on her face Sr. Helen performed her duties with her head held high, duties handed down by God, to be administered in the name of salvation. She wore her pride like a magnificent suit of armor.

Remaining five steps ahead, she led me to the lavatory. Opening the door, she motioned for me to kneel in front of the sink. Pulling my head from side to side, she clipped the longer strands of hair.

When I reached up to feel what she had done, she slapped my hand, warning that vanity was a sin.

"We are done here," she said. "Go to the sorting room. Veronica will get you started."

"Yes Ma'am."

A Sister I didn't recognize sat reading the Bible, just inside the front door of the sorting room. She looked up and directed me to the far corner where Veronica was pulling soiled linens and garments from bags. After hours of sorting, the Sister rang the bell. We stopped our work, and stood in line by the door.

"Not bad," Veronica said, touching my shorn head.

"I must look awful."

"No, just a little ragged. You're lucky, sometimes she'll cut into your face, when she's in a hurry."

The Dining Hall

e walked single file to the dining hall. Dinner was tea with two thin slices of bread. I looked around at the other penitents. Some sat hunched over, stuffing bread into their mouths. Some sat straight, taking small bites and staring around the room. No one had hair like mine. Many had chin length, and a few with shoulder length, only one had a braid hanging down her back. I could read their personality by the length of their hair.

"Are you all right?" Veronica asked.

"Just tired. Thinking."

"Thinking will get you in trouble."

For the first time since arriving, I saw Sara. She wore an oversized jumper, and had a sweater wrapped tightly around her thin frame. The side of her face appeared swollen and red. Strands of hair fell around her face. She brought in steaming pots for the tables. We didn't make eye contact, but she nudged my back as she passed. I had hoped working in the kitchen would provide a safety net, as far from the Sisters as possible. I had been wrong.

From beyond the partition, the voices of the Sisters could be heard. The aromas of supper didn't match the food in front of us. There was no roasted meat, no baskets of fresh bread. Between the panels of the partition, the Sisters could be seen spreading butter on thick slabs of bread.

Along with the rustling of silverware and the shuffling of feet, muted voices could be heard beneath the sound of the gospel being read. There she was slumped over the far end of the table. I slipped in to the empty seat next to her. I soaked the thin slice of bread in the soup and placed it to her swollen lips.

"Thank God you found me. I thought I would never see you again," Sara said, without looking up.

"What happened?" I pushed a strand of hair behind her ear, steadied her shaking hand.

"I'm going to die here Alice… I will."

"Sara, it's just the first day. Look at me. I have no hair."

"But you also have no black eyes," She said turning to me.

"Oh, Sara, you need to go to the infirmary."

"No. I have to clean up, they're watching," Sara lowered her head. "They're always watching."

I left the table and looked for a Sister. "One of the women is sick," I said. "Is it all right if I take her to the infirmary?"

"Who is it?"

"Sara, one of the kitchen help."

"No, she has to clear the tables. When she is done, she can lie down for a bit," the Sister said, without looking up.

"She's not strong enough. I can clear the tables for her."

I didn't wait for a response. Helping her out of the chair, "who did this to you? What happened to your face?"

"I ran into Sr. Helen. I mean right smack into her." She tried laughing, but covered her mouth in embarrassment and pain. "This place is fecking crazy."

I decided against taking her to the infirmary. Sr. Helen would know. I led her to the kitchen instead, helping her to a mattress against the wall. I went back to the hall to clear and wipe down the tables.

Returning to the kitchen, I dimmed the light in the far corner. A woman, who could have been anyone's grandmother, came up behind me. "You go on now, before the same thing happens to you."

I found my way back to the dormitory and an unrestful bed.

I didn't remember falling asleep, but I remember being awakened with an abrupt slamming of the door. Sr. Helen stormed through the dormitory and stopped at my bed. Her black gown, with its thick woolen folds, made her seem like one of the statues from the chapel. Her arms, folded across her chest, frozen in her stance.

"Out of bed. You didn't think I would know? I saw you at supper. If she can't make it on her own, we decide what is necessary. You worry about getting your own work done. Do I make myself clear?"

"Yes Sister. I'm sorry. I thought she needed help."

"You don't think. You do as you are told. Here is a reminder, in case your memory is short."

Before I could blink, my cheek caught the full force of her knuckles. I held the back of my hand to my cheek, trying to pull myself up from the floor. That was my first warning. The second came as a kick to the ribs as I lay on the floor.

She was gone with the slamming of the door. I crawled back onto the bed, and huddled on the thin mattress.

"I thought you were smart," Veronica whispered. "Next time, she's not going to just knock you over. She is going to knock you out."

ꟿy Sister's Keeper

fter two weeks, Sara was still in the infirmary recovering from her visitation by Sr. Helen. The same night she gave me my reminder, she had beaten Sara half to death. I was allowed to help with her care, changing her sheets and her bedclothes.

"How are you feeling, Sara?" Her frailness terrified me. The tight bun that usually held her hair in place had fallen from its place. Strands of gray hair lay across the pillow.

"I'm fine. Don't worry about me."

"Do you remember what happened?" I asked, stroking hair from her eyes.

"No. I was sleeping," turning her head to avoid my eyes.

"I should have been there to protect you."

"You couldn't have done anything," she said squeezing my hand.

"I'm the reason you're here. Sr. Helen got mad at me, and you paid the price. You'd have been safer if you'd stayed in Castlepollard."

"You didn't do anything wrong." Though Sara seemed weak, she pulled herself up in the bed. "Can you help me get up?" She asked.

"Okay. Do you want to walk around a little before I have to go?"

"Yes. I have to get back to work."

I pulled back the cover, took hold of her arm, and helped her put her bare feet on the cold tile floor. Moving slowly, I held onto her, and she held onto the wall. We walked to the end of the corridor and back. As I was leading her back to her bed, the nurse approached and pulled a chair up.

"Sara, you have one more day in the infirmary. You'll have to go back to the kitchen tomorrow night."

"What if I did her chores for her?" I asked.

"You can't be doing that. You have your own work to do," Sara said.

"Here, Sara, let me help you back into bed, and Alice, you get back before they lock the doors."

The nurse was sending me away, so she could protect Sara. I left the infirmary at her insistence, stopping at the chapel before going to the dormitory.

There was no altar of votive candles to be lit for special occasions. I slid into the front pew and stared up to the altar. A crucifix hung from the center wall. Nothing ornate, like the statue in the entry hall. Two candles on separate ends of the empty altar offered the only light.

> *Hey God,*
> *It's me, Alice. Remember?*
> *I keep asking for your help, but I don't think you're listening.*
> *I thought Castlepollard was bad, but this place is not what I expected. I don't understand. Why do You allow these people to do what they do? They are cruel and hurtful. There is no love and tenderness. I'm terrified every time I turn around. Look at me . . .*

"No love and tenderness?"

I jerked around and there she stood in the dim light, her hands, folded in front of her gown. She looked calm, no clenched fist, no tight jaw. She stood tall, almost regal.

"So you have come to the chapel to ask forgiveness, have you?"

"I came to talk to God."

"That is quite bold."

"I wasn't trying to disobey you."

"Of course, you were. You've been going to see Sara every night."

"I'm worried about her."

"I am sure you are, but she is clumsy, if she does not learn to stay on her feet she will keep having accidents."

Sr. Helen turned and walked out of the chapel. I waited for her to return, for one last word, but the chapel stayed silent. There was nothing more to be said. I followed Sr. Helen out the wooden doors and went to the dormitory. I slipped off my jumper and took the nightgown from the cupboard, pulled it over my head and fell into bed.

Three days later Sara was back in the kitchen. Her arm still wrapped. She moved slowly, so as not to reinjure herself. I tried to remain invisible.

*   *   *

One afternoon, with the bright light of the sun coming through, Veronica and I were hanging laundry. When we came to the end of the first row, I turned to Veronica.

"Do you ever think about getting away from here?"

"And going where?" She asked, not even looking at me.

"Why are you here?"

"I fell in love. He wanted to marry me, buy a house, raise our children in the church, everything you dream about, you know." She looked over at me, coming close, spreading the sheet out over the line. "I loved him, but my father decided Daniel was not good enough, so he sent him away. Da paid him to leave, and he left. After I found out I was pregnant, my father sent me to a mother baby home in Dublin, soon after, I was sent here."

"What about your Mum?"

"She died when I was a little girl. It was just the two of us. I couldn't believe he sent me away."

"And your baby?"

"He died. It doesn't matter it's over and done. I just have to find a way to stay alive and not ache every minute of every day."

Veronica took the empty basket inside the building and I was left alone.

*   *   *

Coming around the corner, I stopped when I heard two penitents whispering to each other.

"Rita tried to run away again." The longhaired girl told her companion.

"They found her last night in the shed by the back gate. Badly bruised, swollen everywhere, I don't think she'll make it, and if she does, she'll be a bit daft forever. The girls standing outside the door said Sr. Helen went crazy and had to be pulled off of her."

"I overheard Sr. Helen telling Nurse that Rita had turned simple and therefore of no use to anyone," the other girl said.

I needed to see Rita for myself. I slipped down the hall and up the stairs to the infirmary. Opening the door, I saw her in the far corner, her hands folded across her chest. The blood cleaned away, but I saw the cuts, the swelling and bruising.

"Alice, you shouldn't be here." Veronica came up behind me. She handed the nurse a note from one of the Sisters.

"Is it true?"

"You mean was this girl beaten to a pulp?"

"I didn't mean that."

"Did she do it?"

"She says no. She found her this way, but if she did, it's criminal. If that happened outside, whoever did it would have been arrested, but in here, no one will know, and if they do, they won't tell. Even if they tried, who would listen? You need to go on now. Don't tell anyone you've been here," Veronica said, trying to push me out the door.

I looked at the nurse and saw the despair in her face. Rita's recovery was out of her hands. It was up to God now. I watched her pull up the blanket around Rita's neck. I wondered if Rita was like Veronica, no family, no one to care for her, or if was she like me, with a family who refused to claim her. Looking at her, I almost hoped she would find her peace, that she wouldn't wake up, and God would take her home.

The Conversation

ours turned to days, days to months. Each began the same, starting with the benediction and ending with the blessing. Night after night we sat in the dining hall listened to Mother Michael as she found new ways to tell us we were sinners and our penance would never find salvation with God.

"You girls are the blessed ones, you know. We are here to save your soul and, to that end, we will need to be sure you are rid of all temptations. God has spoken to us, as we are His messengers. We are your only chance for salvation."

Each night they prayed over us, like families pray over their dead. They promised us ways to find forgiveness, but day after day, we found none. The Sisters spoke of salvation but with each encounter, our spirits died a little more. Each morning we saw a new bruise on a cheek, or an arm, or a girl who couldn't get out of bed. Though they told us we were being saved, nothing in our chores felt like redemption.

The work assignments changed from day to day. I was moved from the folding room, to the washroom, to the ironing room. Some girls never worked in the laundry rooms. They spent time in the yard, away from the others, hanging out clothes, or scrubbing the dormitory and lavatory walls, then moved on to the chapel. Some penitents spent time in the infirmary, helping the nurse with girls who suffered sores from the lye, or exhaustion from the long hours.

I was sent to the washroom, steamy with a dense vapor filling the room. Basins full of boiling water, lined the walls of the room. Other girls stood over steaming pots in the middle of the room, swirling the sheets around with a staff, spinning the material one way, then back the other, making sure the folds soaked up the lye-laced water. We leaned into the sinks, scrubbing linen, pushing and pulling the garments across washboards.

For hours we did backbreaking work, saying nothing. Each day a different Sister sat in the doorway watching our every move, while reading aloud from the Bible.

"To do the work of God is to believe in Jesus, the One God sent to save us from sin, harm and evil. That said, don't be insensitive to His communication; He wants, and can enable you to live as He does, and wants to keep you. Believe and be saved."

All the while blocking our way from leaving for any reason. Depending on the Sister in charge, often we soiled ourselves before being allowed to use the lavatory.

*   *   *

Though Veronica refused to acknowledge a friendship, each day she found ways to share more about herself and her time here. Though I only had sketchy details of her past. She kept much private. she filled in many details of the Laundries. Secrets I could never have imagined.

One night, when Mother Michael was away and Sr. Helen took to her bed with stomach pains, I grabbed the empty chair next to Veronica in the dining hall.

"The other night you said something about Monsignor Matthew, but you didn't finish."

"Not here. I'll tell you in the dorm."

We sat quietly and ate. I didn't bother her again. When the bell rang we stood and lined up against the wall, where from across the room, I saw Rita. It had taken months for her to recover from her injuries, and it had only been a few weeks since she returned to the dining hall. Everyone ignored her, not for hatred or revenge, but fear their actions would betray a kindness.

They averted their eyes and left longer spaces between themselves as they walked in line. With Veronica behind me, I watched from my corner of the room as she left the dining hall.

As we headed toward the stairs, our group broke off and went toward the dormitories. Once inside, we lined up at the foot of our mattresses. Under the watchful eye of Sr. Bridget, we changed clothes. I still wasn't comfortable undressing in front of other girls. Even with my sisters, I pulled my nightgown over my head before taking off my clothes. Sr. Bridget had her own ideas about how we should undress. First, she demanded we take our jumpers off, then shoes and socks. She watched as we bent down to place them under the bed. We then unbuttoned our blouses as she stared at us. Left in our slips, she prodded us, first those with pouching bellies, many from just having babies, others from just age catching up with them. When she became bored with that, she poked at our breasts with her ruler. It didn't matter what size we were. She seemed to find an odd pleasure in it. You could see a grin cross her face and her eyes soften. Her biggest pleasure came when we took off our bras and panties, standing in front of our beds naked, with just enough light to show our flaws. She pointed them out to the Sister sharing duty with her. It didn't take long for her to grow tired of our nakedness.

"Go on, get dressed the lot of you."

None of us ever looked over at each other. It seemed the one favor we did for each other.

After they left the dormitory, I watched Veronica steal into the lavatory. After a few minutes of silence, I followed. I found her leaning against the wall. I felt like a schoolgirl, crowding around for silly gossip.

"Okay, I have to ask you, does that happen every night?"

"What? Getting naked in front of Sr. Bridget, so she can stare and poke at you?" I nodded.

"No. It happens at her whim. Not every night or week, but when she gets a new Sister she makes her come with her, makes her watch and tries to get her to participate. They are usually so embarrassed they just stand there."

"I've never seen that happen before and I've been here for a few months."

"Yeah, I know how long you've been here. She goes in stages. I guess she's back at it again."

"Does this have anything to do with the Friday night showers?" I asked as I washed my face. She looked around the lavatory, then back at me.

"Tonight was just the first act. If she doesn't get off on any of the girls, when Friday comes, she'll demand more of a performance from us in the showers. Every other Friday is shower day, but not every girl gets to take a shower. You have to be chosen." Veronica said, going to check the heavy wooden door. When she accepted that we were alone, we sat on the floor, and she began to tell me about Friday nights.

"After dinner, the Sisters pick random girls to go to the basement." She said, leaning her back against the wall. "The Sisters watch and play stupid games, making the girls line up, so they can ridicule until all pride is lost." She fell silent.

"Is Sr. Helen involved with this?" I asked.

"No, surprisingly she's not. This is a game Sr. Margaret and Sr. Bridget invented."

"How do they get away with this?"

"No one knows, except the women. Not even Mother Michael. Sr. Bridget is sick, and she knows no one will ever tell, and if they try, who'd believe them?"

"I don't understand. Why do they do it?"

"Because they can, no one stops them."

I got up from the floor and walked to the faucet. I let the water run through my fingers, then splashed it across my face. I wanted to throw up, but I took a deep breath, and turned back to Veronica.

"A different group of girls is picked each time to go down with Sister Bridget."

"Is it always the two of them? No one else?" I caught my breath enough to ask. "Have you ever been picked?"

"Twice. The first time was unbearable. The second time I made myself invisible so I couldn't see it."

"Why haven't I ever been picked?"

"How about thanking your lucky stars that you were invisible to Sr. Bridget?"

I continued to wash my face, hoping to wash away the memory of everything I heard.

"So what happens?"

"A lot like tonight. You strip down in front of them and stand there as they stare at you and make fun of how you look. I tried to cover myself, but Sr. Margaret slapped me, and pulled my hands away."

"I can't believe it."

"I wouldn't lie about this. You are still fairly new, as it's only been a few months, so if you're picked, be prepared to be ridiculed beyond anything you'd imagine. She'll make fun of everything about you, freckles, moles, too much hair, too little hair. You need to know this. Even though there was nothing I could do about it, someone told me what to expect. It just helped to know what was coming. I thought you should know as well."

"What should I do?"

"What can you do? They'll laugh at you no matter what. And, if you're too slow, she'll hit you. She has a belt wrapped around her palm, the end of it hangs down, and she swings it around for everyone to see. She makes the other girls laugh at you."

"Why would they do that?"

"Because if they are laughing at you, they're not being ridiculed. So she won't pick on them. It's all about survival."

"So they laugh at each other so they won't be ridiculed?"

"You got it."

"What was it like?"

"When it happened, she poked my breasts, and swung the strap around laughing," Veronica continued, as if I hadn't spoken. "When I wasn't looking she swatted me across my back and I fell to my knees on the wet linoleum."

I was trying to imagine all this, but couldn't. How could women do that to each other? Why would they want to? Even in the worst of school days, where girls were mean just because they could, I never remembered girls being this mean. But she was right, they had put us in a situation that we would do anything to survive. What god would allow that?

"If I get picked, what happens?" I asked, afraid to even hear what she would say.

"Don't be the first or the last in line. She picks on them most. Oh, and don't be in the center either. Try to be fifth or sixth from the front or back."

"Does this rage ever stop?"

"You mean her free rein to abuse whoever she wants, in the name of God?"

"Yeah, I guess that's what I mean."

"No. Every day someone thinks of something new, some new way to take us to the breaking point."

"So, everyone just takes it?"

"Look, if you get called, stay calm, don't act scared, or she'll know. Make eye contact with Sr. Margaret. Stare her down. She hates that and, for some reason, she gets nervous and backs away," Veronica said.

"But if I stare her down, and she gets mad . . ." I picked at the dry flakes on my arms as we stared at each other in the cold lavatory. "How did you make it this long?" I asked, though I knew she must have asked herself the same question every day.

"I don't know. You just do it," Veronica said, suddenly getting sad.

"Is there ever a chance of getting out of here?"

"It has to be a male, and he has to have papers from a parish priest."

"I have a brother." I could hear the resignation in our voices, the chance that our only way out was something we'd have to do alone.

"At least you have someone who'll come for you."

"But he doesn't know I'm here." Suddenly his face came back to me right there, thick red hair falling over his eyes, his lanky arms dangling beside him as he walked.

"I wrote letters to a girl from school," Veronica said. "I asked if her father could come for me."

"You got a letter out?"

"I stole some stationery from Mother Michael and slipped it in her postings one day."

"Did she write back?"

"I don't know. I'm still here, so I guess not."

I wanted to hug Veronica, but I kept to myself. As we got up to go back to bed, she turned suddenly.

"Do you think your baby is alive?" she asked.

"She was adopted out, somewhere in Dublin, I think."

"If they told you she was adopted out, they've lied to you. They don't do that in Ireland. They only foster out babies. Unless she went to the States."

"I don't know where she is, but I have to believe she is safe, if I don't, I don't have anything to believe in."

"They've lied to us, about everything. You know she could be here, across the grounds in the orphanage, but even if she is, you'll never see her. The Sisters keep the orphanage very guarded from the likes of us. Only a few special girls work with the babies, mostly, the Sisters take care of them."

The room began to spin, the idea that my baby could be that close. My girl, my black-haired girl who wore my medal could be just across the field from me.

"Come on, we have to go to bed before someone finds us."

I wanted to thank her, for saving me, for reminding me of Finn, for making me feel human again, for just listening, but she had stepped back inside herself and walked out of the lavatory without another word.

I waited until I knew she was in bed, then I left, slid in quietly, and pulled the covers over my head. I heard a raspy voice from the bed next to me.

"I know what you've been doing, and I'm going to tell."

A Night Away from Vigils

fter talking with Veronica, I paid close attention to everything. I stayed in the shadows and attempted to go unnoticed, I had to. I did everything expected of me, and more. I didn't leave my assigned room until everyone was gone. I folded the last of the towels, or wrung out the clothes from the steaming kettle. I was the last in line to the dining hall. I even steered clear of Sara, not talking with her, or helping, as I had often done in the past. I was not going to give any Sister a chance to catch me in their trap. Around the penitents, I kept my head bowed and my hands busy.

After a while, Sara was back to old herself. She did her kitchen chores, along with cooking extravagant meals for the Sisters. Extravagant, meant seasoned meats, with steaming vegetables, and fresh baked desserts. Her talents made it difficult for them to complain. Everything about the Sara I had known returned. Her bun held tight to the back of her head, and her quirky smile beamed across her face, I imagined, to hide her pain.

I stayed close, watching her whenever possible during meals, or in the chapel, but never trying to communicate. I watched out for her in every way I could that didn't draw attention to either of us. Of anyone, she was the most vulnerable. It was too easy for the Sisters to find any little thing in anyone, to defy the blessings of God.

Of all of the Sisters, we learned to avoid Sr. Helen and Sr. Bridget at all costs.

One Friday night before vigils were about to start, I lined up behind Veronica as I had done every day since my arrival. I knelt in the chapel and I prayed to my God, hoping we'd all be kept safe, that Veronica and Sara would survive the madness. And that He would bring my Finn back to me. I prayed that one day Rita would find the key she needed for her freedom.

After vigils, I was glad to be returning to the dormitory. The cold had seeped through the walls causing a chill to run through us for the day, and the hot water we had immersed our hands in seemed even hotter, the lye stronger. We climbed the stairs and from a tiny oval window that looked out over the walls of the compound, in the evening shadows I could see the fields far past the walls that confined us. For a few moments, instead of endless fields. I saw Mum in the yard tending the garden, clearing away weeds for the new spring flowers. Her braid down her back, and her soft smile that made me feel safe. I remembered Fridays when Da would come in late, returning from the pub, when Mum allowed family rules time to be relaxed. We gather around the warmth of the hearth laughing, playing games for an evening of laughter and silliness, all of us together.

Lost in my thoughts away from this place, a tap on my shoulder brought me back. Without a word of direction, Sr. Bridget motioned for me to go back downstairs and wait. I saw five girls standing in the entry, so I went there and waited. I even saw Rita coming around the corner. We didn't say anything to each other, but stood together waiting. Rita picked at her nails, keeping her head bowed. Her wounds had healed and her hair had even grown out, but she was still slouched and moved much slower than the other girls.

Sr. Margaret came around the corner and directed us toward the stairs. As we moved down the hallway in silence, I knew where we were headed. I wanted to throw up, not only to get out of going to the basement, but because the idea of standing naked in front of them sickened me. I looked for Sara, praying that she would not be part of the group. Going against Veronica's advice I moved toward the end of the line, when I felt another tap, but this was more like a nudge. It didn't hurt, so I ignored it, then it came again, sharper. I turned in the direction where it came.

Monsignor Matthew stood behind me. Being the last in line, no one saw, as he moved me away from the stairway where the lights dimmed. Once out of the line, he guided me back downstairs toward the chapel. We went down the center of the aisle to a door behind the altar that I had never seen. Once inside the dimly lit office, he closed the door, and motioned for me to take a seat.

"I remember you, interrupting my sermon at Castlepollard," he said, leaning against his desk, staring at me.

"I'm sorry for that." I tried to turn away. "My baby was coming."

"How did everything go?"

"You must know. You brought me here. You signed the papers."

"You do remember me."

"Yes, I remember you, but I need to get back to my line before I'm missed. I don't want to get in trouble."

"No, you're with me. You won't be missed, and I guarantee you won't get in trouble."

"But Monsignor?"

"Stand up my dear, let me look at you."

"Monsignor, please." The sound of his voice and the words made my stomach crawl.

"Relax. I'm not going to hurt you. Do you like it here?"

"No, I don't." Did he think I was crazy? Of course, he was going to hurt me. I was no longer the innocent schoolgirl. I knew what it was like to be violated, for a stranger to tear at my body, and ravage my spirit.

"Why wouldn't you? We feed you, give you a place to sleep, and in return you help us. What could be wrong with that?"

"I'm sorry."

"So you're not grateful for what we have done for you?"

"No, I am. I didn't mean that." If I thought there was a chance that someone would believe me, I'd scream so loud, the walls would shake, but who would listen. I was a sinner, a penitent, less than human. Instead of opening my mouth, I bit my tongue and endured, and prayed that what I was allowing to happen would mean possible freedom.

"What did you mean?"

"I don't think I belong here."

"If you don't belong here, where do you belong?"

"At home," I said, getting more nervous as he peered at me. I could feel his breath on me. This time I knew what was about to happen. I didn't understand how another man thought he had the right to take what was mine. Before, it had been a stranger, but here, a priest who stood before me in God's name.

He glided me away from the only light in the room a lamp on the far corner of his desk. He pushed me against the wall, moving his hand over the outside of my jumper.

"Monsignor, please don't do that?"

"Why, I've been waiting to be with you for a long time," he said. "I promise, I won't hurt you." He continued to push against me. "I wanted you when I drove you here. I've been watching you. You're a good lass. Maybe we can help each other. I might be able to arrange a release for you."

At that moment, I wished it had been Sr. Bridget who tapped me. Though I would have dreaded it, at least I'd have been prepared for the showers. I was not prepared for this, to be assaulted again. Only this time I'd know the face, I'd know the voice, but every evening I'd have to kneel to him and know what he did to me.

He lifted my jumper, and I felt his cold hand on the inside of my thigh. I smelled the alcohol, doused with an aroma of a sweet, sickening aftershave.

"Relax, dear. I'm not going to hurt you. You help me, and I'll help you."

"Please, Monsignor, don't do this."

I was begging a man of God to set me free, like begging that the dead of winter would bring warmth. While he pushed with one hand, I could feel him fumbling under his robe with the other. I could feel his baby soft skin against my neck.

When I heard the first knock, I froze. He continued pushing against me. I felt the metal zipper on my skin. The second knock came.

"Monsignor Matthew?" Relieved when I heard the voice, yet terrified at what she would find.

"Mother Michael would like to speak with you." She tapped again, but when she opened the door, she didn't look behind, not seeing me in the shadows.

"I'll be there shortly," he said straightening his robe.

"She has requested you now."

"Very well. Give me a few moments. Do you know what this is about?

I don't like to be bothered."

I stood in utter terror, too horrified to even breathe. He moved toward the door as Sr. Helen turned to leave. He closed the door, but turned back toward me.

"Looks like we have been interrupted," he whispered. "You go on back to the dormitory. We are done for tonight. I believe you will keep our little visit a secret."

"Yes Monsignor."

"So that is a promise?"

"Yes. I promise."

"Good girl." He closed the door and left me alone.

There was nothing for me to say. There was no one to tell, even if I tried, who would believe that he would do such a thing? I remained against the wall too stunned to move, but more shamed by what I had allowed to happen.

The stairway was empty and the lights were dimmed. I walked alone through the halls, My footsteps echoed every move I made. Back in the dormitories, still trembling, I slipped into my coarse nightdress. Blurred images of him floated around in my mind. I couldn't fall asleep. I could still feel his soft hands on my skin. I tossed and turned, trying to break free of the memory. It didn't take long for me to realize that, should it happen again, I might not be so lucky a second time.

I pulled my legs up close and wrapped my arms tight around them. I peered across the room, realizing that it wasn't just me. None of us would be safe again. It was not just the assaults, it was the walls that closed us in, the locked doors that kept us hidden.

I had gotten away by luck, protected by the one person who terrified me most, but I'd wake every day in the same cot, the same jumper, no family to call my own, more isolated than any other time in my life, with one more danger to watch out for.

ΜONSIGNOR-IN-CHARGE

t took a few weeks before Veronica and I had any time alone, but without saying a word she figured out how I missed shower night. I felt more on edge than ever. Everyone was watched more intently, but one evening in the dining hall, Veronica feigned an upset stomach.

"Sr. Margaret, can I take her to the lavatory," I asked, as Veronica leaned on my arm. "She's cramping? Her time, you know," I said.

"Go on, clean her up," she said, shooing me off.

With Sara's help, I took her to the lavatory. Once inside, Veronica stood up, instead of talking to me, she looked over at Sara.

"Why is she here?"

"I thought she should know, too."

"Why? He'd never go after her." Sara lowered her head when the words came out, but regained her composure.

"I'm old, but I'm not stupid. I see things," Sara said.

"I'm sorry. We shouldn't be fighting each other. We are here because of Monsignor Matthew," Veronica said.

Sara looked over at me, then back at Veronica. I knew she was wondering why I hadn't said anything.

"I didn't tell anyone. Honest."

"We need to be helping each other, not fighting. Sara can help us a great deal. She sees a lot more going on than we do, and has more contact with Mother Michael, being in the kitchen."

"All right. I'm sorry," Veronica said. "Tell us what he did."

"It was Friday night and I thought it was Sr. Bridget coming to take me to the showers, but as I turned around I saw him and he took hold of my arm and led me through the chapel to a room behind the altar."

"I know that room. I've had to clean it before," Sara said.

"What happened?" Veronica asked, still irritated that Sara would interrupt, or contribute to the conversation.

"He unzipped his trousers, and he tried to get to me, but…"

"Well, did he?" Veronica asked.

"No, just as he began kissing my neck, Sr. Helen knocked at the door."

"What did he do?" Sara asked.

"Well, I couldn't see his face, but his hands came out from under my jumper, and he began to tidy himself up."

"Did she see you?"

"No, I don't think so."

"That bastard. We have to find a way to stop him," Veronica said.

The three of us stood there in the lavatory, powerless against this man who believed he had the blessing of God to put his hands all over us. Veronica never admitted if he touched her, but it seemed if he touched one, he touched us all.

"OK, we have to get back, but Sara you have to get word to us if you know when Monsignor will be on our side of the compound more than for Mass or vigils. We have to protect each other."

No one denied the danger Monsignor Matthew presented. What we feared most was that no one would believe it if we dared to tell, and if no one believed us, how would it stop?

Just as we were about to leave the lavatory, the door burst open and there stood a woman barely as tall as Sara, dressed in the familiar black and white habit, a cross hanging from her waist. Her face, soft, creamy like butter.

"What are you doing in here?" Sr. Agatha asked, leaning against the closed door.

I had seen her before, and she struck me as not much older than either Veronica or myself. Her soft blue eyes darted back and forth between the three of us. There was no puffiness in her cheeks, or pudginess around her waist. She was one of the youngest Sisters in the compound.

"She had cramps, so we were helping her," Sara said.

"You need to get back to the dining hall, before you get in trouble."

"What difference does it make? We're always in trouble, no matter what we do," Veronica said.

"Are you alright?" The Sister asked looking straight at me.

"Yes, I was just helping Veronica."

"I know what happened with Monsignor Matthew. I know where he took you," Sister Agatha said, clutching hold of the cross that hung from her waist.

"Nothing happened."

"Did he hurt you?" She continued to stare at me.

"No."

"I know about Monsignor. You girls have to be careful."

"If you know, then why hasn't anyone stopped him?"

"Because he is a powerful man. Mother Michael thinks he will help her get out of here, so she does anything he wants."

"No disrespect Sister, but why should we believe you?" Veronica asked.

"Because, I believe you. Does anyone else?"

"What do you know about him?" Sara asked.

"I know that he will say or do anything to get to a young girl."

"I don't understand why someone isn't stopping him," Veronica said.

"You do know, he's a priest, very high in the order of the church. No one would ever believe he could do anything so despicable. If you don't think something is true, then it is not a fact for you."

"Wait. I'm sorry, how do you know all this?" I asked.

"That's not important, besides you don't need to concern yourself with that."

Veronica pushed her hair from her face, and looked over at Sr. Agatha. "Why are you telling us this?"

"Because, I know Monsignor Matthew takes advantage of his title." Her words spread like fresh honey poured over a hot biscuit.

Sr. Agatha stood up straight, smoothing out the folds in her skirt. "What I see happening is wrong, and I can't do anything about it, except warn you to stay away from him."

"Will this information do us any good?"

"Sometimes you need to have information to protect yourself, even if you can't do anything about it," Sr. Agatha said. "Monsignor Matthew has presided in St. Patrick's Compound for years and controls everything in the parish. It all goes through him, from the purchase of jumpers, to the transfer of babies, even to the assignment of workers in the compound.

The three of us looked back and forth. Sara turned away, and then locked herself behind the lavatory door. Veronica pulled the rubber band from her hair and regathered the strands, still staring at Sr. Agatha, as she wrapped the band around her fingers, pulling her hair through. I moved away and leaned against the sink more in agreement than shock. This was the first time we'd have to agree with our jailer. It would be important to know what kind of criminal held us captive.

When Sr. Agatha left the lavatory, Sara stepped out in the middle of us, as if taking a bow from center stage.

"I can look out for him. I'll know when he's been invited for dinner, or when he's doing services. Mother Michael always wants special meals prepared whenever he stays over."

"I'll watch out for Sr. Helen and Sr. Margaret. Their terror can be as deadly as his." Veronica said.

"I'll watch out for the new girls who come in, the young ones who have no idea what could happen." I needed to do my share.

We had a plan. We reluctantly became a team, out to protect the innocent. If the thought had not been so laughable, we might have given ourselves a name. By the time we returned from the lavatory, all the girls had moved from the dining hall to the chapel. I was sure we'd have been missed, as somehow Sr. Helen and Sr. Margaret could always sense a lost soul, regardless of the reason, but that night, nothing seemed amiss. We slipped in, taking the row behind the Sisters. Brother Patrick conducted the service. He was a seemingly invisible man, whose voice held no emotion, he spoke in a monotone, regardless of the Gospel he read.

For the rest of the evening, everything was done in an eerie silence. Sara left us at the kitchen door, but as I walked by, she brushed my arm, grasping my fingertips, then letting them slip away. As we changed our clothes Sr. Margaret gazed up and down the rows, watching as our jumpers dropped around our ankles and nightgowns slipped over our heads. After every last girl was in her bed, and covered with a thin gray blanket, the lights went out, the door was closed and for a time, though all together, we were alone with our thoughts.

I tried to collect everything in my mind. I needed to line them up, giving them order and priority. I had survived a year in this place, a beating that had long since healed, a haircut finally growing out to make me look more human, and avoiding an attack with the help of an unsuspecting ally.

Before falling asleep, I was determined, that just because I had survived this long, I couldn't settle in and become too, comfortable. I had to keep guard, watch every turn. There would always be someone trying to catch me in a moment I wasn't watching.

THE SINS

ne Sunday after returning from Mass, all the girls took their seats at the long tables for breakfast. Just three days before Christmas, and Monsignor Matthew had returned from three weeks of traveling throughout Ireland on church business. No different than Reverend Mother had been, though this was his home, Mother Michael laid out the red carpet, while easing up on some of our duties, still knowing Sister Helen would continue the guard over us. Our Monsignor Matthew became a double-edged sword.

We were each presented a slab of ham, an egg and a thick slice of bread. Bowls of butter had been placed around the table. I looked up at Sara as she passed, serving the girls.

"It'll be a good day," she said.

"I hope so," I whispered back.

A few days ago a new girl had been added to our dormitory. I had seen her often, but looking up and down the tables, she was nowhere to be seen.

"Where's Mary?" I asked Veronica, looking around.

"Sister Helen called her away. I saw her going toward the chapel."

"Why would she go to chapel so soon after mass?"

"Did Monsignor Matthew call for her?" I asked. The girls answered with suspicious stares.

"We have to find her," I said.

We knew he picked the most vulnerable of the girls, and used them as long as they were of benefit. Since the day he maneuvered me to his office, we found he had approached four other girls, only two escaped unscathed.

Mary's parish priest had brought her in. No one knew why she'd been left in the doorway. She seemed too terrified to tell anyone of her undocumented sin, remaining silent, even when approached with kindness.

"I have a bad feeling that something happened," I said.

"I'll go to the lavatory," Veronica said. "Sara, can you get back inside the chapel?"

Familiar with everything about the dining hall, Sara knew, from the empty seats, who was missing. Monsignor Matthew hadn't attended breakfast. From behind the lattice, we could see that Mother Michael had taken her seat next with Sr. Helen. They were deep in conversation, often looking to Monsignor Matthew's empty chair.

"Look, here she comes," I said. We looked to the door and knew immediately.

"It's too late," she said, jabbing me under the table.

We looked up and noticed a slouch in her posture, using the chairs for support, as she walked down the row. She brushed the hair from her face, her cheeks blushed, her eyes drooped. I knew the look. When she looked up, we saw red marks, welts beginning to form on her face. Sara filled Mary's plate with eggs and ham, but watching her, we could see that she could barely hold her glass. When she tried to pick up her fork, it dropped to the plate.

"I'm not hungry," she said, barely able to open her mouth.

Sara put the plate on the table and reached for the fragile young girl.

"I'm going to take you to the infirmary."

"No, I don't want to get you in trouble," she said in barely a whisper.

"Don't worry about that. Wait here." Sara left the girl alone and came to our table, bent down and whispered in my ear. The floor Sister was too busy cutting up her slab of meat to notice our conversation.

I nudged Veronica and motioned for her to follow. Sara and I told the Sister in charge that Mary had a fever and asked if I could take her to the infirmary. Without looking up, she approved. Five minutes later Veronica told Sister she needed to use the lavatory. The Sister, scraping her plate clean, didn't seem to bother looking up when Veronica left the hall.

I took Mary to the infirmary. When I opened the door, Nurse wasn't anywhere around, so I led her to a bed, sat her down and helped her get comfortable. She tried to hide the red marks on her arms, and the ones forming across her face, turning away to cover them from sight.

"You fought back, didn't you?" I asked

"What do you mean?" Mary asked, looking up at me.

"Look at your hands." I held one of her bruised hands up in the air. You have scrapes and scratches. We know who did it, we know what he did," I said, letting go, then putting my arm around her shoulder to comfort her.

"No, nothing happened. He just wanted to talk to me," she said, beginning to cry. She sat on the thin mattress, her face buried in her hands.

"Come on, let's clean you up. You'll feel better in a bit." I went to the sink, took a washcloth from the cupboard and held it under the faucet until the water became hot. While I soaked the cloth Veronica came through the door.

"Is she all right?"

"She has scratches on her arms, and she might get a black eye. She is a mess. We need to clean her up," I said.

"Who needs to be cleaned up?" Nurse asked, as she came in from another room, standing behind Veronica.

"It's Mary. She's been hurt."

"What happened to her? Was it one of the Sisters?" Nurse asked.

"No. We think it was Monsignor Matthew."

"Mary can you tell me what happened?" Nurse asked, sitting on the cot next to her.

"Nothing happened. I started my period, and I upset Sr. Margaret, so she grabbed my arm and I tried to pull away. That's why I have the scratches."

"Regardless of what happened, we need to clean you up. Can you stand?"

I handed Nurse the washcloth. She wiped her face and ran the warm cloth down in the creases of her neck. Then she led Mary to the shower, and turned the water on. Nurse, ever so gently, pulled the jumper up over her head, helped her take off her slip and undergarments, allowing a few minutes to wash away Monsignor Matthew's sins. Standing there naked, we saw bruises taking shape on her legs and thighs. He had done more than she was willing to tell.

"You think Monsignor Matthew attacked her?" Nurse asked, turning away from the shower.

"Yes. She came from the chapel, didn't she? Who else could it have been?" Veronica said.

Mary stepped from the shower with a towel wrapped around her. Her arms had turned red around the scratches. She looked so much thinner and younger, wrapped in the towel. She couldn't have been fourteen. Her Laundry haircut stuck to the side of her head.

"Are you alright?" Veronica asked.

"Yes, thank you, but I need to get back before anyone gets in trouble."

"You won't get in trouble, Mary," Nurse said, standing and going to a closet, where she pulled out undergarments and a nightgown, placing them on the cot.

"You can tell us what happened. We will do everything we can to protect you."

Mary looked up at us, as we stood in front of her. "You can't protect me from what is happening here. The only way I can protect myself is to not say a word. If I let it happen, he will get bored and it will stop."

"No, that's the point Mary, it won't stop. It may stop with you, but there'll always be another girl for him to pick on," Veronica said.

"How did you know?" she asked.

"Because, we all have been where you were tonight, at least once, some, more than once," I said.

"Did anyone tell?"

"No, no one ever tells."

"Why?" Mary asked.

"The same reason you don't want speak of it," Veronica said.

"We all know what would happen if we said anything. No one would believe us. It would be Monsignor's word against ours, if they even considered approaching him about it. Remember, he walks on water," I said, feeling braver than ever before.

"It happened to you?" Mary asked looking at each of us.

"I was lucky, Sr. Helen came in and it stopped before it started, but I know what he wanted to do. I didn't tell because I wanted to forget it ever happened."

"Did Sister Helen see you?" Mary asked.

"No, it was dark and I was behind the door. She never knew I was even there."

"What about you? What did he do to you?" Mary asked Veronica.

"He made me take him in my mouth, over and over again. He threatened me with a beating from Sr. Helen if I ever told, then one day it stopped. He never called for me again. I figured he found someone else. I was overjoyed that he would finally leave me alone," Veronica said.

"I can't talk about what he did," Mary said.

"You don't have to, we saw you when you came out of the chapel, but you must say it out loud for yourself," Veronica said, "or you'll never have another night sleep without his face in it."

"I've never done anything like what he made me do, not even with my husband."

Veronica and I looked over at Nurse, then at each other when we heard those words fall from her lips. She didn't look like she could be married. She seemed barely a teenager.

"You have a husband?"

"My Da made me marry his best friend, so someone would be able to look after him. I went to work there when I was ten and we were married when I was twelve. We were married for two years. I had two babies, but they both died. By the end of the summer, he died too. I expected to go home, but my father took me to the rectory, dropped me off, and the priest brought me here. I didn't do anything wrong."

I couldn't look at her as she spoke, spilling the words, like a family sin she had kept hidden. I was just fourteen, with a baby who had survived. Mary made my rape seem merely an unfortunate event. She sat stooped shouldered on the bed, while Nurse helped her settle on the cot. Veronica took a blanket from a nearby bed and placed it over her.

"You rest now," Nurse said.

"I don't know what to say. You have been so kind to me. No one has ever been this kind."

She laid her head on the pillow and turned away from us.

We knew we couldn't protect her, and her saying it out loud, made us feel vulnerable and weak. She had said it all.

"He raped her and she needs time to heal. You girls go on back, so you don't get into trouble. If the Sisters say anything, tell them to come to me. I'm not afraid of them."

"Will she be all right?" I asked.

"Yes . . . for today at least."

We left Nurse and went to our assigned duties. We didn't say anything to each other, after what we had seen. There was nothing to say. Mary's broken body said it all.

THE INVITATION

ate one afternoon after spending hours in the folding room, Sr. Agatha interrupted my day by requesting that I walk with her to Mother Michael's office. She patted my hand as we walked down the hall, but said nothing. When she opened the door, I looked at her and nodded. She turned away with one final pat.

"How are you today, Alice?" Mother Michael asked without standing.

"I'm fine."

"I'll get right to the point, something has come up and I thought of you. Sit down."

I took a seat, looking around the room. Nothing had changed from the day I arrived. A picture of the Sacred Heart hung on the far wall. I stared at the open crimson heart and wondered how it must have felt for His heart to break when His life shattered before him.

"I don't understand what you're saying."

"The caretaker, Jonathan, will come in to explain."

Just as she completed her sentence, I heard a knock at the door, and Jonathan came in. He moved to the far corner of the room. I had seen him before, when I had gone to hang up sheets or meet the delivery trucks. He had a familiar grin known by everyone who passed him in the breezeway or the corridors. A bit nervous and anxious, he seemed uncomfortable standing in a room filled with religious authority.

"Jonathan, this is Alice. She will be working with you in the garden."

I wanted to ask why she had chosen me, but became too frightened, afraid that if I did, she'd decide one of the other girls would be better, so I sat silently, waiting for the catch. There was always a catch.

"He has asked for some help in the garden, and I thought you might be the one to fill the bill, so to speak. I'd like you to work with him whenever he needs it."

The idea of working with Jonathan seemed appealing, but my experiences with men, were not memories I cherished. Da always appeared bothered by the company of his family. He brushed us off, sending us on chores, to bed, then back to school each morning, with barely a mention. In the evening, he came home late from the fields and often ate alone, or with Mum who never failed to have a second dinner ready for him. We never sat next to him in church, instead he lined us up in the pew in front of him, so if any of us misbehaved, he could give us a thumping. Da left the tenderness to Mum, or the Sisters who ran the school.

From early on, I'd been terrified of men, nervous that I'd do or say something wrong. After the rape, I was too broken, and Monsignor Matthew had only added to my disgrace.

I knew that Jonathan wore a constant smile, but kept to himself, and limited his conversations. His greetings, though speechless, were honest and endearing. I needed the freedom to spend time in the cold, country air with someone who'd find no judgment, no ridicule, or insinuations that my life had no meaning.

"I don't understand. Why me?"

"It was not my doing. Monsignor Matthew requested you. You'll be allowed to work two days a week to help in the garden," then Mother Michael turned to Jonathan. "She'll be at the garden gate in the morning. When you're done with her, send her back to kitchen gate. Do you have any questions, either of you?"

Though I didn't let Mother Michael have any inclination, I knew why Monsignor Matthew had requested me. Though he resided in a different building, his back windows looked out onto the garden where I'd be working. He could watch in the guise of keeping an eye on me, but I would know.

Without saying anything, Jonathan leaned across the massive desk, reached out his hand offering a firm grasp. Larger than most men I had ever met, I saw the red weathered hand reach out in what I hoped to be a friendship. His oversized coveralls hung from under his wool jacket. His flannel plaid shirt wedged through the sleeves.

"Excellent. It's settled. Alice you will start with Jonathan tomorrow. Be at the gate after breakfast. But, understand this, it won't be easy. I'll be keeping a close eye on you, as will the other Sisters. Monsignor Matthew will monitor you as well. Jonathan will also report your progress and should you do anything in question, this job will be taken from you."

"Yes ma'am."

On my first day, Jonathan met me at the gate, unlocked it and led me to the overgrown garden, full of weeds and thistles. Wild roses and heather grew along the hedge; the roses were lost among patches of dead vines that had collected over years of abandonment. We didn't talk, in those early days, while working together. He showed me what he wanted done and I did it. If I had a question, I asked, he answered. That was that.

We started by clearing two patches in the massive garden. The sounds outside were so different from the stale stillness indoors. The winds whistled high above us, almost singing through the clouds. It was clean and I was a part of it.

Jonathan worked diligently, bending and reaching, tossing the weeds about to clear a space. Though the cold ground was hard, Jonathan continued to dig. I trimmed back wildflowers and roses.

When I looked over, I saw his hands red from the exposure, digging in the hard ground. He often pushed his hat back, wiped his forehead, and then replaced it, continuing with his chores.

I spent hours raking, trimming, and gathering it all together and taking it to the fertilizer pile. The wind blew and shadows of the sun splintered through the clouds.

I thought about Meadows Glen and how my brothers and sisters ran through the fields as the winds danced about us. We were free then. No harsh rulers coming down on our knuckles, or Da's strap on our backsides. In these few hours, I was free too. Free from the lye soap, the watchful eye of Sister Helen, free to let my guard down.

Our days ended in the silence they began. I went to the garden after breakfast and worked until supper time. Sr. Helen motioned from the window for Jonathan to send me inside. I'd smile at Jonathan as I handed him my hoe, then go through the backdoor to the kitchen. I turned to see him still bent over, pulling the weeds and leveling the ground.

I'd come into the kitchen just as Sara was getting the plates from the cupboards for supper. I washed up, then helped her set the tables. Even after all day in the yard, I was happy to help, before returning to the dormitories for a restful night.

"You seem happy."

"I am," I said, "I forgot how great it felt to be outside. It's the first time since I've been here that I actually felt clean."

"Well, you're not. Have you looked at yourself? You're a mess."

"I'll see if I can sneak a shower in before I go to bed," I said.

I went off to the infirmary where Nurse allowed me a shower and change of clothes without a word of contention.

"You're a lucky one, you know that don't you?" Nurse said, as she handed me a clean jumper.

"I know, but I keep waiting for someone to grab hold of me and toss me about, like I'm not worthy of anything."

"That could happen at any time here. I'd watch myself if I were you. Mother Michael never does anything to be nice. There's always a motive."

"That's what frightens me. No one knows when everything will break apart."

"Just watch yourself, Alice."

A Statistic

When not in the garden, I worked in rooms full of soiled garments belonging to unknown priests, unidentified schoolgirls and random hotel residents. I stood for hours, next to penitents I didn't know, not their Christian names, nor the towns they were born, not even why they were there. If not for Veronica and Sara, I'd have spent my days in silence.

If allowed, I stayed in the kitchen as often as I could. I preferred my time in the garden, but kept a watch out for Sara, who never strayed from my mind.

Sara still collected her share of bruises. In her clumsiness she often dropped or spilled something in an awkward manner that brought about reprisal, or on her own, fell or bumped against the walls.

I saw little of Mary except in the dining hall, but it didn't keep me from worrying about her every day. Sara informed me that she had been moved around a lot, from the ironing room, where steam filled the stale air, to the hot muggy boiling rooms, as the girls often called them. I could only hope that Sr. Agatha kept her word and found a way to keep her safe. My hope for the girl came to no avail. One day, after coming in from the garden, I searched for her, only to learn she had been placed in the infirmary.

"Watch yourself, girl. Monsignor Matthew has been in a vile mood. You heard what happened to Mary?" Sara asked, as she peeled the carrots. Veronica stood over the sink rinsing the vegetables we were about to help Sara peel.

"She's been working in the ironing room," Veronica said.

"When they aren't moving her about," Sara chimed in.

"Why would she be moved around?" I asked.

"So no one will notice that her belly is growing," Veronica said, looking over at me.

"What are you saying?" I asked.

"That Monsignor Matthew got to her," Sara said.

Sara used her place in the kitchen to learn all the secrets. She noticed everything, even the smallest of changes. She knew when the girls were on their periods, or when they had been to the Friday-night showers. Though Sara had observed all this about Mary, she was helpless to do anything.

"Pregnant, she is, four months past." Sara looked up, then went back to her peeling.

He had gotten to her the night we found her. I was sick to my stomach. It knotted and moved up to my throat, and sat there. He had enough time to do something he'd never be blamed for.

"She's been throwing up for the last few weeks, with no one tending her, and still working in the rooms. She's been unable to swallow any of the food placed in front of her, so I've been taking her soup when I can. She's only been sipping on water. Nothing is staying down."

"She's getting weaker and weaker. They don't think she will make it," Veronica said.

"She's already lost two babies," I said.

"From what I've seen of her so far, she won't survive another one," Sara said.

"Have they called a doctor for her?" I asked, still looking at Sara.

"You know Mother Michael would never do that, and if she even thought about it, Sr. Helen would find a way to talk her out of it."

We continued working, knowing that by the following day we well may lose one of our own, and in a few hours after that, she'd be replaced. They'd never tell us, and they'd never tell her family, just bury her somewhere on the grounds, leaving her unmarked. We had seen crosses on the lawns on days we slipped out to meet the laundry trucks, and with no one staring out the windows, we walked about. I imagined the crosses were for the Sisters, not the penitents. I had no idea where the penitents, or even the babies were buried.

"I'm going to sneak into the infirmary," I said.

"No, if Sister Helen finds you, you'll get double of whatever she thought you might deserve. I'm to go up and take her some soup a little later. I'll let you know what I find."

Sara knew so many details of our lives before the rest of us. I imagined being in the kitchen and how the requests for food from the Sisters and Monsignor Matthew let her know the conditions of everyone there. When Sr. Helen came down early requesting a special breakfast for Mother Michael, we knew she'd not be at the table for at least a day.

I helped Sara serve dinner, and after everyone took their places, no one paid attention when I asked to be excused. Sr. Beatrice, sat engrossed in her cross-stitch, paying little attention to anything. I saw Sara stare over at me. I stared back trying to tell her with my eyes that I'd be okay. She motioned me to follow her to the kitchen. She scooped the broth into a bowl and placed it on a tray.

"Here, take it. Tell Nurse, I got held up and that you have permission. I'll cover for you as best I can."

I headed toward the stairs and carefully balancing the tray, I made it to the infirmary in a few minutes. I looked around each corner to make sure I had not been followed. I shifted the tray and knocked on the locked door.

"What are you doing here? You trying to get yourself in trouble?" Nurse said, as she greeted me at the doorway.

"No, Sara couldn't come, so she asked Sr. Beatrice if I could go for her. Where's Mary?" I asked, looking around at all the beds.

"You can't see her."

"Why not? I have soup for her. You told Sara to bring it."

"No, I mean I'll take it to her. She is very sick, and is still throwing up," Nurse said, "I doubt that she'll make it through till morning. She told me about her other two babies. From what she said, I believe they were stillborn. She's just not strong enough to go full term. She is a mere child."

"You stayed with her. You didn't go home. Why?" I asked.

"She needs constant care. She's too fragile. Even if she survives this, I don't think she'll survive the delivery."

Nurse, in the Laundries, reminded me of Nurse Claire at the Home.

She cared about the girls, but felt helpless to change anything. Every night she left the walls of the compound and returned to her own life, so different from ours. When she returned the hours she spent with us seemed to mean something. In her own way she found a way to keep us as safe as best she could.

"You need to call a doctor. Did you ask Mother Michael?"

"Of course I did, girl. Mother Michael won't allow a doctor on the grounds unless it's for the Sisters. And no one else cares enough to do anything. Certainly not Monsignor Matthew."

"Can I see her?" I asked.

"No, leave her be. She's sleeping. I'll give her the soup when she wakes," Nurse said.

"Please. I won't say a word. I just feel so bad for her."

I saw the change in her face. Her jaw softened, her eyebrows relaxed, and for the first time, a tiny slit in her lips crossed her face.

"Very well," Nurse said, looking back at Mary. She must have thought I could do something she hadn't. "Be very quiet. Follow me. She's in the back. In a lot of pain, she is. I've actually been giving her some rum Sara brought from the kitchen, to keep her calm, and to help her sleep. Mother Michael won't allow me give her any medication."

"Can you wake her? She needs to know she's not alone." We stood over Mary's bed. She looked like a wee one, lying under the blanket.

"She finally fell asleep," Nurse said, standing behind me.

"Please, let me try?"

Nurse bent down next to her. "Mary, can you hear me?" Nurse whispered.

"Come on girl, open your eyes."

We each stared down at her. At first nothing, so she called her name out again. Mary blinked, and squinted her eyes.

"Where am I?" Mary asked, slowly opening her eyes.

"You're in the infirmary," Nurse said, pulling the blanket over her shoulders.

"What am I doing here?" Mary looked around at us as if we were strangers to her, which ironically, we were.

"You collapsed on the floor and Mother Michael had you brought here," Nurse said, moving toward the cot.

"How long have I been here?" She asked, barely audible.

"At least three days," Nurse said, staring down at the terrified girl.

A long silence took hold, and she closed her eyes again, but before long opened them and stared at us, blinking once or twice.

"We're going to tell," I said, looking over at Nurse, who leaned down to tend to Mary.

"You must never tell anyone," Mary whispered.

"Mary, you're pregnant. Someone should know, this is not your fault," I said, heartbroken for girl.

"No one will believe you. They wouldn't even believe her," Mary said pointing to Nurse.

"Do you believe her?" I asked, staring back at Nurse.

"Yes, but what can I do?"

"We have to find a way to get her a doctor."

"You have to get out of here. I can't do any of this with you here. You go on now."

I leaned down and kissed Mary on the forehead. She burned with fever. I gave Nurse a hug and went out the door, slipped down the staircase and returned to the kitchen to help Sara finish the cleanup after supper.

Veronica came through the doorway, carrying dishes to the sink and sat at the table. Sara stood in front of the sink and I took a seat next to Veronica.

"How is she?"

"The girl is half dead. Been throwing up for three days now. She's barely alive," I said.

Remembering her face, I tried hard to hold back the tears. I believed I had just seen an angel, a few hours from meeting her Savior.

"It could have been anyone of us, you realize that don't you?"

"She's going to die." Sara broke in. "She won't survive the pregnancy and if she does, neither she nor the baby will survive long after."

The next morning, I left the dormitory early, hoping to get another chance to see Mary, but once in the kitchen, girls were running about in complete chaos. Looking out the window, I saw an ambulance outside the gates and the attendants were coming to the door. They took a stretcher up the stairs and in a few minutes came out with Mary lying, half conscious, under a blanket. The Sisters tried to keep us quiet, but it had been a long time since such a ruckus occurred. Sara and I went to the stairway and watched as they wheeled her out. I saw Nurse come back in and head toward the infirmary without a word to Mother Michael. I approached Nurse before she disappeared behind the infirmary door.

"Did you tell?"

"What would have been the point? I got her out of this place. That should be enough. She won't survive the week."

"Thank you," I said, squeezing her hand.

"For what?" She walked away, with her head down.

After they wheeled Mary out the front door, the whispering increased in all the rooms. Even during dinner, girls gossiped back and forth that Mary had snuck out and met a boy. That poor girl had not met any boy. She had met the devil himself.

A few days later Nurse slipped a note to Sara:

Mary died yesterday.
I thought you and Alice should know.

I could only imagine that her family would never know what happened to her.

THE ATTACK

t didn't take long for the news about Mary to spread throughout the compound. We waited for Mother Michael to make an announcement during one of the evening meals, but weeks passed and she said nothing. Monsignor Matthew did not come around the dining hall, nor did he do services. Brother Patrick took over the daily religious chores.

Whispers came to a halt during meals, and abrupt yelling could be heard coming around corners. The floors were never clean enough, and the stains always seemed to have a shadow that needed more scrubbing.

One evening, about the time everyone seemed to have forgotten Mary, another girl had been brought in to take her cot, and her seat at the dining table. Mother Michael stood up from her chair and came to our side of the partition.

"I know there have been rumors going around concerning our dear Mary, and I have decided that it is important I set things straight. They came and removed Mary from the compound three weeks ago, and took her to a hospital, but unfortunately, she was very sick and did not survive. Her family now has her back and we hope they find strength in her love of God."

"What happened to her?" One of the girls sitting by Mother Michael asked.

"Nothing. She got a fever."

"Was she sick? Will we get the fever?"

"No. She was ill when she came, and we could do nothing to help her.

Our Nurse did everything she could. It was in God's hands."

I looked over at Veronica, and shook my head. Knowing what I knew, I couldn't believe what happened had anything to do with God. I bowed my head and made the sign of the cross in silence. I knew that what happened to Mary could happen to any of us, and in time would happen again because we couldn't stop it.

I decided I couldn't sit still, so I went to help Sara as she continued to serve the meal. I went into the kitchen and picked up a large bowl of soup, carrying it to the Sister's table because Sara couldn't hold the weight. As I approached the table, I saw Sr. Helen's skirt in the aisle, but thought I could step over it and still hold myself upright.

As she sat deep in conversation with another Sister, I tried to step over her, but I lost my balance, tripped and spilled hot potato soup across the front of her skirt. My feet folded around me and I fell to the floor, splintering the bowl as I went down. The second the steaming liquid seeped through to her skin, she jumped up, knocking her chair to the ground.

She stood over me and when I looked up at her, her arms began swinging in all directions. She began screaming in what seemed to be tongues, words I couldn't understand. I cowered at the tips of her black-heeled shoes. Without realizing it, the soup had also scalded her hands, which added to her rage. But what came out of her mouth in the next few minutes had nothing to do with the soup. She began to lash out with hate that I could never imagine.

"What is the matter with you? You pathetic girl, you can't even carry soup to a table? You are as retarded as that bastard child you gave up."

She continued hitting me, first with her fists, and when I didn't move, or fight back, she picked up the ladle from the soup bowl and began to hit me with it. She hit me about the head, arms, across my back, and anywhere she could find. When the wooden ladle disintegrated to splinters, she stood, grabbed the chair and threw it down on me. She collapsed to the floor in exhaustion.

"They brought her back, you know," she screamed, as I lay motionless. "Yes, in God's holy name, left the bastard child on the doorstep, they did. Did not even bother to wait for someone to answer. Left a note, abandoning it yet again. It will never have a home, you senseless whore. It will die here, behind these walls, just like you."

"That is enough, Sister. Leave the girl be," said Sr. Beatrice, a passive older nun who guided us to vigils each night. She moved to where both of us lay crumbled on the floor and reached for the arm of her fellow Sister.

"You saw what she did, she deserves even more." Sr. Helen raged, trying to maintain her balance while holding on to Sr. Beatrice.

I was left lying on the floor, reduced to a heap, like a tumbled house of bricks. No one came for me. They weren't allowed. The beating not only broke my body, but broke me to my very core. She made me believe my daughter was as incidental as she thought I was.

I knew that Sr. Helen might be lying, by just the fact it came from her mouth; but surely some small part of it must be true. My Finn could be here, living just a few buildings away, seeing the same sky, breathing the same air. I had to learn the truth, to know if Reverend Mother had succeeded in sending her away, or if she, too, had lied about everything. I knew I had to do what I could to try to find Finn.

I couldn't concentrate on the pain, not Sr. Helen's outburst. I could only think my baby might be close. She'd be walking now, her small arms reaching out for balance, teetering her weight on her tiny feet. I remembered her black hair and could only wonder if she might have ringlets, or if the shade of her hair had changed. If I were to believe Sr. Helen, then my daughter had been abandoned also. I would do whatever I could to find her.

Sara came to my aid before anyone else. I couldn't see her face, but I felt her hands, the skin cracked and as rough as they had been the night of my delivery, when she patted me in the infirmary at the Home.

With reluctant permission from Mother Michael, Sara and Veronica took me to the lavatory to clean up. Sara used a wet rag from the kitchen to soothe the reddening welts. One of the broken pieces from the chair had punctured my leg, blood oozed down the open wound. My body ached, and rage filled me.

Perhaps Sr. Helen knew she had found the weakness in my heart, or she just erupted from the rage deep in her soul. The cool wet cloth moved across my forehead and I allowed myself to breath.

"You need to listen to me," Sara said. "I know what you're thinking about your wee one, but you get it out of your head right now. We all heard what she said. You can't believe her. She's trying to rile you.

Don't even think about it. She won't think twice of beating you again. She doesn't care the end result. She couldn't care less if any of us live or die. We're merely property."

"Why do they hate us so much? I don't understand. What have we done to them?" I asked.

"I don't have the answers, but I don't want to ever experience what you just did," Veronica said.

"Leave it be. If what she said is true, they'll find her another home, and your baby will be gone before you even know it. Do you hear me?" Sara asked.

I heard the words, but had no clear understanding of their meaning. I could only focus on the memory of Finn, minutes old, her thick black matte of hair, and her delicate fingers. I couldn't explain the sensations of my scant recollections. Somewhere in the memories I found the pieces of my core, and for that I would sacrifice anything.

"Veronica, come and help me, we have to get her to the infirmary. Nurse needs to take a look at you." Sara said, as Veronica took hold of my arm.

"You're not listening to me," I cried, almost delirious from the pain.

"No, we are not. You're hurt and Nurse needs to tend to you."

With both arms wrapped tight around me, Veronica and Sara led me from the lavatory to the infirmary. As we came through the door, the pains in my side became too much for me to bear. By the time Nurse came over, they felt like cuts from a knife. I remember being laid on a cot and covered with a blanket. I heard chatter next to me.

"What happened? The Sisters did this, didn't they." Nurse said.

"Yes," Sara said. "Alice was helping me serve the soup, she tripped, and spilled everything on Sr. Helen. After it happened, Sister just went crazy and began hitting her, with her hands, then the soup ladle, and finally she threw a chair on top of her that splintered into pieces. See, it cut her leg."

"I'll need to examine her. She may have broken something," Nurse said.

"She held her side and moaned as we brought her in here." Veronica said.

"Go on, get back to the kitchen," Nurse said, "let me take care of her. I'll examine her and do what I must. I'll make sure she stays here until she's healed. I'll do the best I can."

Sara came over to the cot, leaned down and touched my arm. "I'll pray for you."

I grabbed hold of her hand as it brushed past me, and squeezed it. I looked up at Veronica standing in the doorway, terrified that they were leaving me alone, but knowing they couldn't stay.

"Alice, listen to me. I'm going to examine you to make sure there is nothing broken. I'm going to lift your arms. If it hurts, let me know. I'm also going to clean the wound in your leg. Do you understand me?"

"Yes."

"Tell me where it hurts."

"My side, it hurts to raise my arm."

"By the sight of the bruises taking hold, I think you may have broken some ribs."

"I don't understand. Why would she do that? I had no intention of hurting her," I said, in a whisper.

"Because she is angry with everyone, and she takes it out on those who can't defend themselves."

"I can't let go of my daughter again."

"Oh you poor girl, you never had your daughter. They had her from the very first day, it was already decided what they were going to do with her. Don't you understand that?"

"No. I let them take her once, and I did nothing. I won't let that happen again. I don't care how many beatings it takes. Do you understand that? I'll regret it, if I don't do something. That's what terrifies me the most."

"You rest now, go to sleep. No one can hurt you anymore," Nurse said.

I closed my eyes and saw her face before me. Sr. Helen may have thought she broke me, in her moment of rage, screaming, for everyone to hear, that my daughter was as useless as I was. I found myself lying broken on the thin mattress like a pile of kindling, but I realized nothing would be gained with anger. I needed to be grateful, for Sr. Helen, in her hatred of me, brought my Finn back to me.

I knew Sara was right, Sr. Helen could very well be lying because she was hateful, but I had to hope, that maybe for once, this woman in her black gown of God was telling part of a truth.

I didn't sleep that night. I lay with my ribs wrapped, my cuts bandaged, and a new sense of myself. I had stopped fighting, too afraid that I would stir the embers of a fire that we all wanted to die. We had all come here crippled, damaged, too frightened to fight back. I knew I had to find a way to keep my wits about me.

RETURN TO THE GARDEN

I t had been weeks since I had seen the light of day. Sr. Helen in her rage had left me with two broken ribs and a cut that required four stitches. I had bruises on my face, my arms, and a tooth had been splintered.

My first trek out of the infirmary took me to the dining hall for supper. I didn't care what the girls saw any more. The purple splotches on my face had turned yellow. It didn't matter if they were turning pink, I had the scars, and they would always be there. We all had the scars. On the other side of the partition, I saw Sr. Helen. My eyes froze on her face. The last time I had seen her, she stood over me in a rage. I didn't see the rage in her eyes this time, but I did see her get up and walk toward the table, suddenly motioning to me.

"Mother Michael wants to see you."

I went down the hallway with a sense of freedom, usually we were escorted wherever we needed to go, but she allowed me to go on my own. I knocked twice on the door and waited.

"Come in."

"How are you feeling?" She asked.

"I'm better, thank you, Mother Michael."

She stood, walked around the desk, and stopped in front of me with her arms crossed over the crucifix that rested on her chest.

"Let me be plain with you. I know what you think, but your baby isn't here. We never allow the babies on the same grounds as their mothers."

"I know that now, Mother Michael." I stared straight ahead, trying to remain strong.

"Do you know what your plans are?" she asked still staring at me.

"I don't have a plan. I just know I need to work hard until I'm allowed to return home. I'd like to go to Dublin, maybe attend university." I said, still staring straight ahead.

"Do you think we should let you go home now?" She asked, circling me.

"Yes, I'd like to go home. I haven't done anything for you to keep me here."

"Well, your parents don't think so. They don't want you back. Did you know that?" A slick grin passed over Mother Michael's face.

"I just want to go home. I'll do whatever you ask of me. I won't be any trouble, I promise."

"Oh, I am certain you'd promise anything. Remember this, I say when you can go. Don't forget that. Though you are in the garden, I still know your goings-on. So don't get any fancy ideas. Jonathan keeps me well informed. Do I make myself clear? If you think Sr. Helen can be cruel, don't push me, girl."

"Yes Mother Michael." Without warning, a quick slap stung my face and I reeled back. Mother Michael made her point.

Mother Michael ordered the Sisters to keep a watchful eye over me when I returned to the garden. It wasn't clear why they were so attentive; perhaps afraid I would escape... but where would I go?

Once allowed back, I reveled in the clean air, but I couldn't tell Jonathan what had happened to me, so I pretended I'd never missed a day. Instead of thinking about myself, I chose to imagine Finn pattering about, waving her arms, laughing, talking her own language and being happy, a happiness I had yet to know with her.

"Welcome back, Miss. A bit of work to be done. Are you up to it?"

"Yes, I'm so grateful to be back."

He reached over and handed me the basket. "We can start with the vegetables, as they need picking."

"Thank you. I'm okay, I can do the work."

"Girl, I don't know exactly what happened, and you never have to tell me, but I know you're not okay. Take it easy until those bruises heal."

"I'm sorry." I said, trying to cover my face. I didn't want to say anything about the beating, or the desperation, but somehow I knew either

Veronica, or Sara had slipped in to the garden while I recovered and told him everything.

"Only a beating would keep you from the garden. Go slow. I'll watch out for you."

While he did most the work, I puttered about picking the carrots and the squash, then moved on to trimming the new buds and seedlings. We continued to work side by side for hours, and with each task I felt myself getting stronger.

My body ached, but under the heavy wool cardigan he couldn't see the last of the bruises that had once covered my arms, only the ones that were slowly healing around my face. Sara had said yellow shadows still remained, reminding her of the rings around the moon.

I needed to keep coming to the garden each day so I wouldn't remember what happened to me. I wouldn't remember the rape, or the beatings, or the loss. I would replace those with planting, trimming, and finding a God I could believe in that would help me find my way back to my daughter and a life I could call my own.

*   *   *

"So, what part of the country are you from?" As he knelt in the black dirt, and continued to dig the holes for the seedlings.

"From the Midlands, born near Delvin," I said, turning my face from him.

"I'm from Cork, but moved with my family to Dublin when I was a kid. Settled in Howth, by the seaside with the Missus."

"You have children?" I asked, as I continued handing him the new seedlings.

"No, the Missus couldn't bear children of our own, but nieces and nephews fill up all the rooms in our house on the weekend. I enjoy hearing their laughter. It distances the silence." He gave a shy smile, but his face was all lit up with joy.

"What about you?"

"I lived on a dairy farm, cows, pigs, and chickens everywhere."

"I imagine you had a lot work to do."

"My brother did most of it, but we helped, as we could."

"Who would be the "we"?" Jonathan asked.

"I have an older brother, and two sisters."

"That is a good-sized family."

"Mum wanted more, but she had problems. After losing two more babies after my youngest sister, the doctor told her to stop."

"So, when you weren't in school, what did you do?"

"We learned to milk, clean out the stables, do all the work Da didn't have the time for. The chickens and the pigs were the most demanding," I said, looking up at him for the first time. He looked down at me, with the sweetest smile, I had ever seen.

Each day, I told him more about the life I remembered. Talking made the work go faster. Sometimes we didn't talk about ourselves. He taught me about the seedlings and cuttings. He showed me how to plant, trim, and the purpose of the fertilizer pile.

One day, out of nowhere, he said , "I've been thinking a lot about you. If you don't mind, I'd like to call you by name."

I smiled at him. "My Christian name is Alice."

"I know. If that'd be okay, I'd like to call you Alice. I know they give the girls different names when they come, but no one ever uses them. Seems, no one but the Sisters are called by their names, and of course Monsignor."

"They use your name."

"Well, yes, I guess they do," he smiled, then tipped his hat.

"I was named for my grandmother."

"Then you're the oldest of the girls."

It felt odd talking to someone about my life, having him smile back at me, as if it was something important, something that he wanted to hear. I was having my first true conversation since leaving Meadows Glen.

"I've been here a long time. I know things that you could never imagine," he said as he went back to digging the cold hard ground.

"Do you know about the babies?" I asked. "Where they go?" I thought I had nothing to lose in asking him. I knew he wouldn't hurt me. He'd tell me yes or no, or tell me not to bother with it.

"Yes. A social worker comes to the Home, takes the baby to the train or bus depot, depending on where it's being sent."

"Have you ever seen a transfer take place?"

"I made a transfer once, a wee one in a basket when no one came for her. She slept the whole way. I took her to the airport where I handed her over to a nurse, who took her on the plane. I believe it was to the States."

"Do the babies ever come back? I mean do the families ever decide they made the wrong choice?"

"Not often, but it can happen, mostly if they are fostered out. A family can change its mind about caring for an infant. They brought a wee one back a few months ago."

"Did you know her name?"

"No, just back from a family who agreed to foster her out, but after a few weeks, changed their mind," he said as he continued to dig.

"Was she in a basket?"

"Lord, no girl, wrapped tight in a blanket she was, held by a nurse. Why do you ask?"

"No reason," I said, fiddling with the cuttings of wild roses I had in my hand. I rubbed the soft petals between my fingers.

"There's always a reason, Alice." I stared back at him.

He nodded his head, walking back toward the shed. He was smart, kind, and if I were to have an ally I would have to trust him.

When I came in that night from the work, I was more silent than usual. I didn't know where my thoughts were coming from, but I felt I was changing in the time I spent with Jonathan. What the Sisters had taken from me, he was giving back, day by day.

"You must know why we're here? All of us, I mean. They call us sinners," I said, knowing it was the one way to get Jonathan's attention. It had been a couple of days since I'd last been in the garden, but I had been aching to talk to him.

"Oh no, dear Lord girl, you're not a sinner. You're a child thrown to the hands of the devil. I don't know the details of your story, but I know that something terrible happened. I know that if they have their way, you'll die in the disguise of penance." Jonathan pulled off his hat, took out his handkerchief, and wiped his forehead.

I had more to say to him.

"I was a good girl. I obeyed my parents. I should have walked home that day with my brother." I tried with my words to convince Jonathan of something that I couldn't even believe.

"Don't be doing this to yourself," he said, stooping down on the ground, letting his shovel drop to the side, as he pulled weeds from the cold ground.

"But it's true. If I had left school with him, I would have made it home safe. I'd still be in Meadows Glen, finishing school, maybe even going on to university someday, but that isn't happening. I'm here.

I got a beating a while back. Sr. Helen in her rage said that my daughter was here." I looked up at him. His face was tight, his lips puckered out, then he took hold of my arm, stopping me before I could continue.

"You stay clear of Sr. Helen. Stay out of her fire. Don't rile her, or you'll never find a way out of here. She's an angry, bitter woman, she is. I've seen what she can do. What she has done to you is just the tip of her rage."

"I'm never getting out of here am I?" I asked, staring straight at him.

"You're not asking me about you, you're asking about your daughter, aren't you?"

I nodded.

"I'm afraid that if anyone tries to do anything for you, and it fails, you'll be sent off to another Laundry. Your baby, who you say is here— and I doubt she is—would be fostered out before you could turn around."

"How do you know that?" I asked.

"I just know. I don't know what they'd do with her. And me? I'd be fired on the spot, and probably arrested. Do you hear me?"

I didn't move at first. I couldn't figure out how he knew what was so deep in my heart. I knew. My thoughts made no sense to me, but I knew I needed Jonathan's reassurance. Without saying a word, he reached over for my hand, patted it, and gave it a tight squeeze. He had seen me. Jonathan had been the first sign of hope I'd had in almost two years. I wanted to jump for joy, but I stood still, and smiled up at him.

Jonathan dropped the shovel he had been digging with, moved over to where I was standing, and wrapped his arms around my shoulders. It was gentle and kind. I allowed myself to blend into his strong, warm arms.

I glanced up to the window in the rectory. Monsignor Matthew was watching. I pulled away from Jonathan, and moved across the yard, as far as I could get. Jonathan looked up to the window as well. He tipped his hat to the Monsignor, picked up his shovel, and went back to his digging. Jonathan motioned for me to go inside. When I got close enough to hear him, he looked up.

"You need to go in now. We're done for the day."

I took the tools I had been using, and put them in the shed. I left Jonathan alone without looking at him or up to the rectory window. I went through the back door by the kitchen where Sara greeted me, holding a bowl with a dishcloth. I closed the door and sat at the table.

"Monsignor Matthew saw me in the garden."

"Of course, he did, that was where you were supposed to be."

"No. When I started talking with Jonathan, it got very serious. He gave me a hug." I could feel myself smiling the same way I had at Jonathan. "It was so special. He made me feel so safe. Then I saw him in the window."

"What are you talking about?" Sara asked, turning away from the sink.

"Jonathan. I'm talking about Jonathan, that Monsignor Matthew saw him hug me, now he's going to tell Mother Michael."

Sara looked up at me as if I were crazy. "You go on now. Clean up. Take that guilty look off your face." Sara went back to her dishes, and I headed upstairs to the dormitory.

"There you are," Sr. Helen grabbed hold of my arm just as I was about to go through the door. "Monsignor Matthew sent word that he would like to see you. He asked that I should bring you to the rectory."

"But, I'm a mess, shouldn't I clean up." I tried to show Sr. Helen my clothes.

"No. He wants to see you now."

I had never been in the home of a priest before. I was shocked to see all the beautiful statues, and the massive, bulky furniture choking the entry. Gilt-framed paintings hung from the wall. Rich velvet drapes, covered the windows, leaving the room dark and mysterious. Small lamps sat on tables giving off a meager light.

"Wait here," she said.

Sr. Helen tapped the door softly with her knuckles, then stepped back, looking at me, with disgust. Her look made me nervous, but what was about to happen behind the closed door, scared me even more.

"Don't touch anything while you are in there. You are filthy. Perhaps you should have taken a shower before you came."

Monsignor Matthew opened the door, standing to the side, first looking at Sr. Helen, then over at me.

"Thank you Sr. Helen. That will be all. I will send her back when I am finished."

I wanted to grab her arm, beg her not to leave me alone. I was terrified to be there with him. I knew what he had done to Mary, what months before, he had tried to do to me, remembering what Veronica said he forced her to do.

"Come in, Alice," he said.

THE REQUEST

ave a seat my dear," he said, easing himself into the chair behind his desk.

"Perhaps I should stand Monsignor. I'm very dirty from being outside. I worked in the garden all morning."

"I know, but don't worry about it. Someone will come in to clean it later. By all means, sit down." He lit a cigarette, inhaled, and gestured for me to sit.

"Why did you want to see me, Monsignor?" I held the edge of the chair, gripping tight.

"I wanted to talk with you about the garden."

"I have so enjoyed being outside working with Jonathan. He taught me so much about planting, new ways of taking care of vegetables." I said, hoping our discussion would be about the garden.

"Let me get to the point, so you will be clear about what I expect. I know how much you enjoy being outside, being a country girl and all. I have a proposition for you."

"Yes, Monsignor."

"You are a pretty girl," he said, getting up from his desk, letting the cigarette smoke swirl about him as walked toward me.

"I'm afraid I'm a bit of a mess. My hands are dirty and my hair is wild and..." I grasped at other excuses as he locked the door.

He came back to the chair where I sat, then slowly began to run his hand down the center of my face, to my chin. I could smell the tobacco on his fingertips. It made me cough. He stopped as quickly as he started, then stared at me. I didn't know what to say to him. He stood in front of me, caressing my face, moving his hand along my jaw, and touching the soft skin on my neck without a word.

"Stand up," he said as he stepped away from me, "Take off your jumper."

"Please don't make me do that," I pleaded. "I couldn't"

"Yes you can. Remember, you are doing it for God."

This had nothing to do with God at all, I thought. He touched me in ways that brought only him pleasure. I was young and inexperienced, but I knew what he wanted, but I also knew, everything about it was wrong.

"Monsignor, please don't ask this of me."

"I'm not asking. I'm telling," he said as he smashed his cigarette in the ashtray on the edge of his desk.

He tightened his jaw and watched with unblinking eyes. He had called me in for a purpose. I couldn't leave until he had his needs satisfied. Sr. Helen wouldn't be coming back for me.

I stood up, took off my sweater, dropped it to the floor, then took hold of my hem of my jumper, and pulled it up over my head. I stood there in my slip, almost naked and feeling vulnerable.

"Don't do this," I begged, trying to cover myself.

He leaned against his desk, staring at me. A slight movement came from his mouth, indicating that he might be trying to smile. Then his tongue came out, he licked his lips. He walked up to me, and ran his hand over my slip, touching my nipples. I should have pushed him away. I should have screamed, but I didn't. I froze.

"You are very pretty. You have beautiful cheekbones and your eyes are quite lovely." He wasn't staring at my eyes. The more he complimented my beauty, the more I wanted to cry.

"Are you nervous?"

"Yes. I shouldn't be here. I don't understand why you're doing this." I felt myself shaking, shivering like a chill had wrapped itself around me.

"No. You are wrong. We should both be here. We are exactly where we need to be. I also know you like to be outdoors, isn't that true?"

"Yes, I told you, I'm enjoying it very much."

"And you want to continue to work in the garden? Am I correct?"

"Yes, Monsignor."

"Well, good. We both want something. You want the garden and I want you."

"No, please don't do this."

"It won't hurt. I promise. Come sit on the couch so you can be more comfortable. You seem sad sometimes, distant, away from everything around you," he said, guiding me to the couch, then sitting next to me.

"Why don't you sit closer?"

"No. I don't think I should. It isn't right. You're a priest, I'm just a penitent."

"Well, while you are here, why don't you just think of me as your very good friend who is going to give you what you want, as long as you give me what I want. Isn't that what friends do?"

"But we're not friends. You are my priest, I'm just a girl doing her time here, soon I'll be going home."

He reached over and slipped his hand under my slip and began to move it on the inside of my thigh. He hands were warm, and soft, much softer than I thought any man's hands should be.

"Let me put it this way. If you want to continue working in the garden while you are here, and you want me to help you go back home someday, then you won't mind doing me this favor will you?"

Before I knew it, he had both hands under my slip, between my legs, moving them up and down, massaging my skin. He touched me in a way I had often dreamed a man might touch me, a man I loved, not my priest, here in the Laundries.

"This is our secret, and you must remember that. You wouldn't want me to get angry with you, or those you care about, now would you?"

"No, Monsignor, but this is wrong."

"No, it's not. I want you to get to know me better, and I want to get to know you better. Do you understand? I can guide you through it."

He pulled me close to him on the couch. He guided my hand between his legs, pulled me on top of him, and began foundling me. I struggled, but he held me tight and forced me to move on him.

"You'll get better at it, in time," he said, letting go of me, and pushing me off him. He got up from the couch, straightened his pants, zipped them, and handed me my clothes.

"Put your clothes on, but you are not leaving yet. Go over and sit in the chair. I want to be sure we are very clear about what is going on here."

He moved around the desk, and settled in to his seat, lighting another cigarette. He folded his hands in front of him.

"You want to continue working in the garden, correct?"

"Yes."

"Good. I will let you continue working in the garden, and I will even investigate the possibility of you going home, as long as you keep our meetings to yourself. That means, not telling anyone, including your dear friends, Sara or Veronica. Do I make myself clear?"

"Yes."

"I will know immediately, if you breathe a word, and if you do, rest assured you will regret that decision. Now go on back. You'll miss supper."

"Monsignor?"

"That is all. I'll be calling for you again in a few days."

I unlocked the door and left his office. I looked back at him, but he had already busied himself with something on his desk. I walked back the way I had come earlier that evening.

I knew I couldn't tell anyone because I never said no to him. I never pushed him away. I never fought back. I should have. I should have run out of that room kicking and screaming, but without saying a word, I had agreed because I wanted to work in the garden, I wanted to find my way home. He could control that, but more important, I believed he could harm anyone I cared about.

THE RAPE

s the weeks passed, I continued to work in the garden. When not with Jonathan, I cleaned the tiles, scrubbed the sheets, and washed dishes. Once a week, when least expected, Sr. Helen rounded a corner, or came through a doorway.

I always knew when it was her, the thumping of her shoes identified her. Their steps were soft, barely touching the tiles, hers pounded the ground with a strong beat, like the sound of a drum. I knew when I heard those footsteps Monsignor Matthew had summoned me to the rectory.

He never called on the same day, or even the same hour, but Sr. Helen always met her responsibilities. No matter where I was working, she found me. In silence, we walked through the breezeway to the rectory door. Expressionless, Monsignor greeted her, demanded that I enter, then excused her with the wave of his hand. Each time the door closed behind me, I feared what new thing he had dreamed up to satisfy his lustful being. I couldn't help but wonder if she worried about what went on behind the door, or just considered it another task to complete for her beloved Monsignor.

"How have you been this week?" He asked, walking back around his desk, as I took my stand in front of him.

"I'm fine, Monsignor."

"Are you enjoying the garden?" He lit a cigarette, held in the smoke, then let it come out in a sliver of a swirl that rose above his head, like a halo.

"Yes."

"Why don't you come over here? Sit on the couch with me."

He'd moved over to the couch with his cigarette between his yellowed fingers. Instead of wearing his trousers, as he had on the first day, he wore a black silk dressing gown that, after seated, fell open. Always naked underneath, he'd call for me to come to him. After a while, I knew what to do. I went to the couch, bending down in front of him. It didn't take long for me to satisfy his needs, but when I finished, he wanted nothing to do with me.

We rarely had any conversation during those times. He kept his word, allowing me to continue in the garden, I kept mine, coming as summoned each week. Sara no longer showed signs of any bruises. She had no idea what happened each time I was called out, Veronica continued to believe, that in a short time, she'd be rescued.

With few of the Sisters bothering to pay me much attention, I changed my ways. As I folded the towels and sheets returned to some distant hospital, I worked slower. I took the last place in line, the last to Vigils, even to crawl into bed. Veronica noticed. I saw it in her eyes, but for whatever reason, maybe to protect herself, she remained silent.

On a cold evening, after a long morning in the soaking room, and an even longer afternoon in the garden, I was exhausted. The freezing wind burned my face and my fingers ached from the cold. Sr. Helen came into the dining hall, tapped me on my shoulder, summoning me in the middle of my meal. I put down the spoon

"He wants you now." I followed behind the tapping of her shoes.

"Should I go alone?"

"Yes, I don't have time for you. You know the way." She turned back to her own table, while I went out the double doors.

I had gotten used to my time in the rectory. I separated myself from everything he did. I took my soul and hid it for safekeeping, so I could get through it. Though disgusted that I allowed him to have at me, it continued. As the weeks went on, he became braver with his demands. The first few times, he never touched me, but expected me to pleasure him. I did as best I knew how. After a while he'd told me to take off my jumper, which I did. Then I moved to the couch, bent down on my knees in front of him in my slip. Sometimes a strap of my slip would fall off my shoulder, when I went to lift it up, he would reach down and stop me, making me let it fall.

I knocked on the door, waiting for him to answer, hoping our time would be over as fast as it started. When he opened the door, he stepped back into the shadows. I walked slowly into the dark, smoke-filled room. His dressing gown was tied around his waist, and with his cigarette in hand, his black slippers glided across the floor.

Instead of going to his desk, he walked straight to the couch and sat down. I waited for his usual directions, but none came. He took a drag from his cigarette, and sipped from a glass he had placed on the end table. Tonight wasn't going to be like the others. The only common thing about tonight would be the cigarette and me.

"I want you to do something different for me tonight," he said taking a sip and lying back. "Take off your clothes."

"You mean my dress?"

"No. Everything, but do it slow."

"What if someone comes?"

"We have never been interrupted before. I doubt that will happen."

"I won't do it."

"Come on now, straightaway."

"Please."

"Oh I think, you will do whatever I ask. You wouldn't want anything to happen to Sara, or for someone else to be assigned to the garden, would you?"

"I'll tell. I'll tell Mother Michael what you've done?"

He laughed out loud, then took another sip of his brandy. Then he stood, went to his desk and picked up the pack of cigarettes. He took one out, lit it, and leaned back on his desk.

"If you won't do it, I'll have to do it for you. I might not be so gentle. Now, first, slip off your shoes and socks."

"I swear I'll tell." I stood frozen as he came over to me. Without any notice, he slapped my face. "Slip them off, then take your jumper off."

As I had done the first night, I pulled the dress over my head and stood there in my slip.

"Now it is my turn." He pulled the strap of my slip down on one side, then pulled the other side down. It fell to my waist. "Pull it all the way down."

I pulled the slip past my hips and it fell to my bare feet. I immediately covered my breasts with my arms, trying to hide as much of myself as I could.

"Move your hands," he said getting up and slapping my hands away. "Let me see you." He moved to the table to turn on the light. The glow of the light fell on me. When he returned to the couch, I moved my hands to cover myself again.

"Please don't make me do this."

"When you do what I ask, we will be closer to being done. I'm not sure what you are waiting for."

I took hold of the edge of my panties, and then paused. "Go ahead. Do it, or I will. Remember, I won't be so nice." I pulled them down to my knees, and stepped out of them. He pulled my arms away, going over to the couch. He drained the content of his glass in one gulp.

"Come here. Sit on my lap."

I slowly moved over to him. He took hold of my breasts roughly pinching them. I could tell he was struggling, getting so angry that he wanted to hit something. I assumed it would be me, but he stopped himself. He took hold of himself, pushing it between us. He pulled and yanked. He tried to push himself inside me, but it wouldn't go. He pushed me off him, demanding that I take hold and rub him until he became hard.

Finally, I felt his hardness grow. He pulled me back on top of him, pushing it up inside me, and the pressure of him made me burn inside. I let out a scream, but he kept pushing. He jerked forward, over and over, finally falling back on the couch. I tried to stand, but he pushed me to the floor.

"Get out of here. Take your clothes. Leave me."

*   *   *

I took a seat at the table in the kitchen, dropping my head in my hands. I couldn't stop my body from shaking. I needed a place to hide, to be alone, so I could figure out what I could do. I looked back, terrified that he might have followed me, but he had been the one to tell me to leave. I thought he might be too ashamed to leave the room.

I heard the girls moving around in the dining hall, so I knew they would be going on to chapel soon. Since Sr. Helen had summoned me, she wouldn't be looking for me, sure to believe I was still with him.

Sara came in through the double kitchen doors, grinning.

"Have you heard?"

"Leave me alone, Sara."

"But it is wonderful news."

"I don't want to hear it, just please go back to work. Let me be."

She went about her work without another word to me. Another penitent, an older woman, came in with dishes piled high in her hands. I didn't get up to help. I didn't move. I felt paralyzed. My body was numb, where he had penetrated me. I remained seated at the table. Sara continued to clean, looking over at me every now again.

After a while, Sara came over, sat at the table and patted my arms, the way she did when she couldn't find the words.

"They're leaving Vigils now."

"Thank you."

Sara touched my arm. I could feel my skin burn at the simple touch of her fingers.

"Don't. Don't touch me. You have to leave me alone right now."

"What happened to you?"

"I can't tell you. Is everyone out of the chapel?"

"I think so. Don't you want to hear?"

"I need to go there."

I left the kitchen without another word to Sara. I could feel her eyes on me, but I couldn't turn around and look at her. I knew I had offended her by not talking, but I could not deal with her incidental gossip, or who had said what about whom.

When I went through the door of the chapel, I was relieved that it was empty. I went up to the front pew and sat down. I knelt as I looked up at the statue staring down at me.

Dear God,

I've come to you repeatedly, but You don't seem to be listening. What do I need to do to get Your attention? You have to know what's going on. What he's done to me. I'm sorry Lord, but I can't believe You can let this continue. I'm feeling broken beyond ever being put back together. I can't do this. You have to

help me. You have to hear me.
I want to hate You for what You have let happen. There was a
time I did, but if I give up on You, I have no one.

My body continued to shake as it had done in the kitchen. I stopped praying to the statues that stared down on me. I could feel someone staring at me, watching me, but I was too terrified to turn around to see whom it could be.

"Alice, is that you?"

I still didn't turn around, even though I recognized the voice. She had been there for Sara when Sr. Helen took hold of her, and when Monsignor Matthew took hold of Mary. I felt her slip in next to me, but I couldn't look at her.

"Alice, you don't have to say anything." Nurse put her hand on my shoulder.

I turned my face away from her. I didn't want her to see me. I felt more shame now than the day I came home after the attack.

"Everything speaks for itself, my dear. The fact that you're here, when you should be in the dormitory, tells me all I need to know."

"I can't tell you."

"Like Mary couldn't tell us?" Nurse continued to stroke my back. Slowly I stopped trembling.

"How could he do that?"

"There are some people who think they don't have to answer to anyone, not even to God. He is one of them. He will get his due."

"When? When will he pay for what he's done?"

"That is not for us to decide, but it will come."

"He can just destroy our lives, like we have no purpose?"

"Yes, he thinks he can, and he knows there is nothing you can do about it now. I'm sorry."

"I have to find a way to get out of here," I said. I looked over at Nurse, but she had turned away.

"You need to come to the infirmary. You'll stay there tonight."

"I can't. I'll get into more trouble."

"No, if anyone comes around I'll tell them you're sick, that it was my choice to bring you to the infirmary. For tonight, you'll be safe," Nurse said.

"I'm scared." I began to shake again.

"I don't know how to keep you from him, but right now I can take you to the infirmary, clean you up, let you get a good night's sleep. Tonight you will be safe."

"I have some news for you," As we came through the infirmary doors, Nurse went ahead of me going into her office. I took a seat on an empty mattress. She came back with an envelope, handing it to me, I saw my name written on the outside.

> *Dear Alice,*
>
> *I hope Nurse gives this to you. I so wanted to see you before leaving, I looked everywhere, but no one could find you. It happened. I can't believe after writing this note, and going out the front door, I will be free from this place. I won't be going home, but they are taking me to Galway, where I'll get set-up in a flat. Maybe get a job soon.*
>
> *I hope you get free from here someday. I believe your brother will come for you. We can't lose track of each other. I'll leave you my new address. You can ring me. I know you'll be free someday. Don't lose hope. Don't let Sr. Helen break you. As for that bastard Monsignor Matthew, the next chance you get, find a way to hurt him anyway you can, maybe throw lye in his face.*
>
> *I have to go, they're waiting for me.*
>
> *I know you will find a way to be free of this shortly.*
>
> *Call me when you get that chance.*
>
> *By the way, my name was never Veronica. My Christian name is Bridget, but since you know me as Veronica, it's okay. I just wanted you to know. I'm sorry I never told you.*

I was overjoyed for her. Someone found a way out. She would never again have to see Sr. Helen, and Monsignor could never get to her.

"Her aunt and uncle picked her up today. They already have a job lined up for her. She will be caretaker for an older woman in her aunt's church."

"How did Mother Michael take it?"

"There was nothing she could say. The papers had been signed, so when the Father showed up with her relatives, she had to sign her out."

"Was Veronica surprised? Did she know they were coming?"

"I only saw her when she came to the infirmary to change clothes. I asked her, and yes, she was very surprised, but she did say, 'I knew someone would come.'"

*　　*　　*

After my night in the infirmary, Sr. Helen never came for me again. I went back to my routine. I paid little attention to anyone. I did my duties, but never more. I kept my distance from Jonathan, trying not to let him see inside my heart.

Since my time in the rectory, Sara had done well for herself. The bruises around her eyes and those on her arms had long healed. Her broad smile swept across her face, and for one night her green eyes held a glimmer of light. I took the chair next to her, and took hold of her hand.

"Sara, how you doing?"

"Just grand. Staying out of trouble as you can see," she said, beaming at me.

"I need to talk to you about something," I whispered into her ear.

"What?"

"I don't want anyone to hear," I said. "Come over by the stairway."

"Okay. What's going on in that head of yours?"

"Listen to me," I said, grabbing her shoulders. "I'm getting out of here."

"What? You've gone loony, girl."

"I can't tell you where or when, but I wanted you to know." The idea had been conceived the last night back from the rectory. I had no plan, but I knew I had to find a way out.

"Yeah, and I'm the queen of England," Sara said, almost laughing.

"Sara. I don't know when it will be. I just wanted you to know." I needed for her to believe me, so I gave her a hard look, tightening my jaw.

"What is going on?" Sara asked.

"I can't tell you. I just have to find a way out of here." I whispered, terrified that someone would walk in on us.

"You're being foolish, girl! No one's ever made it out. Remember Rita? Remember Mary? You know that. Others tried, but they've always been found out, and always dragged back to face Mother Michael, and Sister Helen."

"I'm not doing anything until we have a plan."

"We? Now who might we be?"

"I can't tell you right now, but it'll work, I know it will." I had to be confident that Jonathan wouldn't let anything happen to me, and together, we could devise a plot.

"Take me with you," she said, her voice faint, but pleading. "Take me and I won't tell, but if you leave me here, I'll tell anyone who will listen. I'll tell them to go looking for you."

"And you know what will happen to you? Do you want to even think about that?"

"No. So take me with you."

"I can't do that."

"Why?" Sara said, digging into the palms of my hands with her fingers leaving marks.

"I just can't. If we both try to go, we'd get caught. As long as you don't know anything, they can't hurt you." I knew what they'd do to her. At least here she could survive, if she could stay out of St. Helen's way. If I made a mistake, if she fell behind, there would be nothing I could do, all of us would end up in the infirmary from the beatings. She needed to be safe from them. Sara let go of my hands and began to press her hands down her jumper.

"But I know now. You've told me. I know your secrets."

I saw the pain in her eyes. It wasn't the pain from her repeated beatings, but from having no one to care for her. The years she had spent between the Homes and the Laundries had taken a toll on everything about her.

"I'll tell. I will," she blurted out, angry and afraid.

"No, you won't. If you tell, they will cart you off to the loony bin and you'll never see another new day." I wanted to believe in my heart that she would never tell, but still I knew there was a chance.

"Please, I won't be a bother," she begged. "Alice, take me." She took my wrists in her withered hands and stared into my eyes.

I pulled her close. I felt her trembling as she buried her head in my chest.

"I have family somewhere outside of Kildare," she said, lifting her head. "I can make my own way."

"Okay," I said moving her to a chair in the hallway. "I'll think about it. But don't count on it. You can't tell anyone. You have to promise, you won't tell anyone."

"I promise."

"No, I mean it. See the cross on the wall? I want you to swear by it."

"Okay, see. I swear, that I will never tell anyone your secrets."

The smile came back to Sara's face, her hugs even more sincere than the last. She held me tight. "I knew you wouldn't leave me here. I won't breathe a word. I promise."

I walked back to the dormitory alone. The cold air seeped through the halls, and as I lie in bed, dim lights cast shadows across the room.

That night, sleep played tricks, bouncing around the room like a rubber ball. I should have spoken to Jonathan before telling Sara, before promising her that we would find a way to be free of this place. I would do anything Jonathan asked of me. I knew I had to keep this secret at all costs.

*   *   *

For weeks, the rampage of the storm took hold. The power went out, and the compound was flooded throughout. Nurse requested extra help as the women came in with fevers and infections. I wheedled my way in, and Sara came at least three times a day with soup and tea.

To everyone's surprise one morning, Mother Michael requested the doctor to be called. Nurse informed her that he couldn't travel due to the flooding from the storm. I was feeding one of the women when Mother Michael came storming through the door.

"Ring him back. Tell him to get here immediately."

"Mother Michael, all the lines are down and the bridge he'd have to cross is flooded. There's nothing I can do."

"Then find another doctor, someone who can get here."

"I can't call, but perhaps we could send Jonathan to bring him back?"

"Very well. Call him in immediately."

By that afternoon, Jonathan had returned with a doctor to tend to the patients, both penitents and Sisters. His kind and gentle manner made the work we had to do seem more important, not just another task, like washing the clothes. He stopped and talked with each of the women, asking their name, and how they felt, then bending down to help them all.

The storm destroyed almost all the work Jonathan and I had accomplished in the garden. Branches were blown down from trees, landing on the vegetable plants. Small seedlings, drowned by the rain, were left floating in the puddles.

The storms kept everyone inside, so it took a few weeks before I could approach Jonathan. When I received word that I'd be returning to the garden to work with Jonathan, I couldn't stop smiling

He greeted me by the gates, his eyes filled with excitement. "I have news for you," he said, pulling his cap down over his eyes. "I told Marie about the situation here."

"Why would you do that? I'm so ashamed,"

"You have no reason to be embarrassed for being here. Now, let me finish, girl. Her sister, Evelyn, has an extra room. So if we can figure out a way to get you out of here, you'll have a place to stay. Unless you'd prefer to go home?"

He said, "We." I heard the word drop from his lips. He had been thinking about it, too. I wanted to jump up to hug him, but I remained calm, allowing him to finish.

"I have no home to go to," I said, turning away, starting to rake so I wouldn't have to look at him.

"Evelyn works in a hospital in Dublin. Can't promise anything, but she'll try to help you get a job so no one can come for you. With a job, you'd be respectable. What do you think?"

"You'd do all that for me?" I was almost giddy. Then my mood darkened.

"Does she know where I'm from?"

"Of course she does, why else would I have reason to bring you up in dinner conversation?"

I started shoveling the mud to absorb the water, so we could replant seedlings. I couldn't believe what Jonathan had said. I'd have a place to live, a room of my own, and someday, if all went well, a home, a life I could call mine. I'd be respectable.

"Alice, did you hear me?" he asked.

I dropped the shovel and reached up with both my arms, without even looking to Monsignor Matthew's window. I hugged him as tight as I could, then felt his big arms bringing me off the ground, hugging me back.

"I can't believe you did that."

"I know what's been going on. There is no question that you have to get out of here."

"I should have fought back, given up the garden, but he also threatened Sara and Veronica. He threatened everything I cared about. I didn't know what to do, so I agreed. Every week I went to the rectory on his order. I'm not telling you anything more."

"You don't need to. He's a wicked old man. He ought to be tarred and feathered, but it'd do no good for me to say anything. No one would believe me. He is a man of God."

"You'll really help me? What if you get caught?"

"I'd be fired, I imagine, but I've been thinking of leaving this place, anyway. My brother has a bar in Howth. He's been asking for my help, and the church has been looking for a caretaker. I'd be taking a cut in pay, but with the two jobs together we could make it."

"What about Sara?"

"What about Sara?"

"I can't leave her here, I just can't."

"Then, we won't."

I didn't have the heart to tell him I'd already told her about my plan to escape, but if he was willing to save me, I couldn't imagine he wouldn't save Sara, too. Then I thought of Veronica. She had made it, safely tucked away in Galway.

"I started thinking about what we could do, so I told my Missus. She contacted her sister."

"Is there a chance of Sara coming home with you?"

"No. Evelyn has only one room to let. I suppose I could check around to see what I could find. Does she have family?"

"She says she has a niece, but I don't know where she lives."

"Do you know her name, I mean her real name?"

"Yes, she told me once, it's Katherine, Katherine O'Dea."

"All right, I'll see what I can find out."

Jonathan went back to trimming the shrubs. His silence was louder than I had expected.

"Are you mad at me? I'm sorry," I said, afraid that I had crossed over the line.

"Don't fret, girl. I've seen you with her, and I know how much she means."

A few weeks later, Jonathan spoke to me while we were working in the garden. "I did a bit of work on my own, about Sara. Yes, her name is Katherine. She entered Castlepollard at fourteen, but they never allowed her to return home."

I had never thought that much about Sara having a life outside of these places, but she did. Like me, a mere teenager when her nightmare began.

"She has a younger sister still living outside Kildare, near County Meath. Marie is going to post a letter, to let her know her sister is still alive."

"I can't believe you did that. How did you do that?"

"Never you mind, Alice. You have your secrets. I have mine. I may be an old man, but I have connections, too. After what she has been through, did you think I could leave her behind?"

"Your heart is so kind," I said.

He continued trimming the hedges, moving away from me, as if he needed more space to think. My heart ached for this kind gentle man who didn't give a second thought to sacrificing everything to free us.

"You have to realize that this could all backfire," he said. "I could lose my job, but worse you could be sent to another Laundry." He put the clipper on the ground, took off his jacket, moving over to the wild patch of blackberries.

"I know what you're doing for us. Someday, I'll find a way to pay you back. I promise."

"I'm not looking for a payback. I'm trying to do something that will make a difference."

"Thank you, Jonathan."

"You can thank me when you are out of here. We still have to figure out how to get the two of you out."

The next day, Jonathan greeted me with a smile. "Any ideas?" I asked, returning his smile, and nudging him.

"Actually, yes. I overheard that in a few weeks Mother Michael will be going to Kildare for a special Mass. It could be risky, but I have a plan that just might work." Jonathan took a long pause, walked around the blackberries bushes, to the wild roses and jasmine garden, then turned back to me with a schoolboy grin.

"This might sound a bit loony, but I figured if I could offer to take Mother Michael to the Kildare rectory in my truck, it might be a way to get you out. We still have a few weeks, but if she were to leave early on a Friday, it'd be three days before she'd be back. The other Sisters would be too afraid to call in a runaway to the rectory unless they had approval from Mother Michael, herself. I know that Sr. Helen is having some family issues, so she might be going along with Mother Michael, for an extended visit after the service in Kildare. Sr. Beatrice would be in charge for three days."

"Let me make sure I have this right. If Sara can get a key to the back gate and we get to the driveway, we'll be riding in the back of your truck with Mother Michael and Sr. Helen sitting in front with you? That's insane. Do you know what would happen if they saw us?"

"No, don't you see? It'd be perfect, you and Sara in the back of the truck while I drive them to Kildare. We'd make sure you were hidden inside the bags, so even if one of them did turn around, she'd only see bags filled with dirty laundry. After I drop them off, I take Sara to her sister's, you to Howth."

"Yeah, perfect until she turns around to look in the back of the truck."

"But that is my point. She'll never turn around. We'd make sure you were hidden inside the bags, so even if she did, she'd only see laundry bags."

I wanted to believe him, but I could see her catching us somehow. She'd drag us from the truck, and we would never see the light of another day.

*　　*　　*

For the next two weeks, life in the Laundry went on undisturbed. We washed clothes, hung them out to dry, and folded them at the close of the day. Every chance I was offered, I went to the garden. The rectory visits had stopped. Monsignor Matthew hadn't been seen by any of the penitents. Word spread that he went to Sean Ross Abbey for a few weeks, involved in meetings with church dignitaries.

Sara continued her chores in the kitchen, relieved that she had been included, but upset that as the weeks went by, I had no further details. I didn't tell her anything that Jonathan shared with me. I let her believe that I had no idea how it would happen, or when everything would unfold. Jonathan kept his ears open, remaining on guard in every detail of his work in the compound.

The plan moved forward as scheduled. Mother Michael announced that she'd be going to Kildare for a special Mass with Bishop Connolly from Dublin. Monsignor Matthew would meet with him early in the week, then Mother Michael and St. Helen would follow the Friday next for special services.

"It is quite an honor being invited. They will be sending a car," Mother Michael announced during evening meal, almost giggling. It was odd to see her smile and show human traits. She twittered about in embarrassment. Her cheeks became red, and for just a moment she acted like a shy schoolgirl.

Having a car arrive to pick them up changed everything. There'd be no reason for Jonathan to take them. There would be no escaping. I didn't move, not even to look over at Sara, who tried to nudge my arm. I hadn't told her anything specific, except that she had to find a way to get a key from Sr. Beatrice. If she thought she could get the key, I would give her more details. I brushed her off, not wanting anyone to get the faintest idea that by two weeks end, we'd be gone from this place.

"As the car will be making two other stops at nearby convents, unfortunately there won't be enough room for our dear Sr. Helen, but Jonathan has agreed to deliver her to Kildare, so she can attend the special service also, then go on to be with her family for a few days. We will keep her in our prayers."

I wanted to shout for joy. It couldn't have worked better if we'd planned it. I hurried through supper, and helped Sara with the dishes. It was time to let Sara know as much as I could, especially about the key. Without the key, none of this would ever happen.

"Sara, listen to me carefully. Everything is set for the morning that Jonathan takes Sr. Helen to Kildare." I reached for her hand across the table, to make sure she was paying close attention to everything I was saying. "You're to come upstairs, and unlock the dormitory door, then unlock the door in the breezeway. When we're safely out, you're to hide the key someplace where Sr. Beatrice can find it."

"What do you mean find it?" Sara laughed out loud, like I was telling her a joke. "That doesn't make sense."

"We only want her to think she misplaced it for a few hours."

"You're to tell your helpers that Nurse requested you for some chores. You'll likely miss breakfast that morning. Tell them you don't know how long it will take."

"Then what?"

"After we are outside, we'll wait for the truck. We are to get inside, hide, and then wait. We don't breathe a word. We wait."

"It sounds too simple."

"Simple, if it works. A nightmare, if we fail," I said as I reached to put the last of the plates away.

"In two weeks we'll really be gone from here?" Sara asked, wiping her hands, then brushing stands of hair from her face.

"You can't breathe a word to anyone. Not in passing, not by accident. Nothing. Do you hear me?"

"I'm not a fool. I want out of here as bad as you do." Sara took hold of my hand and I saw tears glistening in the corners of her eyes.

I turned to Sara, caressed her cheek. "I have to look for Jonathan to be sure everything is set." I was anxious to slip out and find him.

There were times after Vigils, when Sara and I sat outside the kitchen door on the bench. We took deep breaths, taking in the cold night air, finding anything to talk about that could make us smile, or give us peace.

Tonight though, I slid out the door alone.

"What are you doing here?" Jonathan asked, seeing me come around the corner.

"Mother Michael just announced the trip. I was so terrified when she said the car was coming for her, but then she said, you're taking Sr. Helen. That's so grand."

"Yes, she called me in yesterday, asking if I'd mind making the trip. I told her it would take me from my chores, but she promised when I was done with deliveries, I could go home for the weekend, rather than return to the compound."

"Okay. What are we to do?"

"Monsignor Matthew is picking up Mother Michael at 4:30 Friday morning at the front gate. You and Sara need to be ready at 4:20 by the delivery gate. I'll back the truck in so I can pack in the bags. I'll put the laundry bags in, including two empty ones. When you get to the truck, get inside. Don't let anyone see you. Pull the bags up around you so if I were to look in back I wouldn't be able to think anything is odd. I'll do the rest."

"Okay."

"Now, mind me about this. For the rest of the week, don't draw any attention to yourself. Tell Sara to stay low. If anything goes wrong, there won't be another chance at this. You can't breathe a word."

Jonathan turned away, and went back around the corner. I looked over at the light coming from the kitchen window. It was one of the older penitents who worked with Sara, standing at the windowsill, staring out into the evening light. Seeing her terrified me at first, but I noticed she didn't have her glasses on, so she didn't really know what she was looking at.

"Who's there?" she called out, opening the back door, and looking around. I knew she couldn't recognize me, but she heard everything within a hundred feet.

"I'm just bringing in some potatoes for tomorrow," I called out, gathering the potatoes from the bin under the window.

"Well, hurry up, girl. It's freezing out there."

"Yes ma'am. Sorry about that."

I passed through the door she had left open, rushing past her. I dumped the potatoes into the sink, then headed straight to the folding room. I told Sr. Beatrice that I was late because I needed to finish a few things in the garden, with Jonathan. She said nothing. Nodded, and waved me away without looking up, going back to her embroidery.

"Sara did you get the key?"

"Yes, I have it." She held out her hand, opening her fingers. There it was, small and gold.

"I don't even want to know how you got it."

"I won't tell you, but I will say Sr. Beatrice is an easy mark. I'll return it tomorrow. She'll find it by accident and wonder how she could be so foolish."

We sat in the chapel without saying anything more. I took hold of her hand and brought it up to my lips. I kissed her fingertips gently and brought them to my face. She pulled me close and held me tight.

"How do I tell you how grateful I am for what you have done?"

"We're not out yet, Sara."

"No, but I've never been so close, and felt so loved."

"Sara, I don't know what's going to happen after tomorrow. I don't know whether we'll make it, but at least we can say we did everything we could to change it."

"Tomorrow will go exactly as planned. We are going to be just fine."

"Come on now, Sara, we need to go to bed. We have a big day ahead of us."

We left the chapel, arm in arm, and when we reached the kitchen door, I kissed Sara on the cheek and left her alone for the last time. I went up the stairs to the dormitory, undressed, and got into bed for what I would have to believe would be my last night in the Laundries.

Another day about to come to a close, the lights had been flipped off. The latches locked for the night. We were one day closer. Sleep, eluded me. Even though Sara had gotten the key, I prayed that no one would get into any trouble, or get sick, to cause a change in our plans.

Lying on my thin mattress I tried to imagine how I would be, away from this place. I didn't know how to live a life that would be totally mine. No one would be telling me where to go, or what to do. I would be alone, making decisions that might be wrong.

I tossed back and forth most the night, following shadows of late night ghosts with my eyes. Just as I found myself dozing off, I heard the latch. The door slammed against the wall. Sr. Helen stomped in, and flipped on the light.

"Who has it?" I looked around the room and saw that a few of the girls had already sat up.

"Sister, what is wrong?" The girl closest to the door asked, almost standing up, by the time Sr. Helen had entered the room.

"The key. The key is gone, and one of you whores has it."

The room fell silent. The girl by the door sat back down on her bed. I was too afraid to move. I knew this had something to do with Sara and the key. I didn't bother to sit up, but when Sr. Helen stood in front of the room, she demanded, that we stand to the side of our mattresses.

"Turn them over," she shouted.

One by one, we each turned our mattresses over and let them fall to the floor. She walked by each bed, examining the floor and everything around it. When she was done, she told us to put them back. We did, and then waited for her next order.

"Open the drawers. Put everything on your beds."

Each of us emptied the contents of the tiny drawers in the nightstands. Again she walked up and back. Nothing. I was about to pass out, terrified that she would do something that would destroy my chance at a new life. She didn't find the key in the dormitory.

"There will be hell to pay, until I find that key. And when I find it, God help you all."

It reminded me of the rant the night Sara had spilled soup on her skirt. She left the room as quickly as she had come, slamming the door behind her. We each picked up the random contents from our drawers and put them back. The girl closest to the door turned off the light, and we lay in silence. There was no chatter among the girls. We all had our secrets.

I didn't sleep that last night. Instead I lay still, remembering the breathing coming from the walls. I imagined myself free of this place, wearing clothes that didn't reek of lye, the sores gone from my arms and hands. Finally, I dreamed of a life filled with kindness and joy.

I heard the footsteps coming closer to the door, then the turn of the key, and finally footsteps going back down the stairs. I looked around to see if anyone moved, but when no one did, I sat up.

*   *   *

Our day of redemption had come. Sara had accomplished the first phase. Without a sound, I opened the unlocked wooden door in the dormitory, slipped down the stairway, to get Sara from the kitchen. She was already puttering about, handing me a hot cup of tea she had made while waiting.

"Did you have any trouble?" I asked.

"When Sr. Beatrice told Sr. Helen she had lost her key, she went crazy. She almost tore the kitchen apart. She even took a swing at me, she only got part of my cheek." I touched the edge of her jaw that was turning from red to purple.

"I'm sorry. She somehow always seem to take her rage out on you."

"That's all right, I just don't move fast enough. I'm grand though. She never found it."

"I'm not even going to ask where you put it."

"I have it safe," she said patting her chest.

We stood alone in the dimly lit kitchen, staring back and forth at each other, then over at the mattresses in the corner of the room. The clock hanging from the wall read 4:15.

We stepped outside so as not to awaken any other penitents. We watched in silence from the breezeway for a few minutes. We heard the tires move across the gravel, taking Mother Michael away. Everything was on time. Phase two was complete. Mother Michael was gone. Now we just had Sr. Helen to deal with, and after last night's outrage, I had no idea what we would be facing.

When we couldn't hear the gravel sounds anymore, we crossed over from the breezeway. Sara unlocked the delivery gate at the edge of the back driveway. After we were through it, she ran back toward the kitchen with the key.

"Where did you put it?" I asked her when she returned.

"Right where she could find it, after searching for a while. I put it under the mat, where everyone puts spare keys. Right?"

We saw Jonathan's truck backed against the far wall. We immediately went to the truck, got inside the back, then stepped inside the two laundry bags he had left for us pulling them up around us, then slouched down.

A few minutes later we heard Jonathan coming toward the truck. We lay still inside the bags he had left for us. He tossed the laundry bags in the back of the truck. They bounced around, falling all around us.

"Are you all right?" Jonathan whispered.

"Yes, we are safe and sound," I said, sure that my voice came out quite muffled.

"Sr. Helen will be out soon. Don't make a sound."

I pushed myself closer to the curtain that divided the truck bed from the driver's seat. Sara collapsed into her bag between the others, so there would be no shadows.

Mother Michael had left the Laundries with no one expecting her back until late Sunday night. If all went as planned, even if they noticed us gone, nothing would be done until the Monday morning bell for breakfast. Mother Michael and Monsignor Matthew would both be away. A strong storm was expected around noon, and predicted to last all weekend. With the enormity of it anticipated, there would be a good chance the power would go out, giving us an additional chance of a safe getaway.

I could hear Sara close by, I could hear her breaths, deep and spaced apart.

Jonathan stowed Sr. Helen's belongings in the back of the truck, while she stationed herself in the front seat. I peeked up and saw her profile through the cloth partition. She seemed different occupying space in the delivery truck. Her power had diminished as she sat hunch-shouldered.

"Thank you again, for going out of your way," she said, kindly. After last night's outburst, I was surprised she could be so cheerful.

"No problem." Jonathan put the truck in gear. "If the storm holds off, it'll be a nice day for a drive through the country." I prayed that Jonathan would arrive in Kildare before the storm, but watching the clouds from the back of the truck I feared they might put a halt to everything. Once Sr. Helen was dropped off, there would be no worry about the clouds. Let the rains come for the entire weekend. We knew there was still a possibility of the Guardia coming in search of two runaway penitents. Where would they look? Who would they ask?

"Are you alright up here, Sister?" Jonathan asked.

What if Sr. Helen took a quick glance around? What if she moved the curtain? In our odd shaped laundry bags we waited for the worst. I'd have thought that I would have been more terrified to be stowed away. Bouncing around inside the truck, I knew that at any minute we could be stopped and checked. Somehow being engulfed in the bag was no worse than lying in the infirmary recovering from the beatings. I had no bruises, or marks as I lay quietly. My throat was tight and my lips dry. There was no pain, just excitement and nervousness, fearful of the chance that we would be returned to the Laundry.

As Jonathan drove along the deserted road, I squirmed around, lifting myself up to watch the gray clouds. The clouds grew darker even as the early-morning light took hold. I looked back at Sara, whose bag was still. Her fear of being found would keep her hidden the entire trip. I could feel each bump as we traveled on toward freedom. I settled back in, wiggling into the space against the wall listening as Jonathan tried to make light conversation.

"I hope your family is well. Mother Michael says you will be staying on to visit with your family."

"My Mum has been ill for a long time. I need to go home, spend some time with her," Sr. Helen said, continuing the pleasantries.

"It is always hard when a family member is sick," Jonathan said.

"She had heart problems as a girl. They got worse as she got older. Now, I think her heart is just giving out." Still peeking out, I could see Sr. Helen looking out the window avoiding Jonathan's face, as she talked about her family.

I never imagined her as a woman with feelings or a family. Here she was talking to Jonathan about her Mum, that she might be losing her. I knew that feeling. I'd lost my own Mum, not to death, but by abandonment. Perhaps someday I would find my way back to her.

"What do you do, when you aren't making deliveries or caretaking?" Sr. Helen asked, trying to show Jonathan she was interested. I couldn't see her face, but my guess was that she couldn't care less about the goings-on of the old driver.

"I spend time with my wife, doing odd jobs at the church and whatever my wife wants me to do. I live a simple life," Jonathan said with pretended earnestness.

"Where in Dublin do you live?" she asked. Without waiting for a reply, she continued. "It must be nice to go home each night. I miss that. I love my life in the convent, but I think I would have liked to have my own place just once in my life." Could she possibly be showing human qualities? Did she know a real world existed outside those walls?

"I've lived in Filgas my whole life, small house near St. Patrick's, off Main Street," Jonathan lied.

A cold mist fell, as we crossed a massive bridge in the center of Dublin. From the back of the truck I could see the streets we passed, with brightly colored doors. The empty streets glistened in the dampness of the early morning. Jonathan slowed as we passed a cemetery.

"My grandparents are buried there." Sr. Helen blurted. I saw the sign as we passed, Glasnevin Cemetery. The headstones stood in a row, some broken, some chipped, while others stood upright. Crosses and angels could be seen across the countryside. I had never seen so many. In Meadows Glen there was a cemetery, but the crosses were small, tiny in comparison, but just as Glasnevin, ancestors from centuries past, lay in the cold wet ground.

"It's a beautiful cemetery, it is. Been there a few times myself, for friends, but my family, they're buried in Kildare."

From the rear, I could see the quieter streets as we passed neighboring villages. We passed the tall steeple of the church and I heard Sr. Helen remark that she had once attended service there.

I didn't know how long the trip would take. I had never been beyond the gate of Meadows Glen, except for Castlepollard and being driven through Dublin to the Laundry, but I felt sure we were half-way there, halfway to freedom.

I nudged Sara's bag and waited for her to peek out. I knew she wouldn't say a word, but hoped she would look. I watched her bag move and soon the top of her head appeared. I motioned for her to look out the back. She smiled. So far, all my fears over the last few weeks had diminished. As we drove slowly down the road, I felt I could have hope that we would be successful, that we would be free.

"I want to thank you again, Jonathan, for taking time away from your work to deliver me to Kildare," Sr. Helen said.

I couldn't figure out where all her pleasantries were coming from, or why. Never, had I seen her laugh, smile, or show any traits resembling humanity. It was strange to hear her acting human, since being cruel and abusive had been all we had known.

"I am happy to do this for you, Sister. You work hard. You deserve time away, even if some of it is for work." She had no idea that just a few feet away, Sara and I listened to her conversation. Listened to her laugh, and imagined the cold wind brushing across her pallid face. We were seeing her in a way none of the other penitents would have a chance to, but it wouldn't change what she had done to us.

Finally, Jonathan pulled into the driveway of the rectory, stopped the truck, and helped Sr. Helen down. Sara and I sat inches from her as we watched her move her skirt around, attempting to step down from the truck. I waited for her to turn and rip back the curtain, exposing us. Instead, as Jonathan gathered everything together, she stepped from the truck and he escorted her to the door of the rectory.

"Thank you again Jonathan. I'll see you soon. Wait, I forgot my box, I think it's in the back of the truck." She moved toward the rear. I could hear her rustling about, juggling her belongings like a circus performer.

"Oh no, I've got your box right here, Sister. I'll carry it to the door for you," Jonathan said.

I peered out between the curtains and saw Monsignor Matthew come to the gate. The sight of him made me gag. A part of me wanted to jump up, find a stick and beat him to a pulp for what he did to me, but I remained still, not moving, not risking my chance for freedom.

He took my God from me, and for that I would never forgive him. He took the boxes from Jonathan without a word, and guided Sr. Helen along the path. Jonathan said his good-byes, and scrambled back into the truck.

FREEDOM

Sara Goes Home

onathan drove out of the curved driveway. I remained in my bag, still peeking out, while Sara settled back in, not moving. He continued on for a while, then turned off onto a dirt road. He pulled over, got out, and came to the back of the truck and helped us out of our bags.

As he opened the passenger door, I crawled into the front seat, and Jonathan helped Sara step up next to me. We looked at each other, but neither showed any emotion. I couldn't speak for Sara, but I still feared there was no reason to celebrate. Jonathan came back around to the driver's side taking a moment to revel in his success.

"We did it, girls," Jonathan said, patting my hand. "You're out. They won't know for hours, maybe even days. Even if they call, being so far from the convent, what could they do? Besides, the other Sisters would be reluctant to report a runaway to the Guardia. What would they say?" Jonathan backed out of the dirt road, speeding down the fairway, knowing that he had just accomplished what Mother Michael considered the impossible.

"I can't believe this. What if she does find out?" I asked. I felt like a butterfly in a jar, with no lid—I had a way out, but I was too petrified to move. I didn't know how to take the next step. I could feel the fresh air of freedom. I just couldn't see the opening above me.

Jonathan dropped laundry bags off at designated places around the city. He pulled into long cement driveways that led to back walls of stone buildings belonging to unspecified rectories and hospitals.

Before our final stop, Sara handed Jonathan a scrap of paper. "Do you know the place, sir?" she asked.

"Yes, I do," he said, "I've known it for a while now. We're taking you home Sara." Jonathan sped along the road, staring straight ahead.

We retraced our route through the streets of Dublin, passing the cemetery we had seen earlier in the day. Jonathan pulled to the side of the road, taking a bag from under the seat. He opened it, and produced sandwiches wrapped in paper, along with fruit, and three jars of water.

"Marie thought you might get hungry on the trip, so she packed a lunch," Jonathan said as he motioned to the feast he had laid out.

Jonathan spread a blanket and we each took a seat. I couldn't find the words to explain why doing something so simple, like eating a sandwich, could mean so much. After being locked away for so long, I was doing something normal.

"Better get going," Jonathan said. "The clouds look as if they are about to wake up."

The thunder would be coming soon, then the rains. We got up, while Jonathan put everything away. We piled back into the truck.

We drove for at least another hour, then turned off on a graveled side road. I saw a woman frantically waving to Jonathan. "Take the next turnoff," she said.

She was younger than Sara, but seemed older than me. She wore a floppy hat, held down by one hand while the other was clasped to her mouth as she ran beside the truck.

"Sara, I believe we are here," Jonathan said, as he turned in to the driveway.

"Oh my God, there she is," Sara said. She clasped her mouth in an unconscious imitation of the woman on the road. "That's my baby sister. How did you find her?"

"Never mind about that. They're here, waiting for you." Jonathan stopped the truck. "Wait," he said, "let me help you out." Like he helped Sister Helen, Jonathan held his hand out to Sara, as if she were royalty. There were no bags to take in this time. All we had, we left behind the walls of the Laundries. There was nothing we wanted to keep, nothing we wanted to remind us. I jumped out after Sara, to hug her for the last time. Jonathan handed her over to the younger woman with the hat.

"Go on now. Straightaway, what are you waiting for?"

"Thank you both," Sara said, brushing away the tears with her wrinkled palm. She grabbed hold of Jonathan, holding him tight around the waist, laying her head in his chest. He patted her back, then stepped away, letting her sister hug her.

"We had no idea, where they took her. No one would tell us anything," said the woman with the floppy hat.

"Jonathan, Alice, this is Emma, my baby sister. The last time she saw me, she was just six."

"Sara, this is my daughter Rose."

I watched Sara stare at the teenager, surely thinking she was a mirror of what she might have been, had she been given the chance. She had green eyes, like Sara, white skin, almost porcelain, with a mass of chestnut curls that fell around her shoulders.

"I don't know how he did it, but a month or so ago his wife wrote asking about Sara, if I might know any relatives. I wrote back telling him I was her sister. I told him to bring her home to us whenever he could," Emma said.

She had been my protector all those years. Taking care of each other had been a reason not to give up hope. Sara let go, standing with tears streaming down her cheeks, in her worn jumper, her gray hair pulled tight against her head, with a smile spilling across her wrinkled face.

"Would you like to come in for tea?" Emma asked, as we stood in the driveway.

"No," Jonathan said at first, then looked at me, I nodded.

"Come in," Emma said, "you can wash up. I have some clothes if you'd like to change, Alice," she said looking at me. "After Jonathan's wife rang to let us know you'd be coming, I shopped in town for what I hoped would fit. I imagine you'd like to get out of those clothes. You must want to leave everything that reminded you of the past behind."

The idea of wearing clothes that didn't belong to the Sisters or the institution, or that didn't smell of lye was something I had long given up on. I'd been wearing a jumper since the day Mum sent me to the Home. I'd been convinced I would die in one someday.

"Thank you, Emma." I felt the tears wet on my cheeks. It was the first time I had let myself cry happy tears. The first time I had allowed myself to feel any emotion that was not absolute terror.

As we walked into the yard, I looked around, thinking it simple, but the most beautiful home I had ever seen. Ivy splashed across the white cottage. Potted plants lined the front walkway. White lace curtains hung from inside the house. A litter of kittens peeked from under the bushes. Sara ran to scoop one up in her hands. As she held the kitten she began to dance around, laughing, as if in attendance of her first party.

"I wouldn't have it any other way. You can't just walk out of Sara's life. You must come in, freshen up. Share lunch with us."

Jonathan cleared his throat. "I have deliveries to make in this area. Why don't I do that, while you ladies have a nice chat? I'll come back to get Alice in a few hours."

"Jonathan, are you sure it would be okay?" I asked, knowing he might want to be going home with the storm coming.

"Of course, it would. You go on now."

Jonathan pulled out of the driveway with a wave while we walked into the house. Sara grabbed us, Emma and me, each on a side, and walked through the door, head held high.

"While you're cleaning up, I'll fix supper. Rose can get the table ready. Will soup and fresh bread be okay?"

"That would be delightful," I said, as we followed Emma through the kitchen.

"You go first," Sara said. "I want to lie down for a bit on a real bed. I'm just so happy that I can do whatever I want."

Inside the bathroom, a small white porcelain sink was surrounded by pink tile with a slab of lavender soap sitting in a ceramic bowl. The water filled my hands. I splashed my face, then lathered up, relishing the silky feel of the soap.

I looked in the mirror at my naked body. Almost nineteen, my body felt much older. I was thin, scrawny, and the yellow rings from the bruises I had received had turned to dark shadows. I looked at the body that I had allowed Monsignor Matthew to have, remembering the slaps and pinches, remembering the grimaces on his face, when he couldn't get hard. I washed my bare skin in utmost privacy, no peering eyes, no inconsiderate poking. I stared at myself for the first time without turning away, without shame. I was no longer a child, now a woman who must learn to move on. My hair, though it had grown, was dull, ragged around the edges. My face showed the years I had survived.

I ran a dampened washcloth down my arms, past my thighs to my knees. I repeated, doing the same on the other side. I slowly cleaned the residue from beneath my nails, then drenched my face in the warm water. I took the clean rain-scented towel, wrapping it around my naked body. I stared at the clothes she had placed on the counter. Simple cotton clothes that for someone else would have little meaning; to me they felt like silk. I stroked each garment as I took hold of them, dressing myself. I did it quickly for fear someone might come in, declaring a mistake had been made, that the Guardia were on their way. The dress hung on my bony body, so I pulled the belt tighter around my waist. I brushed out my hair, letting it fall to my shoulders and slipped on the flat shoes she left by the door.

I gave each cheek a tight pinch, then emerged from the bathroom a new woman, not the broken one who had walked through the door moments earlier. Sara jumped up from the bed, laughing when she saw me. I had my old worn clothes in my arms. Sara grabbed them from me.

"Here, let me have those, we'll burn them later in a ceremony." I laughed at her.

"You look amazing. You're so pretty." I twirled around the room. My dress was a simple shift, lavender, like the lilacs in a spring garden. I knew I wasn't pretty, but I was prettier than I had been in years. At that moment, I felt radiant.

"I know it is silly, but I feel so good, for the first time, I feel clean, not coated in lye. I can smell a fresh scent all over me. I am so grateful."

"Freedom isn't silly, girl. We paid dearly for this. We deserve it."

"You're right."

"Okay, my turn, you go into the kitchen, have tea with Emma and Rose, I might take awhile."

I moved down the hallway, calling Emma's name when I entered the kitchen.

"Oh, come in, have a seat. Just look at you. So grand," she paused, taking my hand, "You are a gift, Alice. You're a beautiful girl. You got lost for a while, but we've found you."

I blushed at her kind words, feeling the tears coming down again, but trying to hold them back. It had been too long since a stranger had spoken with such kindness. "Thank you Emma."

"What would you have in your tea?"

"I don't know. It's always been plain."

"Let me add some sweet milk and sugar for you." I sat at the table, not able to take my eyes off the wildflowers in the vase in front of me. I felt the breeze coming through the windows. Though the sky was getting blacker, the storm was a gift, a curtain pulled over our escape.

"I want to thank you for what you did…for Sara. She is my only sister. Our mother never knew what happened to her. She had a girl, you know. Did she tell you?"

"No, I had no idea. She didn't tell me much about herself, but she saved me from so many beatings."

"No, you saved her. It's because of you she's home. You brought her back to me. We feared she might be gone forever, until the letter arrived from Jonathan's wife."

"Why didn't anyone come for her?" I asked.

"We didn't know where she was. We searched for her over the years, but no one would tell us anything about her."

"The Sisters did nothing to protect us, but even less to help us find our way back home."

"Her given name is Kathleen you know. Sara was her middle name. I only ever called her Sara when I was a little girl. My mother told me she fell in love with a soldier. When she was twenty or so, they ran off to get married. When they moved to Belfast, our father disowned her. He threatened the rest of the family if we ever made contact with her."

"Did she live in Belfast?"

"For a while. He died in a bomb attack before she learned about her pregnancy. She had no family in Belfast, so she tried to come home, but our father wouldn't allow it. The next day he called the local priest and they hauled her away, like a criminal. We never knew where she was. He didn't want anybody to know. Mum begged him to let her stay, but he refused." She bowed her head, as if she were at the end of her eulogy.

I took a sip from the tea, then a bite of the bread Emma had left on the table. Emma continued to unfold the events that brought Sara into my life.

"It didn't matter to him. My father worried more about the concerns of others, than the effect on his family. He had her carted off. No one ever saw her again. My mother went back to the parish priest to learn where she'd been sent, but he turned her away as well, telling her to forget she had a daughter."

I continued to sip my tea, trying to make sense of what she was telling me. I could understand my being sent away, I wasn't married, but Sara did the right thing. She married the man she loved, then found herself pregnant. She never did anything wrong, except the man she loved died.

After a while, Sara danced through the doors of the kitchen in a skirt and sweater. Her hair fell around her face. She had color on her cheeks and her lips, a bright red. She looked beautiful. Her smile filled the room with the hope we thought we had lost. I watched her twirl around the room, laughing, with her arms in the air.

*　　*　　*

I savored the early moments of my newly gained freedom, watching Emma go about in the kitchen. The shifting sunlight coming through the kitchen window reminded me how quickly things changed. The night before last I watched Sr. Helen unleash her hatred for the last time, now I was watching Sara in her own home. Free.

"I had a girl you know. I named her Stella, after my grandmother," Sara said, smiling with such tenderness toward her sister.

"They took her from me after nine days. I didn't know where she was taken. I lost it all, just gone. She would be your age now, almost. I think that is why I was so taken with you. You could have been her." Grief gripped hold of her for a moment, but she hid it by laughing out loud.

"Do you know how old I am?" Sara asked, finishing the last bite of cobbler.

I was embarrassed by an answer I may have given, a day before. She seemed broken and old, but now she was unrecognizable, quite beautiful, in an angelic way. She had let the gray waves of her hair fall around her face. They softened the wrinkles on the curves of her jaw line.

"I'm thirty-seven. A child wouldn't you say?" We all laughed, but there was truth in what she said. She'd been robbed. We'd all been robbed. People, who our families had believed in, took everything from us, never bothering to look back to pick up the pieces. We had lost our children, our faith, and our dignity.

The afternoon slipped away, and after laughing, crying, and hugging, we heard Jonathan driving up the driveway. We went out through the kitchen door to greet him. Jonathan stepped from the truck, a big grin lighting his face.

"Imagine that. Look at you. You both look grand."

"Yes, we do," Sara chimed in, dancing in a circle.

"Are you ready, Alice?"

"Yes."

"Come on then, getting late. The storm will be getting heavier. We had better go."

We said good-bye, promising to write. Sara handed me a note, while Emma reached out to hug me, then laughed as she fell back into the arms of her sister. She would be safe now, away from harm, or danger, or any of the sadness she had known for so long. I reached out for Sara again, but this time I didn't want to let her go.

"I will always remember you." I whispered in her ear.

"It will never be good-bye. I'll never forget you. You saved my life."

Pointing to the note, Sara said, "You have my address. Write to me when you're settled. We can meet for tea, like friends do, like real people do." She smiled at me, and turned arm in arm with her sister.

Getting in the truck I could smell the storm coming, but it was not a storm that scared me anymore. I stared at Jonathan, then reached for his arm. "You're a miracle."

"No, just did a bit of leg work and luck. She'll be happy here. No one will come for her. She won't sleep in the kitchen and she won't have to get up before the chickens. She'll be happy. Now, let's get you home."

"Let's go," I said, smiling such a broad smile that my yellowed teeth showed. I didn't care.

"We are stopping in Dublin on the way back to Howth, and getting you some clothes of your own. You can pick out an outfit, with shoes and undergarments."

"You can't do that, you've done too much already."

"It's done girl. Marie and I set some money aside. We decided together, that you should have it. You need a fresh start, something you can call yours. It's not a lot, but it'll do for now. When you get your own money, then you can buy whatever suits your fancy."

I had never gone shopping alone. I'd never picked out clothes. Mum just went to the retail, and picked out what was least expensive. There was never any choosing.

We drove for a while in silence. As we pulled into Dublin's main street, the rain fell like petals floating to the ground, but within ten minutes it felt like rocks being thrown against the truck. Jonathan pulled up to the curb out of busy late afternoon traffic and pointed toward the store window.

"There's the shop. Marie's already talked to the owner. She's expecting us. She'll be helping you. I'm going to the pub to warm up. She'll ring me when you're done."

I ran into the shop to keep from getting soaked. An attractive young woman greeted me.

"You must be Alice?"

"Yes, I am."

"My name is Patricia, I'm going to help you today. Marie described you to me, so I hope you like the things I've picked out."

Patricia was taller than most the girls I knew, and had blonde hair that fell in ringlets past her shoulders. Her cheeks were rosy, her lips a soft pink. She had on a tweed suit with heels that made her legs look sleek. She had a gold band on her finger and her pink nails matched her lips. I had never seen such simple beauty packaged so elegantly.

She opened the curtain of the dressing room and there were dresses and skirts with sweaters and blouses. Lying on the bench in the corner, were soft cotton and satin undergarments, things I had never worn before. I looked up at the salesgirl.

"It's all right. Try on what you like. When you are ready, call for me. I'll help with anything you need. Don't be shy."

I slipped off the clothes Sara's sister had given me, and put on each garment, first the panties, the brassiere, finally the slip that fell just below my knees. I buttoned the red blouse and zipped up the brown tweed pleated skirt. I didn't recognize myself in the mirror. I pulled the sweater over my head, then stood back and stared at myself.

"Alice you doing all right? Can I come see?"

"Yes, of course."

"You look grand," she exclaimed patting the collar and straightening the skirt. "The color is perfect with your hair. Do you like it?"

"I think so? What do you think?"

"It is wonderful. You must take it. There is enough left for you to get something else, perhaps a scarf?"

"I don't know what to pick."

"Well, what color do you like? How about green?" holding up a green plaid wool scarf.

"Okay." I stumbled around. I was embarrassed that Jonathan had done so much, embarrassed that Patricia noticed how naive I was, and embarrassed that I might look the least bit pretty.

"How is this?" she asked, wrapping the scarf around my shoulder.

"Lovely," I said, unable to look away from the mirror.

"If you like, I could fix your hair for you. Put on a little lipstick," Patricia said, reaching for a tube on the counter.

Just then the door opened and Jonathan walked through. "My goodness girl, look at you."

"Doesn't she look grand?" She added the pink lipstick, and walked around me, while Jonathan stood with his hands in his pockets, a smile on his face.

"She looks like a bit of heaven."

While I gathered my new clothes from the dressing room, I overheard them chatting, their voices calm and easy. Jonathan thanked her. As I came from behind the curtain, Jonathan shook her hand, and reached for the door.

I got into the truck, and as we pulled away from the curb, I looked over at Jonathan. "I don't know what to say."

"There's nothing to say. A girl needs clothes," he said pulling out into the afternoon traffic.

*   *   *

On the final leg of our trip, with the truck empty of laundry, my dress bags held tightly in my lap, we traveled back through Dublin to Howth, Jonathan's town by the seaside. Growing up in the Midlands, I had never seen the ocean, I only knew rolling meadows enclosed by rock fences.

As we drove along the shoreline, I felt young again, experiencing something very new to me. I rolled down the window, hung my head out to take in the smell and the beauty of the beach, even the rain couldn't stop me. I asked Jonathan to pull over so I could just take it all in.

"You'll be living close by here," Jonathan said. "You can walk to the shore every day, if you like."

I stared out at the waves washing up the shore, as they moved in and out, splashing against the rocks.

"We're almost there?"

"Up around a few more corners. You'll be home."

I sat back in my seat, holding tight to my new clothes. Then there were tears. I didn't know what to say to him, so I turned away. From the beginning, he had understood everything. I wasn't hiding anything from him that he either didn't know or in some way had not experienced. This kind gentle man had given me back my life, but I couldn't look at him.

As Jonathan drove through the open gate, I saw a bright red door open. Two women walked out onto the steps waving.

"There they are," he said, "Evelyn, the taller one, is my sister. Marie, with the curls, she's my girl." The women came off the doorstep grinning, twittering about like mother hens.

"Is this your house?" I asked, looking around the yard.

"No. It's Evelyn's. I wanted to bring you home first."

"Oh, Jonathan, so glad you made it." Evelyn reached out and gave Jonathan an affectionate pinch. Marie folded into his arms, as we went through the door.

"We have it all ready," Evelyn said, as Marie reached for my hand. "Hope you like it. Are you ready to see it?"

They directed me along the walkway to the back of Evelyn's house where a tiny cottage stood. Marie opened the blue door, and I stepped into my new life. As simple as it may have seemed, for the first time my experiences were beyond anything I had known—a life I could call my own.

"Do you like it? How are the colors?" Both women chimed in with excitement about their accomplishment. I looked around, trying to take it in. The room freshly painted, had crisp white lace curtains covering the windows, a bouquet of wildflowers, mixed with lavender roses on the kitchen table. A worn tweed couch, sat against the far wall of the room, with crocheted pillows against each arm. Next to the picture window, they placed an oak rocking chair. It was more of a home than I had known since that rainy day Da turned me out.

"You go ahead, settle in to your room, while we get dinner ready,"

Marie said.

The scent of fresh bread came from the oven. A platter filled with baby red potatoes that smothered a roast, sat on the kitchen counter.

"I don't know what to say."

"You don't have to say anything, dear girl," Marie said, her voice, gentle in all the excitement.

Evelyn and Marie took me back to the bedroom they had decorated. In the closet they'd hung a few dresses, and a coat. On the dresser, they had placed a brush, a comb, small bottle of lotion, and a tiny crystal perfume bottle. They opened the drawer of the dresser showing me an embroidered pink cotton nightgown, and several pairs of undergarments and stockings, and two folded pullover sweaters. A second rocking chair sat in the room with two small books of poetry, one by Emily Bronte and the other William Butler Yeats, and a novel I had never read, *Wuthering Heights*.

The incidentals included a silk hankie, a small bottle of bath oil, a square lavender soap bar, and a toothbrush, that I'd use in the privacy of my very own bathroom.

In one breath I was elated, but in the next, terrified. I didn't know how I would do this. The Sisters in the Laundries had never taught us life lessons for the real world. Every minute of every day was filled with someone else's demands and expectations.

"You go on, put everything away. Take some time, we'll get supper ready," Evelyn said.

I took the clothes out of the bag that Jonathan and Marie had bought for me. Looking around the room, I was shocked that I had been given so much. I hung the skirt and blouse in the closet, and placed the undergarments in the dresser. As I closed the drawer and started crying again. I was horrified that I would let them all down. That I'd do something that would make Jonathan regret his decision.

"Alice?" Evelyn called out, tapping on the door.

"Come in, please," I said.

"You settling in all right?"

"Oh yes, thank you for all you've done." She stepped in and took a seat on the bed.

"I know you've had a rough time of it. I want you to know that I won't be intruding on your life. You're free to come and go as you please."

"Thank you, but I'm afraid I won't be having any place to go for a while, except maybe a walk on the beach, or a trip into town. I promise I'll look for a job as soon as I can."

"You'll love walking around Howth. There are many shops to spend your time. You can even take the bus into Dublin," Evelyn continued, "I don't know if you're interested, but we're hiring at the hospital. I can set up a meeting with the head nurse. It will be at the bottom level, but if you're interested, I'll tell them about you."

"That would be lovely, thank you."

"I'm sorry. I'm putting way too much on you for your first day here. Take a few days to settle in. Rest."

"No, I don't want to wait. I don't want to rest. If you could schedule the appointment, I'd love to start work right away. I need to become respectable. It's the only way I can get my life back."

"The job will be menial, changing beds, scrubbing floors, cleaning rooms."

"I'd be perfect for that." I said.

"But not forever, I'm sure."

"Come out when you're ready," Evelyn said.

Evelyn stepped out and closed the door behind her. I continued putting everything away. I went into the bathroom, pulled the rubber band from my hair, then brushed out the knots. I placed the clip in my hair. I dabbed the perfume on my fingers, touched my neck, looked in the mirror, and took a deep breath. Before coming out, I stared at myself in the mirror, pinching my cheeks, just to let myself know all of this was real.

*   *   *

"Alice, I think you should take some time before going to work. Get used to being here. You have plenty of time to work." Marie said.

"No, I need to work. Earn my share, so I can be respectable."

"Ladies, I think we need to let Alice do what she feels comfortable doing. She is free now to make her own decisions. I think we need to clean up here and let Alice settle in," Jonathan said, picking up the plates from the table.

"You two, go on. I'll stay and clean up, then scat, out I go," Evelyn said.

Jonathan and Marie took the dishes from the table. Evelyn put the perishables in the icebox. I sat, still dazed by the entire evening. Jonathan helped Marie with her coat, then put on his own. They both hugged me, and said their good-byes.

"Maybe I could go in to Dublin with you in the morning?" I asked.

"Tomorrow is Saturday, girl. I don't work, except at home. I wash and clean, then have dinner in town. Jonathan's brother owns a pub and we have dinner there every Saturday and sometimes after church." Evelyn began to wash the dishes, but when I went toward her to help, she motioned for me to start the tea instead.

"I'll see," I said, feeling a little uncomfortable. "If it's all right, I think I'll take a walk around town, down to the ocean. I've never walked on a beach before."

"Jonathan told me you'd want time alone. On Sunday we go to Mass in the morning. I usually walk the four blocks, but if it's raining, Jonathan picks me up."

"I don't know about going to church."

"Of course, dear. I'd understand if you never returned to church."

"I will someday, but not for a while."

She gave a quick hug and went out the door, closing it behind her.

*   *   *

I didn't know if fear had overtaken me, not allowing me to venture out, or it was the security of another wall that kept me safely inside. I stayed in the cottage for three days after my arrival. Evelyn dropped by several times, offering to take me to town. I declined. Marie rang when everyone met at the pub for supper, asking me to join them. I declined her, too. It would have been safe to go out in numbers, but a sense of doom crept through my body and kept me behind the locked door.

On the fourth day, when I had arranged and rearranged enough dishes and linens, I decided, the time had come to go out. I dressed in the warmest of clothes, grabbed my coat and scarf and headed down the walkway with a purpose.

Strangers hurried along, catching buses, rushing around the streets, going about the business of their day without taking notice of me. I walked the three blocks and stared out at the massive ocean, I had never seen in person. There had been pictures in books, stories that Da told of his only visit, but nothing I could claim as my own. It overwhelmed me with its awesome beauty, the power of the waves battering the shore. I was standing at the foot of a new world.

I found my shoes sinking deep into the sand, I took them off to free my feet of their confines. The sand melded between my toes, like clumps of oatmeal. I reached down, taking hold of this newfound gift, mushy in my hands, I had never felt such a sensation, watching as the sand trickled through my fingers, dropping to the ground. I seemed drawn to the water. The constant movement of the waves beckoned me, pulling with a promise of rebirth. A moving, ever-changing force.

It was exhilarating. The cold water crawled up my feet and caressed my ankles. Tingles moved up my body, causing goosebumps and shivers. This was not the cold I felt in the Laundries, shivering in bed, numb and hard from the freezing night air and tired muscles. This was fresh. This was free.

I watched people move along on the beach, couples with gloved hands entwined, lingering in the warmth of each other. Red-cheeked children ran ahead of their parents, turning, laughing, filled with the excitement of the cold air and the crashing of the waves. Even dogs, wet and matted, could not contain their unbridled joy.

I didn't make eye contact with people who passed. I kept my face hidden with my scarf, looking up only to find my way. I didn't want to stand out or be remembered by anyone. I stayed on the beach far too long. The light of day was fading and my fellow beachgoers were disappearing. A few were left. Those who lingered were just watching the waves.

As I put my shoes on, a man with a scruffy beard and torn trench coat caught my eye. I froze in that moment, the growling voice rung in my ears.

"Hey girlie, you're gonna like this . . ."

The man was not speaking. The voice came from inside my head, pounding against my brain. The beach became a distant memory as I found myself back on the lane. The gravel digging deep into my back with the weight of him. His stubble rubbed against my neck, the stench of cigarettes and stale alcohol. His hands fumbled beneath my jumper, then the ripping of my panties. He let out a groan, thrusting himself harder.

"Shut up. Don't move."

I heard him only in my head, but my heart wouldn't stay still. I couldn't catch my breath, as the bearded man passed.

A hand on my shoulder startled me.

"Miss?"

I looked up into the eyes of a tall uniformed man standing over me. I looked around, and people stood frozen in their steps, watching, waiting for something to happen.

"Are you all right?" he asked.

I didn't look up. Then I felt him touch my shoulder again.

"Miss, can you hear me?"

"Yes, I'm fine. Is something wrong?" I tried to seem normal, wanting to make him think he had made a mistake.

"You look a bit distraught. You kept staring out, so still. A woman asked me to come have a look."

"I'm fine, Officer. I just wasn't paying attention. Must have been day-dreaming."

"I can't be leaving you here alone," he said.

"Just taking in the fresh air."

"Looks like another storm's coming in."

"When is there not a storm coming in, Sir?" I asked.

"Who might you be?" he asked, finally bringing his eyes back to my face.

"My name is Alice."

"Alice, what?" he asked removing his cap.

"Alice Brennan."

"Are you new here? Can't say I remember seeing you before."

"I've just moved here. Only been here a short while."

"Have you caught your breath? Are you all right?"

"Really, I'm fine."

"Perhaps I should walk you home. Where you living?"

He watched my every move. I didn't know what to say. I knew I wasn't breaking any law. I had a place. I wasn't a vagrant.

My face became tight, I squinted my eyes. I knew how to get to Evelyn's cottage, but I didn't remember the name of the street or her number.

"Do you know anyone in town?" He continued staring. I didn't know whether I should stay still or try to run. Running seemed a bit foolish, but he terrified me with his questions. I didn't want to bring Jonathan into it, but I knew I had to verify that I knew someone in town. If he took me to the station, I had no idea what would happen. I didn't want to think about it.

Mother Michael knew about the escape by now. She would have called the Guardia. Surely notices were sent out.

"I'm family to Jonathan Nolan. I'm living in his sister's cottage."

"I know Mr. Nolan. I don't ever remember him ever talking about family outside Howth."

"I need to be going now. Nice talking to you." I closed my eyes, and took a breath stepping forward. His relentless inquiries made my fingers begin to itch. I held them close, hidden. Not because he continued asking, but because I had to come up with good enough answers that would stop his inquisition.

"Why don't I take you to Mr. Nolan's? He can escort you home."

"He's not home. He's working."

"Is Marie home?"

"Yes, I'm sure she is."

"We'll talk with Marie."

"I don't understand why you have the need to do this."

"It's my job, Miss. You seemed disoriented on the beach. I am worried for your safety. Besides, there have been reports of runaways. I have to be sure. If you are who you say you are, and you're well, then you can be on your way. They're only a few blocks from here."

For a while, we walked along in silence. The clouds parted, shadows danced on the sidewalks. After we passed the first block, the officer continued his interrogation.

"Where were you before coming to Howth?"

"I lived with my family in Meadows Glen, until I finished school. I wanted to get a job or go to university in Dublin. My aunt's brother has family in Howth. That's how I'm related to Jonathan."

"Have you done either yet?"

"Either what?"

"Gotten a job? Attended classes?"

"No, I'm hoping to get a job in a few weeks."

We walked up the driveway and he moved ahead, going through the gate first. When he reached the steps, he turned, waiting for me. As I came up behind him, he knocked on the blue door.

"Good afternoon Officer Leary," Marie said, standing in the doorway. I peeked around to see her face. "Alice, is that you? Is there anything wrong here?"

"Do you know this girl, Mrs. Nolan?"

"Of course, I do." She looked over at me, then back to the officer. "She's my husband's family. She's staying in Evelyn's cottage. I don't understand. Did she do something wrong?"

"No, but when she was on the beach, she seemed to be having a spell. I didn't think she should be alone. We had a report last week of some runaways. Doing my job, Mrs. Nolan."

"Well, you be on your way now. Go on, do the real job of protecting us, not bothering with young girls."

"Yes, Ma'am."

"Now Alice, come on in." By the time Marie closed the door, Officer Leary had already found his way across the street.

"I'm so sorry. He kept asking me where I lived. I couldn't remember the street. When I gave him Jonathan's name, he said he knew him. He made me follow him here. Then he started talking about some runaways. I was sure he knew who I was."

"Don't you worry now, everything is fine. Now that he knows you're connected to Jonathan, he'll leave you alone. He's new on the job, and I do believe he was worried about you. He is a good man Alice, just doing his job. Everything will be grand. Come, sit down, have some tea."

"If it's okay, I just want to go home, but thank you so much. I think I've had enough for one day." Marie laughed, then hugged me before I opened the door.

The sun that once peeked through was gone. The clouds came back together, raindrops slowly starting to hit the ground. I'd been gone from home much longer than I expected. When I reached the corner, Evelyn's house stood out. I was overjoyed to know that once I went through the back gate and through the blue door, I'd be safe. At least until I ventured out again.

I thought about Officer Leary, wondering if he would continue watching me every time I stepped out. I knew there was a real possibility that, one day, he would come knocking on my door.

*   *   *

Weeks passed. I still couldn't get Officer Leary out of my mind. I became reluctant to venture out, afraid that he would search me out, but there was a kindness in him. I thought perhaps if we met in a different time . . .

The rain had stopped for a few days. I opened the windows and doors to let in the light and fresh sea breeze.

"I held true to my word. You have a job at the hospital," Evelyn said, standing at the door with a box tucked under her arm. "It's not the top of the heap, but you'll be making your own money."

"When do I start?"

"Tomorrow. I have your bus pass. It's good for the whole month," she said placing the paper on the table. "You'll catch the bus out of Howth at 5:00."

"Okay."

"You'll take the bus into Dublin, getting off at the Stephen's Green stop. Two blocks past, on your left, is the hospital. You'll be there in plenty of time. Your shift starts at 6:00," she said, taking off her coat, moving to the stove to start the kettle for tea.

"It isn't fancy. You'll be tired at the end of the day, but you can work your way up. In time, if you want, you can enroll in courses, become trained, if you like it—one day maybe find yourself a nurse. To start though, you'll be cleaning, mopping, stripping beds, you know, meeting the needs of patients. It will be important to make sure they're settled in their rooms. When the patient leaves, you clean the room, and prepare it for the next one."

"I can do that. I'm not afraid of hard work." Her description brought me back to a time when choices were never allowed.

"That goes without saying. I would not have recommended you otherwise. Now, here you go. I brought you a present. Hope you like it," as she placed the box tied in twine on the table.

Before I even opened it, I reached out to Evelyn, letting her wrap her arms around me. She whispered into my ear. "There now, girl, never mind, you'll do fine."

"Thank you. I don't know what to say."

"There's nothing to say, get on with it, open the box."

I untied the knotted twine, and lifted the lid. Inside, lay folded a blue uniform, wrapped in white tissue, with white stockings and shoes. I knew uniforms before, from school, from the Home, but worst of all, the Laundries. This one stood out as different, even as I unwrapped it. I knew I would wear this one with pride.

"Go on now, hang it up. You'll be putting it on early tomorrow."

I petted the soft cotton material, afraid it might disappear right before my eyes. I hung the uniform in the small closet, placed the shoes under my bed and hid the two pairs of nylons in the tiny dresser drawer.

"I know you've had a tough time of it, but things will turn around. I'm sorry for what you've been through, but each day is a new start."

"I promise I won't let you down."

"Of course you won't." as she moved toward the door.

"Evelyn, thank you so much for this."

"Thank me by doing a good job."

After Evelyn left, I went back into the bedroom staring at the uniform as it hung in the closet, a symbol of my freedom. I couldn't wait for my new job, and everything it would offer me. I had to believe. I had survived the worst that anyone should have had to experience. I went back into the kitchen, picked up the bus pass. I would need a pocketbook to put my things in. I let out a laugh. I was doing something normal, run of the mill, and it felt wonderful. I grabbed my coat and scarf and headed to town. Passing Evelyn's house, I saw a lone light in the window.

As I walked through the streets of Howth, I kept a watch out for Officer Leary as the skies grew threatening. I stepped into the general store, my eyes wide, overwhelmed by the sheer variety. It didn't take long for me to find the perfect pocketbook, soft, black, with four compartments. The price tag was ten shillings. I could afford that. I took hold of the handles and slipped it across my arm. I looked up, the woman at the counter grinned.

"That is perfect for you."

"Thank you. I've never owned one before."

"Well, this one is perfect. Not too big, but enough room to hold everything a woman needs."

"I'll take it." As I paid for the pocketbook, I noticed a small book on the counter. It was a rich, brown leather worked with a design of a swimming swan. "What . . . the pages are blank?"

"It's a journal. You fill it with whatever you want. Words, pictures, recipes, anything. It's the last one we have, so I can let it go for two shillings, if you're interested."

"It is beautiful. The swan seems . . . I'll take it, also."

*   *   *

The rain that had held up for three days began to come down. I strolled alone, gazing through the windows. Through lace curtains, I watched as wives served tea; passed platters of cooked meals to loved ones. Imagining that one day I'd be the one pouring tea, getting my children settled. I felt a comfort here in this small town.

The streets emptied as the rain fell. I pulled my woolen coat around tighter, grasping my bag. When I decided I couldn't get any wetter, I stepped into a corner pub, to wait out the remainder of the storm, taking an empty table in the far corner, so I could watch what I considered to be the excitement of people moving about. Just as I settled in, the bartender called from across the room.

"What will you have, Miss?" he asked, swiping his towel, across the table.

"Just tea, please."

In a few minutes, he came back around the bar with a tray, heavy with a china cup and saucer, with a teapot, a small glass filled with a caramel colored liquid, and a plate filled with biscuits.

"I didn't order this," I said, eying the shot glass.

"You look a-might wet. Aren't you cold from that rain?"

"Yes, it seems to soak right through everything."

"This might warm you up."

"Is that...?" I paused.

"Yes, Ma'am. It'll warm you to the bone." He grinned. I couldn't help but give him a slight smile back. I felt a heat move up through my cheeks, though still cold from the storm.

"I can take it back, but it will warm you up, at least until you have to go back outside."

"Just tea and biscuits." I said, "but thank you."

"It's on me. Looks like you could do with a bit of nourishment," leaving the plates on the table. He was a small man, with a barrel shaped middle, and spiky gray hair that matched his stubbled-beard. The most endearing, he wore a smile that welcomed strangers. Up close, creases of years fused into his sunken cheeks. His forehead narrowed, his eyes glistened and a soft chuckle rolled from his belly.

I watched him walk away and I wondered who greeted him at the end of his long day. I ate the biscuits, drank the warm, rich tea, then sat back and watched. I allowed myself a few moments to relax, and looked about the pub. Tables were filling up, as men, just getting off work, stopped for a pint after a long day.

I half-hoped that Jonathan might appear, that we could chat, as we did in the garden. I don't think he ever realized how he always made me feel important. I sat alone, imagining my first day at work, how I'd be, wondering if anyone would know, if they could see through my soul.

"More tea, Miss?"

"Yes, thank you." Though the pub was filling, the bartender paid attention to me. He watched as if he was trying to get me to recognize him, but nothing seemed familiar.

"I've seen you in town, on the streets. You're new here aren't you?" He seemed to be searching for something appropriate to say, but as he looked away I could tell he had no idea. Something nagged at him.

"Yes, I'm from Dublin."

"Wait. You're Jonathan's friend?" He said, as he bent low, as if he had found a lost treasure. "I'm Joseph. You're Alice, right?"

"Yes, but how do you know that? How do you know Jonathan?"

"You don't see the resemblance?" He laughed, turning sideways, so I could see his profile. "I'm his brother, younger brother, that is. I hoped it might be you. He told me a young girl would be coming to live in Evelyn's cottage."

"What did he tell you?" I couldn't breathe, hearing this stranger say he knew about me.

"He told me you were coming from a bad situation, needed a place to stay. We're a small town. None of us ever move away. We know when someone new comes around. A stranger is not a stranger for long," he said.

"Well, Joseph, very good to meet you."

"Good to finally meet you, too. You tell Jonathan and Marie to bring you to Sunday supper. You are welcome whenever you want to come." His eyes scanned the room, "I guess I should get Hollings his pint before he pounds the bar down. Really, Alice you are welcome here anytime."

"Thank you, Joseph."

Watching him serve his customers, I realized he shared the softness of his older brother, not as strong in features, shorter in stature, but I saw they shared a gentleness that I would learn to cherish.

"I need to go now before the next storm, Joseph."

"Very happy you stopped in. I'm glad you're safe, that you've found a home here in Howth. You come see me when you'd like something special with your tea. Here, take my umbrella, in case the rain starts again."

I laughed out loud, taking the umbrella. "Thank you, I'll bring it back." I walked home in the early-evening light. Though I kept an eye out, to my disappointment, I didn't see Officer Leary coming around any corner. Much had changed since my arrival a month earlier. I had a place to live, a job, people who knew me, people who cared about me. I no longer stood out as an outcast to be pitied, no longer a penitent to be abused. Tomorrow, I would meet people who knew nothing about my past. They would think of me as a young girl starting a new job. Nothing more, nothing less. To me at that moment, it all seemed too good to be true. A dream, maybe? Something would tear it apart; something would shatter the chance at normality. When I turned up the drive I saw the lights to Evelyn's cottage. Her door stood a jar, but I wasn't in the mood to share the evening. I was ever so grateful for everything she had done, but I needed to be alone. I needed to prepare for my first day at work. I needed to be ready. I slipped past the open door around the corner.

After dinner, I took my uniform from the closet. The wrinkles had mostly fallen out, but I decided to iron it, so I would present a good impression on my first day. I buffed my shoes and laid everything out, so I didn't have to take time in the morning. I made sure the bus pass lay snug in my pocketbook and looked around my tidy room, letting my eyes fall on the journal. I opened the front cover and sat down on the couch mulling about what I might write. Would I tell the truth of what I experienced over the last few years? Who would read it? How would I explain the feelings of having my daughter ripped from my arms, knowing that I would never see her again? How would I write about the hatred and cruelty of Sr. Helen?

I took the journal and went to my room, placing it on the nightstand.

As I undressed, the memories came back. They flooded over me as I began to write. I didn't look at the clock. I didn't stop when I felt my eyes getting heavy. I also didn't turn back to the pages to see what I wrote. I could only write it once, and there would be no reading the words again. When I woke the next morning the journal lay closed on the bed, hidden between the covers.

* * *

"I'm Alice Brennan, I start work today. Do you know where I'm to go?"

"Down the hall to the second door. Ask for Bernie. She'll tell you what to do."

I opened the office door and found two women folding towels. Both looked up when I came through, then went back to their task.

"Excuse me, I'm looking for Bernie. Could someone help me?" I asked.

"I'm Bernie," the taller woman bellowed. She dropped the towel and took hold of my hand, shaking it with all her strength. "Are you Alice? Put your things over there in one of the empty lockers." With rosy cheeks, bright-green eyes, and large square shoulders, I couldn't help but like her the minute I laid eyes on her. She was larger than any girl I'd ever seen. I'm sure she'd have given Reverend Mother and Sr. Helen a run of it. I doubt they'd have ever cut those massive chestnut curls pulled piled high on her head.

"You do as I say and everything will be just grand," she said.

"Thank you. I won't let you down."

"It won't bother me none, just doing Evelyn a favor. Got other girls to replace you anytime."

After explaining the tasks I'd be responsible for, she guided me to Room 11.

"You start there," she said. "Do each room on one side, then go back down the hall on the other side. Help the patient get out of bed, change the sheets, and mop down the floor, clean the bathroom. Don't dally. Move on when you're done. Don't touch personal belongings. If the patient's in the room ask them before moving anything, so they won't blame you for stealing. Some patients like to blame aids for taking things they've misplaced." She barely took a breath as she gave the list of my duties.

I took a mop, bucket, and all the cleaning supplies and went to Room 11. An old man sat up in bed reading the paper.

"Morning sir, I'm here to clean your room. Is that all right with you?"

"Sure, if you could help me up, I'll use the lavatory, then go for a walk. I'll be out of your way, Miss."

I took the arm he held out, while his other hand secured his gown in the back. After finishing in the bathroom, I helped him with his robe.

"When I'm done with my walk, you can find me in the chair by the nurses' station."

"I won't leave you there for too long, I promise."

I moved through his room, noticing that he had been here a long time. His belongings were lined up along the window. I dusted between them, careful not to move or drop anything. I sloshed the mop around under the bed to pick up all the dust, when something shiny caught my eye. Reaching for it, I realized that a money clip overflowing with bills had fallen to the floor. I laid it in the windowsill with his other things.

"Were you going to steal that, girl?" I heard his voice coming from behind me.

I turned to face him, "No, I found it on the floor. As you can see I put it back with your belongings."

"You know I could turn you in, I saw you holding it."

"It was on the floor, I picked it up. That's all."

"Go on now girl, finish your work."

I wanted to tell Bernie, but too afraid a confession might get me fired on my first day. What would Evelyn think if I got fired before the day even ended? By lunchtime, I had cleaned eight rooms. Three of the patients were asleep, never waking while I worked. Most of the other rooms were empty, making them easier to get through. It was the next to the last that lingered, fretting my mind for days to come. A frail girl, barely a teenager, sat tied in a chair by the window, her hands folded in her lap. Her blue eyes sunken deep. She didn't turn when I passed. I progressed into the bathroom, closing the door. There were random items that represented her life. I picked up the towels and became terrified when I saw the blood. I had not seen so much blood since the Laundries. I tossed them in the linen bin, then scrubbed the floor where they had been.

When I came out of the bathroom, a nurse was standing over her brushing her hair.

"You'll need to help me bathe her," she said, starting to untie the girl from her chair. "We are short-handed today."

"I'm only supposed to clean the room, and help move the patients, not bathe them. Bernie said to keep to myself."

"I understand, but I need help now. I'll let Bernie know when I see her."

"I guess it will be all right. You promise to tell Bernie?"

"Take hold of her arm. We'll guide her to the bathroom. You hold her tight. I'll wash her, then you can help me put her back in bed."

"I saw the towels in the bathroom. What's wrong with her?" I asked, still holding on.

"She had a stroke. She can't talk, or use her hands. She's pretty much bed ridden."

"No, I meant the blood."

"It happens when she menstruates. We put towels under her. See?" nodding her head toward the wheelchair. Blood had come through her gown. "That's why we bathe her so often. That is why I'll be needing your help."

I didn't know what to say. I couldn't take my eyes off the young girl and seeing her so fragile unable to move tugged at me.

"What's her name?"

"Her name is Maggie. I talk to her every chance I get. Sometimes I think she hears me. She'll blink, but she never responds. Her eyes just stare straight ahead."

After placing her in bed, the nurse took lotion and rubbed it down her arms and legs. We pulled the covers up to her waist. The young nurse took a tube of lipstick from her pocket, and slid it across her lips.

"Someone has to make her look pretty," she said.

"You look beautiful, Maggie," I said, smiling.

"Go on now, you can finish the room. Thanks for helping me. I appreciate it. I'll let Bernie know how helpful you were. A lot of the assistants don't like to come in here. It bothers them the way her hands are gnarled and the look she has in her eyes."

The nurse patted the sheets before leaving the room. "Oh, my name is Nora. You must be the new girl? What's your name?"

"Alice."

"Nice to meet you Alice. I'll see you around. You did a good job today."

By the time I finished Maggie's room, it was past 11:00. I went into the locker room, got my lunch-bag and went looking for the cafeteria. I found Bernie and another girl dressed like me sitting at a table next to the window.

"Is it all right if I sit here?"

"Well, where else would you be sitting?" Bernie asked, "How is it going?" Setting her sandwich on the waxed paper, giving me a broad grin. "This is Stella, she just started yesterday, so you two are the new girls."

"I have some things to talk to you about."

"Is everything all right?" Bernie asked between bites of her sandwich.

"No, it's good, but Mr. Blake in Room 11? I thought I'd better tell you. I found a money clip on the floor, but I immediately put it with his belongings. When he walked in, he accused me of trying to steal it. I wasn't."

"Mr. Blake does that all the time, even to the nurses, tries to get a rise out of everyone. Scares the devil out of all the girls, he does, but now and then he catches one."

"Has he been here a long time?" I asked unwrapping my sandwich.

"Oh, yes. He goes home for a while, then he has a spell, they bring him back. Goes in circles it does. I'm afraid he'll die here someday soon. He's been sick a long time. After a few days he gets restless, so he plays tricks to pass the time."

"There's one more thing."

"You've had quite the morning, I see."

"When I was doing Maggie's room, Nora asked me to help bathe her. I hope that was alright. She said she would tell you about it later, but she needed the help right then."

"Oh, that's fine. Just don't do anything when a nurse isn't around, in case something goes wrong."

As I finished my sandwich, I couldn't help thinking how things had changed. Here I was with a respectable job, a place to call my own. No one would be coming to look for me. I was safe. I was free. My heart leapt.

I had one room left on the first floor, so I excused myself from lunch, telling Bernie that I wanted to go back and finish the rooms.

"Hard worker, we have here I see," she said to Stella, then they laughed. "That's fine." Bernie said, "Go ahead to the second floor and do the same with the rooms there."

I finished the last room on the first floor and took my supplies to the second, continuing with the directions Bernie had given me. Even as I worked through the afternoon, I could still picture the transparent skin and coarse thin hair crowning Maggie's head.

The day slipped by with no disturbances and with a smile on my face I returned my keys to the girl at the front desk. As the bus turned toward Howth, I stared out the window thinking about the girl who didn't even know she had a life, tied to her chair, barely holding up her head, with fingers twisted like pretzels.

I was torn between feeling grateful and guilty for all that I had. I stared at people on the street, realizing for the first time that I was no different from them. I had carved out a life, and like them I would find a way to make it work.

*   *   *

I walked the five blocks from the bus station, not stopping at the pub or even talking to anyone. I saw it on the porch as I turned the corner, a stark white reflection of the sunlight. I proceeded to the porch, picked it up, turning it over in my hands. There was no return address.

> *My dearest Alice,*
> *I have looked everywhere for you. I left Meadows Glen two months after they took you. I attended university in Dublin and have a job in London now. I wrote Mum to ask where they sent you, but she never answered. I never really expected her to, not with Da there. He wouldn't even let us mention your name, so I'm sure he wouldn't let her write. I have been look-ing for you forever. I heard rumors about Castlepollard, but they told me you were gone. I found a convent in Dublin where someone finally talked to me. I showed a picture and asked if*

you had been here. He asked me why I was looking for you. I told him I was your brother. He said to write you a note, and he would try to get it to you. So if you're reading this, I guess he found you.

I'm sorry about everything that happened. I'm sorry that I wasn't there. But I'm here now. Whatever I can do, just let me know. I hope this finds you.

Connor

I folded the paper, put it back in the envelope, and placed it on the table. I went into the bedroom and changed my clothes. There was too much to think about. I thought about calling Jonathan, but I held off. I wondered how it got to my door, but it didn't matter. My brother had found me. He'd gone out to make his own life, but he never forgot me.

The cat mulled about in the garden, randomly coming up on the porch and rubbing herself against my leg. I leaned down and scooped her into my lap. We sat alone, staring out in the cold night air. I had thought about my brother a million times, hoping he'd come looking, but as each day passed I let pieces of him go, giving up hope of ever seeing him again. But now, here he was, after all this time he had come for me.

I laid in bed with everything ready for the next day. I took Connor's letter and read it again, and again. I wondered if Jonathan might bring him to see me, or would letters be our only form of communication. I put it away into the drawer and took out my journal, opening it to where I had left off. Tonight I went back through the pages, reading them slowly, wondering if I'd ever let someone have it. I didn't write anything, but I did slip his letter between the pages.

I wouldn't think about him anymore, at least until tomorrow.

Weeks passed.

*   *   *

While the rain came down, one afternoon, I was sitting in the rocker on the porch. The damp air was refreshing. The cat had settled in my lap and I was about to begin reading, when I heard tires on the gravel.

"Alice, come on over here. I have a bit of a surprise for you." I heard Jonathan say, walking up the drive. "I found someone along the road who wants to see you." I moved closer, peering over his shoulder and realized the tall shadow standing behind could only be my Connor.

It had been weeks since his letter. I tried to forget him, knowing that we might never see each other. Afraid that time and space would divide us. I gave Jonathan a quick hug, crying as I grabbed Connor so tight we almost fell over. He held onto me as well, lifting me off the ground.

"Oh, my God, you're here." I looked back at Jonathan grinning into his blue eyes. "I can't believe it," I cried.

"No thanks to the Sisters," Connor said, letting me down and slipping his hands in his pocket, and dropping his head. "I went to the door, but they kept turning me away. At first, they said you weren't there. Then they said you ran away. They told me to never come back," he said dragging his feet in the gravel. He spoke as if he had to get it out all at once, without a breath. The words came out like pleas of atonement; begging me to forgive him. He didn't know there was nothing to forgive. When I saw him last, he was just sixteen, about to start university, not a man at all. Now, he stood in front of me, my brother, who hadn't forgotten me, a man in every right.

"I let you down," he said, burying his head in his hands.

"You never let me down."

"I think it's time, you two have some time alone. I'll be at the pub. Connor ring me when you're done, or come to the pub."

"Jonathan I can't thank you enough for bringing him to me, for finding him."

"I'm afraid he found me, and wouldn't let go."

"I'll bring him down to the pub in a few hours, when I'm done with him." Jonathan walked down the gravel path to his truck, Connor and I walked arm in arm into the house.

"I should have been there. If I had waited just a bit that day, you wouldn't have been alone."

"Connor, stop. It wasn't your fault, none of it. What could you have done? You were a boy."

"I could have knocked him down."

"Then what? He would have beaten you as well."

"And the Sisters kept turning me away. Finally, I found a priest at university. I told him what happened and he filled out a document telling the Sisters to release you to me. He said it gave me guardianship. That they would have to turn you over. But when I went back, she took just the document and slammed the door."

Standing in front of me, my dear sweet brother had tried to be a prince.

"Connor, it's over. Thanks to Jonathan, I'm free. I don't have to think about those times any longer."

"Alice . . ."

"So tell me about Mum and Da."

"They wouldn't talk about you. And if I ever tried to bring it up, Da told me to shut my trap."

"That's because he knew where I was."

I could tell Connor needed to talk, and let go of the burden he had ladened himself with for such a long time.

"Do you want to take a walk?" I asked him.

"That would be grand. Could we stop at a pub? Is there one close by?"

"I think I can find you one." I laughed, realizing my brother was no longer the awkward teenager I once knew. "But I want you to myself for a while. Let's go down to the shoreline. We can talk."

I grabbed my jacket, and we walked the long pathways around town. I linked arms with my brother, and let him tell the story he'd held in for so long.

Connor pulled his cap down from the brisk wind. As we strolled around the streets, he told of waiting on the steps of the Home for a sight of me. He said one of the girls in the yard told him I'd been sent somewhere in Dublin, but didn't know where. For weeks he came back to the different Laundries in Dublin looking for me, until he found Jonathan.

I didn't know what to say to him. My beloved brother, stood broken in pieces because he couldn't help me. I wondered if I should tell him what really happened. What I went through. Or had Jonathan told him enough. I never wanted him to hear from my lips what I had experienced. I was ashamed that I'd not been strong enough to fight back.

"I can't tell you what they did," I said stopping in the sand, looking up at him. "For now I just want to spend time with you. I want to be happy."

"Where's that pub you know so well? We've been out here for hours, let's get warm."

He sat at the table, drank his Guinness, and gave me a wide grin. In that moment, I knew he understood.

While waiting for another Guinness, Connor reached into his trouser pocket, pulled out a small gold-plated mirror and placed it in my hand.

"Keep this with you."

"What is it?"

"Remember the mirror?"

"Where did you get it?"

"I went through your things after they took you away, and I kept it, so I knew I could always keep you with me. Now, every time you look it, it will remind you that I'm always here."

Staring at the mirror folded in my hands, transported me back to a time long forgotten, like the faint scent of honeysuckle. It took me back to that time when our lives were filled with only fun and laughter.

Clouds moved across the sky, covering us like a blanket. At my beckoning, we left chores unfinished, going to the dilapidated house our parents had forbidden us to go near.

"You're going to get us in trouble if you don't get down right now," I called out, as he crawled through the upstairs window.

"No one will know if you don't tell." He popped his head up, showing that he made it through the small casement just below the eaves.

I stood in the garden looking up at him, when I heard him bust out laughing, "I'm okay!"

"Someone is coming, hurry up. You have to get down."

"This place is amazing inside. You have to come up and see everything. I'll come down and open the door."

When I got to the front door, there stood Constable McGrath, arms folded across his chest, cap tipped to the side, sneering as he caught us red-handed.

"Well, what do we have here?" he, said, grabbing my ear, almost lifting me off the ground. He tapped his baton against his thigh, waiting for my co-conspirator to appear.

Connor swung the door open to the Constable still holding my

ear, showing no amusement. Neither did Da, by the time the
three of us landed at our front door. Connor never told anyone
that I had been the curious one about the abandoned cottage.
I asked Connor later, about the whipping, but he said drop-
ping his trousers was simply a mere challenge to overcome. He
laughed, saying his hide was tougher than most. Days later,
in the barn, when we were alone he gifted me with a small
gold-plated mirror he had pilfered from the cottage.
"Here, so you never forget us."

We drank and chatted about everything that didn't matter. We
laughed with Jonathan and Joseph and for a while, we were normal people, doing what normal people do.

"Tell me I'll see you again." I called out as he boarded the train.

"I'm a call away." He stepped back, and handed me a slip of paper.
"I'm that far away," he said, touching my cheek.

I continued waving long after the train pulled away. We'd been given
the chance to say good-byes. I knew this was not the end. He was back in
my life and would remain so, forever.

Instead of going home, I went back to the pub. I took a seat by the
door, but instead of bringing my usual tea, Joseph came to the table with
a pint.

"Would you like a little more than tea? If it doesn't suit you, I'll bring
your regular."

"No, it's perfect." I took a slow sip of my first Guinness. It felt warm
going down, smooth.

"Mind if I have a seat?" he asked.

"No, not at all," I didn't want to be alone.

"He's a fine young man, your brother."

"Yeah, he is, isn't he? He never gave up on me, you know. Look, look
what he gave me." I held out the mirror he had saved.

"He kept it all this time, thinking about me."

"Not sure what that means, but it must be important."

"It was something he gave me as a kid, when I went away, he found it
and kept it with him. Never mind, it's a long story."

"All that counts is that he came back for you. He loves you, as a
brother should."

"I gotta get back to work now," Joseph said, giving me a wink.

I watched as Joseph interacted with others along the way. I listened to the banter of strangers, catching snippets of conversations. I imagined them listening to Connor and me, speculating on the shifting tones, wondering how we could be so happy and so sad, so lighthearted, so intense. He'd drink a Guinness, while I sipped tea. Should Officer Leary come by, I'd introduce them, so he would know I wasn't a homeless waif. Maybe he would start looking at me with something other than pity.

A knock on the window startled me. Jonathan waved and came in the door.

"How did it go? Have a nice visit?" He asked, motioning to Joseph for his usual.

"I couldn't imagine it being better."

"He is coming back soon, isn't he?"

"When he can. He's living in London, but I'll see him at least, on holidays."

"He's a fine young man. After meeting him, I knew I had to bring you two together. Sorry I kind of dropped him at your front door. I thought it was important."

"I really should thank you. I never answered his letter because I was worried how he would react. I'm not the same."

"No, you're not. You're a fine young lady who doesn't need to rely on anyone. You have a job; you have a life. You should be proud."

"I am, Jonathan, I just worry. Da kept calling me a whore. Connor . . ."

"Connor is a young man that knows how to think for himself. He saw how your Da handled the situation and he heard enough stories to get an idea of what you went through."

"So you think he knows?"

"I don't think he knows everything, but I'm sure he has an idea."

"Should I tell . . . I mean, do you think people should tell their secrets? All of them?"

Jonathan took a long drink, then set his glass on the table.

"Do you think people should tell secrets?"

Jonathan took another drink and wiped his brow. "You know, Alice . . ."

"Never mind, you don't have to answer. I figured it out. I'll be going now." I left coins on the table for the pint, leaned over and gave Jonathan a quick kiss on the cheek. "Thank you."

"For what? What did I do? I didn't even get to answer the question." He looked confused.

I smiled back at him. "I'll see you in a few days."

I took the road along the seaside where sandcastles filled the shoreline. Some had toppled, bridges broken, moats destroyed, while others stood tall, unscathed. I took myself to the edge of the ocean, looking out at a world I would never see, clutching the mirror. I had to believe that Connor's train hadn't taken him away from me forever. Along with that, I believed if Connor had found Jonathan, then someday, I would find Finn. Lights flickered in windows, people busy with the tasks of getting on with their lives.

I, too, was getting on with life.

*   *   *

I took the mirror from my pocketbook and placed it on the bureau. Every day I would think of Connor as I saw it. I went back to the kitchen opened the cupboard, took the bottle of brandy and a glass and placed them them on the table.

I took three blank sheets of paper and sat at the table. The cat curled up next to the papers. The words spilled out everywhere. Didn't he deserve to know, or at least, what I could find the courage to tell him? He was my brother and, outside of Jonathan, there was no one I trusted more. I took the words and put them on the paper.

12, February

Connor

Being with you today, took me back to the years when we were free to be ourselves. I loved you so much, then one day, everything was gone. I was alone and terrified.

No one ever came for me. I delivered my baby alone. Then Mum signed the papers that gave us away. Her daughter and her granddaughter. I never felt so betrayed.

My true horror began in Dublin behind even higher walls. We were whipped for asking about our babies. We worked through sickness, and ate food that wouldn't be tossed to stray dogs. They ridiculed and abused us. These were people we had been told to trust. Jonathan saw it all. My wounds healed on the outside, my hair grew back, and the scabs peeled off, but my heart never healed. I think of my dear Finn every day. Through all the abuse and the shame, it was Finn who cradled herself inside my heart.

Please tell me we'll never lose each other again. I can't go through life knowing that I would be alone.

You must know that I can't tell you everything that happened. I'm ashamed that I allowed those things to happen, I couldn't stop them. I didn't know how. They had broken us all.

I'm so proud of you, brother. How you didn't let Da get in your way. Going to University. Becoming a man. Listening to how you came to look for me, how hard you tried. Hearing everything you went through filled me with so much love. I cherish my mirror. You remembered me. You never forgot. You found me.

I promise you, Connor, I will find her. You have given me a purpose, a will. There is nothing more I can tell you about those times, so I will leave the rest unsaid. My dearest Connor, please visit me often.

Your Sister,

Alice

I reread the letter and took a sip of brandy. Before I lost nerve, I addressed an envelope and sealed the letter inside. Safe in my pocketbook, I would post it in the morning. The day was over.

I went to the bedroom and picked up the journal that was slowly filling. I had found a peace I hadn't expected, when I started writing. Somehow, the hurt eased a little.

The Decision

he newness of my life in Howth wore off, though I still relished my walks to the beach and my strolls about town, it all fell into a familiar pattern. Over time I was ready to move forward, to take chances. I wasn't going to travel the world, but with little steps, I would be making small decisions that I had been avoiding.

Bernie trusted me with more responsibilities. I spent more time with Maggie and the other high-maintenance patients. I paid Evelyn rent, though she protested when she found the envelope under her doormat. My cottage finally became the home I had always imagined. I found company with a stray cat, who now claimed me as her owner. And Officer Leary always greeted me with a smile and a tip of his hat. Surprisingly, we were bumping into each other more and more often. I would round a corner and there he was, talking to a clerk, or crossing the street. More often than not, he caught up to me as I walked along the shore.

Instead of posting a letter to Sara, I rang her up, asking if we could meet. So, come Sunday after church, we were to meet at a small café in Dublin. Sara found solace sitting in a pew, I took to the seashore to find mine. Black clouds spread across the sky. A few unleashed dogs splashed in the shallows. Sheets of rain unfurled. An old man bundled in a coat, with his woolen cap pulled down, hurried past. Coming from the opposite direction, a shirtless young man with tattoos on his forearms strolled by with his dog.

I waited until the rains slowed, then turned toward the bus station.

I left the bench, kicking my way along the beach, stooping to examine every rock or pebble, believing that instead of finding God on an altar, He was here among the rocks and shells.

The bus stopped at O'Connell Street and I walked the two blocks to the cafe. It had been well over a year, I wondered if I'd recognize her, if she'd look different from when we left her at her sister's. The tables began to fill, but I saw no one I recognized.

"Excuse me, Alice?" I heard a fragile voice from behind me. Just as I felt the touch on my shoulder, I turned. There she was, her gray hair wrapped high on her head, petal red dots of rouge on her flushed cheeks, and cherry stained lips staring at me.

"Is that you?"

"Who else would be tapping you on the shoulder?"

"You look stunning," I said, turning to see her in full view.

"And look at you." Sara said, touching the lock of hair that lay on my shoulders. "So what is this about?"

"Come sit, let's catch up first. It's been over a year," I said.

"We can catch up later. You worry me. What's this all about?" She asked again.

"I'm going back," I said.

"Going back where?" Sara asked, taking a sip of tea.

"To the Home. I want to find out where they sent Finn. I can't stop thinking about her. If I know that she is safe, then maybe I can let her go. I need to stop feeling guilty, that I didn't fight for her. Can you support me on this?" I was anxious to get my point across to Sara.

"You don't need my support. You've already decided. Do what you have to do. I just don't want to see you hurt. Didn't they hurt us enough?"

"They did . . ."

"So do you have a plan?"

"I'll take the train," I said, shrugging. "Do you think Nurse Claire might still be there?"

"Maybe. But what will you do if Reverend Mother opens the door?"

I hadn't even thought of Reverend Mother being there. I was sure everything would go easy. Nurse Claire would open the door, greet me with open arms, and tell me everything I wanted to know about Finn.

"Do you think you'll ever let go?" Sara asked.

"Did you let go?"

"A long time ago, but it doesn't mean that she isn't with me all the time. You'll understand that someday."

"I think I already do."

"If you did, you wouldn't want to go back."

"I need to stop feeling guilty. I didn't fight enough."

"Alice, when you fought for you, you fought for her. You have nothing to feel guilty about," Sara said.

"Am I wrong to want to know that she's okay?" I asked.

"No, I think you're wrong to think once you find out, everything will be over. She'll still be in your heart." Sara said, taking hold of a wisp of her hair. "You will never be free of her. Nor should you be. It won't change anything."

I sat back, realizing she was right, everything she said was true. I'd never quit thinking about Finn, and I'd never stop feeling guilty.

For the rest of lunch, I remained silent. Sara had set me wondering, what would happen if Nurse Clare didn't open the door? What if it was Reverend Mother or Sr. Beatrice?

"Come on, let's walk a bit before I have to catch my train," Sara said, realizing she had struck a chord.

We walked down O'Connell Street, like sisters, arm in arm.

"Call me when you learn something."

"But that's why I wanted to see you. I wanted you to go with me?"

"I promised myself, I'd never . . . I can't go back."

She caught her train and I walked the two blocks to catch my bus. For twenty-five minutes, I sat watching the countryside pass. I understood Sara's feelings.

I knew of only one other person I had to tell about my plan, and telling Jonathan would give me a sense of order.

I stopped at the pub on the way back, finding my usual table empty. Joseph waved and brought me a Guinness. I didn't have to order things anymore, he just brought what he saw fit.

Before I even took a sip, I spotted Jonathan charging through the double doors, in his usual woolen cap, and navy jacket tucked around his broad shoulders. Watching him come through the door, with a grin and hug for his brother, I knew I could never forget the chances he had taken for us. He had saved us from sure death, a true friend.

"Well, what are you doing here?" he asked, with his cap tipped to the side of his head, standing tall in front of me.

"You were just the person I hoped to find. Can we talk?"

"And what would you be wanting to talk about?"

"I want to go back to Castlepollard, to find Finn." Jonathan was silent. "She would be almost six." My words tumbled from my mouth. "I need to know about her. She might still be in the orphanage, or maybe with a family in Dublin. Maybe I could go by her house, or see her walking with her Mum."

"Maybe I'm the man on the moon . . . she's not in the orphanage, or in a house in Dublin. She's gone, my guess, they sent her to the States." Jonathan leaned over, taking hold of my hands.

He motioned to Joseph, putting two fingers in the air. In a minute or so, Joseph would bring two shots to the table.

"Okay, but she's somewhere, right? Maybe they'll tell me. Maybe Nurse Claire is still there. Maybe Reverend Mother is gone. Someone else might be in charge." I touched the sleeve of his arm so he'd look at me.

After a long pause, "You have so many maybe's, girl. You know they're going to lie to you, like before," he said, leaning back in the wooden chair. "They have no reason to tell you the truth. None. You've got to understand that, girl." I saw the anguish in his face.

"Connor found me. Doesn't that mean we can find her, too?" He twisted his cap in his hand, then straightened it back on his head, pulling it down, tight over his forehead. "Jonathan, I think about her when I see a carriage, or when I pass a schoolyard. At work, during lunch, I go to the nursery, standing there peering from behind the wall at the babies. Did you think I could forget? If they lie to me again, they'll have to do it to my face. I'm not the same. I'm not broken anymore. I'm stronger. I can do this."

"Then why are you telling me? If you are so set, just do it, take the train, take the bus, go back to the Home. Learn everything you can, then what?"

"I just wanted you to know. It seemed important that it be okay with you."

"You're living your own life, now. You don't have to ask my permission for the decisions you make."

"I'm not asking permission. I just didn't want to do anything behind your back."

"Just think about this, okay? Do you really think they care about your feelings?"

"That is all I've been doing. She's my daughter, at least I can know where she is, know that she is safe."

"You signed papers. She's gone. You're right, she may well be in Dublin, but you'll never have at her. By my guess, she's long gone."

My heart ached at the words I heard. I had to look away, then turned back to him. He placed the shot glass in front of me.

"Here, you need this more than me."

"I don't want it."

"Yes, you do, then you're going to listen to me."

"Okay." I took a deep breath, swallowing the caramel colored liquid. It turned hot going down, but felt smooth. I put the glass down, staring at Jonathan.

"You need to let her go. What happened to you and all the others, can't be undone." He touched my arm. "It's over."

"No it's not. It'll never be over. Jonathan, I need to find out where they took her. They can't hurt me anymore."

"You don't think so?" He downed his shot without taking his eyes off me."Girl, have you lost your senses?" Jonathan finally said. He shook his head, looking away from me, but seemed to understand that nothing could change my mind. "When are you going?"

"As soon as I can. I don't work on Saturday."

"Then, if you have to do this, let us take you to the doorstep."

"Why would you do this?"

"Because, you can't be coming back alone. What if it all goes wrong? You'll need Marie's tender friendship to guide you through."

"I can't ask you to take me."

"Alice, I know you have to do this, truth be told, I'd be shocked if you didn't, but we both know they'll lie to you. They will say whatever they have to, to get you on your way."

"I know that." I reached out for his hand. "But if I don't try, I'll hate myself for the rest of my life."

"Come on, let me take you home. I won't talk about it anymore. I promise."

"I need to walk by myself."

I rounded the corner toward home, kicking bright shiny pebbles down the street, like a kid reliving childhood.

RETURNING TO CASTLEPOLLARD

e said little as we drove across the Midlands. I sat between Marie and Jonathan, with Marie gripping my hand. He pulled through the open gate, down the driveway of the Home. The gravel crunched beneath the tires as he parked. I stepped from the truck, staring at the brick building, as I had done six years previous.

I stole away from them, knowing that if things went off-course, they would help collect the pieces, to make me whole again. Until then, I was on my own.

The pillars still loomed in front of me, but I knew the secrets behind the walls. I knew the lye smell seeping through our hands. I knew the bruises and scrapes that came from scrubbing the tile floors, or being shoved against a wall. I straightened my skirt, brushed my hair away from my face, and stepped forward.

"You be careful, sweet girl." Jonathan said.

I stood tall at the convent door tapping twice, composing myself. Nurse Claire opened the door and I saw her connect my face, with the picture in her mind. "Oh, my God. Alice, what are you doing here?"

"I've come to learn about Finn."

Claire ushered me in. "She's not here. They went to a funeral in Kildare. Reverend Mother, all of them."

"Good. Then you can help me."

"Come in. We'll go to Reverend Mother's office." I didn't see any girls in drab jumpers cleaning the entry or down the hall, but the same smell of lye filled my lungs when I tried to breathe.

I could tell, not much had changed as we entered the office. Claire took the chair behind the desk, motioning for me to sit down. When I had come through the first time, she had no chairs. Today, I took a seat in a plush velvet upholstered straight back. Looking up at the same framed pictures hanging on the wall and the cross behind the desk. I remembered Him.

"Alice, I don't know what to say. How are you doing?" she asked.

I knew if I took the time to answer her question, I'd lose my nerve. I hoped she understood that my rudeness was not personal, but desperate.

"Please, I didn't come for small talk, if I may. Can you show me her file?"

"I can't do that. You know that." Claire rubbed her white hands together, then laid them back down on the desk. I reached over touching her cold fingers.

"No one is here. No one will know. You could look in the file."

"I don't have the files."

"You can help me. I need to find out where she is."

"I would love to help you. What they did to you and all the other girls was wrong, but I don't have access to anything. She locks all her cabinets, and takes the keys with her everywhere."

"If you don't tell me, I'll keep coming back until someone does." Claire got up from the wooden chair, walked to the door, opened it, peered out, then closed it again.

"I don't need a file to tell you what I know. They fostered her out, three times in Dublin, but each time they brought her back, with no explanation. Each time she returned her condition worsened. She was sicker, weaker than before she left. Finally, Monsignor Matthew took her, along with Reverend Mother, to a Dublin orphanage, where she remained until being adopted. I'm sorry."

"Ironic that it'd be the two of them to take her."

"What do you mean?" Claire asked, watching my every move.

"After what they did to me, they take the one thing that is mine to somewhere I'll never know." I stared up to the cross and wondered if He heard me now.

"How old was she when they took her? You've got to tell me something."

"Just three when they transferred her to Dublin. After that, all legal papers stopped coming here. But I can tell you while she was here, I saw her as often as I could."

"What was wrong with her? I mean why did they bring her back?"

"The Sisters foster children out to local families all the time. They hope the families will agree to continue fostering until they're of age, but for some reason they kept returning Finn. They noted in her file that she had a fall, and spells followed. I was with her on her last day here, even dressed her before they took her."

"Thank you."

Walking to the window, I moved the curtain with my hand, looking out, realizing I didn't have to search the eyes of children on the street anymore.

"How could they take our babies from us?"

"They took your babies because they could, they were a commodity. They were worth money, and the convent needed money."

"But they had no right."

"Alice, you have to realize that if Finn had not been adopted, when she got older she would have been sent to an Industrial School, then likely off to a Laundry when she became a teenager."

"It doesn't make it right."

"No, it doesn't, but pray she has a good family and that she's away from the abuse. Would you want her to have gone through what you did?"

"No, I wanted her to be with me. I wanted to raise my daughter, not have her live in an institution all her life."

"You can't change what they did."

I sat back down, taking a deep breath. Claire brushed strands of hair from my face and a chill ran through me.

"I am sorry, Alice."

"I know you are."

"Claire, why are you still here, knowing what you know?" I asked, getting up from the chair.

"I come here every day, because of girls like you. I know if I'm here, instead of the babies being dropped in a toilet, I can wrap them in blankets and keep them safe, at least for a while."

"You took care of us." I blinked back the tears.

I opened the door heading to the foyer. As we reached the front door she handed me a folded scrap of paper, "I wish you luck, Alice. Here's my number, call me if you need anything."

"I will. Thank you for everything," I said.

I heard the truck on the gravel, looked up and saw Jonathan. I patted the paper in my pocket knowing that when I was ready, I could call. I was no longer the terrified teenager.

"Well?" He asked, as I got into the truck.

"She's gone."

"Gone where?"

"I don't know."

"I'm sorry, Alice."

"I just wanted her to know her mum loved her," I said, forcing back the tears.

On the drive home neither Jonathan nor Marie said anything. Jonathan stared ahead at the road. Marie reached over and took hold of my hand.

"Would you like to come for supper?" Jonathan asked.

"No. I need to go home."

"We understand. Go on Jonathan, take her home," Marie said.

He drove the remaining blocks to the cottage. As he pulled to the curb I reached over kissed Marie on the cheek and jumped out. Slipping past Evelyn's lights, I opened my door, relieved to finally be alone.

I took the brandy from the cupboard, poured it into a glass. The sip felt just as warm as it had the first time. I left the glass on the counter, went to the bedroom, and pulled back the covers, falling into bed.

I took the journal from the nightstand, opening to the last page. Could I write about this? That I had lost her forever? Would I describe what Claire looked like at the door, or how everything looked different?

I stood tall at the convent door, tapping twice. I composed myself. Nurse Claire opened the door and I saw her connect my face with the picture in her mind.

Aidan

irst I saw the blood seeping through the towels. A short balding man lay on the gurney, moaning. Another officer held the towels in place, the blood covering his hands. "He tried to get the children out of the street. He didn't see the taxi rounding the corner. It came too fast."

"We'll take care of him officer," Bernie said, taking hold of the side of the gurney, following it behind the curtain.

"His name is Sean . . . Officer Gallagher," the officer stammered, staring as Evelyn wheeled him behind a curtain.

"It's all right. Aidan we know who he is."

"Evelyn, I didn't see you. Sorry, a bit confused," Aidan shook his head.

"He's in a terrible mess. I think he might lose his leg,"

"He won't be losing anything if we can help it," Bernie yelled back at him.

The tall officer didn't notice me, but when I saw him straight on, I recognized him immediately. I moved over, helping Evelyn with the man on the gurney.

He stepped back, watching from the corner, refusing to leave. The muscles in his face tightened; his voice strained, anxious like a terrified child lost from it's mother.

Bernie came in with a clipboard. "Aidan can you contact his wife?"

"Yes, Ma'am. He lives off O'Connell Street. I have the number. I can ring it if you like."

"Alice, take Officer Leary to the desk, so he can make the call," Bernie said.

"I know you," Officer Leary said, staring at me.

"You almost arrested me a few months ago."

"Sorry, just doing my job."

"It's all right. Come this way, Officer Leary."

"You can call me Aidan." He followed me to the front desk. His thick wavy hair hung down over his forehead. It was winter, but beads of sweat rolled down his temple. He smiled back at me, but I looked away embarrassed that he remembered me.

I couldn't hear the conversation, but when he hung up, he smiled at me.

"She's coming down as soon as she can," Aidan said, his jaw relaxed. "She had to find someone to care for the baby." He took a cigarette from his pocket, and lit it.

"What are you doing here?"

I pointed at my uniform, then looked at him. "I work here."

"I didn't mean that," he said, his face turning red. "I meant what do you do here?"

"I'm a nurse's aide."

"That's grand."

"Well I don't know about that."

"No, I mean it's grand you found a job."

Evelyn came from behind the curtain, "He has some cuts and scrapes, and a broken leg. It looks like he may have a few broken ribs, also, but he should be fine. He won't be tripping around O'Connell Street for a while, but when he heals he'll be good as new."

"That's good. His wife will be relieved. How long will he be in hospital?" Aidan asked.

"At least for a few days, just to be sure it's only his leg that we need to worry about. He'd like to see you, so you can go back in, if you like."

"Thank you Evelyn."

I watched Aidan go behind the curtain, while Evelyn made some final notes on her clipboard.

"He's cute isn't he?"

"Who?"

"Don't tell me you didn't notice him," she said, going back to her clipboard.

"I'm going now. Good night." I went out the two doors. Oh yes, I had noticed.

*   *   *

Sean Gallagher spent six days in the hospital. I looked in on him every day, even though I didn't do anything medically. I brought him meals, changed his sheets, and passed time between shifts. He laughed despite his pain, always greeting me with a smile. I looked forward to seeing him, but more, I looked forward to the early evening when Aidan came in, after getting off his shift, to visit with his partner.

"How's he doing today?"

"Quite well, I must say. Doesn't he ever get mad?"

"No, he's a pretty jolly guy."

"He has a long recovery ahead, you know. He'll be on crutches for at least two months."

"Oh, he'll be fine. He doesn't take things too seriously, always the light side of everything. So Miss, how are you today?" It came out of the blue, almost scaring me.

"You can call me Alice. I'm doing fine. I'll look in on Sean when I can."

On the day Sean went home, Aidan, and Sean's wife came to pick him up. Aidan stood in the corridor like a schoolboy holding his hat in his hand, asking if he could call on me. Before I could even answer, Evelyn blurted out, "Aidan, I'm having a few friends over next Saturday, why don't you come? Sean, you and your wife should join us, too." Her smile spilled over, unable to contain herself.

Aidan fumbled with his hat, dropping it to the floor. "That would be fine ma'am. I'd like that, thank you."

"Don't be so nervous Aidan, you've known me your whole life. Dinner will be easy, you can relax." Evelyn laughed as she wrote the address down to her house, handing it to Sean, as Aidan wheeled him toward the hallway.

First Date

hough I hoped for a simple dinner to get to know Aidan, it turned into a grand party. Evelyn had told me Aidan had, what she called a "twinkle in his eye," when he watched me go about my work at the hospital. For whatever reason, he had agreed to spend an evening with the only people I called family. I wasn't all that comfortable with that.

Had we gone to the pub, it would've been dark. We could have had a nice meal and a Guinness. If the conversation died, we could have left, and that would've been the end of it. But inside the candlelit cottage, people talked in small groups, waiting for dinner to be served. From across the room, Aidan and I watched each other, pretending we weren't.

After dinner Aidan stepped outside to have a smoke. I followed him and sat on the ledge looking out toward the ocean.

"A little stuffy inside, I needed to get a smoke," Aidan said, as I watched the swirls of smoke rise above his head. "Are you having a good time? There are a lot of people here. She invited more than I expected."

"I'm not good at parties. Really don't know that many people. Some of them are from the hospital; others are friends from Dublin." I tapped my fingers on the ledge.

"So, Alice, what do you do when you're not walking along the shoreline, or working in the hospital?" Still holding the cigarette between his fingers, he looked around everywhere, but at me. I had even colored my face with rouge and lipstick to turn his head.

"I live right behind Evelyn. She has a small cottage that I rent from her. I've been here almost two years now. Outside of work, I don't do much. I have a small garden, and a stray cat. And, as you know, I walk the shoreline."

"Yes, you do, I see you there a lot." I smiled.

"Since coming here, I've learned to knit, even made a few things. I'm afraid I am quite boring," I said, self-conscious about the simplicity of my life.

"That's alright. I'm not too exciting outside of work either. I go to pubs with the guys, but I usually take on any extra shifts I can find. What else is there about you that I might like to know?"

In front of me, nervous in a different way, a hat pulled down tight over his emerald eyes, stood a man with friends, a hard worker, and for whatever reason, he had taken an interest in me. I didn't know what to expect. This was something new.

Jonathan came out to the porch, interrupting the conversation, our history lesson with each other. "Why don't the two of you go on, take a walk?" Jonathan said. "The waves are calling out to you. Go on, have some time alone. We'll be fine without you for a while." I already had my sweater wrapped tightly around me. At Jonathan's urging we headed past the gate and down the lane.

Jonathan was right, a beautiful night, with the stars hanging like ornaments, glistening from the sky, and the shadows of the trees dancing around us. A stray dog ran ahead of us, his tail flopping from side to side. He laid low waiting for us to catch up to him, then ran ahead again.

"Since we were interrupted, shouldn't we pick up where we left off?"

"By all means," Aidan said, as he slipped his hand to my elbow, guiding me toward the beach.

"You know how old I am, can I ask the same of you?"

"I'm 27. I guess I'll just tell you everything, so it won't come back to haunt me. I married at 24, but while giving birth to our first child, my wife died. It was a difficult delivery; he didn't make it either."

After the sentences slipped out, I took a deep breath. A loss, such a horrific loss for one man. "I'm sorry," were the only words I could find.

"That was three years ago. I spend all my time working. I thought I could forget them, if I worked hard enough. I've been Sean's partner since leaving Howth."

I watched him telling me his life. He didn't seem the insecure police officer stopping me on a cold rainy day because he thought me to be a vagrant.

"I might as well spill it. I am looking to find a wife, I am. Losing Charity changed everything for me. I want someone to come home to. I want the sound of babies at my table."

"I've been alone too, but not so sure I'm ready for that sound at my table," I continued taking a deep breath, "being alone has been good for me, at least for now."

"Now why would such a pretty girl want to be alone?"

"Because I don't know what I want yet."

"You don't want to be a Mum? Don't all young lasses want that?"

The words stopped me cold. I could say nothing to him. Would I tell him I'd been a mum for nine days? Would I tell him that while the wife and child he loved, died, that my child and I had survived?

"Of course I do," I said, "but not tonight. Tonight I need to go home. So, if you'd like, you can walk me back to my flat."

"Can I kiss you?" When I said nothing, he took hold of my hand, and we walked back to Evelyn's. We went inside, said good night to Jonathan and Marie. He then kissed Evelyn lightly on the cheek, thanking her for the evening. We followed the walkway to my cottage. It saddened me to think my first true kiss might only be a brush on the cheek. Instead he, gently pushed my hair away, took my face in his hand, lifted it and touched his lips against mine. Sweet and smooth like warm syrup. I closed my eyes. I wanted to feel every sensation of his lips, his fingers. It made my heart leap.

"I'll call you tomorrow."

I wondered if that was how love started, slow, tumbling down, like the waves, rolling up to your feet, then slipping away, back out to the vast ocean. The love I had known to this point was nothing of what I felt in my heart when his hands touched my face. My Da loved me by putting clothes on my back, and food on the table. Connor loved me with tricks and teasing. I suppose Mum's love had been the closest feeling to this, her pulling me close, softly moving my hair across my face.

He would call tomorrow.

*　　*　　*

I cherished my Thursday evenings with Marie. Just the two of us, taking away the pains of the week, by sipping tea, mixing ingredients, and laughing out loud. When I first moved in, Marie gifted me with a bottle of brandy, hidden among clean sheets and towels. It didn't take long for it to become an integral part of our evenings together.

While we cooked she often talked about her life, with Jonathan, and the world she had carved out for herself. She believed she had paid her dues to her God, and happiness could now be hers without guilt. She never worried about laughing too loud, so infectious, when her eyes glistened, as if angels had come down and anointed her with pure joy.

"Evening, Alice." Marie called out as she walked through the garden, up the steps to my front door.

"Good evening, what are we making tonight?" I asked, as I stepped aside, so she could come into the kitchen.

"How about we make lemon cake. My grandma taught me when I was a wee girl."

She went to the table taking the items from her basket. I watched as she placed them on the table, like the nurses at the hospital laid out the instruments for the doctors before surgery.

"So, can I ask? How is Aidan?"

"He's fine." I could feel myself blushing.

"You like him?" she said looking up at me, as she poured everything from the mixing bowl to the pan.

"I do, but it scares me."

"Love can be pretty terrifying. It catches you up, ties your tongue in knots, and gives your cheeks a beautiful blush."

"I can feel that blush sometimes when we are together, and he is holding my hand."

"You've got something on your mind? Something isn't sitting quite right?" She opened the oven door, and slipped the pan inside.

I took a long pause, not planning to tell anyone so soon. "He asked me to marry him."

"Oh, love, that is grand. I've known him his whole life. He is a nice man and will make a grand husband. Tell me how he did it."

"We walked along the shoreline, he held my hand, then suddenly just stopped, turned to me, still holding my hand, and he asked me to marry him. Simple, straightforward."

"Did he offer you a ring?"

"Yes, but I couldn't take it. I couldn't give him an answer. I told him to hang on to it, that I had to think about it. Oh Marie, I don't know what to do."

Marie took the kettle, poured two cups of tea, and reached for the brandy.

"You could use this right now. I remember when I was proposed to," Marie said.

"What did Jonathan say?"

Laughing as she added the brandy. "Oh it wasn't Jonathan."

I looked at her puzzled.

"Jonathan never told you?"

"Told me what?"

"Of course he didn't. He's too much a gentleman. Jonathan wasn't my first love." She took a deep breath, then a sip. "Oh, I loved him from the first day we met. But, not as a lover. He cared for me a great deal. But I never got that feeling, you know, the one that makes you blush, you can't keep a thought, you can't sleep?"

Aidan did all the things Marie had said. He made me blush, rattled my thoughts; he was the last thing on my mind when I feel asleep, and the first when I awoke.

"When I was young," Marie said, "I found myself in a bit of a spot, like you, back then, well, not the same. I brought mine on through unbridled love."

I took a seat across from her, drank my seasoned tea, and listened.

"At the end of my sixteenth year, I meet a lad who took my breath away, made my skin itch, and gave a blush to my cheeks. Oh Lord, he swept me off my feet, he did. He was my Prince Charming, my love, my heart." She looked up, with her cheeks blushing red and smiling, lost in the memory.

"He was a soldier, and when he came around in his uniform, even Mum took a deep sigh. I loved him so. At seventeen, he asked me to marry him. I immediately said yes. We decided we'd be married on his first leave home, when he returned to his duties, I was pregnant. I never told anyone, not even Mum, but I wrote him straight on telling him the news. A month after sending my letter, a telegram came, 'I've decided to stay in Belfast. The best to you.'"

"How awful. What did you do?" I took a sip of tea, but I couldn't take my eyes off the old woman sitting across from me. Here she was baking a lemon cake in my kitchen and sharing what I thought to be her broken heart. We all had our secrets, the moments in our lives that turned us upside down and left us broken, but watching her, she wasn't broken. She had come out from the other side whole.

For a few seconds her hands froze and I could see she transported herself back to that moment.

"I had known Jonathan since my schooldays, a few grades older he was, but always my best friend, like a brother, I told him everything."

"You told Jonathan what happened?"

"Oh yes, I went to his work, and walked right in. I told it all to him and cried like a babe, as he put his loving arms around my shoulder. He walked me home without saying a word. The next day he came to our back door, not asking for me, but Da. In front of my family he asked for my hand. No one said anything to anyone. In three weeks we were married. I lost the baby a month later, and never had another pregnancy. I don't think it ever bothered him that we didn't have a child of our own. If it did, I never knew. He loved me as if he had picked me out for himself, never treated me like a hand-me-down."

"That is so terrible."

"Yes, but I got the best of the deal. I got Jonathan."

"Why did you tell me all this?"

"I don't know. You deserve to be happy. He treats you kind. He loves you. I think you're ready to take a chance."

"Do I tell him?"

"Only you can decide that. Aidan is a good man. He loves you. I would tell him, but it's up to you," Marie said, cleaning up the counter.

"Do you ever think about what might have been, if things had worked out?" I asked.

"No, things worked out just fine. I have what I need. I have what I love. You will have it someday, too." She said it with great clarity.

"It is time for me to go. Take the cake to work tomorrow."

"Thank you."

I was grateful for her telling me. Could I keep a secret, or would I let go? Marie stepped out into the cold night air.

"Marie," I called out. "I think about her all the time. Not a day goes by that I don't wonder what could have been."

"I'm sure you do, but you do that long enough Alice, you won't have room to let anyone else in."

Beginning Again

ven after panic set in, and advice from Marie taken, Aidan continued calling. He came each day to the hospital, where we went for dinner when our shifts were done. We sat in candlelight, talking about everything from growing up in Howth, to meadows as playgrounds. I told him about Meadows Glen, Connor, and being a schoolgirl. He told me about being a part of the Guardia, how he and Sean had been next-door neighbors for as long as he could remember.

I told him I wanted to finish my training at university, then someday travel outside Ireland. We held hands in the candlelight. Often he reached across the table taking my face in his hands, and kissing me. He owned a car, so after dinner he drove me home so I didn't have to take the bus. He would come in for tea and cake.

On our days off, we packed a basket, went off to the beach like children, playing for the day. We laid out a blanket, sat wrapped in each other's arms, talking about our dreams.

"I want a house someday," I said. "Not a flat, a place to have a yard, maybe near a park."

"How about a meadow in the backyard?" He said, laughing. "How about a house in the country?"

"No. I lived in the country most my life. I'll visit, but I want to be close to things, to people, to work."

"How about maybe outside Dublin?"

"Aidan, what are you saying?"

"I found a house. It's on the other side of Dublin. We could raise our family, but still be close enough for work. If you want to continue working in the hospital, we would be close enough."

Our courtship lasted six months, then in front of Jonathan, Marie, Evelyn, and Joseph at St. Joan's we said our I do's. I still said nothing to Aidan about my time in the Home, or The Laundries. I told him nothing about sweet Finn, who, by now, had started school.

Joseph gave us a reception at The Pub following the ceremony. Connor came from London, and Jonathan drove to Kildare to pick up Sara and her sister. Claire came from Westmeath with her husband. I could only hope they would promise it would be my decision to tell or not tell Aidan—now or ever.

I hadn't seen Sara since our tea in Dublin, before meeting with Claire at Castlepollard. Thrilled to see her looking as happy as she had that day. Dressed in a blue suit, with a bonnet to match. Her green eyes glistened. The fragments of the world in the Laundries, no longer connected us. We were dear friends who had created new lives and prospered from them.

"Oh my, dear girl, look at you," she said, greeting me at the pub "More beautiful than ever."

"Sweet Sara, thank you for coming."

"I told you we'd make it, didn't I? That we'd get our lives back? Is he a good man? Does he treat you right? Did you tell him?"

"He's wonderful," I said.

I leaned into her shoulder, whispering. "No, I haven't said a word. I can't. Please do the same, if you will. Not a word, I'm happy. I don't want to lose it." Sara grabbed my arm led me out the front door.

"Tell him Alice. If he loves you, like you say he does, he will love you more after he finds out." She turned me so we were eye to eye. "Don't keep this secret. It will beat you down, maybe not today, not tomorrow, but someday it will keep you from living your life."

"And who might you be? Hadn't I met all Alice's relatives?" Aidan asked as he came up behind, grabbing me around the waist.

"This is Sara. She's Evelyn's cousin, from Kildare," I said, trying not to look at either of them. When they shook hands, Sara darted a look of contempt in my direction. "I'll be inside in a moment," I told Aidan, as he pecked me on the cheek.

"You see. It's already started. You're not married three hours, and you've lied to him already."

"Sara you don't understand."

"No, girl, you can say that to anyone else, but not me. This is your chance to be free of it. He loves you. Tell him. Give your daughter a face in his life."

"I can't, so stop. Please, just enjoy yourself." I gave her a quick hug, then whispered, "I know what I'm doing. I love you." She hugged me back.

The men drank, the women danced. The next day with a gold band, a simple diamond on my finger, I packed my belongings from Evelyn's cottage, and moved into the house Aidan bought on the other side of Dublin.

I started back to Sunday Mass, having made my peace with God, realizing that if I found him at the doorstep of the ocean, I could find him anywhere. Every Sunday, after services, we packed a cake and drove to Howth for dinner with Jonathan and his family. Once a month I met Sara in Dublin for tea.

At night in the dark, we cuddled under the quilt Marie made as a wedding gift. He kissed me, held me, and loved me. He shared the family he had lost touch with, his mistakes, and his best days. I shared little after leaving Meadows Glen, talking more about my work at the hospital, and my life in Howth. The first time we made love I didn't find myself on the gravel road. He whispered in my ear, caressed me with clean hands. With my past gone, I had no reason to resurrect it. Each time we made love, the memory became further and further removed.

"We'll have lots of babies, fill our house with laughter," Aidan said between kisses.

"What if I can't have a baby?" I asked, pulling away from him, to see his face.

"Why would you be thinking that? Of course, you will. It takes time. Don't worry about it."

We didn't talk about having babies for a while. We settled in to our life together, went to work, and invited family and friends to our table. On my days off, when Aidan worked a long shift, I met Sara or Claire in the city. Everything fell into place. Day by day our house became a home.

As the months passed, Aidan, asking more about how I was feeling, or more to the point why I wasn't pregnant. He stopped on the streets in front of carriages, leaned down, cooing at the babies in their strollers. When Sean and his wife came to dinner with their children, he couldn't get enough of the little boy, cuddling, roughhousing every chance he could. I could tell his heart ached.

"Aidan, I'm sorry, I haven't been able to give you a baby."

"Don't worry, it will happen all in good time."

"But it's been a year. I don't want you to think you made a mistake."

"I could never think that," he said.

My life with Aidan brought me the contentment I had longed for. He gave me complete freedom, from decorating the house, to keeping my job, to what I made for dinner. Aidan had created a garden that turned into such a blessing, a haven where he let me be.

Roses were planted in the spring. A neighbor brought over cuttings of wild thyme, then helped me prepare the soil along the back garden path. Aidan took me to the nursery, where we bought azaleas and hydrangeas of every color. He made a wooden bench, setting it up in front of the newly planted bushes. My time in the garden, with vines laced through the trees, the sweet faint smell of gardenia in the air, seemed a gift from God. In the garden I brought life to things that had been left by the roadside to die. As everything flourished in our garden, nothing grew inside me.

Because I didn't get pregnant, the rape came back to me; maybe it had damaged me somehow, or the delivery, because it had been so hard. Maybe it had done all that, and more.

At the hospital babies filled my days. I watched, and learned, but it didn't take long to realize that if Nurse Claire had not been at the Home, many of the girls and our babies, wouldn't have survived. I wrote her often, though we hadn't gotten together since the wedding, I cherished every letter. I told her about my concerns about not getting pregnant, but in her delightful way, she'd respond that like Aidan, "it would take time," so I waited.

Often in the evening sitting under the moonlight in the garden, Finn came into mind. There were a million reasons I should tell Aidan, but for all of them, I knew I never would. Loving him enough never appeared to be a problem. The shame put on me from my past overtook me, like a disease. I had to believe I could change things, but I could never turn back.

A Second Chance

n one of the hottest days of the summer, he walked through the front door, announcing he had been promoted to Captain. I, in turn, confirmed that a baby had been growing in my belly for three months. He beamed, dropped his hat, and swung me around the room. "We are having a wee one. I knew it would happen."

I should have told him about Finn then, but I didn't. Too content, too much in love. I was still unsure how he would take it. I didn't know how I would take it.

As the seasons changed, we settled in to a loving existence, the three of us. He patted my belly when he walked by, leaned in, kissed me, then went on his way. This pregnancy, nothing like the first, made me feel fragile. After each visit, the doctor reminded me I needed to rest, to be off my feet. I knew in my heart something must be wrong, but the doctor seemed unwilling to disclose any problems. I worked through my sixth month, but finally at the doctor's insistence, I put in my notice at the hospital.

The possibility of losing this baby became a reality for me. I imagined if I had lost the baby in the Home, the Sisters would have been more than overjoyed. It would have meant, one less baby to care for, one less baby needing nappies.

Since Aidan never went to the appointments with me, I had another secret to keep from him. Afraid if he knew, it might shatter the safe life we had built for ourselves. He never questioned my life before him, nor I, his. I let the months slip by, wrapped in his love, nesting in our home. I let him love me, hold me safe from the world. I let the memory of Finn go. I settled in to the new world with Aidan, but she was never completely gone.

*   *   *

"Aidan, it's time. The baby's coming."

"Are you sure?"

"Aidan, I think I'd know. I work in a hospital. I've helped deliver babies, besides, believe me, it's time," I said, trying to smile through the pains.

"Sometimes with the first, they don't know for sure."

It could have been the moment right then, to tell him that this was not my first. I chose to keep my history buried. I believed with all my heart that I had made the right decision. I had found my own ways to remember her, planting flowers, baking random cakes on cold November days that served as a treat with dinner. Aidan ate with sheer delight, never asking what brought on the urge, and I never told him.

When my water broke, it was much different than the first time. Here in the garden of my home, safe, loved. Before, it was in front of God and his servants, but in shame and despair.

"Be sure to ring Jonathan, then Sara, if you would."

"That I will, but I'll be ringing Sean first, for support, you know."

It took ten minutes down the main streets of Dublin to the hospital. They settled me in to my white room while Aidan filled out the paperwork. A familiar wooden cross, hung from the wall, but this time I had no problem staring at it.

"Evelyn will be here in no time. Everything will be just fine. It'll be over before you know it," Bernie said, leaving the door ajar. I saw a swirl of a black gown go past the door. For a second, the blur took my breath away. I closed my eyes to hide the image. When I opened them, the room remained empty.

Doctor O'Hara came in with a broad smile. "How we doing, Alice?"

"We're doing just fine, Dr. O'Hara," I smiled, rubbing my belly.

The pains that had started early that morning had progressed at a steady pace.

"Bernie's going to get you ready. It looks like you're getting close. Let's take a look here."

Bernie slid me down, placing my feet on the edge of the bed. The pains were coming harder and stronger. Though I would have preferred Claire, by my side, Bernie, in her clumsy but endearing manner, brought all the comfort I needed. While she held my hand, and wiped my forehead with a cold washcloth, Dr. O'Hara moved to the foot of the bed, beginning the examination.

"So, this is your second, Alice?" Dr. O'Hara asked.

"No, Doc, this would be her first. Remember the wedding over a year ago?" Bernie said.

Dr. O'Hara didn't respond to Bernie and her attempt at humor. He looked up at me, but with a contraction coming on, I paid more attention to the pain, than to the man who knew my secret.

"Bernie, can you go to the front desk, bring me Alice's file? Knock before you come in."

"Sure." I waited for Bernie to look over at me, but she hustled out the door.

"You can slide back now, you have a while. You're not as dilated as I thought, but we need to talk."

"What is it?"

"I think you know what I'm asking. Let me try this again. This isn't your first baby is it?"

"Why would you think that?" I asked.

"You've had severe tearing on your cervix. Though it's healed, tearing like that only comes from a difficult delivery."

I said nothing.

"Alice, you can stay silent if you wish, but I've seen this before. They never sewed you up, did they?"

He heard everything he needed to hear, without opening my mouth.

"There's no mistaking, you birthed in a mother-baby-home."

"You can't tell anyone. Not ever."

"Does your husband know?"

"No. He won't understand."

I pushed myself up on the bed, just as I did, a gentle tap came at the door.

"We'll talk later, but if this baby is anything beyond six pounds, I'll have to take it surgically. You ruptured. It never healed, as it should. Had you been sewn up, I wouldn't be so worried."

"I don't think I understand what you're telling me."

"You had a lot of damage after your first delivery and you should have seen a doctor. Do you remember the pain?"

"I don't remember anything. They told me I had a difficult delivery, but they didn't do anything for me. Reverend Mother wouldn't allow it."

Dr. O'Hara looked at me sadly.

"You rest. I'll be back in a few minutes. Your contractions will be getting closer."

He opened the door, and motioned for Bernie to tend me until he came back. "Come get me when her contractions get three minutes apart," he said.

"Everything all right, Doctor?" she asked.

"It will be," he said, closing the door, nodding to me.

I couldn't look at Bernie when she came to the bed.

"What's he talking about?"

"Nothing," I lied. "Just telling me the pains would get worse. Preparing me, I suppose."

"Will you be needing anything?"

"Bernie, could you go see how Aidan's doing?"

"Sure, I'll be right back."

Lying on the bed, I rolled over, away from the cross that hung in front of me. It had been my secret. Almost ten years passed.

Just fifteen. Late November. Pains coming with only Nurse Claire by my side. Terror that Reverend Mother would burst through the door.

But in this room, with a band on my finger, a home to call my own, lying here alone, the pains felt natural and right. I curled up, grabbing the blanket that covered me. I woke up to a contraction, then another a couple of minutes after. Bernie left to find Dr. O'Hara.

"All right, Alice, I expect it's time for this little bundle to meet its mum. You ready?" Dr. O'Hara said, coming through the door.

I followed everyone's directions, taking deep breaths, pushing as ordered. I remember Dr. O'Hara coming in, checking the chart, then leaving as quickly as he had come.

Bernie nudged my shoulder. "Just one more push."

"Okay." She took hold of my hand, holding it tight while Dr. O'Hara took over. I felt the pulling and the tugging, like he was reaching deep inside. Part of me wanted Aidan there, another part wanted to be alone when I took my baby in my arms for the first time. The pulling and tugging stopped. The room was silent, then I heard it.

Dr. O'Hara leaned over. "God was on your side, Alice. The baby is fine, but you and I need to talk later."

A Realization

ears streamed down my cheek. Dr. O'Hara handed my naked screaming daughter to Bernie who wrapped her in a blanket, then handed her to me.

"Got a pair of lungs, she does." Bernie said as she arranged my pillow, pushing my hair from my face. I held my baby close, taking in everything about her. She had stopped crying, and gazed at me with her green eyes, wide open, taking in everything she could see. She had Aidan's eyes, with his puckered lips. There was no matte of black hair this time, but red shades of blonde fluffs, soft, like the touch of a rose petal.

"I need to take her now. Doc needs to finish you up," Bernie said reaching for the bundle, so secure in my arms.

"I'm going to sew you up now, so you lie back," Dr. O'Hara announced, returning to the bed. Bernie handed the baby to another nurse, then fitted a mask over my face. Before I could even protest, everything went silent.

I don't know how long I slept, but when I woke, the room was still. Dr. O'Hara had left. Bernie stood in the far corner with her back to me.

"What happened?" I called out.

"Everything's fine, Alice. We cleaned you up. Your baby is perfect."

"Can I see her? Hold her?"

"Of course you can. I just bathed her. You think you might want to try feeding her? Do you want some help?"

"No, if it's okay, I'd like to be alone," I said, anxious to hold my daughter. "Where is Aidan?"

"Aidan's still in the lobby with Sean, Jonathan and Marie," she said. "But he wants to come in."

"Can you tell him to wait a bit, just until I feed her?"

"By all means. You need time alone with your girl."

I held my daughter in my arms, as she burrowed deep against my breast. Her mouth nuzzled around, then she grabbed hold with little or no help. It took a few seconds for the sensation to come. I felt the muscles tighten. I stroked her face, remembering the first time. Her lips rounded on my skin. I listened to the sweet suckling. I kissed her soft head, settling down in the bed.

"My dear girl," I said into her ear. "There will be days you might think me gone from you, but I'm not. Though not my first, you will always be loved. I will watch over you, and guide you. Not a day will go by that I will not be there for you. No one will ever take you from me."

It felt odd for me to lie in this bed, this room, feeling so safe, knowing no one would burst through, damn me to hell, or grab my child from my arms. I stared at the ring on my finger, realizing what a difference it made in the eyes of the world.

I should have had a man for Finn, but the only man had been the one who created her in his rage. We would never know him or his kind. Deep in my heart, in a small crevice where I never let anyone see, I was thankful to him for what he had given me. Someday I would see her, hold her in my arms. She would know I never forgot.

I shifted the baby to the other side, adjusting her as I had done before, but she had fallen asleep. Even touching her cheek didn't wake her.

"Hello, my beautiful Missus," Aidan said, greeting me as he came through the door with a bouquet in one hand, a teddy bear in the other, looking as if he'd just won the sweepstakes. His cap tucked under his arm, he held out the flowers and the bear. Bernie came in after him, taking both from him. He reached down, kissed me, stroked my cheek, staring at the baby in my arms.

"She's beautiful, isn't she? I had no idea we'd make such beautiful babies. Oh, my dear Alice, I love you so."

We were alone, such a perfect time. I handed our daughter to him, watching, as she lay secure in his arms, not moving or waking. A silence filled the room while he stared at her. "Aidan, I need to talk to you," I said in a trembling voice.

"Alice, you all right?" he asked.

"I'm just happy. I can't believe I found you, that we're here with our baby."

"I always wanted a girl, you know. She won't want for a thing," he said. "We need to pick a name for her. You had said you liked Rose. That would be fine, if you still want it."

"Your mother's name was Rose, wasn't it?" I asked. "I'd like to carry on her heritage. This baby is in her rightful place to take her grandmother's name, as she should. I'd like to name her Rose, for you."

"Then that would be your mother's name?"

"No. You deserve this."

"Are you sure?"

"I've never been so sure. Aidan, I need to tell you something."

"You need to rest love."

As I grasped hold of him to pull him toward me for a kiss, the door flew open.

"Look who's come to see you," Jonathan said, holding the door for Sara with Marie at his side. Sara rushed in, scooping the baby from my arms. "Oh, she is fine, just fine.

Has your eyes, she does," Sara paused, caught herself, then brought her attention back to the baby.

"No, she has Aidan's. Look how green."

"Gorgeous, isn't she?"

I looked back and forth at Jonathan then Sara. Afraid, that accidently, they would tell Aidan, not even realizing. Jonathan caught my glance. I saw a bit of a nod of his head, as if he knew my thoughts. I hadn't told them they couldn't say anything, I just expected they never would, but I could see how easy it would be to slip.

"Oh yes," I said. I looked over at Aidan, but he had missed the silent conversation, mesmerized by the baby.

"How are you feeling, girl?" Sara asked.

"I'm good, a little tired. Isn't she beautiful?" I asked, beaming, as I watched her sleep in the arms of my dearest friend. In a few moments, Sara handed her back, then turned to guide the traffic that stood about the room.

"Come on now, let Alice have some rest. Out, all of you. You can see them after they've had a nap," Sara said as she began to push everyone through the door, then turned back to me.

"Oh Sara, I can't believe she's here."

"Are you going to tell him?" She asked, taking the chair by the bed, watching my every move.

"I almost did. He kept telling me how much he loved me, then we talked about names, then the door opened, and everyone rushed in. Sara, can I tell you something?"

"Of course. What is it?"

"Dr. O'Hara, the doctor who delivered the baby? He knows I had a baby before."

"How could he know that?"

"Dr. O'Hara said there had been damage. I'd healed, but he was worried that if the baby was too big, I'd tear again."

"Did you tell him?"

"No, I didn't have to. He knew what happened. He said he'd seen it before. What if he tells Aidan?"

"He can't be telling him anything. You're his patient, not Aidan," Sara said.

"I don't know. Dr. O'Hara said we needed to talk later. I don't know what to do."

"Tell Aidan, so you aren't so haunted by it. I'll go get him. You need him now."

"No. I can't do it here. I'll wait until we're home, alone."

"Are you putting it off?"

"Don't you think she looks like Finn? They could be sisters, except for the hair."

Sara turned abruptly and with a stern face she replied. "No, they don't look alike at all. She has Aidan's nose, his green eyes. Finn had your nose, your blue eyes. This baby girl is here because of love," Sara wouldn't stop staring at the bundle in my arms. I heard the anger in her voice.

Finn would always be in my heart, even more now that I had Aidan's baby. "Sara, I need to be alone for a bit."

"Do tell him," she said, steadfast.

"You're making me jittery. Go on now, I need to rest, leave me be," I said, patting her arm.

*   *   *

As I packed my bag and checked the room to be sure I had left nothing behind, Dr. O'Hara came into the room. "You ready to go home now?"

"Yes, Aidan is waiting for me. Everything okay?" I fumbled with the latch on the suitcase. I hoped he had forgotten.

"Can you drop by my office before you go. I just want to go over a few things before you check out."

He left me alone and I latched the suitcase, taking a deep breath. I knew what it would be about. I left the room with my suitcase in hand and walked down the hall to his office. I tapped on the door and heard him rustling with papers. I opened it and peeked inside.

"Come in, sit down. This won't take long."

"What is it?" I said, trying to seem relaxed.

"I'm glad the delivery went so well. Rose is a beautiful baby."

"Thank you." I said. I decided I would bring it up before he had the chance. "I know what you...."

"Stop. You don't have to explain anything. I know what happened. My sister was at Sean Ross and Bessboro. She never made it home. We learned later that they buried her in a communal grave on the grounds, no burial Mass, no headstone. When I learned of this, I was a kid, but I knew I had to do something in her memory. I knew if I went into medicine I could make a difference, so other girls wouldn't have to go through what she did."

"I'm sorry what happened to your sister." I whispered. "But you still can't tell Aidan. You have to promise me that."

"Did your family send you there?"

"Yes. I was raped." I felt tears on my cheeks, my voice cracked. He stared at me without moving. "I named her Fionnuala, but they took her and sent her away. Reverend Mother said the pain was our penance. In the Laundries, we were punished and told that only God could forgive us."

I saw the sadness build in his eyes for everyone he hadn't been able to save. "I never knew what my sister went through, but I imagine she didn't survive the delivery. I never understood how they could do what they did in God's name."

He composed himself. "You were lucky, no life-or-death decision had to be made with this baby. I'm not telling you that you have to tell Aidan, but he is your husband. He loves you and you shouldn't have a secret like this separating you."

"He could leave me, maybe even take Rose."

"I don't see Aidan doing that. Give him a chance. Think about it."

"I'm afraid. I saw what Da let happen before he even knew the truth. I was his daughter and he turned me away."

"You go on home, love your baby. Maybe in time, you'll find a way to tell your husband."

In a quick moment, he came around the corner of his desk, and hugged me. Then I heard a soft voice in my ear.

"Tell him Alice. Times are different. He's not your Da."

LETTING IT SLIP AWAY

efore long Rose toddled across the floor, grabbing hold of tables, her blonde wisps grew into golden ringlets. In an odd way, it pleased me to think they didn't look alike, because their differences separated them in so many ways. I couldn't love them more than I already did.

"Look at you, baby girl," Aidan said to Rose, who waved, "in no time you'll be walking on your own." Then he scooped her up, propping her on top of his shoulders. Her face lit up, she giggled, as her curls bouncing around her face.

"Give her here, it's her bedtime," I said, reaching up to take hold. As he leaned down, I kissed him suddenly on the cheek. He laughed out loud and pulling me even closer. I allowed myself to take in this moment, with no judgment, no task at hand.

"Aidan, do you have a minute before you go out?"

"I always have time for you. I won't go if you don't want me to."

"No, I didn't mean that. I just need a few minutes. Sean would be disappointed if you didn't show up."

"I'm only going because of his invite. I can stay if you like?"

"Let me put the baby down. Don't go just yet."

I headed to the nursery, putting Rose in her crib, leaving the door ajar just enough to keep the darkness at bay. I pulled her blanket up around her, kissed her gently on the forehead, then slipped downstairs.

"What is going on?"

"I've been wanting to tell you something."

"What is it?"

"Rose is going to be a big sister."

"Your pregnant?"

"Yes. I haven't been to the doctor, but I know it. I want you to go with me, so we can hear the official news together."

Aidan never had trouble saying things out right, but when it came to sharing his heart, he blushed, then stammered. "You know, I love you."

"And I, you," I said, grinning at his blushed cheeks.

He had found the key to my locked door. I could open it, and tell him, allowing myself to be free of it, but something caught up in my throat, as always I let the opportunity slip away.

Dr. O'Hara shook Aidan's hand first, then reached for mine, taking hold with both his hands. He looked up nodding his head, then took a seat behind his desk.

"So, might we be here for another baby?"

"Yes. I've noticed some changes, you know." I blushed looking over at Aidan as he watched me.

"Well, let's have a look. I can tell you in no time. Aidan if you will excuse us." Dr. O'Hara stood up, moving toward the door. I patted Aidan on the shoulder, leaning down, whispering into his ear.

"I'll be right back, love," I said, kissing him on top of his head.

"So, Alice," Dr. O'Hara said, coming through the door. "When was your last period?"

"Three months ago."

"Are you regular?"

"I have been since I stopped breast-feeding about five months ago."

"Everything else been okay?"

"Yes, perfect," I said, almost gloating that I had such a good time with Rose. No unexplained sadness, no mood swings. Everything had gone right this time.

"How is the little one?"

"Growing like a weed. Starting to walk."

With his nurse's assistance, I slid down on the table, holding my feet on the edge. I felt him insert the cold metal instrument, immediately my body tightened. The nurse took hold of my shoulder, patted me gently until he pulled it out, then my muscles relaxed.

"Okay, I'm done. Alice, get dressed. You can wait here."

"Am I?"

"I'll talk to you in a minute."

The nurse helped me down. I quickly put my clothes back on, then leaned against the table. She finished taking some notes, then left the room. I knew the signs of pregnancy, as most women did, but still needed confirmation from Dr. O'Hara. I knew he'd be coming back in to give me more than just a nod to my pregnancy.

"You know what I want to discuss. I have the same concerns from the last time we talked."

"You said I was fine. Rose's delivery went so much better than the first."

"Yes, I know, but with another pregnancy. Yes, you are pregnant. You're facing the same problem because more scar tissue has grown around your cervix. There could be more unforeseen complications. Don't you want Aidan to know? In case something happens, he will understand."

"Don't you think he'll worry no matter what he knows, Doctor?" I took a deep breath. "I know you have the best intentions, but you have to stop this. This is my family. It is my place to tell, when I find a good enough reason."

"Okay, think about this. If this was his secret wouldn't you want to know? And, if you knew, would it change things for you?"

"No, of course not. I'd love him always."

"Then why can't you believe he will do the same?"

"Because, it happened to me, not him. I vowed after I left those places, I'd never tell anyone what happened."

"He is not anyone. He is your husband, and you love him." Dr. O'Hara clenched the file in his hand, as he stared at me.

"Of course I do."

"Then for the love of God, Alice, tell him, so you won't be haunted by the memory of your past."

"Doctor, please, leave this part of my life to me. I'm haunted by the past every day, but my fear is stronger than the need to share."

"I'm sure you have been thinking about it since the day it happened. I understand how dreadful it was for you. Believe me, I'm not trying to minimize it."

"Thank you. Can we go tell Aidan the news?"

"Yes, of course."

He left the room and I gathered myself together. I took a tube of lipstick from my purse, coating my lips in bright pink. I needed color so Aidan wouldn't think I was worried.

When I walked in, Dr. O'Hara was already behind his desk. Aidan was sitting where I left him, looking amazingly calm.

"Everything all right?" He asked, standing up, helping me to my chair.

"Of course it is," I said, once again touching his shoulder.

"Well, Alice is definitely pregnant. About three months along. Baby should come at the end of February. I want to watch her though. There were some problems with her last delivery that might affect this one."

"You sure she's okay?" Aidan asked, taking a seat on the edge of the chair.

"Aidan, she is fine. Don't worry. I just want to be sure I don't miss anything. Go home, celebrate with your family. Tell everyone. She is fine. I'll see you in a month."

Aidan held my hand as we left the hospital. I could tell he was bubbling over with excitement, waiting to find the right words to say. Once in the house, Aidan couldn't contain himself when Marie met us at the door, coming forward before we could even get in the front door.

"Oh, we are so thrilled for you." Marie gushed.

Aidan came over putting his arm around me, hugging me tight. Jonathan walked up holding Rose, who immediately reached out for Aidan. While we were gone Marie had prepared a light supper. We moved into the dining room, while Aidan placed Rose in her high chair. We sat down, chatting lightly through supper.

I watched Rose play with her food, letting the conversation float past me. It was Dr. O'Hara's words embedded in my mind, set on my telling Aidan everything that had happened. If everyone believed in Aidan, why couldn't I?

After Jonathan and Marie left, I cleaned up the kitchen, while Aidan gave Rose a bath, then put her to bed. Having an early shift in the morning he was already in bed. I slipped in next to him. Laying together, he wrapped his arms around me, holding me close.

"Aidan, if I told you I did something terrible when I was young would it change how you felt about me?"

"Nothing would ever change how I feel about you. You changed my life."

"And you mine. You are so good to me. You help with Rose."

"Of course. She is my girl, too."

"Most husbands don't do that."

"Alice, you brought me love. You brought me Rose. I could never walk away from my life."

I moved closer to him, letting him wrap himself around me. I laid in his arms feeling safe and loved.

"Is there anything wrong?"

"No." I closed my eyes, knowing I'd lied to him again.

Connor Comes to Terms

he weather warmed, the sun stayed out longer each night and we had just finished supper. Aidan had gone next door to talk with Frank McGuire about summer planting. Rose heard Connor coming through the door, arriving for his usual visit. His face drawn and tense, as he walked out the patio door. His eyes fell on Rose, toddling toward him. His face beaming as she reached for him. He took her up in his arms before she even realized it, tossing her high in the air. She giggled until she couldn't breathe. She called out, "Onn-ur, more, more pea-se."

"Connor, don't toss her about, she needs to go down, it's getting late and you're getting her worked up."

"She loves it," Connor said

"Between you and her Da she'll never settle down."

"Okay. Mummy is such a poo."

"Poo-oo," she giggled, sitting tall on his lap.

It was her Da and Connor, she saved her endless giggles for, never getting enough of either one. Starting my fifth month, I took a seat in my chair and watched Rose take ownership of Connor as he continued to bounce her around. I rubbed my belly as the new life inside reminded me that though my children would never know grandparents, they would always have Connor to turn to for everything in their lives.

After a while Connor carried a very sleepy Rose up the stairs with her arms wrapped around him, her head gently nuzzling in his neck. She gave a simple wave of her fingers. He leaned into her soft white neck, and I smiled to see Connor's fingers match her wave. When Connor returned, I motioned for him to follow me to the living room.

"Let me get you something to eat."

"No, I'm fine. I ate on the ferry."

"OK, what's eating you up brother?" I asked as I motioned him to the couch.

Connor took a cigarette from his pocket, and lit it while staring out the window. I went over and stood next to him, reaching for one as well before he put the package back in his pocket. A calm filled the room as we watched Aidan and Frank from the window. Their conversation animated, waving their hands motioning to plants here and there in the garden.

"How long have they been friends?" Connor asked, as smoke rings moved toward the ceiling.

"Frank has been our neighbor since we've been married."

"What do they talk about?" Connor asked.

"I don't know, I've never asked. Frank helps him at church, and I think he joins Aidan and Sean at the pub, now and again."

"Look at them," Connor said, almost in awe. "They look so natural."

"What's going on here?" I asked, putting my cigarette out.

"I miss that."

"What?"

"A best friend."

"I don't know if they're best friends. Actually Sean, Aidan's partner is his best friend. He's over here all the time." I caught myself, realizing what he was trying to say.

"You have friends at work right?"

"Sure, but we talk shop. They don't know anything about me. They don't care."

"I can't believe that."

"You were my best friend, " Connor said, taking another cigarette.

"Are you kidding? You hated me. You made me do all your dirty chores, and you boxed my ears all the time. I don't get it. Where is all this coming from?"

Connor turned from the window, studying me. There were no tears. It was matter-of-fact, straight-faced. Sad.

"They never explained what happened. Da told me to never bring it up, unless I wanted a crack across my trap. So I remained tight-lipped, nudging the girls to hush whenever they asked. After a while the questions stopped coming."

"I always wondered what it was like for everyone after I left."

"Things weren't good. Da went downhill fast. For days on end, he wouldn't come home. There were even nights Mum went out to find him. After she brought him home, they'd fight, and yell at each other. The babies would cry, then for days on end there was a discerning silence."

I don't remember that," I said, "I remember Sunday dinners, birthdays, and laughter. I remember being happy."

"After you left, that happiness went with you."

"No, I didn't take any happiness with me."

"I missed you, Alice. You were the only one who really knew me, laughed at my stupid jokes. I was lost without you. I didn't know how to be, anymore."

"I was lost without you, too."

"But we're supposed to make believe you had never been here. Da got rid of everything of yours."

"I can't do this Connor. I have your back now and that's what I want to remember."

"You've never talked to them since then, have you?"

"No. Jonathan took me to Howth and I stayed there."

"You know what, this is supposed to be a fun trip," Connor said. "Let's not talk about this any more."

"Good. Let's talk about your future. Tell me about your plans."

"Not what I hoped. I thought it would be different." He took a long pause, walked across the room, and came back. "I'm thinking of moving back to Dublin. I've been offered a job, and I think...." I didn't even let him finish, but jumped into his arms as my body allowed.

"You're coming home? Oh my gosh, you'll be so close."

"I haven't made my decision yet, but I'd have a flat, choice of my stories, but everything would be local."

"Is that bad?"

"I won't be traveling as much."

"Had you been traveling that much?"

"I went to Paris...."

"But it wasn't your story. You told me you did backup research."

I watched as Connor tried to defend his choices. My poor brother faced a decision that he thought would be the end of his career. I knew I was being selfish, but I wanted him back. I had lost him for so long and I needed him in my life.

"When do you have to decide?"

"I need to let them know in a week. My first story would come out the week after."

"Do you already know the story?"

"Yes, the history of Manor House."

"Maybe you could write about them someday."

"Who?"

"The Church . . . expose them for what they've done."

"I think I need to stay pretty simple, I need to get established before I take on the Catholic Church."

"You know what, when Aidan comes in why don't you guys talk about it."

Aidan came in, pushed his wiry hair from his face and moved to shake Connor's hand.

"Have you had a drink yet, Connor?"

"Just talking to Alice, thought I'd wait until you came in. Didn't want to interfere your conversation with Frank. How is he anyway?"

"He's grand. Telling me about some bushes that we could plant in the yard that would bloom all year."

"It must be nice to have someone to talk to."

"Yes, it's nice to have a friend. He's always been there for us."

I excused myself while Aidan and Connor continued their conversation. Taking a last look out the window, Frank tipped his hat as he looked up. I returned to the kitchen, setting up my tea. Aidan came in, kissing me on the cheek.

"We're going to the pub for a pint or two. I won't be long," he promised.

"That's a great idea, Connor has some things he wants to talk about. And get him some supper, he won't eat here."

"Anything for your brother," Aidan laughed.

"You take care of him Aidan, he's going through a tough time. He needs an ear." He rubbed my belly and left the room.

After climbing the stairs, I checked on Rose who lay curled in her crib. I closed my door, set the tea on the nightstand and began to change. After settling in bed, I took the journal from the drawer opening it. It had been a while since I had time to write. Tonight had been more than I planned for, usually the visits from Connor were light and silly. He talked about London and the research he did on the articles, saying one day he'd have his own by-line. But tonight was different. Maybe it was Rose, or seeing Frank in the garden with Aidan. I didn't know what triggered him, but I saw it on his face as he came through the door.

I covered my smile with the sheet. My Connor would be coming home. As I looked through the pages, pausing on certain ones.

For a reason I couldn't explain, Dr. O'Hara's words came to mind, as if they were mine. The pen slid across the paper.

> *"Stop. You don't have to explain anything. I know what happened. My sister was at Sean Ross and Bessboro."*

I didn't hear Aidan crawl into bed, but I felt his arms curl around our baby. I felt his legs melt into mine, his hand brushing my hair away. On this night, I felt more loved than I ever could have imagined.

A Request

he seasons changed, and as each year passed I woke to my husband and my children considering myself lucky. I survived. I had survived it all. But there were moments; moments when split seconds flashed, glimpses of cold wet gravel beneath me, the Home, where the cross offered no safeguards. The Laundries, where hatred flowed like spilt milk, seeping through the cracks of the floor. Da came into my nightmares, cold and hard, without a blink of his eye. Mum, still standing in the doorway, terrified.

Perhaps the final apology would come when we meet beyond this world.

*   *   *

We decorated for Christmas every year since being married, but this year seemed different. I wanted to do something more, a floor-to-ceiling Christmas tree. I wanted to celebrate the tradition of the holly wreath on the front door, and a white candle in the window. The tree Aidan brought in stood tall in the corner with cranberries and popcorn wrapped around, mixed with the lights and the tinsel.

In those days I baked every recipe I could find that would fill the house with the smells of Christmas. Most of the recipes I learned from Evelyn and Marie during my days in Howth. Their recipes over the years became legend, or so Aidan always bragged when I placed them on the table.

The girls filled the house with laughter, chaos and a peace my spirit devoured like a sweet dessert.

Rose, our first, blonde ringlets, pink cheeks, did everything right, never questioned authority, protected her sisters with a fierceness, and believed the world was her oyster.

Catherine, our chestnut haired rebel, rosy blushes, dashes of freckles across the bridge of her nose, fought for every cause, brought home lost puppies and kittens, and sat for hours with Aidan telling how she would change the world.

And the youngest, with ginger colored ringlets, the most free-spirited, Francine, her Da's favorite, could do no wrong. Even when she lied, he'd give her his look, she'd smile, he'd pat her head and they woul laugh.

Finn, her presence floated in my mind, lingering like a late snowfall. Grown, perhaps married, I could only hope she had found a life.

*   *   *

Connor's visits had become routine since his move to Dublin. As the girls grew so did his relationship with each of them. He spent hours helping Rose study, making her school projects perfect. Catherine would lead him to the shed giving the details of each wayward animal she found, and asking what he could do for her to make them better. And Francie, from the time she could talk, he laughed at her jokes, and together they talked about his stories and she always told him how to make them better.

He never missed birthdays, anniversaries, school events, every chance he had, he spent with the girls.

After settling in to his new job and flat in Dublin, he met a woman, he called "magical." They married in a small private ceremony, honeymooned in London and returned to his flat. They were happy, both writing for the same paper. They traveled when they could, but Dublin was home. Jenny folded into our family like sweet cream into tea. Her warm touch gave Connor everything he needed to take hold of his life. When they came, we talked about anything and everything, but never about Meadows Glen, or our parents.

Before Christmas, he promised the girls he and Jenny would come for Sunday dinner, but it wasn't Sunday, and dinner was hours away.

I could tell the minute he came through the door that this visit would be different. This conversation would not be about the girls' school work, or his newest articles, or even Jenny's accomplishments. He didn't waste time, barely taking off his coat.

"Mum wants you to come home for Christmas."

"How does she know about me?"

"She has called a few times and asked about you."

"Why would you tell her anything?"

"She knew more than I told her."

"She has no right."

Enraged that she even had the nerve to ask, but I couldn't be mad at Connor for being caught in the middle.

"She knows you've been married a long time and that your girls are growing," he continued, "I think she's afraid that she won't be around for much longer. She wants to see you."

"Why, after everything, would I go see her? If she knew about our girls why didn't she ever call or come see us?"

"I don't know, maybe she thinks she isn't wanted?"

"Of course she isn't wanted. Why would I want to see her? She never came for me. When she came to Castlepollard, it was to tell me that I'd never go home again," I said.

"Alice, she's sick. She said she's been seeing a doctor, but wasn't clear about it. Said she's having stomach pains, not eating well."

"Connor, what would you have me do? Parade my family back to Meadows Glen like we're on holiday?"

"But what if she's really sick?" he asked, turning away from the window. "She wants to see you. Come with me. Bring the girls."

"Have you gone back yet?"

"No."

"But you want me to go."

"It's different. You're her her firstborn daughter, no matter what she did, she has always loved you."

"So, I should always love her? I'm not going. She has no right to my family."

"Come on, grant Mum one last wish." I saw the pain in his face, the redness that formed around the rim of his eyes. I knew his heart ached for the past, to reconnect to a life we once had. "Okay. What about just you and I go. If you and Mum can stand to be in the same room for more than five minutes, then you can bring the girls back. We can take my car to Meadows Glen. We don't have to spend the night. You'll be home before the girls get home from school."

I watched as the rain beat against the pane. The cat sat on the windowsill, looking up at me while I scratched her ears. I wanted to shout that I'd never walk back inside that house. She'd never see any of my girls, since she never cared about seeing Finn.

"Alice, it's different now," Connor said, moving behind me, placing his hands on my shoulders. I could feel the weight, the tenderness of his embrace all at the same time.

"Why? Because I'm respectable now? I have a ring on my finger, a husband in my bed?"

"No, I didn't mean that," he said.

I turned to face him. "You may not have meant it, but that is what I heard."

"I just mean that maybe it's time for you to go back. Time for you to forgive her. You have a family, a husband who loves you. You've won. Don't you get it? You have nothing to be ashamed of."

"What did I win?"

"You survived. You beat them all. Can't you forgive her?"

"Forgive her? How willing would you be to forgive, if it happened to you? You have no idea what it felt like being sent away, having to give up my baby."

"No, I don't, but you have children now."

"Oh, my God." I swirled to him. "Do you think I could replace one with another? Pretend Finn never existed, that I never carried her or held her in my arms? Fed her at my breast. I can't believe you're asking this of me."

"You know what, let's not talk about this anymore. Let's just have a nice evening. We can talk tomorrow."

"I don't think I can have a nice evening thinking about Mum."

"Come on, I hear Aidan in the drive."

Aidan came through the front door with the girls following behind.

"Just in time for supper," Aidan called out as the girls circled Connor.

We each took our places at the table and for a while we laughed and talked and never mentioned the past, or the heartache. We were a family together, with no regrets, no bitterness. I sat back and watched the two men I loved more than life, laugh and play with our girls and fill the holes in their lives.

After dinner, the girls pushed Connor through to the living room. I heard the giggling and shouting from the kitchen, as he roughhoused with them as he had done when they were small. I remained in the kitchen cleaning up and listening. Aidan stayed behind to help me finish the last of the details and allow the girls undivided time with Connor.

"God, the girls love your brother," he said, coming up behind me.

"He is the only uncle they have."

"That is too bad, but at least they have him."

"His visit is different this time. You notice he didn't bring Jenny?"

"Yes. How long is he staying?"

"I guess it depends on me. What he wants me to do."

"What does he want?"

"He didn't just come to see the girls. He's on a mission."

"He wants you to go back to Meadows Glen?"

I turned around, took the towel from the counter, and dried my hands.

"Yes he does," I said looking quizzically at Aidan. "He wants me to take the girls. How did you know?"

"He called me a day or two ago to see what I thought."

"Why didn't he call me? I'm the one going."

"He wanted to know how you'd be with it?"

"What did you tell him?" I asked, starting the water for tea.

"I told him, I thought maybe it was time for you to resolve things. You're happy now. The girls are doing great. We're good. You have reason to be proud."

Aidan poured the water into cups, then went to the table as I put everything away so there would be nothing left in the morning. Before long, the cat came through the doorway and curled up on the floor next to my feet. I stared down, as I scratched beneath her chin.

I took a sip of the steaming tea, but put it down because it burned my lips. "Everything Connor says sounds logical. I know she's my Mum, but does it mean I have to forgive her?"

"What do you have to forgive her for?" he asked, taking a sip of the steaming tea. I stared at this man I had kept so many secrets from and wondered if I would ever find the strength.

"Are you ever going to tell me what happened?"

"There's nothing to tell," I lied. I had become good at lying about my family, keeping it private, burying it so deep I was close to convincing myself of my own falsehood.

"This, 'nothing to tell' sure has you worked up."

"It's a daughter thing. We always fight with our Mums."

"So is this what will happen when the girls grow up?"

"No, I will never fight with our girls."

"Alice, come here. Sit down," he said, taking hold of my hands. "What happened?"

"Aidan, I don't want to talk about it." He stared back at me, waiting. "She accused me of a lie, something I never did. She threw me out of the house and told me to never come back. I left. There, I'm not saying anymore about it." But what I didn't tell him was that forgiving Mum would be a betrayal to Finn. I couldn't do that.

That night curled up with Aidan by my side, the girls, safe and loved, secure in their beds, I laid in a contented silence.

"I think you should go to Meadows Glen. I don't know who did what to who, but if it means you can let go of this deep dark secret that has tormented you for so long. I say, go."

"I already told you."

"I figured when you were ready, you'd find the words to tell me the truth."

"And if I can't find the words?"

"You will stay tormented. I will love you no matter, but, but it breaks my heart that you can't tell me."

"What if it was bad?"

"It's not for me to forgive you. It sounds to me, you have to forgive each other first. I should be the least of your worries."

I sat up in bed, turned so I could face him, but could only look at his face in the shadows, so as not to see his disappointment in me. "When I was fourteen, I was raped. They didn't believe me."

Aidan pulled me down, holding me close, saying nothing. In that one second, he took my fear, rolled it up, and put it away for safekeeping.

He didn't ask questions. He held me close, stroked my hair, and kissed my cheek. I lay my head where he kept my heart.

In the morning, he was gone. I found a note on the dresser.

Go to Meadows Glen. Come back when you're free of it.
I'll always be here.
Love you still.
Aidan.

Back to Meadows Glen

took the note, folded it, put it into my pocket, and headed to the girls' rooms. All the beds were empty, but I heard the giggling coming from downstairs. When I came around the corner, I saw Rose hugging Connor's shoulders, and Catherine and Francine were snuggled under each arm. I leaned against the wall smiling.

"All right girls, upstairs get ready for school. I'll have breakfast done in no time."

"I'm leaving for Meadows Glen in a few hours," he said.

"I'll fix breakfast before you go."

"So you aren't going?" he asked.

"Why should I? Because she wants me too? I told you last night, there's nothing there for me."

"It's your home."

"No, Connor. I have a home right here."

"Just tell Aidan you're taking a ride."

"And lie to him?"

"Haven't you been lying to him all along?"

"No, I haven't. I told him about the rape. I told him about Mum and you wanting me to go to Meadows Glen with the girls."

"And the Home, the Laundries, and Finn?"

"No, just the rape. That was all I could do."

"What did he say?"

"I didn't let him say anything. He just held me tight. What would you have done, if the woman you loved told you she was raped? What would you say?"

"I would tell her I loved her."

"He agreed I should go," I said, scowling back at Connor.

"So come with me," Connor said, after sipping the tea I had placed on the table for him.

"What are you waiting for? We can leave before lunch."

I went back to the counter to get things ready for the girls, thinking about what I would say to Mum after all this time. I wasn't that child anymore. I had promised myself I'd never go home, but here I was, on the brink of returning to the place I had spent years trying to forget.

"Connor, here's the deal. I'll go with you, but we stay a few hours and like you said, be back by supper, so the girls don't know."

"Mum . . ."

"No. This or nothing."

"You're sure?" Connor asked, as he lit a cigarette.

"That's the only way."

"You win."

The girls came back down and Connor said his good-byes, heard all the things he had not heard the night before and promised he would be back before they could miss him.

Connor opened the door of his rental car, while I slipped in to the front seat. I could only hope Aidan was right, if I could find a way to let it go, I'd be free. I looked at him, nodding as he started the engine.

We drove to Kildare, and took the dirt lane that led to Meadows Glen. As the rain fell, we passed the school, past the overgrown bushes that looked the same as they had back then, but today, the bushes were empty. I was safe. As the unpaved road became narrower, I saw the wrought-iron gate, and the house behind it. Everything came rushing back, the memories of childhood, like yesterday, running across the meadow, barging through the front door.

Sweet smells filled each room. Evergreen, from the tree we had dragged through the meadow to the front door, and the holly that Mum would use for a wreath. The smell of bread, fresh from the oven, steam rolling up in circles in the windowsill. After placing our treasures on the table, we watched her weave together the wreath that would hang from our front door. Sometimes Mum would add a ribbon, usually white, remnants from years past.

She washed the cranberries we had picked over the days, placed them in a ceramic bowl, and threaded a needle for each of us. After our threads were filled, we draped the strings around the tree like a necklace.

That same evening Mum retrieved a hidden white candle, putting it in the kitchen window, then wrapping leftover holly as a holder. We huddled around as she lit it, watching the glow of the light reflecting off the walls.

"Now," she said, "no one will get lost."

"Is that for Da?" Connie called out, watching the shadows dance in the window light.

"No, silly, your Da will be home before you know it." But we watched her face change from delight, to concern, as she stared out across the meadow wondering why her husband had not made it home to be with his family, on Christmas Eve.

We sat at the window waiting. Before long, we saw Da come through the gate with a handful of packages. Connor ran to open the door, while the other children bolted out.

"What's all the excitement?" Da asked, standing with reddened cheeks, and a faint scent off alcohol lingering off his coat.

"You're home," we cried in unison. "We put the candle in the window, so you'd find your way."

"Why? You think I don't know my way?" He said gruffly.

"Where you been?" Mum asked.

"Did some extra work for Doc O'Shea, so I could buy gifts for the children."

"Did you have yourself a pint?"

"Not tonight," he said, looking around the room.

We didn't bother with what was said between our parents, just waited for the rest of the packages to tumble from Da's arms.

"No, these are for tomorrow. No peeking," he said pulling away from Mum's glare.

Da took the presents, and laid them around the tree, then looked over at Mum, and took a seat in his chair.

*"I think it's time for a story. Do you have the cookies made?"
Da asked, as we gathered around his chair.*

"They're on the counter cooling off," Maggie cried out in excitement.

"Well, come on, settle in now."

*Connor and I stood back watching as the tension slipped from
Mum's face, a smile sliding in its place. The wee ones tucked
themselves into his lap, barely allowing him to take off his
jacket. Mum dimmed the lights. Da read the story by the glow
of the candle from the window.*

The broken gate brought me back.

Mum Reveals Her Truth

1971

The house was in shambles. The gate hung by a hinge, the garden overgrown with wild weed vines. No sign of flowers or vegetables. The shutters torn from the windows, and clumps of peeled paint scattered on the ground.

Connor tapped on the door, but no response. Harder the second time and the door opened, slightly. In the subdued light, I saw matted strands of her hair around her shoulder. She saw Connor first, then peeked around at me.

"Oh my God, you've come," she said.

"Mum." Connor gasped.

"Come in," she said, opening the door just enough to let us squeeze through.

Mud clots, from boots littered the floor. Dishes piled up in the sink, clothes strewn about. A stagnant smell filled the room. Mum continued to cling to the door for balance, until Connor took hold of her, leading her to the table. Though she shut the door, I opened it again to allow fresh air to filter through. A rancid odor came from the pot hanging in the hearth.

"How are you doing Mum?" Connor asked.

I stood in silence, taking in all the filth. I didn't know this woman in front of me clutching her son's arm with a death grip. The Mum I knew would have never let her home—her pride and joy—fall to such shambles.

"I'm sick. My stomach."

"What'd the doctor say?" Connor asked.

"He said I need to watch what I eat, but I can't keep much of anything down."

"Where is Da?" Connor asked, still looking around the room.

"I imagine he's working a few fields over. He comes home late after stopping at the pub for a pint and bowl of stew. Sometimes he doesn't come home at all. I think he passes out at the pub."

"Does Da know you're sick?" Connor continued trying to make sense of the world we used to know.

"He thinks it's in my head. He tells me to rest, but he doesn't understand the pain. I don't talk to him about it anymore."

"Mum, you can't live in this filth." Connor moved toward the kitchen window. "Maybe this is why you're sick. We'll clean it up for you."

"Why don't I take you for a drive," Connor said, looking toward me. I motioned for him to guide her toward the door. "We'll stop in town, buy some food, and when we get home we'll fix a nice dinner. We can come up with a plan for you," Connor said.

I nudged Connor. "We're not staying that long."

"That is a grand idea, I'll clean things up here, when you get back, I'll fix dinner."

I watched as they walked down the cobbled path, through the broken gate. Connor helped her into his car. I took off my coat, hung it by the door, and began to look around to see where to start.

I opened the windows, took the pot from the hearth, and carried it outside, almost throwing up as I poured the contents into the ground. I found towels and soap under the sink. It took all afternoon to scrub the floors and wash the table. I cleaned off the counter and put the dishes away after they dried. I went back over things a second time, to be sure the smell had dissolved in the air.

After I finished I went upstairs, and opened the windows, swept the floors, hung her clothes, and rearranged the clutter on her dresser. I opened the dresser drawers, trying to put things away and bring some order back. Under a sweater, I found a faded brown envelope with Mum and Da's name on it, from Castlepollard, marked a month before my transfer to the Laundries.

I took the yellowed handwritten letter from the envelope.

Dear Mr. and Mrs. Brennan,
We need to make arrangements for her transfer as she is due
any day now. As we told you upon her arrival, the fee is ninety
pounds. We will need the money before she can be released
to your custody. If you are unable, or refuse to pay, she will
be transferred to Dublin to a Magdalene convent, where she
will work off her debt. The work will be strenuous, but she will
be provided social skills, classes and when we feel the time is
right, and when her debt has been paid, she will be released.
Please note though, she can only be released to her father, an
adult male relative, or parish priest. If not, she will remain
until something can be arranged.
We feel we are doing everything in her best interest. She must
learn the consequences of her actions. With due penance and
atonement, I'm sure God will forgive her of her transgressions.
We will notify you of the birth. After that, you may come on
the ninth day, with the money, to collect your daughter, or sign
papers for her transfer. We expect to hear from you soon.
May God be with you.
Reverend Mother
Castlepollard

I guided myself to the bed, still holding the letter. I sat down so I wouldn't fall to the floor. For years, I'd believed she really didn't understand. I was wrong. She had written it all down. She knew. I placed the letter back in the envelope, put it where I found it, and closed the drawer.

I went back downstairs, managed to find nails and a hammer in the barn to repair the gate, I walked to the meadow, picked wildflowers to bring a scent back into the house. In a drawer I found a used white pillar candle, lit it, and placed it on the windowsill. People could sit on both sides of the table, even on the couch.

By early evening, Connor's rental pulled up to the repaired gate. Mum smiled when she entered, looking around the room, at the sink, empty of soiled glasses and plates, and the debris swept from the floors. Connor led her to the couch, pulling the afghan around her shoulders and went back to the car to bring in the groceries.

"Connor, could you go to the pub for a while, maybe look for Da?" Mum said, "I need to talk to Alice? Alone."

I nodded to Connor. "Are you sure, Mum?" Connor asked. "What do I do if I find him?"

"Just tell him Alice is here."

She didn't start the conversation until she heard the engine of his car rumble down the graveled lane.

"Mum, we have nothing to say to each other. Connor told me you were sick, so I came to do what I could. I've cleaned your house, I'll even fix you dinner, but after that, I need to go home."

"You must hate me."

"Mum, it's done."

"Alice, please."

"What?"

"I'm sorry. I'm sorry for everything that happened to you. I believed we were doing the right thing. I was terrified that if you came home that it would be too hard for you, that people would ridicule you."

"Did you tell Connie or Margaret?"

"No. We told them you were at university, having a grand opportunity at the new convent in Dublin." She clutched the afghan weaving her fingers through the yarn.

"So you made up a life for me?"

"I didn't want them to know what you had done."

"What I had done?" I turned away before she could even answer. My anger escalated, but I stifled it.

"I'm sorry," she said. I turned back to her and saw tears roll down her creased cheeks.

"I'm dying," Mum pulled the afghan around her, brushing the strands of gray hair from her face.

"We're all dying."

"No, the doctor told me I have a few more weeks at best, that I should get my life in order. I need to tell your Da, but it never seems the right time."

"You haven't told him?"

"Not yet. When I see him, he's either too tired, or has already fallen asleep."

"Do the girls or John know you are sick?"

"No," she said, looking down. "I didn't want to worry them."

"Mum, it has nothing to do with worry. They need to know. They need to take care of you."

"I hoped you would do that," she said, still not looking up.

"No. I have a family, babies to care for. The girls are closer. They could take turns."

"Alice, I need to lie down, I'm more tired than I expected to be."

I took her arm, and led her up the stairs. I pulled back the covers and placed her in bed, scooping her feet from the floor, and folding the blanket over her.

I went back downstairs and started putting dinner together from the groceries that Connor had brought back. I flipped on the radio sitting on a small table by the door.

From upstairs I heard a loud thump, then silence. When I entered the room, I could barely hear her breathing. I imagined her doctor had been off on how much time she might have left. Her heartbeat weak, I didn't think she'd last till morning. Looking around I realized her Bible had slipped to the floor. It lay open and an aged envelope had fallen out. I picked up the Bible and put the envelope back inside. Just as I closed the pages, I saw my name scrawled across it. I tucked the covers around her, took the envelope and went downstairs. As I entered the kitchen, Connor came through the door.

"Where's Mum?"

"Upstairs, sleeping. I don't think she'll last through the night. What about you? What did you find out?"

"Da's been gone for weeks. At the pub, Mrs. Finley said she's been looking in every now and again, but Mum rarely answers the door."

"How could he leave? What's wrong with him?"

I hid the envelope from Connor. I motioned for him to stir the kettle on the stove while I went back upstairs. Mum laid curled under her covers where I had left her, her hair unwound from its braid, her eyes wide open, staring. The creases of stress that once covered her face were gone. Her skin, cool. No blankets in the world would warm her. I took pennies from the drawer and placed them over her eyes, and wept for what we had lost.

BURYING THE PAST

he cold winter days took a turn for the worse. Storms came from all sides, and because of the weather, Aidan had agreed that, it being just a week before Christmas, it'd be best that I go alone with Connor to Mum's funeral. The girls were finishing up school before the holidays. I saw no reason to introduce Aidan to anyone, or let the girls be handed around like trinkets on display. I had no desire to face the past. Being with Mum on the day she died, being in the house, finding pieces of my history had been enough for me. I would represent my family, but I'd walk out the wrought-iron gate for the last time and be done with it all.

"I changed my mind," Aidan said pouring tea. "I'll be going with you to the service after all. We'll be bringing the girls as well. We are a family. I'll support you as you would me."

"Aidan, it is a long way for them to go in a day, besides they'll have to be pulled from school, and they'll miss their parties."

"There'll be other parties they can go to. I won't be talking about this anymore. We'll drive down with Connor, or meet him there. That's how we'll do it."

I watched him holding his hot mug, not flinching. He had made up his mind. I'd seen it before; when he had me tow the babies to Howth, stand in the rain, so he could tip his hat to his fallen Da, then leave without a word to anyone. I knew when Aidan set his mind to something nothing shook him, so I accepted that we'd all be going.

I dressed the girls in their Sunday best, Aidan in his black suit, and before we went out the door, I took the envelope that had fallen from Mum's Bible, and tucked it safely in my coat pocket. Something told me to take it home; maybe it would be the one thing I could use to confront Da one final time.

Connor and Jenny headed down the street in their car. We followed a few minutes behind, the five of us in silence, with the sun fighting its way through the clouds. It would rain before the end of the day. As a family, we would go to Meadows Glen for the first time and the last time. The girls talked quietly back and forth. I turned to the backseat and looked at the girls, each dressed in their Sunday best, clean and neat. I had done well with my family. I could be proud.

Aidan patted my knee. "You have no reason to hang your head, Alice. You go home walking tall. I'm right there with you." He put his hand back on the wheel and continued to drive.

"I'm grand," I said back to him, half-smiling, half-turning away.

We arrived at the church well before services, and even with the torrential rain, the church overflowed with neighbors and town folk. I recognize many from my childhood, even after being away for so long. They nodded as we walked through the door, whispering to each other, nudging to those in front of them. Some may have known, others unconcerned of my history, just there for something to do.

The blessings were made. The Mass performed as a ritual for the attendees. Mum lay cold inside her coffin, wearing the only dress suitable for a time like this. I looked around, then over at Aidan and finally to my girls. Connor held Francie in his lap and Jenny sat between Rose and Catherine, holding each of their hands. They'd never known my Mum, never know how she could laugh from deep inside, that she had the kindest eyes, told the greatest stories, Legends that I'd passed on to my girls, but they would never hear her voice. For that I ached, more than I realized.

Mourners proceeded to the burial site, wailing over our loss. As expected Da didn't show up in the church, nor did he show up under the grey sky standing behind the trees, taking a drink from the bottle he hid in his coat.

The mourners came through the wrought-iron gate, past the front door, and wept for Marie as if she were their own. Margaret set platters out on the table, but the house was empty within two hours. I had one last thing to settle before leaving Meadows Glenn. I kissed Aidan on the cheek, hugged the girls, and squeezed Connor's hand. A part of me hoped I wouldn't find him, but in my gut, I knew such a coward wouldn't go far.

I walked down the center of the road, peering behind every corner, inside open doors. Nothing. I walked back toward the church, went through the open door. I blessed myself, and lit a small white candle. It would be for her, for everything we lost, for everything we could have been.

From the altar, I looked around. There he sat hunched in the far pew of the empty church, where the altar remained decorated with Mum's flowers. His head dropped in his hands. His torn coat stunk of country life and neglect. Staring at him from the back, he reminded me of a time, years ago when I struggled to get free.

"Da?" He didn't move. "It's Alice." He still didn't move. "Da, you can't ignore me."

"I got nothing to say. Go away, girl."

"No. I won't go."

"Get out of here."

"No, you listen to me."

"You have nothing to say that I want to hear," he said turning away.

"All these years, you blamed me. You allowed them to take me from our home, as if I were nothing. God, I was your daughter." I could feel the tears, hot on my cheeks, I couldn't stop. "But you kept me imprisoned, four years in the Laundries, beaten, forced to work until exhaustion, but I made it." I grabbed hold of the pew so I wouldn't collapse in front of him. "You have grandchildren, you'll never meet. And after today, you'll never be seeing me again."

"Wasn't my fault," he slurred, almost falling over as he tried to look up.

"You don't get to talk now. I was a child. I loved you. I had a home, but you took it from me, telling Mum you wouldn't have a bastard child, or a whore in your house. How could you do such a thing?"

"You want me to say I'm sorry?"

"No, it's too late for that."

"You shamed me girl. You shamed us all."

"I shamed you? You stupid old man."

"You can't be calling me that."

"I can call you anything I want. You disowned me remember?"

"You look no worse for the wear," he said regaining his balance.

I took in the features of his face, and for the first time, I saw him as he was. A broken man. His cap pulled down over his eyes, he wiped his nose with the sleeve of his coat. The dirt from the coat rubbed off on his face, leaving a mark, like a scar. I saw no color to his eyes, just red from the cold, swollen from the drink. His cheeks sallow, and his lips puffy from the sores.

"Is this how you want it to end?"

"I got nothing to say. You're no daughter a mine. Whore is what you are."

He finally said the words out loud, and hearing it made a difference. Standing in front of this man, who refused to acknowledge me, I found the strength to turn away, ready to grant him what he wanted, but I still had more to say.

"We buried Mum today, as I'm sure you know. All her children and grandchildren were there to honor her."

"Leave me be, girl," he shouted, turning away.

He pulled his coat tight and walked out. At that moment, I realized it would no longer be my choice to see him again. I pulled the envelope from my pocket. Here I would find the words that she couldn't say while alive. I held it tight, continuing to stare at it. Hearing an echo, I turned to see if Da had returned, but the doors had closed.

Clutching the envelope, I left the ghosts to their haunts and moved to the church garden. He was nowhere to be seen. I took a seat on a bench and opened the envelope. Inside among the pages, I saw a glint of gold. I pulled out a sliver of a ring, her wedding band. As a child, I would run my finger around the small, engraved wings of the swan that encircled the gold band, the one most valuable item she ever owned. I clutched the ring as I read Mum's last words.

> *Dearest Alice,*
> *Connor has told me in bits and pieces what they did to you, and I imagine, you never wanted to hear from me. If there is any consolation, I know how much I wronged you. I knew it*

the minute I saw you in the car, and could do nothing about it. Your Da didn't see it that way. You have to know, it didn't matter how it happened. You shamed him, and he couldn't bear to live with it.

I loved you as any Mum would love her daughter, but I couldn't defy him. I was the one left to face the years alone with him, to try to keep our family together. I understand if you can't forgive me, I can't forgive myself.

Connor told me you married a fine man, I hope he treats you right. He told me of your babies. First came Rose, though disappointed you didn't name her Marie, but I understood you couldn't have the reminder. Then came Catherine. Connor said she has chestnut waves. And Francie, red ringlets tumbling down around her blushed cheeks. He shared pictures of them. They are beautiful. I imagine I will never see them, but at least you have your girls and won't feel so lost. I hope you never have to make a decision like I did. Be a good wife and mother.

I imagine if you have this letter you have also found the letter from Reverend Mother, and you know the truth. I could only hope you will find a way to forgive me.

Love your babies.

Mum

There were the last words Mum and I would share, written before we came for the last time, written after Da left her. I folded the stained yellow paper and returned it to the envelope. We had nothing more to say. I walked slowly back through Meadows Glen to the house, pulling my coat tightly to block the torrential rain. I pushed open the wrought-iron gate to gather my family, and leave this place forever.

The girls greeted me at the door, anxious to get back to their lives. Connor and Aidan were in the corner, deep in conversation with my sisters and Jenny. The neighbors were gone, the kitchen had been cleaned, everything put away, cleaner than I had ever remembered. Everything was empty of the life I had known.

Francie led her sisters out the gate with Connor and Jenny close behind. Aidan and I followed, closing the door for the last time. As I latched the gate by the roadside, the rusted metal handle fell to pieces, just like everything in the house.

Da died four months later. None of us attended the services. Connie and Margaret took care of the details of the inheritance, and six months later to the day, I received a check in the mail. I slipped it in bottom draw layered between the wool sweaters, never opening it.

A Decision in the Garden

inn had found a way to crawl into the edge of my mind, maybe because it was almost her birthday, or it had been raining for too long and melancholy had settled in, or because not a day went by that I didn't think of her. One morning in an empty house, holding a mug of tea, wondering how, if ever given the chance, I could let Finn know the place she held in my heart. I had done so well, almost twenty-four years. My journals held my secret, but never, not even in a moment of weakness did I spill anything.

While the girls were at school and Aidan on his shift, I slipped past observant Mr. McGuire and took the bus to the gate of Castlepollard. Someone I didn't know answered the door.

"I'm here to see Reverend Mother."

"She is busy, give me your name and I'll have her ring you."

"No, can I wait? I have a letter, if that helps."

"I'm sorry it is not our job to promote communication, besides she won't be seeing anyone today."

The woman closed the door before I had a chance to give her my name. I went back in two days. A different woman tried to turn me away.

"I'm here to see Reverend Mother."

"She's not seeing anyone."

"Leave your name, and she'll ring you back." She closed the door, I had assumed to get paper so I could write my name. The door never opened. I waited, but she didn't return.

I was sure they knew everything, even how to contact her. I hoped they might even call her, talk to her in person, but with the response I received, I doubted that even if they knew, they would do it. I allowed my mind to jump to the next possibility. If they couldn't do anything, maybe there was something I could do.

My hands fumbled with a dangling thread hanging from my skirt, as I sat on the bus heading home, dejected twice in one week, and trying to imagine the alternative. Staring out at strangers on the street, I realized the possibility that she could well be dead. I would not allow that thought into my head. I had to believe that she was alive, living somewhere in the States, happy unaware that someone thought of her every day. The ride was long, stopping at each light, watching people I would never know wondering what secret they sheltered in their lives. I had my own that I had kept so long.

Mr. McGuire was by the gate keeping guard even as the rain poured down.

Bringing in an Outsider

1984

I went to the drawer and pulled out the phone book. I flipped through and found a section in the yellow pages, there on Nevin Street. I jotted everything down on a slip of paper, then put the phone book back in it's place. I walked out into the yard, never making important decisions unless I had time in the garden. Aidan called me silly, but I reminded him it had been his gift to me, so it was mine to do as I pleased. Silly or not, it was in the garden where we talked about babies, my work, and where, when alone, I conjured plans about Finn.

After finishing my tea, I went back into the house, stared at the slip of paper on the counter and decided. I had to trust someone, perhaps it was time to trust a stranger. I had to believe he would help me without judgment.

I went up to the bedroom and opened the drawer where I had hidden the letter that had come from Magaret after Da died. I opened it, took out fifty pounds, then put everything back. I had found a way to put his money to use. He'd roll in his grave thinking I used it on her. You owe her this, I thought.

The clouds moved across the sky, and rain fell on my empty house. Everything was in order. I picked up the receiver, dialed the number, but replaced it before anyone could answer. What if it worked? What if I found her and she wanted nothing to do with me?

I dialed the number again. I didn't hang up.

"I'd like an appointment this afternoon at one o'clock, if possible."
I'd take Sara with me for support. "That would be perfect," I said to the
lady on the telephone. Everything was falling into place.

"My name? Yes, Alice Leary. No, I'm sorry I can't give you my number. I will definitely be there at one this afternoon."

It was just past 10:00, plenty of time to be back and have supper prepared. I rinsed the mug, grabbed my coat and umbrella by the door, and
looked in the mirror. The fresh curls from earlier in the morning had
drooped a bit, but after a touch of lipstick, I felt ready to go.

"How is Emma?" I asked Sara as we sipped tea in the café. I knew her
niece must have had a family of her own.

"Married, she is," Sara said grinning.

"Oh grand."

"What is this all about? You're jumpier than a bumble bee."

"I have a surprise for you. Would you like to go on an adventure with
me this afternoon?"

"Where will you be taking me?"

"I've decided to get help finding Finn."

"I thought you were done with this?"

"I can never be done with this. She's my girl."

"Have you gone bloody mad?"

"No, it's perfect. He is a private investigator, and he can get access to
places I never could. I have the money to pay for it."

"And Aidan?" Sara asked.

"No, he doesn't know. I only want to see if I can learn anything.
Maybe nothing will come of it," I said, finding my own justification for
not telling him.

We gathered our coats and pocketbooks together, without another
word walked arm in arm down the block. In a few minutes I saw the
sign.

"There it is." I said, staring up in awe of it.

MALLOY PRIVATE INVESTIGATOR

"I have an appointment at 1:00," I said.

"Have a seat," the young receptionist said. "Mr. Malloy will see you
in a few minutes."

"Good afternoon Mrs. Leary. How can I help you today?" He was short and balding, with puffy cheeks, a smirky grin, and a stain on his tie. I didn't care what he looked like. His ad said he could find people, anywhere. That was all that concerned me.

"I need to find someone. She may have been sent to the States sometime in the 50s."

"That was a while ago," he said, taking notes on a pad as I began to talk.

"I don't want to meet her or anything and she can't know I'm doing this. I just need to know that she's all right."

"Many just want the security of knowing their loved ones are well."

"I can pay you up front. This is my home address. You can send your findings there," I said, pointing at the address. I handed him a small slip of paper and an envelope with the fifty pounds.

"Ma'am, slow down, one step at a time. Who would it be that you're looking for?" He asked.

"Her birth name was Finnouala Claire Brennan. I believe they adopted her out, but I don't know her adopted name, but she might still be going by the name Finnouala. She was born November 20, 1949, at Castlepollard. I don't know when or if she was adopted. They told me they placed her in a Dublin orphanage for at least three years. She may have even been sent to an industrial school. I'm sorry I don't know much. Is that enough?"

"I'd be happy to help you," he said, handing back the envelope, "I don't require a full payment, just a retainer until I find her, then you come back in. We go over everything. If you're satisfied, you pay the balance. I charge fifty pounds for a complete job, but every client is different. If I can't find anything, I usually just keep the retainer, ten pounds. Before we begin, let me ask you, what have you done to find her?"

"I've gone back to Castlepollard repeatedly, but they've refused to talk to me about her. They told me I had no right to this information, because I had signed a paper releasing all my rights. I thought that maybe if they received a letter from you, they might feel a sense of urgency and give you the information they wouldn't give me. Shouldn't there be records available there for you?"

"I can start with the government records and see what I find. It may take a few weeks. I think I'll make a visit first, then follow-up with a letter. I'll need your number." Though he talked to himself, I could hear the words and a plan forming in his mind.

I picked the envelope off the desk and handed it back to him. "It's all here, but you can't call me. That wouldn't be a good idea."

"Ma'am I need to have a way to get a hold of you."

"You can call me." Sara spoke up without looking at me. "It's 860-715700."

"I will do everything I can to find her, but you do know that I may come back empty-handed. The church doesn't like to discuss international adoptions. But like I said, every client is different. Thank you, Mrs. Leary. I will call in about three weeks."

"Thank you, Mr. Malloy."

We shook hands. I placed the envelope back on the table, and Mr. Malloy led us to the door. As we passed the front desk, the receptionist didn't bother to look up from her magazine.

"Are you all right?" Sara asked, reaching for my hand as we walked out the door.

"Yes, I'm fine. Thank you for this. I don't think I could've done it alone."

"I'm sorry you haven't been able to tell Aidan yet."

"I told him some. I told him about the attack."

"And if you find her, will you tell him?"

"I don't know. It has been so long. Maybe I won't have to."

"I don't understand. He loves you. Why can't you trust him?" she said squeezing my hand.

We had a second cup of tea, while the rains showed no signs of letting up. We stayed much longer than I expected, lost in the past and present, running together like the rain gathering in the gutters and flowing down the street. By the time I caught the bus home and passed Mr. McGuire's house, the rain had stopped.

*   *   *

In three weeks, almost to the hour, from sitting in Mr. Malloy's office, the doorbell rang. Looking out, I watched as his head drooped down, an envelope in his hand, Sara stood next to him on the doorstep.

"Mrs. Leary," he said, as I opened the door.

"Mr. Malloy? Sara? I don't understand."

"I didn't feel right having this news delivered by post. So I called Sara's number," he said motioning to her. "I need to tell you what I found in person," he said fidgeting with the envelope. Sara agreed to meet me at the bus station in town, then she brought me here. So here we are."

"It's bad news isn't it?"

"I wish it could have been different. May we come in?" he asked.

"Yes, of course." He took a seat, and Sara sat down next to me. He opened the envelope clenched in his hand, and spread the contents on the glass coffee table.

"I did my best to learn what I could about your daughter. I went through all legal records I had access to. I talked with the Reverend Mother at the Home. Reverend Mother is… Well, I found her to be interesting. She said she never spoke to you about the child, nor did you ever visit."

"Why would she say that?" I asked in confusion.

"Reverend Mother had little memory of you, but she did bring out a folder. She wouldn't allow me to see it, but pulled out a couple of letters. The first had your signature on it. She said a release form was required after all births. The second, she said came from the adoptive family, showing the details of…"

"What? The adoptive family wrote to her at Castlepollard?"

"Yes, she had letters in the file signed by the adoptive mother. Reverend Mother said the families often sent donations to the orphanages."

"What were the details of the letters?" I held tight to Sara's hand, knowing if he had come all this way, it would not be good.

"I'm sorry. From the information I received from Reverend Mother, your daughter has passed."

"Passed? She's dead? Did you see a death certificate? There has to be a death certificate doesn't there?" I looked over at Sara squeezing her hand even tighter.

"Did you do any other research?" Sara asked, speaking up for me, since I had lost the words.

"Yes. I did find records that your daughter arrived in Oregon in 1954, where she remained her entire life. She graduated from college, married, and had her children there."

"She had children?"

"Yes," he said, his face softened around the creases of his mouth.

"Did you find a death record?"

"No. I searched through all Oregon and Washington death certificates from 1960, until present. Nothing. I even searched in Canada. Mrs. Leary, there is no record of your daughter's death."

"Then maybe…"

"With all due respect, Alice, may I call you Alice?"

"Of course."

"With all due respect, I don't understand why that woman would lie to me, especially about a death. I think your daughter might well be alive, but you also must consider in this one instance, the Reverend Mother may have been telling the truth."

I stood up from the couch and walked to the window. His words tumbled around in my head, even as he continued to ask if I believed she would lie about such a thing. Looking out, I saw Mr. McGuire sweeping his walk. He didn't look to the window. Could I answer this question? There was no doubt she had lied.

I spun around, "Yes, I believe she is lying. This woman has lied about everything to everyone I know. I have to believe she's lying now."

"Alice, I wrote down everything I found and what she told me. I even found pictures."

"Pictures? Of who?"

"Your daughter? They're in the envelope."

"Thank you, Mr. Malloy. I appreciate you coming here, and everything you've done, but I'm afraid I must excuse myself."

"I understand, this must be difficult for you. I'll leave everything here for you. You can take your time going through it."

"Thank you so much."

"Mrs. Leary, I left your money in the envelope. I can't take your money for this."

Coming back to the couch, "Oh no, Mr. Malloy, you did everything I asked you to do. You keep that money. You have been very helpful. "

"I'll take the ten pounds for the retainer, the rest is yours, I didn't earn it."

"Whatever you think is right, Mr. Malloy."

Mr. Malloy found his way to the door. I heard his steps down the sidewalk to the gate. I went back to the sofa, where Sara sat.

"Alice, I'm sorry. He didn't tell me what the news was, but implied that it was bad. I didn't think you should be reading about it, so I offered to bring him here."

"You did the right thing," I said gathering up the papers as I sat down on the couch next to Sara.

"I can go if you'd like to be alone."

"No, I'd like you to see the pictures. He did say there were pictures didn't he?"

"Yes. Do you have time? When is Aidan coming home?"

I looked up at the clock, realizing I had plenty of time, before my life would start back up again. On Fridays, Aidan didn't come home until after nine, and the girls always shopped with their friends after school on Friday. I picked up the pictures, looking at them one by one: a passport photo, naturalization copies from government records, a high school picture, and a wedding picture from a local paper. There in black and white, sliver eyes, olive complexion, with hair much darker than mine had ever been. I realize I wouldn't have recognized her had we passed on the street. Here was her life, lying out in front of me, summed up with a list of dates:

```
Birth Name: Finnouala Claire Brennan
Adoptive Name: Claire Grace Fischer
DOB: 20-11-49
Transported to Oregon September 1953
Graduated Westwood College December 1973
Married Name: Claire Hamilton
Date of Marriage: April 4, 1973
Daughter born 4-4-78 Devon Hamilton
Son born 23-7-79 Adam Hamilton
DOD: 15-1-84 St. Patrick's Hospital, complications from surgery.
```

The list told me everything, but it told me nothing. The print blurred. I blinked. Blinked again, hoping the words would change. I would never believe she could be dead. Reverend Mother had lied. I would find some way to prove it. I gathered the papers, knowing everything would have to be hidden away before the girls returned home.

"Alice, I'm going to go, you need some time before everyone comes home."

"Thank you Sara." I reached my arms out to her. She pulled me close.

"You'll find the truth. You will. I know it."

I led Sara to the door, kissed her once again. I took my secret upstairs to a drawer in the dresser where Aidan would have no access. I placed the second envelope with the pictures on top of the first, with the ring and documents. Both lying beneath my red cashmere sweater, I straightened the wrinkles, closed the drawer, and after a deep sigh, went back to my life, downstairs.

I took the bottle from the cupboard that Aidan didn't think I knew about. I poured the rich brown liquid into the glass, and walked out into my garden. I stood alone in the dark afternoon with my half-filled glass and took a sip.

The news of Finn swirled in my head. My breath caught hold in my throat. The ache came from so deep inside, I gripped my stomach. The glass slipped from my hand and my knees buckled. I slumped to the wet grass.

I was barely aware of the rain, or the thunder as it ripped the clouds apart. I had always known that one day I might lose one of my children, but I never expected to lose one twice. Suddenly I felt arms around my shoulders.

"Mum, what are you doing out here?" Catherine called out.

She pulled me up, leading me back to the house, pulling wet strands of hair from my face. In a daze, I saw the shock in Francie and Rose as they stared from the doorway.

"What happened out there?" Rose asked, tossing the sweater to the floor.

"I don't know. I'm fine now. I just went down."

The girls forced me into a warm bath. Stepping into the tub, I let my body sink down, with the pictures of Finn floating around in my head. I submerged myself in the steam and closed my eyes. I could smell the lavender oil Francie poured in as the water filled to the top.

I knew the girls were downstairs waiting, and I would have to have an explanation. I had none. I'd find a lie to tell, to appease them and satisfy Aidan, who I knew they would tell the minute he walked in the door. Migraines had plagued me since Francie's birth and often left me stricken to my bed in the dark.

After my bath, I slipped on my robe, and crawled into a peaceful silence. I couldn't face going back downstairs. In a few moments, under the covers, I heard their footsteps on the stairway. There they stood, my girls in the doorway, Rose holding a tray of tea and toast. Francie moving over to fluff the pillows, helping me sit up.

"Are you all right?" Catherine asked.

"Yes, I just had a spell with a migraine, and it dropped me to my knees."

"Okay, Mum we're going to let you rest. We'll make sandwiches for dinner. Here, have some tea."

I drank the tea and listened as the girls did their best to make me comfortable, finally leaving me to sleep. With the pictures tucked safely away, I knew there would be questions to answer and explanations to make, but for now, this moment, I would forget all that. I let sleep overtake me.

*　　*　　*

I rose early the next day, before Aidan, anxious to get things in order. The girls acted no different than any other morning, just seemed to be watching me a little closer.

"Rose, did you and your sisters tell your Da about yesterday?"

"No, we decided it was yours to tell, but we are worried about you."

"Don't be. I'm grand. Look at me now. Headache is gone, I'm ready to go."

I felt relieved that the girls had provided some discretion in not telling the events of the day before. I would explain the headache to Aidan later, for now I had a lot on my mind, things to do. After Aidan left for work, I rang Claire, asking her to meet me at our usual place at eleven. I called work; informing them I wouldn't be in for my usual volunteering, as I wasn't feeling well. As much as I hated migraines, they did come in for a well-needed excuse.

I went upstairs after cleaning the kitchen. I opened the dresser drawer, pulling out my red cashmere sweater. I slipped it over my head, and took a brush to my hair. I grabbed my handbag from the dresser, and hurried downstairs. I left the house at ten, greeted Frank, once again guarding the neighborhood.

"Morning Frank."

"Good day, Alice."

"No umbrella this morning?"

"No, ma'am looks to be a nice day."

"Well, enjoy your day."

 "You have a nice one, too, Alice. Give Aidan my best."

"Will do, see you later, Frank ."

I found Claire already seated at the café when I walked up. She rushed to greet me.

I reached out for her. "So glad you made it this week. I need to talk about something."

"Come on now, girl. Sit, tell me all about it."

"Okay, where do I start?"

"How about at the beginning?"

"Last month Sara and I went to meet with a private investigator. I needed to see if I could learn anything about Finn.

"What did he find?"

"Finn. She's gone. Dead. He had papers that said she died due to complications in surgery." Claire's face went white. She reached out for my hand, but unconsciously, I pulled it back.

"Did he have a death certificate?"

"No, but he searched for one. He spent weeks going through Oregon and Washington files."

"Oregon? Washington?"

"Yes, Reverend Mother told him that was where she had been sent. He went back to the Home and Reverend Mother flashed a document declaring that she had died from some surgical complications."

"I don't know what to say," Claire said.

"What is there to say? If I believe him, she's gone." I took hold of the napkin, twisting it tight, hoping to hold in the sadness.

"Alice, why did you do this? I thought you were done with it."

"I wanted to be done. I tried, I really did. After I delivered each of my girls, I did let go, but when the milestones came up, she was always there. She haunted me then, she haunts me still. I had to do something. I paid him to search for her. I thought he'd come back empty handed, but he didn't."

The waitress Claire had waived away, returned with two cups of tea and a plateful of tiny sandwiches. As the waitress left the table, Claire took hold of her arm, and patted her hand. I looked up at her and nodded. She returned the acknowledgement, leaving us alone in the corner.

"How do you know where he got everything? Maybe it's a lie. You can't take one man's word for something so important, especially if the words came from Reverend Mother."

"Claire, he has no reason to lie. He did this for money. It wasn't something personal to him. He went back to the Home, He talked to Reverend Mother."

"No. She is not there anymore. I meant to ring you, she was transferred last year. Her health has declined quickly in the last few months so they transferred her to a convent in Dublin. She no longer has anything to be with the babies or adoptions or anything. Sr. Helen took over her spot."

"Do you think he met with Sr. Helen, thinking she was Reverend Mother?"

"She is. She took the title the day they transferred Reverend Mother."

"So, she told the truth about not meeting with me. I never did meet with Sr. Helen, but Reverend Mother never came to the door either. A new sister greeted me, one I had never seen."

"You know that Sr. Helen would lie. Did anyone show him a death certificate?"

"No, he couldn't find one."

"That being said, there is a chance that Finn is not dead."

"So, what can I do?"

"Go to the convent in Dublin, where she is living. Maybe they transferred the old records? There would be no use for them at Castlepollard. I'll go with you. I'd love to see the old bat again, let her know what I thought of her treatment."

While Claire took bites of the sandwiches, I watched, trying to process what she suggested.

"He gave me pictures of her, her married name, where she went to school. I know more than I ever thought I would . . . she has children. She goes by the name Claire. I thought you would want to know that."

"Oh, my." Claire placed her sandwich back on the plate, took a sip of tea, and brushed her hair away.

"Now that I know about her, it is hard to imagine that she could be gone. That I was too late."

"You can't believe that. I've already told you. You need to confront that bitch. You need to learn the truth, or it is going to eat you up inside."

"Why should I go see her? If I go to see her, she'll lie to me again, just like you said."

There was a long pause. Claire looked up. "Did you tell Aidan?"

"No. Years ago, I told him of the attack, but nothing more."

"No. I meant did you tell him about the private investigator?"

"No. How could I do that if I never told him about Finn and the Home?"

"Are you going to tell him?"

"I can't. God, Claire, I have wanted to every day, but when a moment presents itself, I fall silent. I know he loves me, but telling him about her, what happened, all the shame of the Laundries. I can't do that."

"Don't you think this might be the time? Don't you think you've hung on to it long enough?"

"What if it's too much for him? The girls, they would never forgive me."

"You have to know he loves you. I might not have my own children, but if my Mum came to me with this secret, I'd find a way to forgive her. In fact, I'd love her even more."

"I'm scared." The young waitress returned to our table with a fresh pot of tea, setting it down, without a word.

"We all have things that scare us, but Alice, hasn't this haunted you long enough? It's a perfect time to tell. God you have paid your dues. You need to be free of this."

"You know what, Claire? I can't talk about this any longer. I have to get home. I know you're right about everything, but I'm not thinking about Aidan now, or even how he'd feel. I'm thinking about Finn. She's my daughter, and no matter what they say, they took her from me."

"You're running away and it's tearing you apart."

"I'm not running from anything. I just don't think this has anything to do with Aidan. If she is gone, why tell him at all?"

"Okay, let's say you're right. First things first. You need to find out what happened to her. Look, I'll help you find out if she really is ...." She paused.

"It's okay, you can say it."

"Find out first, if she is gone. If she is, you can deal with that. You don't have to tell anyone, but if she's not, we'll do what needs to be done. You never know, she might be alive, looking for you."

"You don't know that."

"But we do know the Sisters lie."

"Thank you."

"For what?"

"For being a friend over all these years. I couldn't have done this without you and Sara."

"Does Sara know?"

"Yes, she went with me to the private investigator's office. She brought him to the house with the news. She has been a part of this every step of the way."

"So what will you do next?"

"You're going to ring me the address of the convent where Reverend Mother is. We're going to make a visit. I have to go," I said, gathering my coat and handbag.

I motioned for the waitress to bring our check. She laid it on the table, smiling as she turned away. I reached for it, but Claire grabbed it out of my hand.

"This one is on me," she said. She turned it over, read it, and handed it to me. "You have to see this."

I read it and before I even realized, tears came down. The waitress had written across the bill "paid."

I stood and walked inside the café. I found her at the counter.

"You didn't have to do that," I said, reaching for my pocketbook.

"Yes ma'am, I did. I'd do it again. I'm sorry but I overheard your conversation. I hope it works out for you. Ma'am, if you were my Mum, there'd be nothing to forgive." I reached over hugging this stranger.

I met Claire outside, where we walked arm in arm for the next few blocks. We had nothing left to say, at least about this, so I asked about her life and we rambled on in easy conversation.

"Alice," Claire said, reaching for her bus token. "I'll call in a few days." I reached for Claire, and she held me tight, whispering in my ear.

"We'll find a way to work this out. We'll find Finn."

Spring Comes to the Garden

pring came to the Dublin countryside, filling the rain-soaked fields with flowers galore. The city baskets that hung from the pillars overflowed in rainbow colors. It was time for the Leary garden to bloom, as well. My garden had become a sacred ground for me, but it needed finishing touches.

As I locked the door, I waved to Mr. McGuire, as he swept his walkway. He could never be mistaken for a gardener. He moved leaves around while watching the neighbors' homes when they went on holiday. He swept the walkway, watered flowers and weeds alike, always on vigilance. Mr. McGuire knew more about us than we knew about ourselves, but we felt safe. No one came down our lane who could not be identified.

"Morning, Frank."

"Morning, Mrs. Leary."

"Nice day," I said watching as he swept the leaves from the walk.

"Might be a bit of rain later."

"Well, guess I'd better hurry on now."

I was anxious to put my plan into place. The backyard needed some color. I needed a secret hiding place. From the movement of the clouds, it looked as if Mr. McGuire would be right about the rain, so I knew I had to hurry to be done in time. The nursery, a few blocks down from the house doubled as the corner grocery.

"Morning, Mrs. Leary, out before the rain comes?"

"It would seem so," I said, stepping through the doorway.

Mr. Scully had owned the nursery for as long as I could remember, but in the last year his son had taken over, but that didn't prevent Mr. Scully from standing at the entrance every morning, greeting everyone who came through.

"Can I help you find anything?"

"Yes, I'm looking for some trailing roses? Yellow or white."

"Just got them in. All ready to be planted. Over in the corner," he said, pointing to the mass of multi-colored blooms bunched together like bouquets.

I picked the two white ones with the most buds. As I began to pay for my purchase, I eyed some interesting ceramic statues under a broken wooden shelf. Pointing to them, I motioned.

"How much?" I asked.

"They're on sale, if you're interested," he said.

There were the usual Saints, St. Patrick, St. Francis, replicas found in almost any garden or rectory walkway. Behind the statues stood a ceramic form, two white swans entwined, like the family I had seen, so long ago, driving over the Liffy River to the Laundries. They were coated in dirt, but a good scrubbing would freshen them up, make them look new.

"Is this one for sale?" I asked, reaching for the ceramic figurine.

"Had that a long time, ma'am. You interested in buying it?"

"I might be, but it looks a bit weathered. What will it cost to take off your hands?"

"You know ma'am, that's the last one I have of that one. Let me see," he said. "You know you'd be doing me a favor. Not too many people wanting dirty swan statues these days."

"Well, I think it's beautiful, if you don't mind I'd like to buy it."

"Since you're buying the rose bushes, I'll throw the figurine in. If you can wait a few minutes, I'll wash it up for you. Will probably look much better than it does now."

"Thank you," I said.

I waited while he took the figurine back behind the shed. In a few minutes he emerged, holding it up for me to see.

"How is that?" he asked.

"It's perfect." I watched him wrap the swans in plain brown paper.

He tucked the wrapped swan figurine in a bag, gathered the two rose bushes together, placing them in my arms. I walked the six blocks home with purpose and intent, basking in the bright sun that seeped through the clouds. As I rounded the corner, Frank still held the broom, moving the leaves around like puzzle pieces.

"Find what you were looking for?"

"I sure did. Doing some planting this morning, Frank. Roses will be nice this time of year, you know, never die, not even in the cold. See you later." I hurried past him, excited with the task at hand.

I went through the side gate, heading straight for the backyard, not even bothering to step into the house. Along with my pocketbook, I set my cherished purchases on the wood table and retrieved the shovel from the shed. The ground was wet, so it was no task to dig two side-by-side holes for the bushes. I planned to place the roses where they could be seen from every window of the house that looked out on the backyard.

I placed the plants in the holes to be sure the holes were big enough but I didn't bury them, not yet. Instead, I went back to the patio, slipped off my shoes at the entry, and stepped into the house. I went up the stairs and pulled out the bottom dresser drawer, and retrieved the manila envelopes from under my cashmere sweater. I took the smaller envelope that held what was left of Da's money, opened the flap, flipping through the bills inside. I knew there'd be enough to make some repairs to the house, and I had the right to the money, but I wanted nothing to do with it, since Mr. Malloy gave me back all but ten pounds. I'd bury it as if I'd never had it. I didn't want pieces of him looking back at me in the privacy of my home. If I ever needed the money, I could always dig it up.

I opened the other envelope, examining the three pictures. I knew if I risked keeping them in the drawer for too much longer, Aidan or the girls would find them. I flipped through them, taking the time to stare at each, so I would never forget them in my memory. I put the pictures back into the larger of the two envelopes. Finally, I went to the jewelry box and took Mum's swan ring, putting it in with the pictures. I'd bury her too.

I walked back down the stairs, through my empty house into the kitchen. I opened the drawer and pulled out plastic wrap. I cut off two pieces. First, I wrapped the money up tight. After that, I took the ring and the papers from Mr. Malloy, wrapped them in the second sheet, and returned to the patio. Before securing the rose bushes in their new homes, I raised each bush from the hole, placed the wrapped envelope in its respective hole, packing it down in the cold wet dirt. I patted down the black soil around the new bushes, standing back, admiring my work. I took the ceramic swans, and placed them directly under the white blooms. There it would be for her, always for her, Finnouala Claire Brennan.

After putting everything back into the tool shed, I went inside to the sink and washed my hands, overjoyed with my accomplishment. As I entered the living room, the phone rang, but I didn't answer it. I didn't want anything to spoil my moment. In the living room, I looked out the front window. Frank still puttering about in his yard. Every now and again he looked up to the window and I would offer a wave, he would smile and return to his duties.

In the dining room, looking through the picture window onto the backyard, I admired my handiwork. There they were, white roses draping the entwined swans. I went upstairs to look through the bedroom windows, and there they were, the same swaying white roses in the breeze encircling the swans.

From each window, the swans slept in my garden. They were home. I doubted anyone would notice the changes, unless I pointed them out. I gazed on it, my own swan garden, secrets safely buried. Forever.

A Decision from the Past

or months, Francie and I could not have a civil word. We argued over everything, her grades, attendance, her new boyfriend, even the clothes she wore when not in her uniform. Her tardiness had not gone unnoticed. She'd been coming home past midnight despite her father's warnings.

Sitting at the dining table, with a cigarette in one hand and a drink in front of me, I stared at the front door, like waiting for my husband to explain his absence. However, this had nothing to do with my husband, instead, my sixteen-year-old daughter, had decided life should be lived by her own rules. Just past eleven, Aidan had retired because of an early shift in the morning. For the fifth night in a row, she had slipped in just past midnight.

"Where have you been?" I heard myself shouting. "You should have been home at eight."

"Geeze Mum, calm down. I stayed at Connie's. We're studying for that big exam on Thursday. You want me to get good grades don't you?"

"No, you weren't at Connie's," I said mimicking her whine. "Not to-night nor last night, or the night before. I rang her Mum and you weren't there."

"It's not a big deal."

"Yes, it is, a big deal. Where were you?" I watched as Francie put her books on the table and turned toward me, taking a deep breath.

"OK, fine. I spent the evening with Collin. Now you know. Does that make you happy?"

"Francie, can't you at least let us know where you are?"

"Because, one, Da hates Collin. Besides, we weren't doing anything wrong. We were having fun. What's wrong with that?"

"That is not the point."

"So what is the point in all this?"

She was right. I'd been protecting her every way I knew how, telling Aidan she was everywhere but where I knew her to be. I never worried about the other girls, Rose never stayed out past dark, instead, bringing her friends home with her. Catherine never left the house until she moved out to attend university. But Francie? She never worried about a thing, believed everything would work itself out. She did what she wanted, then waited with glee for the hatchet to fall.

"Why are you doing this?" I pleaded. "You know how you're Da feels about you."

"No, Mum, I don't. We never talk about me. We talk about what I'm going to do, where I'll go to university. He doesn't know how to ask about me."

"He worries about you." Even as the words came out, I knew she spoke the truth. Though a tender and compassionate husband, he knew nothing about his girls. He left them in my charge because he couldn't handle the emotions of teenage girls.

"Mum, there's nothing to worry about."

"I worry about everything, don't brush it off. You're my daughter."

*   *   *

A few weeks later our family had the opportunity for all of us to be at the same dining table. Francie didn't have much to say during dinner that night. Sitting at the table, she stared over at her father, then at me as she moved her potatoes around the plate.

"You all right, girl?" I asked, watching her fidget in her chair.

"I'm good, Mum. Just a lot on my mind."

"I'm surprised you're even here for dinner," Aidan said, scooping slices of roast into his plate.

"Well, matter of fact, I need to talk to you and Da."

Aidan pulled off his glasses, set his fork on the table and looked over at his youngest daughter, "Frances, is there a problem we need to know about? School?"

"No, school is fine."

"Well, if not school, what is it? Are you sick?"

"I'm fine Da," she said looking back at her dinner plate. "It's of a personal nature. You and Mum have to promise you'll let me explain everything before you get all crazy. You have to let me just say it. Will you promise that?"

Aidan and I looked at each other.

"I'll not be promising you anything." Aidan said, picking up his fork.

"Come on now," I said, reaching over, touching his hand.

"Get on with it, girl."

"It's about Collin."

"Your boyfriend, right?" Aidan asked

"Yes, well no, it's not about him exactly."

"He seems to be a fine enough lad. Did you come here to tell us you want to get married?" Aidan almost chuckled as the words came out.

"I mean it's more about the two of us," she said, taking a sip of tea.

"So … what about the two of you?" Aidan sounded perturbed.

"Collin and I are going to have a baby."

"What? What did you say?"

"No, it's a good thing. He loves me and wants to marry me, just not right now."

"You'll not be getting married." Aidan said, throwing his fork down on the table. "You're a child."

"We will, just not right now. He loves me. He has a job and if you and Mum could help us out for a while, we could make it."

"No daughter of mine will have a bastard child."

Francie stared at her father in shock. He had called her child a bastard. She looked over at me, as if I should say something. He reached for her arm, but she pulled it away.

"They have homes to go to. After delivery, you'll sign the baby over to the convent."

"No, I won't. This is our child. We will decide. You can't just make a decision like that. You can't take our baby from us."

"Mum, say something,"

"Why isn't he here with you?" Aidan asked.

"He's waiting for me to call. I told him I needed to do this alone."

"If this is so important to him, he should be here."

"It was my decision to do it this way."

He got up from the table, pushed the chair back, and leaned into her.

"Well young lady, these are not your decisions to make. You're still a child, so we'll be deciding whether we send you to a home, or give the baby up for adoption."

"You can't do that," Francie said. Her face red, her eyes tearing up, but she held back the tears.

"If he still loves you after all is said and done, when you turn eighteen you can marry him." Aidan sat back down, satisfied, believing he'd made a decision, it was over.

"No, Da, it is my choice. It's our choice."

"I forbid it. This conversation is over."

"No. Aidan it is not over," I said. "We're not sending her away. If they want to keep their baby they will, and we will help in every way we can. Now it's said and done," I said, getting up and taking the plates from the table.

"Are you out of your mind?"

I didn't know whether Aidan was more upset by the pregnancy or my reaction.

"No, I'm not. I am her mother. I will not let that happen. She will stay here. We will help her, as she decides what is best for her and the baby, but she's right, it is her decision. We'll take it one step at a time, but right now, we need to get her to Dr. O'Hara."

"I've already been," Francie said, bringing her plate to the sink. "I'm healthy and the baby is fine. Oh Mum, thank you so much." She came over and wrapped her arms around me. I could feel her body meld with mine. I whispered to her.

"You will never lose this child, I will see to that."

Aidan watched as we embraced, then left the room. He went into the living room and I could hear the rattle of the paper. I didn't know whether it was anger or disgust, but if it was toward me, I was fine with it.

"Mum, what just happened?"

"I think it's pretty simple. You announced you're pregnant, and I said that we're supporting you, whatever decision you and Collin make. That's what happened."

She hugged me again. "Go on, call Collin."

"Mum, can I ask, why did you do that? I expected it from him, but to be quite honest, I expected you to go along with whatever he said."

"I guess you don't know your Mum as well as you thought. Go on now."

I turned off the lights and moved into the living room where Aidan hid behind his paper. I sat and grabbed the first magazine off the table. I stared at it, every now and then, peeking over the top to see what he was doing.

"Do you want to watch the news?" I asked.

"No," he said, continuing to read the paper.

"Aidan I know you're upset, but how could we let our grandbaby be taken away?"

"How could you do that?" Aidan said, this time letting the paper fall to the floor.

"What exactly did I do?"

"Defy me in front of her."

"Is that what you think I did? Aidan, I didn't defy you. We can't make our daughter give up her child. It is her choice to make. I've seen it happen before. I won't let it happen to Francie."

"You've seen it before? Who?"

"It doesn't matter. I'm not losing my daughter or grandchild. We will do whatever she needs."

He looked away from me, picking up the pages of the scattered paper. I left the living room and walked out into the yard. I took a seat on the bench in the garden.

Air came up through my chest and my whole body trembled. Francie asked where it came from, and I couldn't answer her. I knew it had come from Finn. Losing her gave me a strength I never realized I had. I needed to defend my own. The evening chill filled the air and calmed my tremors. Aidan came through the double doors and sat next to me.

"Why would you do that in front of her?"

"Are you still going on about that?" I said, not looking at him.

"There was a time you would never have done that, yet you do it now, without even a second thought."

"No. You're wrong. A million second thoughts ran through my head, but by everything Holy, I won't lose a daughter again, and I won't let Francie have regrets."

"But they aren't married."

"I don't care if she was raped…"

"Wait a minute, what are you saying? Daughter? Again? Raped?"

"I didn't mean that. I just meant the circumstance should not make any difference. She's our daughter and her child belongs to us as well."

"If I didn't know better, I would say this has nothing to do with Francie."

I should have told him right then, with no hesitation. I wanted to tell him that my daughter had been taken from me. I turned to him, but remained silent. He moved closer on the bench, and I took hold of his hand.

"Aidan, I understand your feelings. There was a time that this would have brought shame, and she would have been sent away, but not anymore. What if this happened to us? What if someone tried to take our daughters from us?"

It took a few minutes before Aidan even moved, then he turned, still holding my hand. "I'll have Francie invite Collin to the house and we'll make plans."

"Aidan?"

"Yes?"

"Thank you."

"It wasn't me. Had you not spoken up, she'd have been gone by the end of the week. You saved our daughter from me."

"No, our daughter saved us."

He looked at me, and I knew he had no idea what I was saying, but it didn't matter, I'd been clear.

"Are you coming in?"

"I'll be there in a few minutes. You go on ahead." I needed to understand what it meant to me. I stared at the swans nuzzled around the white roses. They trailed across the garden, symbols of purity.

Reality C⊕mes Calling

1990

he white roses bloomed through the seasons and overtook the garden. The cold months and the rain had worn the figurine down, but the swans still stood regal and beautiful to behold. The envelopes remained hidden beneath their guardians. I had decided for whatever reason I'd let go of Finn, for a while. I still met with Claire and Sara, and we talked about everything but what was foremost on our minds. I hadn't realized the while, had taken five years.

The message had come night before last, while Aidan was with Collin and Frank McGuire at the pub. I played it over and over, knowing it would eventually be erased.

> Alice,
> This is Sister Gabriel, from St. Patrick's Guild. This is a delicate matter, so I will try to be as brief as possible. I received a call from a woman named Claire Hamilton. She says her birth name is Finnouala Claire Brennan. She would like to meet with you. She believes you are her birth mother. From the information she gives, we thought it best to call before she attempts to locate you on her own. You may reach me at St. Patrick's Guild in Dublin. My number is 013-440897.

Each time I listened to the message, I wondered how I could have let it go. Could it be? Could Claire have been right? Mr. Malloy had papers saying she had died, but when I played the tape, Sr. Gabriel said she was alive. She had been looking for me, as I her, but could I see her now? Would this be the right time? Could I let her ring my house, let the girls answer the phone? Though I knew I could never let that happen the idea of her danced in my head, the fantasy from all those years passed.

I rang Sr. Gabriel's number and waited. There was the voice, the same one on the message.

"Sister, this is Alice Leary, you called me earlier about Claire Hamilton. I wondered if you might give me an address where I could send her a post."

After a long pause, I could hear the irritation in her voice.

"I'm not allowed to give it to you. You can send one to the Guild. If she requests it, we can forward it to her," she said in short crisp sentences.

"Thank you I will. Can I drop it off in a day or too?"

"Of course. Good day Mrs. Leary."

I took the stationary from the drawer and placed it on Aidan's desk. I went into the kitchen, and poured a glass of wine.

I settled in and wrote the words I never thought I would.

Dear Claire Hamilton,
I just received a call from Sister Gabriel at St. Patrick's Guild.
I understand you contacted her in hopes of finding your Mum.
She tells me you think I am who you are looking for?
I lost my daughter years ago at Castlepollard and, based on your dates, you would both be the same age. It broke me into so many pieces when I lost her, I couldn't find myself. I searched for her, but I lost her again. I was told she had died. So from what I learned years ago, you can't possibly be her. I wish you well and may you someday find the peace you so desperately seek. I ask that you not try to contact me. My family knows nothing of this, and I wouldn't want them to be harmed in any way. I am sure you can understand. My best to you.
Sincerely,
Alice Leary

I almost posted the letter to Sister Gabriel on the same day so I wouldn't change my mind, but I couldn't. Too much time had passed. What I once thought I wanted had been buried long ago. I couldn't be pulled back in. I buried the letter in my journal and deleted the call so no one could ever know.

Rose came over randomly, often pushing the button when she saw the blinking light. Aidan avoided the phone, so I was not so worried about him, but stranger things could happen. It was gone; no one would know about it.

I thought of calling Sara or Claire, but I no longer felt the need to run to them. Sara was getting older, it was difficult for her to come to the city, and hearing a conversation on the phone was hard for her. Claire had left Castlepollard and gotten a part-time job as a nurse and adopted an older girl. She was busy with the workings of being a mother. I didn't want to bother her if I could help it. We often met in the city, but the conversation was filled with her new life.

Rose was coming by to drop the girls off for the day. I would try to convince her to let them spend the night. I missed the sounds of babies in the house. I looked out the window, but it was not Rose, instead, a tall Sister in a black habit stood at the step. I opened the door.

"Is this Alice Brennan?" She asked.

"I'm sorry, and you are?"

"I'm Sister Gabriel, from St. Patrick's. May I come in? It looks a bit odd for me to be standing on your step."

"Yes, of course." She walked in, setting her briefcase next to the couch. "I thought it would be best to talk to you in person."

"What could you need to talk to me about?" I asked.

"Are you her mother?"

"Sister, all due respect, it is a private matter."

"Do you think I could have some tea?"

"My daughter is due here any moment. I don't think you should be here when she comes."

"In the past two years I have received four letters from this woman. I went through the records at St. Patrick's. You are her mother. She was born November 1949, at Castlepollard. She says her birth name is Finnouala Claire Brennan. Her records show they dismissed her from St. Patrick's Orphanage in fall of 1954. Her American family continued to send donations but in 1961, everything stopped. No word from them since." She recited her information. as if she were reading a litany, knowing it by heart.

"Sister, did you receive a letter mentioning her death?"

"No. As I said all contact from her family stopped back in '61."

"Would the Reverend Mother at Castlepollard have any contact information from the adoptive family?"

"No, once a baby is transferred, the files are sent with the children, wherever they go."

"So there is no possibility of error?"

"No, all mail is sent directly to St. Patrick's."

"Thank you. One more thing before you go Sister. I have a letter I wrote for her, but decided to keep it. Do you think you could send it to her, perhaps before she comes all the way over here?"

"No, I don't think I can do that."

I led her to the door, and as I looked up, I saw Rose turning up the road.

"Alice, this woman is very determined. She's coming to Dublin in a few months and wants to meet you. I have talked to her and I have her letters. She is quite serious about this. She has been searching for you a long time. I don't know whether she knows where you live, but she seems determined to find you. She has been writing to anyone who will answer her letters. I wanted you to know."

"Do you have the letters she sent you?"

"Yes, I do."

"I wondered since you won't take mine, and hers are directed to me, if I could have them?"

"No, she didn't ask that they be forwarded, they cannot be divulged."

I thanked her and she turned toward the door. By the time she reached the bottom of the steps, Rose had parked and was getting the girls out of the car. They exchanged greetings as Rose walked in.

"What was that all about?" Rose asked, looking back down the road.

Rose's two girls bounded through the front door. The girls barely two years apart, with pink cheeks the color of spring roses and long flowing locks that bounced as they laughed. She dressed them alike with ribbons tied in their mass of curls. She kept them tidy and never left them outside unattended, except when they stayed with me. We tossed balls in the yard, buried our fingers in the rich soil from the garden, and ran after the geese in the park, everything that Rose never allowed.

"Just Sr. Sophia, from church, came by to check some schedules."

"Mum, I saw the look on her face. Why would she come all this way for schedules, when she could ring you?"

"It's nothing girl."

"Why are you so flushed?"

I walked back into the dining room to move away from her prodding questions. I looked out over the backyard, staring at the flowers and the swans huddled beneath them. As long as they were there, my secret remained safe. Trying to wipe the blush from my cheeks, I accidentally knocked the flower vase to the floor. I dropped to my knees picking up the shards of glass and petals that fell from the roses.

"Mum, what's going on?"

"I'm fine dear, just turned a bit too fast, and tipped the flowers."

Rose waited for me to say more. What could I say; that the visitor my daughter walked in on would change everything in my life? A truth that had come to be a lie? A truth that the daughter, before her lived?

I steered the girls away from the glass as I picked up remnants of the vase and headed to the kitchen.

"Nina, your flowers are broken," Julie said laying the stems on the counter.

"That's okay. I have plenty more outside," I said, gathering her in my arms.

"Mum?" Rose said, standing in the kitchen doorway.

"I'm fine," I insisted, wiping the perspiration from my forehead. "Come on now let's get the girls settled in to serious playtime, and you off to your chores."

She leaned in with a hug, and whispered in my ear. "I know that wasn't about schedules."

"Never mind," I said.

I looked away not letting her see the eyes that would betray me. My second born daughter could see right through me. Her green eyes now sad, always knew well beyond her years.

"You're lying. I can tell. Look at me."

"Rose, enough. It was a private conversation. I'm allowed to have things that belong to just me, aren't I? Come on girls, let's get your Mum on her way."

I watched as she pulled away from the driveway. I walked back into the house, with a girl on each arm. I would have to think about our conversation later, now it was time for the girls.

I split my time between Rose's girls and Francie's son Paddy. I was more relaxed with him, not so worried that I might say or do the wrong thing, or that I might slip and call him Finn. I squeezed him tight and let his red mop fall over his face. I let him squeal with delight. Perhaps if Finn had been a boy, things might have been different, we might not have been sent away.

Facing the Abyss

eeks after Sr. Gabriel left my doorstep, I informed Claire of the goings-on. I decided, it was time for me to make the final trip to learn my truth. Claire volunteered to come, but I knew I had to make this visit on my own. The front entrance didn't look like the office of an order of nuns. I saw a bright-green door that greeted those who took the steps. Flower pots filled with geraniums and heather climbing the walls of the old brick building gave a false sense of serenity to those who never walked up the steps. I rang the bell. A voice came through the intercom.

"Who is it?"

"This is Alice Leary, I have an appointment at 2:00."

"You're late."

"No, ma'am, I'm not."

"Come in." A Sister I had never seen greeted me. A diminutive woman with bland crème-colored skin, not a wrinkle to be found and glasses that sat at the ridge of her nose. Gray strands of hair creased against her head secured by her white habit. Her black gown, heavy with its folds seemed to overpower her, making her seem even smaller.

"I'm Alice. I'm here to see Reverend Mother."

"Yes, come in," she said, opening the large green door.

Though abrupt at the door, she acted more agreeable once inside, reaching out her white veined hand.

She guided me to a long table, past the sitting chairs in the living room. A massive gold filigree framed painting of the Sacred Heart hung over the fireplace. Everything in the room was immaculate, with the smell of evergreen disinfectant lingering in the air. Crystal figurines decorated shelves throughout the room. A file folder lay closed on the table, looking out of place.

"Reverend Mother could not be here today. She had an unexpected meeting with the Monsignor this afternoon. She is at the rectory."

"Perhaps I could wait," I said.

"No she told me I should conduct this meeting. I have the file, so I believe I'll be able to answer any questions you might have," she said folding her hands on the table.

"Sister, five years ago someone notified me that my daughter had died, but since then I have received calls from a Sister Gabriel that she is indeed alive and is searching for me." The tiny nun had taken a chair across from me, listening as I began to explain.

"I wanted to see where the information came from, or if you could help me. I was hoping to speak with Reverend Mother. She handled everything or so I was told."

"Well, all there is, is what's in the folder. You know I can't tell you much of anything of her family, or any correspondence. We have laws protecting privacy."

"You don't need to protect me. I am here in person. I can prove who I am. The file is about me, or did I misunderstand you."

"It is information about your daughter in America."

"Don't I have a right to know what happened to her?"

"You don't have any rights, I'm afraid. You signed them away, remember Mrs. Leary?"

"No, I didn't sign them away. They were signed for me. I had nothing to do with it."

"Is this your signature?"

"Yes."

"I would say you did."

"The person who gave me the information, said he got it from this office," I continued, "I wanted to know how you found out about her?"

"I don't know what you are talking about. No one came here to ask about your daughter. Do you have the documents you speak of?"

"No, there were no documents, just dates, information about her being in America. That's why I'm here. He told me he had talked to someone at Castlepollard. I assumed Reverend Mother met with him."

"I don't believe I can help you." She started to stand, but I reached out, barely touching her fingers.

"Please, Sister," I could hear pleading in my voice. "I'm hoping you can tell me why you would tell a stranger, before telling me."

"No one came here."

"I don't believe you. You have a responsibility to explain this."

"I don't know what you are talking about. I do know that your daughter has talked to Sister Gabriel. She has been looking for you, saying she is coming to Ireland soon. You told Sister Gabriel you didn't want to see her."

"You're lying. You know he was here. His name was Mr. Malloy."

"Excuse me? If you're going to be disrespectful I will have to ask you to leave. I will not tolerate rudeness."

"I'm sorry. Forgive me. But why would he lie to me? He doesn't know me. I paid him for his services. When I received the papers, he told me he met with Reverend Mother. I know for a fact that all files were transferred here with my daughter."

"He was wrong. I never talked to anyone about your daughter. I'm sorry you've wasted your time with this, but there is nothing more for us to discuss."

"I want to see the papers that have the information he gave me. Can you understand that?" I sat up straight, folding my hands on the polished table. I was not budging.

"You must go now if you are going to continue to act in this manner."

"I beg your pardon Sister, but I have the right to know. I've been lied to since the first day. My Da forced me to sign papers that sent my daughter away. You owe me this. Your church took my daughter."

"Like Sister Gabriel said in the phone calls, she is not dead. She has contacted us, saying she wants to meet you."

"Can I see her letters?"

"No, those are private. She sent them to us. They are now property of the church. I'm sorry."

I sat straight in the chair, refusing to avert my eyes from the Sister sitting across from me with her arms folded across the file that held the history of my daughter. In holding her hands steady, she squeezed her knuckles so tight they turned white.

"Alice you violated God's law by your actions. Perhaps God is seeing this as your penance."

"Please tell me how a rape violates God's law?"

"A man will not attack a woman unprovoked."

I could feel the rage building up in me. "I was fourteen. It does say that in my file doesn't it?"

"I know God has found a way to forgive you your sins, but surely you must be willing to hold some blame in your actions."

"I hold no blame for what happened, except that I could not stand up to you and your kind."

"Back to the issue at hand, you're the one who said that you didn't want to see her. We offered you the chance, but you said no. In fact we offered, repeatedly."

"I know those letters are about my daughter. I have a right to know how she lived, where she's been," I said pointing to the file. "Look at the dates. She was already in America when those letters were sent."

"I can't show them to you."

"There is an envelope with my name on it. See, right there." I said, pointing at a sealed white envelope slipped between the pages of the file.

"Mrs. Leary, please take a seat," the nun demanded as she stood. "That is not for you," she said, slapping the file closed. Too shocked by her response to move forward, I returned to the cushioned seat behind the table.

"It has my name on it," I said, looking up at her stern face. "You're the only one who can help me. Please, I'm begging you!" I could feel the tears well up in my face. It took everything in my power to hold them back.

"I'm sorry. I can't tell you anything."

"Please, anything. I'm begging you."

"She had been ill her early years." she said in a calm, reserved manner.

"What do you mean ill?"

Stunned, I wanted to grab the file, run as far as I could, but I sat in silence. I took a deep breath, laying my hands in my lap, twisting my fingers together. I sat back in the chair, listening to her read from the file, no emotions, a bland recitation of facts.

"They signed her out to a convent."

"Signed out? What does that mean?"

"They sent her to an orphanage in Dublin. I don't have the date of her release. The Sisters fostered her out soon after her arrival, but she was brought back."

"Fostered out? Brought her back? I don't understand."

"No reason was given for her return to the orphanage."

I heard the words, but I went numb. She spoke of Finn as a statistic, an object that had been broken.

"What kind of sick? What does it say there?"

"There were many children, and few sisters to care for them. The babies spent a great deal of time in cribs."

"What are you talking about?" I asked. It seemed she read from a cue card. I wanted her to stop. I wanted her to talk to me like a real person. I wanted to see her hand reach across the table. She continued talking, and even as the tears streamed down my face, she sat stoic, flipping the pages.

I had to stand, to walk around, too afraid that if I continued to sit at the table I would have ripped the files from her slender hands.

"Could you open a window or something? I need some fresh air." I asked leaning against the back of the chair.

"Would you like some water Alice? We can stop for a while."

She softened. I could see in her movements and gestures. She rang a bell and a server came in the room. She whispered into her ear, then went to open the French doors that led out to a patio.

"Would you like to sit outside?"

"Yes, thank you, the fresh air would feel good, but I'd like to finish this." I felt like I had been stabbed with a double-edged sword. I walked around the patio. The cool air fell against my face.

"Sister, again with all due respect, that file is about us. My daughter and I. I don't understand why I can't look at it on my own. I will sit at your table. I won't take it anywhere. I just want answers. And the envelope addressed to me, why can't I see it?"

"Alice, I can't let you see any of the papers in this file. I can't violate the privacy rules. You do understand don't you?"

"No," I wanted to scream in her ear. "I don't! I don't understand any of it." Instead, I took a deep breath. "Sister, I need to know about my daughter."

"I've been given bits and pieces of her life. I've been lied to at every turn. I know you have the best of intentions, but it's my life. No one has been willing to tell the truth. I just want the truth. That's all."

She sat back in her chair staring at me.

"Why do you think you have been lied to?" She asked.

"Where would you like me to start? I was forced to sign papers I didn't agree to, I was sent to the Laundries against my will. It wasn't until my escape that I found any peace. Everything I learned about my daughter has been a lie. You tell me what you would think."

"I'm sorry what happened to you, but I have not lied to you. And my not allowing you to have the file does not constitute a lie."

I believed she didn't have a clue about anything I had said. As if she was listening to a foreign language, but didn't want to be bothered with the translation. Being a nun she would never know the loss of a child, or the sensations of it growing inside you, so how could she understand what that file sitting in front of her could mean to me, words on paper.

"Sister, what I'm searching for has nothing to do with my family. I love my family; my children and my husband, but I need to know about my daughter."

"I'm afraid I don't understand all this emotion. She will come to Ireland in March hoping to have a chance to see you, but you told Sister Gabriel that you could not meet with her. Why would that be, if you claim to love her so?"

"It is my choice."

"This has gone on longer than I expected. I'm afraid I must excuse myself. Thank you for coming." She stood up, leading me back to the door.

I stood on the step as she closed the door behind me. It was done. No one else to see, no one else to plead my case to. I'd go home as I had come, empty-handed.

Letting G⊕

1998

sat down at the desk feeling my legs weaken. I knew if I remained standing I'd collapse. One phone call and it all came back. My Finn had found me. Every year on her birthday, I lit a candle, begging God to keep her safe. Once a year I made a special cake, pretending I was hungry for sweets, never telling anyone the cause of celebration. When the swan roses bloomed, I picked bouquets and placed them on the dining-room table to be admired by all. My silent actions honored her in every way. I had not forgotten her, or given up, but I was smart enough to know the consequences my actions could bring.

Could I do more than a letter? I could meet her at the convent, where no one would know. We could talk and she could tell me about her life. Finn Hamilton would get the letter. I didn't know what I would say to her. Would I tell her she was in my heart every day; that I had been too terrified to tell anyone about her? Would I send her away without even being able to see her face, hear her voice? When I examined all the possibilities, I knew I had to do what was best for both of us.

Dear Finn,
I am sending this letter in care of Sr. Gabriel and I hope that
after you read this, you will understand. I know you came for
me, and for that I am forever grateful. Not a day goes by that
I don't find a way to think of you. I never let you go; it was not

my choice. You need to realize there was never a choice. You were taken from me. I had no say.

I had no place to go and no way to care for you. I was told you would be safe with the Sisters. They would find you the home I could not provide. I can't tell you what happened to me after we were separated. I don't think I can ever tell, not anyone. Not my husband, my children, not even my parish priest. I can barely say it out loud to God.

I found a life after you, a life that brought me children, security, everything I needed to survive. I lived that life, but you were always there, in the back of my mind. I never forgot about you. I celebrate your birthday, alone each year. I say a prayer to God and ask Him to keep you safe. I light a candle each Christmas morning after mass, hoping it would get to you. Your name was the last word I said each night.

I am glad they kept Claire for you. You were named for a woman who saved me. She saved you, too. She loved you when I could not. She held you after I was sent away. She gave me back my faith, and I will forever be grateful for what she did for you.

I have learned that you're well, educated, and have a family. You are a beautiful woman and I am so sorry, but I can't do this. As I said earlier, I never told anyone what happened to me once I left that place, that includes my husband. He has just come home and he thinks I'm writing a letter to my sister in London.

I tried to tell him, but I was never brave enough. So you must know we can never meet. I can't let you into my world, and not because I don't want to. I can't. I hope you understand why. You are a dear one, look a bit like my Rose, you do. I must go, almost time for supper. I will continue to pray for you every day and hope that God keeps you in the hollow of His hand.

Please don't write, as I can't afford for any of my children to find your letters. They would be too hard to explain.

Yours,

Alice

I read the words again. How was it that I could tell my daughter that I could never see her, knowing that just the idea of her had haunted me for years? There was also a truth she had to know, if indeed this was her. I slipped the letter into an envelope, sealed it and walked out into gray cloudy afternoon sky. I waved at Frank, and felt his stare seep through me as I rounded the corner. I caught the bus and would arrive at St. Patrick's Guild in thirty minutes.

Losing Aidan

2005

idan, just seventy-three, had long retired from the force, but two days a week he arrived at the precinct helping with odds and ends, but mostly getting in the way, I imagined. I saw how his health was dwindling. Shorter walks, longer talks with Mr. McGuire, instead of strolling the neighborhood, they sat on the porch. He took longer naps, and stopped more often to catch his breath. Though I urged him to go to the doctor, he refused.

The call came just after four o'clock, supper about to be put on the table. He had gone back to the church to help set up the funeral mass for Mr. Scully.

"Alice, this is Monsignor James. It's Aidan. He collapsed inside the church. You need to meet the ambulance at Dublin Memorial."

"Is he alive?"

"You need to hurry. Ring the girls."

This was the third time I'd been called to meet an ambulance at a hospital.

My throat tightened as I listened to the words over the phone. Dread fell over me. The sense of doom that had lingered for so long, now stood front and center.

I rang Rose, who in turn rang Francie in Dublin. I called Catherine, knowing that I had to be the one to tell her. She had married and moved to London. For reasons neither of them explained, their relationship had fallen apart. She no longer asked to speak with Aidan when she called on Sundays. Though I knew in my heart he had passed, I told her he had taken ill, and was in the hospital. I asked her to come home.

In fifteen minutes, Rose was at the door.

"Mum, did you hear any more?"

"No, but we need to hurry. It's not good, he may not make it."

Rose, with the wheel held tight in both hands, stared at the road ahead, every now and again patting my arm.

"He is going to be fine Mum. He'll get through this like always." I turned and smiled, but couldn't hold it. The sense that overtook me was now almost strangling me.

Rose loved her Da and she did everything to protect him, even beyond what I could understand. She was his first. I saw tears sitting on the top of the round edges of her cheeks. We drove the rest of the way in silence. As we walked through the front doors, she took hold of my hand.

Francie met us in the lobby. "They won't tell me anything," she said.

"I'll go to the desk, and you girls take a seat. We may be in for a long wait."

"Mum, how can you say that?" Francie asked, grabbing hold of my hand.

"The doctors are with him, Mrs. Leary. They will come out as soon as they can."

Here I was, at the same hospital where we had met so many years before, where our children had been born. Now, waiting to see if my husband would make it through the next hour. The longer doctors stayed with him, the worse I knew it was. It was an hour before anyone came out.

"Alice." Dr. Langley said, walking toward me. Monsignor James came from the desk at the same time, and stood by my side. I knew he was trying to protect me, in case I should fall apart.

"I knew this time would come," the doctor said. "He has suffered a major heart attack. He is still alive, but I don't know for how long."

He had warned Aidan previously about his drinking, eating, and his overall habits, but it never worked. Aidan shooed him away, telling him he was a worrywart.

"Would you like to see him?"

"Yes.

"Only one at a time, though."

"Would it be all right, if I go? I won't stay long."

Francie took hold of my arm. "You go on, Mum. We'll wait."

"I won't be long I promise."

Tom led me to the room on the farthest side.

"He probably won't hear anything you say to him, but take hold of his hand, he'll be able to feel your touch."

"Thank you."

Tom opened the door, but didn't follow me inside. There was my Aidan with tubes everywhere. His skin ashen, his eyes closed. I held his hand, slipping my fingers between his. I felt the vibration of the machines as they filled the room. He looked fragile. I couldn't see his eyes, but when I leaned into him, laying my head on his chest, I knew he was slipping away.

"Aidan, my love, can you hear me?" I muttered to him, squeezing his hand tighter. I wanted to crawl up on the bed, wrap my arms around him.

"Aidan, I have loved you since that first day on the beach. You provided me with love, security, and tenderness, everything a frightened girl needed."

I looked at the machines as they pumped up and down. Nothing I did would change things, the machines were the only things keeping him alive.

"I kept a secret from you because I was too terrified. I should have known you loved me enough. I should have known I could've trusted you, but over time I let it slip away, never telling you."

The room fell silent, the vibrations of the machines stopped. The pumping came to a halt. In the stillness red lights flashed. The door burst open and I immediately moved away from the bed. I watched as they worked over him, bringing in different machines, bodies moving around the bed.

They all left, until only Dr. Langley remained who ushered me out the door. "I'm sorry. We did everything we could. Is there anyone I can call for you?"

"No, I have the girls with me. What happens now?" I was numb from his words.

"We will remove all the tubes and clean his body. He will then be delivered to the funeral home."

I'd need to call Aidan's family. Maybe Jonathan would know who I should call. Aidan had lost contact years ago; there would be a wake. The girls would help me prepare the food, and clean the house. All these thoughts running through my head, as the doctor was explaining the details.

"I'm so sorry, Alice. As soon as we release his body, you can make arrangements with the funeral home. They'll come and take care of everything. We have his clothes and personal belongings here. Would you like them now?"

"Yes, thank you."

"Could I have a moment with him?"

"Of, course. I'm sorry, I wasn't thinking. I'll be outside when you're ready."

I stepped back inside the room. Finally, I was alone with Aidan and could tell him anything. Though he was covered with a sheet, I reached for his hand. He was still warm. I pulled the cover from his face. He looked no different than watching him sleep, late at night or early morning.

"Aidan, I wish I could have told you about my Finn, about the rape, the Home and the treatment in the Laundries. I wish I could have told you how broken I was, but I was afraid you wouldn't love me, that you would turn me out. After each of our girls, I buried my secrets a little more. I had held them so long, pretending they never happened. I kept the truth from you."

I didn't realize the tears were falling. I wanted him to wake up. I didn't want to say good-bye to the man I adored. I took a deep breath and took my broken heart out the door. Monsignor was leaning against the wall.

"Are you alright?" He asked, handing me his hankie.

"As best I can be. I knew I would find myself here someday. I just thought I had more time."

A nurse held his belongings, all wrapped in a plastic bag. As we walked down the hallway, he remained silent. Aidan was gone, and tonight I would lie in our bed alone.

As we came back to the lobby I saw the girls, Jonathan and Marie were coming through the double doors of the hospital, greeting us with open arms. They wrapped themselves around us and I could feel tenderness, as I did that first time in Howth. Together we left the hospital, my girls on one side, Jonathan and Marie on the other.

The cold rain beat down as I started my new life.

THE WAKE

he night before services for Aidan, I sat in my garden and wondered where I would find the strength to get through the next week. The girls stayed at the house and together we shared our most favorite stories of him. This man who meant so much to each of us, but in such different ways.

"When Da walked me down the aisle," Rose said, beaming as she continued, "just as we entered the church he leaned over, tightened the grip on my arm and said 'I have always loved you,' then he stood tall, straightened his tie and whispered, 'let's do this.'"

"You were the most beautiful thing in the world to him. He didn't want you to see him cry, so he sucked on a Lifesaver, thinking that would hold back his tears."

We all smiled and I saw each girl dip into their own memories for the moment they would hold in their hearts. Francie was next.

"The day Da picked up Paddy and when he thought I wasn't listening, and whispered in his ear, 'and to think I was going to let you go.'" Tears streamed down her cheeks.

"I think when he saw Paddy, he saw the baby boy he lost and it filled him up with love," I said.

There was a long pause, and both girls looked at Catherine. "It's your turn," Rose said, "What was your moment?"

"I don't think I ever had one. Da and I didn't get along so well."

"How can you say that? You did everything he wanted to do. You went to University, you traveled outside of Dublin," Francie said.

"Come on Catherine. I can't believe you can't think of one moment that will stay with you forever," I said.

"I lied. We met in Dublin one day for lunch. I never told anyone, and Mum I don't know whether he told you," she said, looking over at me. I nodded my head, remembering the day he headed to Dublin, tumbling over himself because he was going to see his girl.

"We met in the city, a little shop by Stephen's Green. We were just talking about everything and nothing, when suddenly he took hold of my hand and said, 'Catherine, I read the article you wrote; in fact, I've read them all. You are a smart girl. I hope you know that. Don't let anyone tell you any different.' He looked up at me and from his pocket he pulled out an envelope. Inside was a picture. It was Da and I; taken when I was about ten. I had won a contest at school. He had his arm around me, while I held up my certificate. 'I thought you might like to have this. It is one of my favorite pictures of the two of us.' I took the picture, turned it over and on the back he wrote the date, and place, with a small note. 'To the smartest girl in the world.'"

He had loved them each so differently and they would carry him with them long after this week was over.

The evening had slipped away with our conversation. The girls cleaned up the kitchen and I went to bed. It was a night to remember him. I took the journal and began reading where we had met on the beach, and where he held Rose for the first time, and when he reminded me about my family.

> *Go to Meadows Glen. Come back when you're free of it. I'll*
> *always be here. Love you always.*
> *Aidan.*

The Rosary, Mass, burial, then the wake all went on for three days. Neighbors brought food, left envelopes and heartfelt condolences. People I didn't know walked through my front door, many of them, fellow officers took hold of my hand.

I couldn't have gotten through it without everyone's support. I knew I had married a fine man, but I didn't know everyone had held him in such high regard. Until he was gone, their voices had been silent.

Of all the people who came, Frank touched me the most. He didn't join in the storytelling or bring a plate of food. Never did I see him with a drink in his hand, but instead he brought over chairs so people could sit outside. Of all the days, instead of rain, the sun shone high in the clouds. Watching from the window, I saw him scoop up Paddy in his arms and walk him to the bench in the garden. He sat with him on his knee and rocked him, until finally Collin came and took him upstairs to bed. At the end of the day, as the mourners began to leave Frank took his chairs back, cleaned up the yard and went home without a word to any of us.

After everyone left, Catherine sat with me to go over the legal issues; the will, bank accounts, and the money that Aidan had put aside.

"Since I have to leave in a few days, I thought I'd go over Da's papers. I'm sure you'll be fine," she said. "Da paid off the house, and there's a solid pension from the Guardia. You'll need to process the paperwork, with a death certificate, but you should have no problems. In a few weeks, a check will start to come, each month, benefits from Da's retirement. He didn't leave you with any bills, and even made arrangements for his burial, and yours. Did you know that?"

"No," I said, but it explained why the undertaker wouldn't take the envelope for the service. "He never talked about money much. He always said there was nothing to worry about."

"Well, Da was frugal, and he made sure everything was in order." Catherine folded her hands over mine, and for that moment she looked the most like Adrian on the day we met. She was my moppet, a head full of curls, loving and tender to me in every way, always making sure, as Aidan had, that I was safe.

A Bit of the Truth

eeks and months passed. Catherine returned to London, but called every Sunday to check on me. Rose and Francie fell back into the routine of their lives as best they could. I knew the girls would be over all the time, and with the grandchildren my days would be busy.

I went through the motions, and each day I picked up the pace. After six months, Rose asked if I wanted to move his things so I might have more room in the house. With Rose and Francie by my side, we went into his closet, and together picked through suits and shirts, labeling two boxes for charity, and one for storage that I was not ready to hand over to someone else.

Everything in order, as his life had been, lined up and coordinated. Rose folded the shirts from his work, while Francie packed away his shoes for charity. As the afternoon moved on, and the sun came through the upstairs window, we finished our task at hand.

"Mum, I've got everything packed way."

"Did you check his pockets?"

For the first time since they had called from the hospital, Francie smiled. "Yea, Mum, I checked them all. I put the coins on the dresser, with a few tattered bus stubs. I even checked the inside of his shoes."

"How are you doing, Rose?"

"Good, the shirts are folded and in the box. I put some of his sweaters on the bed, the ones you might want to keep."

"Only the green pullover, with tattered, sleeves," I said, pointing to the bed. "Always loved that one."

"One of my favorites too," Francie said. "He wore it almost every Sunday. After church, he would settle in, that green sweater snug around his waist."

"That was my first gift to him. I bought it at Cleary's, for his birthday."

"Surprised you didn't bury him in it," Rose piped from the corner.

"No, I need the smell of him close," I said, "now it's my turn to wear it."

"Mum, don't be silly it will swim on you," Rose said, "but if you must," laughing she handed me my treasure.

"All right, back to work. I have to pick up Paddy pretty soon."

We continued going through things, but I was stopped in my tracks when I saw a white envelope on the bottom of the drawer. I slipped it into the pocket of my sweater without a word.

"Girls, let's call it a day. I can finish this later in my own time. All you have to do is take the boxes downstairs. I appreciate your help. I couldn't have done this by myself."

We hugged as each girl took a box, and went downstairs. We said our good-byes at the door and for a while I relished the quiet, just me and the old orphan cat from Howth. I gave him a scratch and walked outside. I flipped the envelope around. It was sealed, and age had yellowed the corners.

The late afternoon sun dimmed and I wrapped my sweater around my shoulders. I strolled to the bench in the garden looking out over the yard. Hydrangeas, lavender, and roses covered the garden. The bushes planted the day the manila envelope arrived filled the yard with a shower of roses.

I held tight to the envelope, looked over at the swans still wrapped in each other, but chipped over time. As I opened the envelope, pictures I had never seen slipped out. I turned each picture over, but there were no names, no dates. I stared, looking for something familiar, but found nothing. The same young woman was in each picture. I could only imagine these were pictures of his dead wife.

I held up the pictures, inhaling the smell of age for anything that might seem familiar. Just as his sweater filled me with him, so did the envelope, faint tobacco, mixed with toilet water. The smell lingered, making me miss his arms around me, his gentle nudges, the smell of his pipe. I ached for him.

In my grief I was interrupted by the presence of Frank McGuire standing on the walkway, hunched over.

"I knocked on the front door but no one answered. I saw the girls leave, so I knew you were home. Am I bothering you?"

"No, not at all. Just some quiet time after the girls."

"Is there a problem? Did something happen?" I asked.

"No, no problem," he said, walking into the yard. "I was wondering if I might talk to you a bit?"

"Is it all right if we talk here, or would you prefer to go inside, maybe have some tea?"

"No, I don't want to be a bother. Here'll be fine. I have something for you."

"Okay." I gathered the pictures and slid them under my sweater and waited for Frank to sit down.

"You know, Aidan and I've been friends for a long time, even before you came to live here."

"Yes. I know." I stared at Frank and could see beads of sweat sitting on his temple. He brushed them away and continued.

"He shared a great deal with me over our time together. I knew his first wife. It nearly killed him when he lost her. But he found you. He loved you so Alice, and the girls; they took him to the moon and back. You made him happy. He loved his life here."

"What did you talk about?" I asked.

"Life. Work. Troubles. All the things a husband doesn't want to bother his wife with."

"I'm glad to know that. Aidan didn't talk a lot about his feelings so I often wondered how things were for him. I mean I knew he loved us, but a woman always wonders."

"Well, a while back he came over and asked me a favor. He had an envelope and asked if I'd keep it until he needed it back. It didn't seem much, maybe some documents. Men do things that they don't want their wives to know." He took a cigarette from his pocket, asked if I wanted one, then lit one for himself, and continued.

"He never came back for the envelope, so I waited until it seemed things had settled and decided you should have it."

He took the envelope from his jacket pocket and handed it to me. It looked like the envelopes that I had buried in the garden. I took hold of it and looked back at Frank.

"He loved you, he did, ma'am. He asked me, if anything happened to him to watch over you, to keep you safe. I best be going now. Good day ma'am."

"Frank, thank you for this. Do you know what might be inside?"

"No, ma'am, I don't. He handed them to me sealed, and I'm handing them back to you sealed as well. Good day to you." He tipped his hat and went back out the yard the way he came.

Inside were two folded papers, my birth certificate and Finn's. A hand-written letter, and a picture I had been given years ago. The note read:

Dearest Alice,
If you are reading this, God has seen fit to take me. I've written this letter in two parts. It's winter, I'm in the park behind the house. So why am I writing you must be asking? I'm writing to let you know I have solved the riddle that sat in our house for so long. You kept pieces of your heart from me, but you need to know, I knew long before that night you lay in my arms barely able to breathe the words. I knew because Jonathan took me for a long walk one day. It was after I fell in love with you, after I knew I didn't want to live another day without you, your crazy blue eyes and wiry chestnut mane. I loved you from that first day. Jonathan knew, as I acted a fool around him. One day we took a walk, I'll never forget, along the shore alone. I want you to know what he said to me that day. I want you to know how much he loved you, and so he began:
"You love her, do you?"
"I believe so."
"Got to be sure. She is an odd one she is."
"Oh, but she is grand."
"I have to tell you something that you must promise you will take to your grave."
"Why would I promise that?"
"If you can't promise I won't be giving her away to you."

I have to tell you Alice, he had me there. What could it be that I would have to promise for a girl I was falling in love with?"
He continued.
"When she was fourteen, she was raped, became pregnant, she did. When her family found out they all but threw her out— sent her to a Home."
It started to make sense what you had tried to tell me, but couldn't find your way.
"She had a baby, a girl, but the Sisters took it from her, sent her away to Dublin, to my convent."
"How did you meet her?" I asked.
"They allowed her to work in the garden with me. They did terrible things to her—things she'll never speak—things I could never tell. Sara, her friend, you will meet soon, was with her."
He pulled a cigarette from his pocket, offering me one, and continued.
"I couldn't stop what was happening to her."
"Who was doing all this?"
"The priests, the sisters. They took advantage, and brutalized these girls they did."
"So what happened?"
"We found a way to escape. I got them out, in my truck. I promised her I'd never tell anyone, but you need to know."
We fell silent, Jonathan turned away, heading down the beach.
"You can never tell her you know this, even if she comes to you, as I doubt she will. She'll take it to her grave, she will. But if you love her as you say—you'll treat her no different. Love her as if she were pure. If you don't and I find out about, it'll be me your dealing with."
So there it was. The woman I loved had a past, but I thought about my past and if you could love me, then I could you too, with a pure heart.
All these years I waited, waited for you to believe enough in me to tell, but you couldn't. I just want you to know I'd have loved you, loved you as I do now. I hope you find her someday. And oh yes, I knew about the garden and the pictures. I saw your beloved and when the day comes I hope you have the strength

to tell our girls. They deserve to know. They deserve to meet their sister. You didn't do anything wrong. You have no reason to be ashamed.

The second part of this letter came the night Francie gave birth to Paddy. I was so angry that you defied me in front of her the night she told us about the pregnancy. But the minute I laid eyes on him, my heart melted right there. I was putty. He made me think of my boy, who never saw his first day. I knew that you had been right to defend Francie as you did. But something you said stayed with me, "that you'd never let it happen again."

My second confirmation came from Dr. O'Hara, who must have thought you would have been too afraid to tell. He was reluctant at first, but after an accidental meeting in the hospital, he thought you had told me, he explained his concerns. I ached that, as your husband, you couldn't tell me. I wasn't your Da, and never would be.

I went back and talked with Dr. O'Hara, we spoke repeatedly to help me understand. He told me about his sister, and explained why you'd be reluctant to tell me.

It took a while for me to understand, but with Jonathan's explanation before we were married, and Dr. O'Hara explaining your reasoning. A part of me felt betrayed, but over time I came to understand.

I couldn't let it end there. I did research of my own. You wouldn't have had to contact a private investigator. I learned a great deal from the precinct and from you. I know you're reading this and hating me, thinking I betrayed you. I had to find out more, so one day while you were out, I looked in your nightstand and found your journals. I picked up the first one and read. I promise I only read about five pages, but it told me everything I needed to know. I finally understood your heartache.

I have loved you Alice, with all my heart. If you're reading this, Frank has gotten up the nerve to bring it to you. I imagine you're sitting in the garden, going through each page slowly, looking at picture you have already looked at, and knowing

*you probably buried them somewhere in your garden so I
wouldn't find them.*

*I hope you find her someday, and that finding her brings you
peace.*

*I've asked Frank to look after things for you. Find faith in your
life and know I am always with you.*

He had known. After all that time, all that fear of telling, but he had
known all along. I realized there was no secret to keep.

I went to the shed for a shovel and carefully dug around the roses, the
roots having spread throughout the garden. I lifted the wrapped packages and cleaned them off and took them upstairs where they belonged.

I was free.

Death of the Devil

urse Claire and I had kept contact over the years, rarely visiting in person over tea, but long soothing letters that set the heart right. She and Sara arrived for Aidan's funeral and even stayed over at the house helping with food, cleaning and making last-minute church arrangements. They were a great comfort to me. It also gave me a chance to introduce them as long-lost friends to the girls, as they had never come to the house.

In time I sent her pictures of the children and grandchildren and she provided me with tidbits of her life, which I relished. She had been there for me at a time that would have been hard for even the Mother of God, but her gentleness and patience got me through, nothing like the Reverend Mother who believed her job was to be the handmaid of her God.

It had been months since Aidan's death and slowly I was getting back to the order of my life. I had left a few messages, but never heard from her. Her last letter included a picture of her youngest she named Alice, and her wedding. I didn't keep it out on the mantel, no one could know who she was. I kept everthing she sent me in the drawer with all my documents. I kept my secrets hidden.

It was the beginning of the month, so the only mail I was expecting was bills, or the newsletters from the church, but tucked in with all the bills, it sat, addressed to me. I went through the other mail, sorted it and put it in its place. Escaping to my garden, I sat at the bench and unsealed the envelope.

My dearest Alice,

I hope you're well and finding a way to move forward after losing Aidan. I should have been there for you more than I was, but life has been more active than I would care to admit. I am fine, but I have no pictures for you this time. This is of a different nature.

Reverend Mother passed away this last weekend. Though I left the Home years ago, I'm still working with the special children who God sends to our care. The Sisters in the school often tell me about Reverend Mother and some of the other Sisters especially when something happens. She told me Reverend Mother had been ill for the last few months, but refused medical care. She said she often came to the infirmary, burning with fever, but would rest a short while on the bed, then go back to her office. Each day she was getting worse, not eating and finally the last few weeks took to her bed. Only sipping on hot broth, rarely even taking any tea.

They begged her to let the doctor come, but she refused. Her last night on this Earth was nothing anyone would want to see. Sister Helen came down from Castlepollard and sat with her while she was burning with fever and throwing up throughout the night. She prayed, as there was nothing left to do. By morning Sister Helen called Castlepollard and informed them of her passing.

I debated writing, wondering if you would care about her passing, but there was a nagging sense I felt the need to write you about this, maybe perhaps so you could rest now, knowing she couldn't hurt any more girls. The suffering is over.

There will be a service, come Friday. I hope you receive this in time. I am taking the train from Kildare into Dublin and I wondered if you would like to meet me there. You wouldn't have to go to the service mind you, but we could meet later for tea and catch up. The service is at 11:00 at The Church of the Holy Family. There is a cafe across the street. We can get some tea and chat. I understand if you don't want to come, but it has been a long time, since that dreary day. I would love to see

you. Ring me if you can come.
Always
Claire

I folded the letter back into the envelope and held it on my lap. Reverend Mother dead, so was her wrath, along with all the lies. She could never hurt another girl, never separate another mother or baby, and never strike out in the name of her God. I didn't have anyone to ask if I should go, I just decided I needed to see her one last time. I had survived her and her reign of terror. And she... she had died a painful death. Perhaps God did have a sense of humor.

I wore the same dress I wore for Aidan. I waved at Frank as I headed down the walkway and moved across the street. I'd have a few minutes to wait before the bus, enough time to collect myself before facing my past. I waited outside a few minutes for Claire, but when I didn't see her I went inside the massive cathedral.

I sat in the back of the church, behind the habited women. I didn't see Monsignor Matthew, but I imagined him to be long dead. I saw Sr. Helen sitting in a row with a some of other Sisters. Sister Gabriel sat a few rows back. The closed casket stood between the aisles of the massive walls. No flowers were draped across the top of the casket, or sprays on either side of the altar. The church was cold. Not from the weather that blew in from outside, but the air that filled the room, the lack of mourners.

Though there was no reason for me to stay for the rest of the service, I did. There were no condolences from me. No words that I could say that would have brought either of us any peace. I was glad she was gone, so there would be no one else she could hurt. In time I would forgive her, but now it wasn't possible.

I found the café across the street that Claire described, and took a seat at an outside table. I ordered two cups of tea and waited. In about fifteen minutes I watched her cross the street, I waved and she took the chair next to me.

"I didn't think you'd go inside," she said.

"I didn't think I would either, but I wanted to see what they do for their own."

"Were you satisfied?"

"No, I wanted an open casket. I wanted to see her ashen face, and veined hands. I wanted to see the devil up close."

"They never show the devils up close."

We drank our tea, laughed at what we had expected, and shared what had been left out of our lives.

"I have something to tell you."

"What is it?" Claire asked.

"He knew. All that time I thought I was keeping a secret from him, he knew about her, and the Home."

"What are you saying?"

"I'm saying that he knew what happened to me and that I was at Castlepollard, and that I had a daughter. He knew everything about her. All that I had learned and more."

"How did you find out?"

"He left a letter and it was given to me after he passed. He had our birth certificates, her passport picture and a letter explaining how he knew."

"Do the girls know?"

"No. I've barely processed it myself. How could I tell them? What would they say if they knew?"

"Alice, how can you ask that question? They would love you just as they do now."

"I can't tell them. So drop it."

"OK, maybe you feel like you can't tell Rose, I mean from everything you've said, she is pretty conservative, but of all the girls, Francie would understand. Do you know how much your girls love you?"

"Yes, and I want to keep it that way."

I could see the look on her face, a mixture of shock and disappointment, her brow was showing wrinkles and she kept pushing her bob up and away from her face.

"You know what, you're right. Let's drop it. I need to catch the bus back to Kildare. I didn't think we would stay talking so long."

We paid the tab, collected our coats and walked to the nearest bus stop.

"Alice, just think about it for a while. You don't have to do anything about it now, but when the time is right, when you feel safe think about it."

"You had better get on your bus before it takes off without you. I'll call you next week."

"No you won't," laughing as she stepped on the bus.

I crossed the street to wait for my bus. I had never thought about telling the girls. I had been so worried about Aidan knowing, I buried it too deep to even bring up. Now it was sitting right at the edge of my heart. I was back to thinking about it and thinking about her.

The bus dropped me at the corner and Frank was in the yard, as usual.

"Good evening Frank."

"Evening Alice."

"Frank, I want to apologize for not thanking you for giving me the envelope from Aidan. I am so grateful."

"You're welcome Ma'am."

"I'll see you later." I walked through the gate and unlocked my door. Once inside I took off my coat, started a fire and poured a glass of wine. I went back to the living room taking a seat next to the cat. I threw a blanket over me, scoped him up in my arms and sat back.

I needed time.

Notes at the Door

2008

he had found me. She had even sent pictures. I had to stand still for just a moment to catch my breath. For months I had known about her coming, attempting to call, to meet, but I had put it out of my head. It was November now, barely a day went by without drenching rain. I could feel the air coming up through my body, but it wasn't coming out. It was the same feeling I had in the back of the truck with Jonathan, getting away from an unspeakable hell. Anxiety and terror. I wasn't running away from anything here. She was running toward me.

I wanted this I told myself, in my dreams, and when I held my girls close, I wondered where she was, or who she had become. The pictures she sent showed such a fine girl, not a girl, I corrected myself-a woman. She looked the most like Rose, chestnut hair, freckles splashed across her face.

I had allowed myself to forget her. I had buried her daily between the Novena prayers and the linen handkerchiefs of my life. She had crossed the world for me. That had to mean something. I opened the letter again, even having read it a thousand times before.

Dearest Alice,
I don't believe I should call you my mother, but I feel it in my
heart. What can I say that I have not said over and over in
my mind? When I first learned of you, they told me you had

died, so I imagined what you may have been like. Later, from the Sisters, I learned you had not died, but alive and well in Dublin. I searched everywhere for you, and surprisingly by chance I found you. I have thought about you every day in the oddest ways. In my saddest moments I have wondered how you could have let me go. In my rational moments I think you had no other choice, you were but a child yourself. We are no longer children, and we must make our own choices. There is no judgment here, but know when I look in the mirror and I touch my cheek, I am touching you and when I see my sea blue-green eyes, they're yours handed down to me. You didn't leave to have a life away from me, but so that I could have a life, and for that I am so grateful.

I have idolized you, hated you and feared you, but I have never forgotten you. I am you, the best and worst.

I will be coming to Ireland soon, and I will not leave until I do everything I can to find you. I have had so many doors closed, but I vowed there would be no obstacles to stop me. Once we meet, you'll be free to do as you please. My goal will have been to meet.

I look forward to a chance to be together, to talk, to tell you of my life and learn of yours. I will call you when we arrive in Dublin and hopefully we can make arrangements. I'll be bringing my daughter with me.

My love to you, I can't believe it's finally happening.
Claire

Evening settled in, no rain today, but cloudy skies. I nipped at some roses, and trimmed the lavender, but could not concentrate. I walked back into the house, thinking I had heard the bell. I saw the napkin notes pushed through mail slot. How had I missed them before? From The Legend Inn, just up the highway. Had she dropped them all at once, or did she come last night, then this morning, a few minutes ago? It didn't matter. She had come, after all this time. I picked up the first napkin.

We're at The Legend Inn, arrived on Saturday, anxious to see

you.
Please call. 013-241123.
Claire

Sorry we missed you today. Hope you are well. Please call.
013-241123.
Claire

I hope we found the right house. It's Claire. We are at The
Legend Inn. I guess you know that. Please call, you have the
number.
Claire

I needed a walk to get away from the closeness of it, but I needed to make two calls. Hopefully, I could just leave a message. I dialed Sara. It rang five times, no answer. I left the message. "She is here."

The same with Claire, no answer, the same message. "She is here." I gathered the letter, pictures and napkins, and put them in my pocket. I needed a walk in the park . . . my park. I went as often as possible over the last forty years.

"Good day, Alice," Frank said, as he swept the walkway.

"Afternoon, Frank," I said, turning to close my gate.

"Out for a walk?"

"Yes, going to the park before the rain comes on."

"Have you got your umbrella?"

"Sure do," I said, holding it up for him to see.

"You've had some visitors, you know. Two ladies said they were from the States. Came late in the afternoon, then again in the evening. I saw them this morning also."

"Yes Frank, friends of my daughters," I lied.

"They have been here for four days in a row, finally, yesterday they went up to the door."

"Yes, Frank, I know."

"Told them you were visiting your daughter in London. You got back early. You all right?"

"Yes, I'm fine. She had to work, so, I decided to come home." I couldn't tell him who they were. I knew it was Claire and her daughter.

"I told them to call first, next time."

"Don't worry Frank, I don't think they'll be coming back."

I headed down the block, turned the corner and went through the walkway to the park.

Emerging from the hedge I was met with a carpet of glorious green, lush and rich, a mixture of shades. Children were everywhere, playing and running across the lawn, dogs dashing behind them, lovers, holding hands strolling, everyone enjoying the late afternoon. There, sitting on a bench, two women talking, their arms waving about. One in a navy raincoat, the other a heavy cream sweater. Both brown hair, as I could see from a distance.

I pulled the picture from my pocket. Could it be? Could they have just left my door and found the park. Suddenly, they got up and started walking toward me. I thought about turning away, but why? I could be anyone, just an old woman walking in the park. I stayed the course and couldn't take my eyes off them. As we passed, they looked my way, smiled.

"Good evening," the taller one said.

"Hello," the other nodded.

"Lovely evening," I said, nodding back, sure I had just greeted my Finn.

Meeting Finn

Making the phone call was easy. She didn't answer, so I left a message.

"This is your Mum." What else was there to say?

Walking into the empty hotel lobby, I saw the café sign over the entrance. I turned toward the double doors and a waitress led me to an empty booth. I had time to compose myself before her arrival. I told the waitress I'd be waiting for a young lady who'd be arriving around one o'clock. I slipped off my sweater, then ordered tea and cakes. I waited.

I couldn't help but wonder how the rest of day would unfold. In my dreams, I imagined that we'd know each other at first sight. She had sent a picture with her letter, and after the park, I knew what she looked like, but she had no way of knowing me. I felt comfortable, knowing that I'd recognize her brown shoulder-length hair, the freckles and blue-green eyes.

A young brunette woman stood by the doorway, looking from side to side. There she was, looking as she did in the park, almost the same as her picture, except longer hair. The young waitress came over and touched her shoulder, pointing across the restaurant to the only occupied booth in the room.

"Ma'am, I believe your party is there," she said, pointing in my direction.

She saw me, as we locked eyes. Did she see the small gray-haired woman, with the scarf hanging from her neck? I moved to the center of the aisle still watching her. She walked toward me. I froze in that moment.

"Alice?" she asked.

"Oh God, it's my Finn. I'm sorry you're Claire." I promised myself, not to cry, but I knew it was a promise I couldn't keep. We stood together, mother and daughter for the first time.

Tears streamed down my cheeks. She reached over wiping them away. All those years of wondering, disappeared. "Don't cry." she whispered. She took a deep breath and squeezed my hand as we took our seats across from each other.

"You called me Finn. I remember that name from the birth certificate Finnouala, right?"

"Yes, but your name is Claire. That's what you called yourself on the phone, and how you signed your letters. You know, I chose both your names, Finnouala from an old Irish folktale, and Claire, in honor of someone who saved us both."

"It's okay . . really. Please, call me Finn. Being here in this place, now, it fits. I may never be called that again." She bowed her head, covering a smile, and I realized she understood more than I ever imagined about the meaning of her name.

"Look at you, you're grand." I didn't know what else to say to her. "Let me look at you." I couldn't help myself. I reached out, stroked her hair and touched her cheek.

"So are you." She didn't avert her eyes from me this time.

"Except for the freckles, you look much as I did at your age. You're my daughter."

"I didn't have any freckles until I turned six. My mother told me they were kisses from the Sun." Claire blushed, covering her cheeks. My sisters had freckles. Connor still had his. I could only hope, somehow, her's came from me.

After the initial visit from the waitress with tea and cakes, she left us alone. As Claire sat in front of me, I saw a sadness move into her eyes. She opened my hand and cupped in her palms was the medal. I placed my hand over hers. My last memory had been the medal, placed around her neck to keep her safe. Without ever knowing it, she had kept a piece of our history.

"You still have it?" I opened our hands and stared at the medal attached to the same string I hadn't seen for more than fifty years.

"My mother saved everything from the day I arrived. She gave them to me, but I kept this hidden so nothing would happen to it. I hid it in a box, so no one would find it."

"The medal had been a prize as a little girl. I brought it with me when I came to the Home. I don't know how, but I found a way to keep it hidden. The day I left, Nurse Claire, your namesake, promised that it would stay with you. I can't believe you still have it."

"It's one of the things I've cherished my whole life. My mother told me that when I came off the plane, it was around my neck. She didn't know who had given it to me. When I got older, she gave it back to me; along with the shoes and dress I was wearing when I arrived."

Still clutching the medal, I knew it was my turn to share. "It's important that you understand why things turned out the way they did."

I began to talk, but refused to let my eyes focus on her. I stared at the wall, as if avoiding eye contact would prevent the pain that penetrated me.

"You don't have to do this."

"Yes, Claire. I'm afraid if I don't do it now, I'll lose my nerve."

"Early spring, but bitter cold, I stayed after school to help my teacher prepare her classroom for a special event coming up the next day. Rain fell throughout the day, much as it is now." I stared out the window.

"I hurried along knowing my mother would be worried and upset. I heard someone behind me, so I walked faster, and began to run, but I fell on the slippery road. As I got to my feet, he grabbed me from behind and dragged me back to the ground. I tried to get away and fight him off, but he was bigger, stronger. I kicked and swung my arms, but I couldn't free myself. He tore at my clothes and I couldn't stop him. Wish I could have. Maybe none of it would've happened."

I paused and stared at her. "I didn't mean it that way."

"It's okay. I understand." She let go of my hands. "It must have been terrible for you. I can't imagine," she said.

It didn't seem real, telling this woman, my daughter, things I'd never said out loud to anyone. Between each sentence, I paused, fingering the silverware on the napkin as the words spilled. I ran my fingers through my hair and squirmed like an anxious child, but I had to finish. If anything, I owed it to myself to say it out loud.

"Just fourteen, I didn't understand anything, too immature. He left me with torn clothes and blood streaming down my legs. I hid in the bushes praying he wouldn't return." I needed to tell her everything, so I pushed my plate to the side and leaned in. She moved closer. I could feel the warmth of her breath.

"He left me there, alone, in the dark. My back ached from being pushed down on the gravel."

Her eyes watered, but she didn't wipe them, and she didn't turn away. It didn't matter why I told her, just that I had found the strength.

"I didn't know what to say when I arrived home. I was too afraid no one would believe me, that my mother would get mad because of my torn jumper and the blood on my legs. I went to my room and washed up, stuffing my clothes under the mattress. By late spring, it didn't take long for her to notice I was changing. I kept my secret as long as I could." I took a deep breath and continued. "In a couple of months, she took me to the doctor. He asked if I had been with anyone. I lied at first because I didn't know what to say. I told him about the stranger in the rain. He called my mother in to the room, and confirmed her fears. Embarrassed by the word pregnant, she swung me around, yelling, 'what did you do, girl?'"

Claire sat in silence watching my every move as if my face were the screen at a movie theatre.

"She made me sit outside while the doctor discussed what would happen. She told the doctor that everything had been my fault. The doctor never said anything in my defense." I felt the ache in my throat as it tightened around me. What could she be thinking? Had her throat tightened like mine?

"That night my parents talked in the kitchen while I sat on the staircase. Two weeks after I met with the doctor, they woke me in the wee hours of morning and told me that within the hour, a car would come for me."

"It must have been awful," she mumbled.

"We were never taught anything about sex," I continued. "My sisters and cousins talked about boys all the time. My parents made me promise to never tell anyone. I kept their promise until now."

Claire began to cry. She covered her eyes, sat up straight, and wiped her cheeks.

"When I searched for you, they told me there might have been a rape," Claire said. "But no one seemed to believe it. The Sisters wrote that you must have done something to bring it on."

She already knew all the pieces of how we got to this place. I felt the flame in my cheeks, almost more embarrassed this time, than so long ago.

"I'm sorry, I shouldn't have said that, but the thought of you being raped somehow made things different. It made me want to find you even more. It helped me understand why things went the way they did," Claire said.

"No one seemed to understand anything, they just kept calling me a sinner, only penance and hard work could save me from the Gates of Hell."

I took off my glasses, cleaned them with a hankie from my purse, and continued. I had come this far. She had a right to know.

"They came for me on a cloudy day before sun-up. The parish priest drove me to Castlepollard, four parishes away. When I arrived, the Sisters seized my belongings and took me straight to Reverend Mother's office where she told me the rules and explained what would happen if I disobey them."

I stopped and took a sip of tea. "While behind their walls, she told me I couldn't talk about my past with any of the other girls. She had a meanness that went straight to her core. She forced me to tell her what happened, and when I did, she called me a liar. I vowed to bury my secret as far as I could. Until now."

I stopped. I couldn't tell her everything. I couldn't let her know what they did to me. That would be my secret. I sat up straight and collected myself.

"Would you like more tea?" I asked, motioning to the waitress. "Have I said too much?"

"No, I've wanted to know what happened since I learned you were alive. When I was little, they told me you died. I guess they did that to protect me."

I gave her a shy smirk. "I'm not surprised."

"Every time I brought up the idea of you, they hushed me up. As I got older, somehow in my heart, I knew you had to be alive."

"Well, yes, I am." Still, after all these years, Claire never gave up. I reached and touched the tips of her fingers, the edges of her painted nails.

"What was it like for you when I was born?" she asked, interrupting me for the first time.

"We weren't allowed medications. No one ever screamed out in pain."

"Why not?"

"No one wanted Reverend Mother to be near them when their time came. Rather than scream, we suffered through chores, or slept in silence, hoping Nurse Claire would be there."

"I don't understand any of this. Why didn't you have a doctor?"

"They didn't allow doctors on the grounds, just Nurse Claire, the only one whoever showed any kindness to us. It was her I named you for, her kindness and compassion."

"I'm sorry."

"I made it through the night, and, when the time came, Nurse Claire took care of me. You had a mat of black hair, and when I held you, you wrapped your fingers around mine. I stayed with you as much as I was allowed. For seven days, I fed you, rocked you, and named you. I stole every minute I could to be with you.

On the seventh day, Reverend Mother took you from me, and we were sent in different directions. That medal, Nurse Claire put it on you and promised she would do everything she could to keep you safe. I wanted you to have something from me." The words stopped coming and we looked down, pressing our hands together. A trait we shared.

"They told us daily we had to repent, to return God's good graces." I looked up at Claire with a weak smile, perhaps relieved that I had let it go. I brushed away the tears that streamed down my cheeks, and my embarrassment slipped away. Somehow, saying it out loud made things different for me.

"I'm sorry what happened to you."

"The Home I was put in was nothing like our homes. We worked every day, no matter how far along we were. My hands withered from the lye soap. The Sisters took liberties, ridiculed and abused us, all in the name of God, but I found a way to survive."

Telling her, made it come back, as if it were yesterday. I had put all those years behind me, but here they were, still lingering, still haunting. I couldn't find any more words. I saw the tiny lines embedded around her eyes fill with tears. The waitress came toward the table, but when I looked up at her, she nodded and turned back to the counter.

"They told my brothers and sisters I went away to school. At that time, if you were poor and sent off to school, everyone knew it meant you had gotten yourself pregnant. Everyone blamed me, saying I must have done something to lead him on; that what happened was my fault. I was fourteen, how could it have been my fault?" I asked my daughter a question neither of us could answer, nor did we want to. "I didn't know what to do," I continued.

My secret became her history, and I wanted to reach my hand across the table to touch her as if a friend who had listened to a sad story, but no words could describe what happened between us. It wasn't about losing a boyfriend, or misplacing a wallet on the bus. It was about pieces of my life that might never be found again, but even more, I told my firstborn daughter about the most private moments of my life.

"My mother came for me, but the Sisters told her I couldn't go home. I was sent to a convent in Dublin." I stopped. I had told Claire all I could for now. I needed to know about her life away from me.

Her Turn

ow that I have told you my deepest, darkest secret, I want to hear about you. Tell me about your life. What do you remember, if anything? How did they treat you?"

"They sent me to the States when I turned five. I learned in my research," she began, "that my years in the orphanage didn't start out so good. They fostered me out, but brought me back on multiple occasions. By the time someone wanted to adopt me, I couldn't leave the country."

I watched as she spoke about her past as if a story she had heard once and remembered all the details. The words came in order and made sense, but seemed to have no connection to her

"When I met with one of the Sisters in 1990, she told me the original plans had me going to Portland, Oregon at three. But I didn't meet the health criteria to be adopted out. A few years later, a woman from Washington came, picked us up and took three of us on a plane to America." She allowed a long pause, and I saw her face change, her eyes dropped and her jawline arched back.

"I didn't walk or talk for a long time. My mother had a picture of me being carried off the plane. I don't remember anything from Ireland. My parents told me I had a hard time adjusting to my new life. Being older, I guess I had become set in my ways. It took a while for us to understand each other. They didn't know what I had been through. No one did."

I didn't want to hear about the bad things that might have happened to her. I couldn't imagine her experiencing pain or heartache. I wanted her life to be a fairytale. Sitting across from my daughter with our fingers touching, I only wanted forgiveness for all the things I hadn't been able to give her and for every sadness she experienced because of me.

"But, you're good now, right?" I asked.

"Yes, I've been fortunate." Claire took a sip of her tea, brushed her hair out of her face and smiled at me.

Just as they had broken me, she had been broken by the same experience. All this time I had been so busy trying to forget, I never thought about what she experienced, going across the world, everything new. I bowed my head, ashamed that I had failed to understand what any of this meant to her.

I needed to change the subject. "Where is your daughter? Is she here? You said, "we" on the phone."

Her face lit up, like a secret she had been hiding that would only come out when called upon. I wanted to see my daughter's child, for it to be complete, the three of us together for the first time.

"She helped me put together an album for you. It starts with my passport picture and goes through until the week before we left." She stared at me as I leafed through the pages. Here were the pictures, her passport, high school graduation, the wedding photo, everything I had buried beneath the swans. Hidden, afraid that Aidan would ask, not something I needed to worry about now. Hidden, so I could forget. I thought about telling her that I had been told she died, but sitting with her there, I saw no purpose in, intentionally causing her pain.

"I'll call for Devon now. I just wanted some time alone with you. Thank you for coming, for telling me what you did. That must have been so hard for you, but I am so grateful. You have no idea. At least now I know and I understand. I believe you."

She said the words I had waited decades to hear. She believed me, and she didn't even know me. Why couldn't they have done the same? It would've made things easier. Maybe I could have found the strength to tell Aidan. I wouldn't have lived with so much shame.

"Dear, why would you say thank you?"

"Because, I know you didn't have to do this. The Sisters told me so many times I should just forget you. That you had gone on with your life and forgotten me. They said you wanted nothing to do with me."

"Oh my dear girl, I never forgot you."

"The Sisters made me feel very different, dirty and shameful that I was looking for you, as if I wasn't grateful for what I had. I never told my husband what happened, or anything about you. As the years passed, I tried, but fear overtook me, and it got easier to stay silent. I'm sorry."

I looked up at her and tears bubbled in the corner of her eyes. She sat tall, wiped her eyes. "It's okay. I understand. I do," she said. "They made me believe you had forgotten me. They made me feel worthless . . ."

"I'm going to call my daughter down, if that is okay."

Claire picked up her phone and left the table, going to the end of the aisle. I turned through the pages of her life. Some of the pictures were familiar. The school photo the Mr. Malloy found, and the wedding picture that had been in the paper. Her life lay out before me. She survived it all without me. She grew into a fine woman and I had missed it. Sitting alone with these pictures, I realized for the first time, that losing me had broken her heart. I had my daughter taken from me because of a sin that was not even mine. With her here now, I could make things right.

I stood when I saw Claire and my granddaughter come down the aisle. Taller than her mother, long straight hair, with ocean blue eyes, a fetching young woman. Without a word, I pulled her close and whispered in her ear. "You are your mother's daughter." A hug, a moment wrapped in each other's arms left me weak as Devon slowly stepped back.

"These are for you," she said, handing me a bouquet of wild lavender. She took a seat next to Claire. Our conversation still bore the frailty of a first meeting. I sat in awe of my daughter, there with her daughter in front of me. I reached across the table for Devon's hand, and caressed it in ways that broke my heart, but in another way I had never felt so much love. I asked about her life and her family. Devon showed great pride sharing her world, being so intimate with someone connected to her by blood, yet a stranger.

The hours passed and we divulged both histories with great care. Had someone walked by, they would have been embarrassed by the intensity of the body language. I leaned in to be close, not to miss a word so vital to my new family. I could say that now. I had her back, and she had a history, my history, and a bloodline that could be traced. In moments, I felt memories poured out as she attempted to make them mine. I would be forever changed because of this day.

Though I had looked at the album while Claire was on the phone, when she returned, my daughter and granddaughter went page by page as she retold her life, and shared their memories. One of the pictures was Claire holding Devon as a newborn, with a flock of black hair. I paused.

"You had the same hair," I said, remembering that moment with her. I had captured it in my mind, and as much as I had once tried to forget, it would never be gone from me.

No one wanted the time to be over. When there was a silence, someone would pick up the conversation, so no one might suggest leaving. The café emptied and the hours flew by.

The conversation moved to incidentals, beliefs, life in Ireland, and intermittent laughter that allowed us to relax. Stories were shared of special occasions and lightness filled the room.

I realized though, as she shared the times of her life, we each held our own secrets. I believed just as I had my secrets from her, she may well have kept secrets from me. Maybe her life had not been as grand as she hoped to present. For now, I would let that go. We would have another place.

"Claire, thank you so much for this afternoon, but I'm afraid I must be going. I have an appointment and I need to catch the next bus. This has been grand." I picked up the bouquet flowers and photo album. "When are you leaving?"

"We leave Sunday morning. We spent most of our time trying to find you."

"I wish we could meet again, but I'm leaving for London for a few days."

"Didn't you just get back?" Claire asked."

"Yes, but my sister has been sick, so I need to go back and help her."

"Can we see you before we go?"

"Yes, how about if I come Saturday night, before you leave. I'll call the hotel and leave a message, but expect me about six."

Finn and Devon together reached around me and I buried my head in their shoulders.

I left them alone in the restaurant and went back out the way I came. On the street people smiled at me, looked at the flowers, then averted their eyes. I decided, against taking the bus, I needed to walk in the rain as it came down. I needed to hide the tears.

The Last Night

 heard the phone from the garden, so I strolled back through the open patio door, closing it behind me as the clouds made faces in the sky. I stood over it waiting for another ring, or a voice to talk without my having to do anything. After the third ring, I picked up the receiver.

I could hear the sounds of the city around her, the mumbling of strangers on the sidewalk, and the horns from the cabs that filled the streets. My dear friend Claire must have been calling from Dublin.

"I'm fine, just off to see Finn for the last time before she returns to the States." I took a seat at the dining table and fumbled with the petals from the roses tucked in the vase on the center of the table. All her questions came out at once. I answered them as I could.

"She's splendid, long chestnut hair, blue-green eyes, and freckles. Not a baby, anymore. Her daughter resembles Francie. If Francie ever has a girl, she'd look like Devon, with thick straight hair, olive complexion, and a broad smile that just eats you up. She reminds me a bit of me while I lived in Howth."

I took a long pause after each question, as we talked, the sounds of the city grew louder, so I waited for the noise to settle.

"I told her as much as I could. I told her about the rape, and the Home." I twisted the cord around my fingers and looked out over the backyard. I heard the sigh come over the line. I had disappointed her. Without her saying, she wanted me to tell Finn about the Laundries and the repeated rapes, I couldn't tell my daughter the shame I had lived daily.

"No, I didn't tell her. I told her what I thought she could believe."

Claire's words echoed in my head. I could hear her voice. "Why not? Do you really believe anything would be different if she knew? She came such a long way to meet you. My God, Alice, give your daughter, a chance. She just might surprise you. Aidan's gone. The secrets can stop."

In the silence, I heard another sigh, then the quick blare of a distant horn.

"I've made a life for myself, Claire. I'm safe and protected from the past though it haunts me still. I can't let her know what they did to me. I can't go back. I just can't. There are no words to express what finally meeting her means, but I can't let her interfere with the life I have built here. No, I won't let her meet the girls and I will not tell them about her."

Again I heard her frustration. I remained seated at the table trying to convince myself that enough had been said. I believed in my heart, everything I had said to her.

"I told her the truth, I didn't lie. I just never mentioned the life I have tried to convince myself never happened." The petals from the day-old roses dropped onto the table. I pressed them between my fingers, knowing everything my friend said was true.

"I'm embarrassed, Claire. Embarrassed that I could never stand up for myself, couldn't stand up for her. I let them take my daughter from me. Me. No one else did it."

I heard the words loud and clear. "Alice, you survived."

"But you stood up to her," I said. "You kept us safe when she wanted her revenge. You kept Finn away from her." I had never said it out loud before, and though stunned, I found myself relieved to say the words.

"I felt guilty that the Sisters treated me like crap and that I found a way to save myself, but I couldn't save her."

I looked over at the clock hanging from the dining-room wall, and realized that if I didn't hang up soon, I'd miss the bus to the hotel. "I can't talk about this anymore, not on the phone. I need to go." I ran my fingers through my still damp hair, took a deep breath, and promised to call in a few days.

I put the receiver back, and took a deep breath. I walked from room to room in the empty house. I moved the cut flowers from one table to another, and straightened the magazines. I picked up Aidan's pipe that I displayed on the table by his chair, rolled it around between my palms, inhaled his scent, and pushed it in my pocket. I closed the drapes and turned on the entry light.

I went back out to the garden, staring at the rosebushes where I had buried my past: the documents about Finn, the letter and money from the private investigator, my sister's letter about Da and my inheritance. I buried everything that I never wanted Aidan to find. The bush had flourished over the years, the white blooms trailed like ribbons around the arbor with my secrets protected below.

I would set Finn free, though it might not be a freedom in her eyes. I could imagine her thinking have I abandoned her again. She had been someone else's daughter for too long and seeing her took me back to a place I could not stay, a place that crushed me. I experienced a hell in the Laundries that I couldn't allow myself to go back too, not in person, not in memory.

Just as I was about to latch the door, I recalled I had some things for Finn that no one else could give her. I went back upstairs, opened the drawer with the cashmere sweater. I pulled out my three leather-bound journals. Mum's ring, I put into a tiny black jewelry box.

I had started writing in Howth to understand my newly found freedom. I wrote when my heart ached, when I had to recapture every moment that had broken me. I wrote with joy about the events that happened that made my life worthwhile. Everything about my life was in there, except the end. I'd finish the last chapter on the bus, then she'd understand everything. She wouldn't have to question my feelings through all the time we had been apart. I not only wanted her to have them, she needed to have them.

In the kitchen, I gathered the gifts I had bought for Devon and her children. Maybe with the present, I could make up with lost time. I'd find a way for her to forgive me for not being able to continue what we had found.

The warm, grey autumn evening filled with clouds that traded places in the sky like chess pieces. Streets buzzed with children and families. Even with dark clouds, no one seemed concerned about the pending storm. I took the seat behind the driver and watched as passengers settled it. I was thinking of how I would say my final good-bye.

Had it not been what I hoped for since the day I let her go? Now, I'd let her go again. I took the last of the three journals and opened to the first blank page. I wrote about the garden for the last time, about my walk to the bus, and about how hard it would be to say good-bye.

I saw Finn and Devon step from the elevator as I entered the double doors. Devon's cheeks were red in contrast to her mother's pale freckles. The young woman's damp hair hung to her shoulders. Her smile spread across her face when she saw me, her arm entwined in her mother's as they came toward me.

"Sorry I'm late," I said, as they approached the foyer. "My daughter and I were chatting over tea. I couldn't tell her where I was going, so I do apologize for my lateness." Just in my words, I had deliberately sent Claire another reminder, that again, she's remained my secret.

"The clerk at the desk said they'd call us when you arrived, but we didn't want to miss you." Claire said. "I wasn't sure."

"You weren't sure I'd come."

"I'm sorry," Claire said.

"Of course, I'd come. I have to say good-bye. I've come with gifts, a present for both of you." Claire tried to smile, but I saw the disappointment in her eyes. "So dear, did you have a grand visit?" I asked, taking her hand.

"Yes." Tears streamed down her cheeks. "It's been remarkable."

I looked at Claire sitting on the couch, a world away from her home, telling me how remarkable their trip had been. My breath caught so deep inside, it hurt to speak. I wanted to tell my daughter that we required one last time together alone, so she could learn all the truth. I wanted more time, but I had squandered it.

I hadn't gone to London at all. I sat home, alone, losing precious time I could have spent with her. I was a liar, but it was too late to do anything about that. They were leaving tomorrow, so we would make the best of tonight. We had more to say to each other, but I let go of her hands and rummaged through the bag for the gifts.

"Dear one, don't cry," I said, watching Devon, try to hide her tears. "I've made you sad. I'm sorry."

"You didn't make us sad. We just don't want to leave because we don't know if we'll ever see you again," Claire said

"Maybe I could come to America sometime." I said, knowing that would never happen.

"That would be fantastic. You could meet everyone, even drive up the West Coast."

"Come sit, it's getting late, I have to leave soon. The rain is coming down and I don't want to get drenched on my way home."

I handed Devon a book, Irish Tales and Sagas. You can read this to your children, so they will know your history."

"They will love it. My daughter is always asking me about tales from Ireland. Thank you."

"I have something for your birthday." I said looking at Claire. "I should have given this to you on the first day we met, but I decided to save it for last."

I opened the small black box, and took out the swan ring my mother had worn. She remained still as I pushed the gold band over her knuckle, though not snug, it fit her finger. Claire petted the swan engraving and beamed at her daughter.

"How does it look?" Claire asked, holding out her hand.

"It is stunning."

"Oh, it's grand. I hope you like it." I said, still staring at her.

She tried to answer, but no words came. I smiled and leaned in, folding my arms around her shoulders. "I wanted you to have something so you wouldn't forget me. This was your grandmother's wedding ring."

"I can't keep it," she cried, "Your eldest daughter should have it."

"You are my eldest daughter. You deserve to have this. She was your grandmother, just because you never met, doesn't mean you aren't connected."

I had to pretend that her finding me was secondary to everything else in my life. I knew that this moment was nothing less than extraordinary. She searched for me, but now I had to let her go in the cruelest of ways. I could feel her pull back as I wiped the tears from her cheeks. I could see in her blue eyes that she didn't want to go home. I half expected that if I'd asked her to stay another day, she would have jumped at the opportunity, but I said nothing. I knew once I walked out the door, we would go back to our lives, and I'd leave her again, this time by choice.

"The rain's coming down harder, I must be going soon. Here are toys for the children," I said as I looked through the window handing the bags to my granddaughter.

"We could call a taxi for you, if it's too late, so you could stay longer."

Devon said.

"Oh no, dear, I'm fine. I do need to go soon."

We stood together. I embraced my daughter again. Her eyes were intent, as if she had something to say that would change everything, but just as I had done, she remained silent.

"Thank you," I said, cupping my hands around her face and grinning as though I'd found a treasure. I didn't want to forget her face.

"I don't want to let you go," Claire said, her hands shaking.

"Thank you, for finding me. You never gave up. I gave up because I had to, but you didn't."

"I'll never forget this time, ever," Claire said.

"Nor I, but I'll always be here. Read the stories about the swans, they never go away."

"No, they don't. I know the story, The Children of Lir?"

"Yes. Good-bye, dear one." I let go of her face, but pulled her close to me for the last time.

I stood in front of Claire, wondering if things would change, if in time, I could tell her everything and let her into my life?

"You know I can't write or call don't you? You do understand?" I asked.

"No, I don't," she said. Unable to avert my eyes, I stared at this dear girl who had no idea what secret I held from her. Too ashamed I couldn't find the courage to let her in.

"I'll always love you and I'm so glad we had this time together, but my children can't know." Even as the words came out, I knew they broke her. Her eyes dropped, her mouth twitched, though no one heard, a faint sound came from deep within. I had broken her heart with those few words, just as I had fractured my own.

"Alice," Claire called out.

"Yes," I said, turning toward her, before I reached the doors.

"I'll write, if it's okay. You don't have to write back. I'll just let you know how everyone is. I'll send pictures."

"I can't put them out, you know that."

"I'll send you presents, you know, for your birthday and Christmas."

"No dear, you don't have to do that."

"But I want to."

"Wait," I said. "I almost forgot. I have this for you. Come here, step outside." I stepped into the cold night air. Claire followed me. "This is for you," I said, pulling the leather-bound books from my bag. "I wrote it all down. I know you might not understand, but my journals will help explain everything."

"What are you talking about?" she asked, holding the books in one hand and stroking the ribbon with the other.

"I wrote this so someday, I could understand. I need you to understand. It is the best and worst of me that I have to give you. I call it *The Swan Garden*, because of my love of swans and what I believe they represent."

"Thank you," she said, wrapping her arms around the leather covers.

I felt tears, or maybe rain, streaming down my cheeks, but I didn't bother to wipe them away. I let go of her arm, walking down the steps, pulling my parka tight around my shoulders. I opened my umbrella, and glanced back where Claire stood, one arm wrapped around Devon, the other clinging to the books.

Dark clouds and heavy rain punished the streets. I braced my umbrella against the wind, and trudged into the night, into the life I had chosen. Away from the life I left behind.

Good-bye my dear girl, my dear Finn.

Acknowledgements

This novel, in its final form, took over twenty-five years to write. It was written to give my birthmother a voice. She survived her stay in a mother-baby home, and over time found a life for herself. This story grew from what I learned about my past and the research of a world I didn't even know existed.

Thank you to my family.
To Billy, for loving me through it.
Aaryn, for never letting me give up, and your amazing artistry.
Kyle, for coming to understand how important this was to me.

My parents, for what they lost and gave up, to provide me with a future.

Mary Kaye and Phil, for giving me a new direction when things weren't working.

To my writing family, for listening.

To my friend, Janice, who changed the course of my life, allowing me to take the first real step.

Tom, for reading and rereading, to be sure I never lost my voice.
Gayle, Karen, and Kathy for being the best of friends I could imagine.

Janet Wile, who sat one night with tears in her eyes as she listened to my first draft, and asked for more. Dr. Gandolfo, for helping me heal my heart. Bonnie, who provided me immeasurable tools.

To the HBE Publishing family for absolutely everything.
Dan, for taking a chance on me, and Joshua for your creative design.

THE CHILDREN OF LIR

The Children of Lir

An Irish Legend

ong ago there dwelt in Ireland the race called by the name of De Danaan, or People of the Goddess Dana. They were a folk who delighted in beauty and gaiety, and in fighting and feasting, and loved to go gloriously apparelled, and to have their weapons and household vessels adorned with jewels and gold. They were also skilled in magic arts, and their harpers could make music so enchanting that a man who heard it would fight, or love, or sleep, or forget all earthly things, as they who touched the strings might will him to do. In later times the Danaans had to dispute the sovranty of Ireland with another race, the Children of Miled, whom men call the Milesians, and after much fighting they were vanquished. Then, by their sorceries and enchantments, when they could not prevail against the invaders, they made themselves invisible, and they have dwelt ever since in the Fairy Mounds and raths of Ireland, where their shining palaces are hidden from mortal eyes. They are now called the Shee, or Fairy Folk of Erinn, and the faint strains of unearthly music that may be heard at times by those who wander at night near to their haunts come from the harpers and pipers who play for the People of Dana at their revels in the bright world underground.

At the time when the tale begins, the People of Dana were still the lords of Ireland, for the Milesians had not yet come. They were divided it is said, into many families and clans; and it seemed good to them that their chiefs should assemble together, and choose one to be king and ruler over the whole people. So they met in a great assembly for this purpose, and found that five of the greatest lords all desired the sovranty of Erin. These five were Bóv the Red, and Ilbrech of Assaroe, and Lir from the Hill of the White Field, which is on Slieve Fuad in Armagh; and Midir the Proud, who dwelt at Slieve Callary in Longford; and Angus of Brugh na Boyna, which is now Newgrange on the river Boyne, where his mighty mound is still to be seen. All the Danaan lords saving these five went into council together, and their decision was to give the sovranty to Bóv the Red, partly because he was the eldest, partly because his father was the Dagda, mightiest of the Danaans, and partly because he was himself the most deserving of the five.

All were content with this, save only Lir, who thought himself the fittest for royal rule; so he went away from the assembly in anger, taking leave of no one. When this became known, the Danaan lords would have pursued Lir, to burn his palace and inflict punishment and wounding on himself for refusing obedience and fealty to him whom the assembly had chosen to reign over them. But Bóv the Red forbade them, for he would not have war among the Danaans; and he said, "I am none the less King of the People of Dana because this man will not do homage to me."

Thus it went on for a long time. But at last a great misfortune befell Lir, for his wife fell ill, and after three nights she died. Sorely did Lir grieve for this, and he fell into a great dejection of spirit, for his wife was very dear to him and was much thought of by all folk, so that her death was counted one of the great events of that time.

Now Bóv the Red came ere long to hear of it, and he said, "If Lir would choose to have my help and friendship now, I can serve him well, for his wife is no longer living, and I have three maidens, daughters of a friend, in fosterage with me, namely, Eva and Aoife[9] and Elva, and there are none fairer and of better name in Erin; one of these he might take to wife." And the lords of the Danaans heard what he said, and answered that it was true and well bethought. So messengers were sent to Lir, to say that if he were willing to yield the sovranty to Bóv the Red, he might make alliance with him and wed one of his foster-children. To

Lir, having been thus gently entreated, it seemed good to end the feud, and he agreed to the marriage. So the following day he set out with a train of fifty chariots from the Hill of the White Field and journeyed straight for the palace of Bóv the Red, which was by Lough Derg on the river Shannon.

Arriving there, he found about him nothing but joy and glad faces, for the renewal of amity and concord; and his people were welcomed, and well entreated, and handsomely entertained for the night.

"There sat the three maidens with the Queen"

And there sat the three maidens on the same couch with the Danaan Queen, and Bóv the Red bade Lir choose which one he would have to wife.

"The maidens are all fair and noble," said Lir, "but the eldest is first in consideration and honour, and it is she that I will take, if she be willing."

"The eldest is Eva," said Bóv the Red, "and she will wed thee if it be pleasing to thee." "It is pleasing," said Lir, and the pair were wedded the same night. Lir abode for fourteen days in the palace of Bóv the Red, and then departed with his bride, to make a great wedding-feast among his own people.

In due time after this Eva, wife of Lir, bore him two fair children at a birth, a daughter and a son. The daughter's name was called Fionnuala of the Fair Shoulder, and the son's name was Hugh. And again she bore him two sons, Fiachra and Conn; and at their birth she died. At this Lir was sorely grieved and afflicted, and but for the great love he bore to his four children he would gladly have died too.

When the folk at the palace of Bóv the Red heard that, they also were sorely grieved at the death of their foster-child, and they lamented her with keening and with weeping. Bóv the Red said, "We grieve for this maiden on account of the good man we gave her to, and for his friendship and fellowship; howbeit our friendship shall not be sundered, for we shall give him to wife her sister, namely Aoife."

Word of this was brought to Lir, and he went once more to Lough

Derg to the palace of Bóv the Red and there he took to wife Aoife, the fair and wise, and brought her to his own home. And Aoife held the children of Lir and of her sister in honour and affection; for indeed no one could behold these four children without giving them the love of his soul.

For love of them, too, came Bóv the Red often to the house of Lir, and he would take them to his own house at times and let them spend a while there, and then to their own home again. All of the People of Dana who came visiting and feasting to Lir had joy and delight in the children, for their beauty and gentleness; and the love of their father for them was exceeding great, so that he would rise very early every morning to lie down among them and play with them.

Only, alas! a fire of jealousy began to burn at last in the breast of Aoife, and hatred and bitter ill-will grew in her mind towards the children of Lir. And she feigned an illness, and lay under it for the most of a year, meditating a black and evil deed. At last she said that a journey from home might recover her, and she bade her chariot be yoked and set out, taking with her the four children. Fionnuala was sorely unwilling to go with her on that journey, for she had a misgiving, and a prevision of treachery and of kin-slaying against her in the mind of Aoife. Yet she was not able to avoid the mischief that was destined for her.

So Aoife journeyed away from the Hill of the White Field, and when she had come some way she spoke to her people and said, "Kill me, I pray ye, the four children of Lir, who have taken the love of their father from me, and ye may ask of me what reward ye will." "Not so," said they, "by us they shall never be killed; it is an evil deed that you have thought of, and evil it is but to have spoken of it."

When they would not consent to her will, she drew a sword and would have slain the children herself, but her womanhood overcame her and she could not. So they journeyed on westward till they came to the shores of Loch Derryvaragh, and there they made a halt and the horses were outspanned. Aoife bade the children bathe and swim in the lake, and they did so. Then Aoife by Druid spells and witchcraft put upon each of the children the form of a pure white swan, and she cried to them:—

"Out on the lake with you, children of Lir!
Cry with the water-fowl over the mere!

Breed and seed of you ne'er shall I see;
Woeful the tale to your friends shall be."

Then the four swans turned their faces towards the woman, and Fionnuala spoke to her and said, "Evil is thy deed, Aoife, to destroy us thus without a cause, and think not that thou shalt escape punishment for it. Assign us even some period to the ruin and destruction that thou hast brought upon us."

"I shall do that," said Aoife, "and it is this: in your present forms shall ye abide, and none shall release you till the woman of the South be mated with the man of the North. Three hundred years shall ye be upon the waters of Derryvaragh, and three hundred upon the Straits of Moyle between Erinn and Alba,[10] and three hundred in the seas by Erris and Inishglory, and then shall the enchantment have an end."

Upon this, Aoife was smitten with repentance, and she said, "Since I may not henceforth undo what has been done, I give you this, that ye shall keep your human speech, and ye shall sing a sad music such as no music in the world can equal, and ye shall have your reason and your human will, that the bird-shape may not wholly destroy you." Then she became as one possessed, and cried wildly like a prophetess in her trance:—

"Ye with the white faces! Ye with the stammering Gaelic on your tongues!
Soft was your nurture in the King's house—
Now shall ye know the buffeting wind!
Nine hundred years upon the tide.
"The heart of Lir shall bleed!
None of his victories shall stead him now!
Woe to me that I shall hear his groan,
Woe that I have deserved his wrath!"

Then they caught and yoked her horses, and Aoife went on her way till she reached the palace of Bóv the Red. Here she and her folk were welcomed and entertained, and Bóv the Red inquired of her why she had not brought with her the children of Lir.

"I brought them not," she replied, "because Lir loves thee not, and he fears that if he sends his children to thee, thou wouldst capture them and hold them for hostages."

"That is strange," said Bóv the Red, "for I love those children as if they were my own." And his mind misgave him that some treachery had been wrought; and he sent messengers privily northwards to the Hill of the White Field. "For what have ye come?" asked Lir. "Even to bring your children to Bóv the Red," said they. "Did they not reach you with Aoife?" said Lir. "Nay," said the messengers, "but Aoife said you would not permit them to go with her."

Then fear and trouble came upon Lir, for he surmised that Aoife had wrought evil upon the children. So his horses were yoked and he set out upon his road south-westward, until he reached the shores of Loch Derryvaragh. But as he passed by that water, Fionnuala saw the train of horsemen and chariots, and she cried to her brothers to come near to the shore, "for," said she, "these can only be the company of our father who have come to follow and seek for us."

Lir, by the margin of the lake, saw the four swans and heard them talking with human voices, and he halted and spoke to them. Then said Fionnuala: "Know, O Lir, that we are thy four children, and that she who has wrought this ruin upon us is thy wife and our mother's sister, through the bitterness of her jealousy." Lir was glad to know that they were at least living, and he said, "Is it possible to put your own forms upon you again?" "It is not possible," said Fionnuala, "for all the men on earth could not release us until the woman of the South be mated with the man of the North." Then Lir and his people cried aloud in grief and lamentation, and Lir entreated the swans to come on land and abide with him since they had their human reason and speech. But Fionnuala said, "That may not be, for we may not company with men any longer, but abide on the waters of Erinn nine hundred years. But we have still our Gaelic speech, and moreover we have the gift of uttering sad music, so that no man who hears it thinks aught worth in the world save to listen to that music for ever. Do you abide by the shore for this night and we shall sing to you.

So Lir and his people listened all night to the singing of the swans, nor could they move nor speak till morning, for all the high sorrows of the world were in that music, and it plunged them in dreams that could not be uttered.

Next day Lir took leave of his children and went on to the palace of Bóv the Red. Bóv reproached him that he had not brought with him his children. "Woe is me," said Lir, "it was not I that would not bring them; but Aoife there, your own foster-child and their mother's sister, put upon them the forms of four snow-white swans, and there they are on the Loch of Derryvaragh for all men to see; but they have kept still their reason and their human voice and their Gaelic."

Bóv the Red started when he heard this, and he knew that what Lir had said was true. Fiercely he turned to Aoife, and said, "This treachery will be worse, Aoife, for you than for them, for they shall be released in the end of time, but thy punishment shall be for ever." Then he smote her with a druid wand and she became a Demon of the Air, and flew shrieking from the hall, and in that form she abides to this day.

"They made an encampment and the swans sang to them"

As for Bóv the Red, he came with his nobles and attendants to the shores of Loch Derryvaragh, and there they made an encampment, and the swans conversed with them and sang to them. And as the thing became known, other tribes and clans of the People of Dana would also come from every part of Erinn and stay awhile to listen to the swans and depart again to their homes; and most of all came their own friends and fellow-pupils from the Hill of the White Field. No such music as theirs, say the historians of ancient times, ever was heard in Erinn, for foes who heard it were at peace, and men stricken with pain or sickness felt their ills no more; and the memory of it remained with them when they went away, so that a great peace and sweetness and gentleness was in the land of Erinn for those three hundred years that the swans abode in the waters of Derryvaragh.

But one day Fionnuala said to her brethren, "Do ye know, my dear ones, that the end of our time here is come, all but this night only?" Then great sorrow and distress overcame them, for in the converse with their father and kinsfolk and friends they had half forgotten that they were no longer men, and they loved their home on Loch Derryvaragh, and feared the angry waves of the cold northern sea. But early next day they came to the lough-side to speak with Bóv the Red and with their father, and to bid them farewell, and Fionnuala sang to them her last lament. Then the four swans rose in the air and flew northward till they were seen no more, and great was the grief among those they left behind; and Bóv the Red let it be proclaimed throughout the length and breadth of Erin that no man should henceforth presume to kill a swan, lest it might chance to be one of the children of Lir.

Far different was the dwelling-place which the swans now came to, from that which they had known on Loch Derryvaragh. On either side of them, to north and south, stretched a wide coast far as the eye could see, beset with black rocks and great precipices, and by it ran fiercely the salt, bitter tides of an ever-angry sea, cold, grey, and misty; and their hearts sank to behold it and to think that there they must abide for three hundred years.

Ere long, one night, there came a thick murky tempest upon them, and Fionnuala said, "In this black and violent night, my brothers, we may be driven apart from each other; let us therefore appoint a meeting-place where we may come together again when the tempest is over-past." And they settled to meet at the Seal Rock, for this rock they had now all learned to know.

By midnight the hurricane descended upon the Straits of Moyle, and the waves roared upon the coast with a deafening noise, and thunder bellowed from the sky, and lightning was all the light they had. The swans were driven apart by the violence of the storm, and when at last the wind fell and the seas grew calm once more, Fionnuala found herself alone upon the ocean-tide not far from the Seal Rock. And thus she made her lament:—

"Woe is me to be yet alive!
My wings are frozen to my sides.
Wellnigh has the tempest shattered my heart,
And my comely Hugh parted from me!
"O my beloved ones, my Three,
Who slept under the shelter of my feathers,
Shall you and I ever meet again

Until the dead rise to life?
"Where is Fiachra, where is Hugh?
Where is my fair Conn?
Shall I henceforth bear my part alone?
Woe is me for this disastrous night!"

Fionnuala remained upon the Seal Rock until the morrow morn, watching the tossing waters in all directions around her, until at last she saw Conn coming towards her, and his head drooping and feathers drenched and disarrayed. Joyfully did the sister welcome him; and ere long, behold, Fiachra also approaching them, cold and wet and faint, and the speech was frozen in him that not a word he spake could be understood. So Fionnuala put her wings about him, and said, "If but Hugh came now, how happy should we be!"

In no long time after that they saw Hugh also approaching them across the sea, and his head was dry and his feathers fair and unruffled, for he had found shelter from the gale. Fionnuala put him under her breast, and Conn under her right wing and Fiachra under her left, and covered them wholly with her feathers. "O children," she said to them, "evil though ye think this night to have been, many such a one shall we know from this time forward."

So there the swans continued, suffering cold and misery upon the tides of Moyle; and one while they would be upon the coast of Alba and another upon the coast of Erinn, but the waters they might not leave. At length there came upon them a night of bitter cold and snow such as they had never felt before, and Fionnuala sang this lament:—

"Evil is this life.
The cold of this night,
The thickness of the snow,
The sharpness of the wind—
"How long have they lain together,
Under my soft wings,
The waves beating upon us,
Conn and Hugh and Fiachra?
"Aoife has doomed us,
Us, the four of us,

To-night to this misery—
Evil is this life."

Thus for a long time they suffered, till at length there came upon the Straits of Moyle a night of January so piercing cold that the like of it had never been felt. And the swans were gathered together upon the Seal Rock. The waters froze into ice around them, and each of them became frozen in his place, so that their feet and feathers clung to the rock; and when the day came and they strove to leave the place, the skin of their feet and the feathers of their breasts clove to the rock, they came naked and wounded away.

"Woe is me, O children of Lir," said Fionnuala, "we are now indeed in evil case, for we cannot endure the salt water, yet we may not be away from it; and if the salt water gets into our sores we shall perish of it." And thus she sang:—

"To-night we are full of keening;
No plumage to cover our bodies;
And cold to our tender feet
Are the rough rocks all awash.
"Cruel to us was Aoife,
Who played her magic upon us,
And drove us out to the ocean,
Four wonderful, snow-white swans.
"Our bath is the frothing brine
In the bay by red rocks guarded,
For mead at our father's table
We drink of the salt blue sea.
"Three sons and a single daughter—
In clefts of the cold rocks dwelling,
The hard rocks, cruel to mortals.
—We are full of keening to-night."

So they went forth again upon the Straits of Moyle, and the brine was grievously sharp and bitter to them, but they could not escape it nor shelter themselves from it. Thus they were, till at last their feathers grew again and their sores were healed.

On one day it happened that they came to the mouth of the river Bann in the north of Erinn, and there they perceived a fair host of horsemen riding on white steeds and coming steadily onward from the southwest "Do ye know who yon riders are, children of Lir?" asked Fionnuala. "We know not," said they, "but it is like they are some party of the People of Dana." Then they moved to the margin of the land, and the company they had seen came down to meet them; and behold, it was Hugh and Fergus, the two sons of Bóv the Red, and their nobles and attendants with them, who had long been seeking for the swans along the coast of the Straits of Moyle.

Most lovingly and joyfully did they greet each other and the swans inquired concerning their father Lir, and Bóv the Red, and the rest of their kinsfolk.

"They are well," said the Danaans; "and at this time they are all assembled together in the palace of your father at the Hill of the White Field, where they are holding the Festival of the Age of Youth.[11] They are happy and gay and have no weariness or trouble, save that you are not among them, and that they have not known where you were since you left them at Lough Derryvaragh."

"That is not the tale of our lives," said Fionnuala.

After that the company of the Danaans departed and brought word of the swans to Bóv the Red and to Lir, who were rejoiced to hear that they were living, "for," said they, "the children shall obtain relief in the end of time." And the swans went back to the tides of Moyle and abode there till their time to be in that place had expired.

When that day had come, Fionnuala declared it to them, and they rose up wheeling in the air, and flew westward across Ireland till they came to the Bay of Erris, and there they abode as was ordained. Here it happened that among those of mortal MEN whose dwellings bordered on the bay was a young man of gentle blood, by name Evric, who having heard the singing of the swans came down to speak with them, and became their friend. After that he would often come to hear their music, for it was very sweet to him; and he loved them greatly, and they him. All their story they told him, and he it was who set it down in order, even as it is here narrated.

Much hardship did they suffer from cold and tempest in the waters of the Western Sea, yet not so much as they had to bear by the coasts of the ever-stormy Moyle, and they knew that the day of redemption was now drawing near. In the end of the time Fionnuala said, "Brothers, let us fly to the Hill of the White Field, and see how Lir our father and his household are faring." So they arose and set forward on their airy journey until they reached the Hill of the White Field, and thus it was that they found the place: namely, desolate and thorny before them, with nought but green mounds where once were the palaces and homes of their kin, and forests of nettles growing over them, and never a house nor a hearth. And the four drew closely together and lamented aloud at that sight, for they knew that old times and things had passed away in Erinn, and they were lonely in a land of strangers, where no man lived who could recognise them when they came to their human shapes again. They knew not that Lir and their kin of the People of Dana yet dwelt invisible in the bright world within the Fairy Mounds, for their eyes were holden that they should not see, since other things were destined for them than to join the Danaan folk and be of the company of the immortal Shee.

So they went back again to the Western Sea until the holy Patrick came into Ireland and preached the Faith of the One God and of the Christ. But a man of Patrick's men, namely the Saint Mochaovóg,[12] came to the Island of Inishglory in Erris Bay, and there built himself a little church of stone, and spent his life in preaching to the folk and in prayer. The first night he came to the island the swans heard the sound of his bell ringing at matins on the following morn, and they leaped in terror, and the three brethren left Fionnuala and fled away. Fionnuala cried to them, "What ails you, beloved brothers?" "We know not," said they, "but we have heard a thin and dreadful voice, and we cannot tell what it is." "That is the voice of the bell of Mochaovóg," said Fionnuala, "and it is that bell which shall deliver us and drive away our pains, according to the will of God."

Then the brethren came back and hearkened to the chanting of the cleric until matins were performed. "Let us chant our music now," said Fionnuala. So they began, and chanted a solemn, slow, sweet, fairy song in adoration of the High King of Heaven and of Earth.

Mochaovóg heard that, and wondered, and when he saw the swans he spoke to them and inquired them. They told him they were the children of Lir. "Praised be God for that," said Mochaovóg. "Surely it is for your sakes that I have come to this island above every other island that is in Erinn. Come to land now, and trust in me that your salvation and release are at hand."

So they came to land, and dwelt with Mochaovóg in his own house, and there they kept the canonical hours with him and heard mass. And Mochaovóg caused a good craftsman to make chains of silver for the swans, and put one chain between Fionnuala and Hugh and another between Conn and Fiachra; and they were a joy and solace of mind to the Saint, and their own woe and pain seemed to them dim and far off as a dream.

Now at this time it happened that the King of Connacht was Lairgnen, son of Colman, and he was betrothed to Deoca, daughter of the King of Munster. And so it was that when Deoca came northward to be wedded to Lairgnen she heard the tale of the swans and of their singing, and she prayed the king that he would obtain them for her, for she longed to possess them. But Lairgnen would not ask them of Mochaovóg. Then Deoca set out homeward again, and vowed that she would never return to Lairgnen till she had the swans; and she came as far as the church of Dalua, which is now called Kildaloe, in Clare. Then Lairgnen sent messengers for the birds to Mochaovóg, but he would not give them up.

At this Lairgnen was very wroth, and he went himself to Mochaovóg, and he found the cleric and the four birds at the altar. But Lairgnen seized upon the birds by their silver chains, two in each hand dragged them away to the place where Deoca was; and Mochaovóg followed them. But when they came to Deoca and she had laid her hands upon the birds, behold, their covering of feathers fell off and in their places were three shrunken and feeble old men and one lean and withered old woman, fleshless and bloodless from extreme old age. And Lairgnen was struck with amazement and fear, and went out from that place.

Then Fionnuala said to Mochaovóg, "Come now and baptize us quickly, for our end is near. And if you are grieved at parting from us, know that also to us it is a grief. Do thou make our grave when we are dead, and place Conn at my right side and Fiachra at my left, and Hugh before my face, for thus they were wont to be when I sheltered them on many a winter night by the tides of Moyle."

So Mochaovóg baptized the three brethren and their sister; and shortly afterwards they found peace and death, and they were buried even as Fionnuala had said. And over their tomb a stone was raised, and their names and lineage graved on it in branching Ogham[13]; and lamentation and prayers were made for them, and their souls won to heaven.

But Mochaovóg was sorrowful, and grieved after them so long as he lived on earth.

Text and images for "The Children of Lir" are public domain and/or appear courtesy of the original work in Project Gutenburg.

Rolleston, T.W. *The High Deeds of Finn and other Bardic Romances of Ancient Ireland.* n. p. n.d. Project Gutenberg. Web. Nov 2015.

CPSIA information can be obtained
at www.ICGtesting.com
Printed in the USA
LVOW07s1449030517

532929LV00001BA/254/P